Jen's Story

The Changing World
of Jenifer McKay

Stephanie Mathivet

1

Synopsis

In the rapidly changing social climate of the 1970s, Jenifer McKay is stepping out into the world as an independent young woman, making plenty of slips and trips along the way. She leaves the dull suburbs of North West London and finds herself living and working as a nursery nurse in the poorer end of London's trendy and radical Notting Hill. Drawn into the world of Black Londoners by her love of the rock steady music of the era, Jenifer becomes enmeshed in the life of a Caribbean family and wider community where she learns stark lessons that help shape her developing political consciousness. She meets young radicals in the 'Black Power' movement as well as the growing 'Women's Liberation' movement and together they form connections and develop bonds that enable them to contribute to a growing social politic. Threaded through the story is also a sinister character who seems to dog her life as she outgrows false friends, as well as a keen young man with whom a romance blossoms. There are twists and turns to the story, ending in a mind-blowing revelation that changes her life for ever. All of the characters are fictitious and while some of the events were inspired by things that happened, the rest is pure fiction that is engaging and compelling.

About the author

This is a first novel from Stephanie Mathivet who is more used to writing books about aromatherapy or child development. Her venture into fictional writing began with chapter one of the book, initially written as a short story. But the characters seemed to 'speak' to her and through her, wanting their story to be told in this way. The sensible advice often given to first time novelists is 'write about what you know.' Stephanie has used her own life experience to create characters and events that mirror familiar experiences of the early seventies in this part of London..

Table of Contents

1   The Ladies

It was Saturday night and, as usual, I was at Liz's place, getting ready to go out. What a performance! The ironing board, taking center place in Liz's small bedsit flat, had served its main function and had now become the Make-up Zone littered with tubes and pots of all sorts, brushes, mirrors and the prized false eye lashes. Mine were green, to match my eyes. I liked to match it with thin green eye liner, and dark green eye shadow to create the big-eyed look that we girls loved so much. We were eighteen then, grown up, already confident that we knew, better than anyone else, whatever there was to know. We were headstrong and daring, rebellious girls, with long lashed big eyes, feeling like we were the bees knees in our leather hot pants, wedge shoes and flappy-sleeved blouses. It was the early seventies and the music was Rock Steady. The club to go to was The Hot Forties in the middle of Soho. There the DJs played the sounds never heard on Top of the Pops or out in the little provincial social clubs and pub dances that white girls like us had grown up in. This was where the grown up, smart, where-it's-at-girls went. It was where you went to be daring, in the after hours for late night to early morning dancing and was frequented by the West Indian clubbers and the smart hustlers. The clothes worn by some of the girls attested to their earnings far higher than our regular wages. We looked up to them, but we were also a bit wary. You had to know how to handle it, being a fish out of water, so to speak.

Thankfully, it wasn't raining that night so our hairdos were safe. We boarded the last Bakerloo line train from Queen's Park down to Oxford Circus. The rattling sound filling the almost empty carriages as we sat there feeling the excitement og going out at this late hour when most were going home to their beds. Arriving at our destination, we turned out into a deserted West End, quickly turning down the narrow side streets to get to our hallowed venue. After a brief queue outside where, from the top of the stairs, we could feel the vibration of the bass line that raised our excitement to get inside we would be totally enveloped in the deep easy sounds of that Rock Steady rhythm. We paid our seventeen shillings and sixpence to get in, parting with a further bob to leave our coats in the cloakroom, just keeping hold of a small bag holding keys, lipstick, comb and some small change for drinks and our cab fare for later.

As we entered the darkened club, Liz looked around to see if she knew anyone there. It was still early, at just after midnight, so the floor was quite empty.

"Let's go to the loo first," said Liz, knowing we both needed to check our appearance was perfect. "There will be no-one in there, with a bit o' luck".

We nipped up the three stairs that led to the Ladies room, stairs that later would be crowded with girls lining up to get into or out of the loos and those who liked to stand on the stairs to gain a view over the dance floor or just for the sheer pleasure of being in the way.

"There's not many people in here," I observed to Liz. "Is anyone here that you know?" I didn't know the West End characters as well as Liz did. I felt a bit nervous, but knew I was safe with her as she had been to the club many more times than me.

"Oh, it will fill up about 2am. You have to be careful you're not dancing with someone's man then, as the hustler girls are coming out of the clubs where they hostess, and meet up their guys in here," she said. "Don't forget, the Paradise and Soulbox close at two, so lots of people come here after that. Don't worry it will get packed, and there'll be loads of guys to dance with, and they are not all hustlers. You never know, you might meet another postman."

I ignored this not-so-subtle dig from Liz about my ex-boyfriend, Ben. We settled our hair, admired ourselves and went back down the stairs into the clubroom and walked to the bar. "Two Cokes please" I said. We never drank alcohol. We didn't have the money for one and being sober was a definite advantage in that club, where there were no lights other than the back lights of the bar. We then walked back to the wall near the Ladies and near the exit. According to Liz, "so we can find the loo in the dark and get out quick if there is a fight". Strategy. We clutched our bags, lit a fag and sipped a little bit of our Coke while it was still cold. It had to last all night, unless we got lucky, and by later on, after being held in our hands for hours, it would be hot and flat. Sometimes we filled them with water from the Ladies, but it tasted foul.

I liked it being dark. You could dance and no-one could really see you. Liz was more confident than me and would use the piece of floor we stood on really well. I was shyer, and ached to dance like she did, but mainly I just stood, looking nonchalant and hoped someone would ask me to dance. Liz knew a few faces there and I got to know them too. If a guy was a good dancer, you could get in a groove all night and not say a word; you'd say good night at the end and hope you might see him next time. African Jimmy was like that. Liz said he had a woman and that was why he never pestered me for my phone number. I didn't fancy him that way, thankfully, but loved to dance with him. Liz liked to dance with Tempo. He was tall and black, and very handsome. She fancied him - that much was clear - and was waiting for him to make a move. When African Jimmy and Tempo were in the club, we knew were ok for a smoke, a cold bottle of Coke and someone to dance with all night.

Being near the Ladies was critical if you were stoned. Trying to work your way in the dark through a crowd of standing and dancing people and ending up at your destination was a feat indeed. Liz's strategy always worked; the stairs were right there which was comforting to know! There was another side to the strategy. If you weren't too stoned, you could sort of vaguely judge if the Ladies was empty or not. We went to the loo together. Always. You had to be careful. Sometimes the black girls in there were ok, but sometimes they did not like white girls being in the club and could give you a hard time.

5

Anyway, always was the rule, but sometimes the rule got broken. That night, Liz was ensconced with Tempo, glued to him in this slow, sensuous dance to an Alton Ellis track – *'I'll be waiting'*. I sang along to the words and sipped my Coke.

> *By the time*
> *by the time you leave*
> *i'll be waiting*
> *i'll be waiting*
> *i'll be waiting*
> *i'll be waiting*
> *waiting there for you'* [i]

I was dying to pee. The stairs to the loo were clear. I hoped it would be empty. But no. Three black girls were in there, smoking a spliff. I lowered my head and made for the empty cubicle.

"But wayt!" said one, sitting on the counter where the sinks were. "Watch 'ow de gyal 'ave no manners." I gathered she was referring to me. "Yu no hask if is a queue 'ere?" She sucked her teeth.

"Sorry," I replied. "I thought you were chatting and that the loo was free."

"Is a queue, luv, an' is me firs'". With that, she heaved herself off the counter and went into the cubicle. Her friend, a big built girl in tight jeans and a suede top, took her place on the counter. "An' is me nex'" she commented. I fiddled with my hair and make-up while I waited, hoping whoever was in the other cubicle would soon come out. I asked the third girl if she was waiting too. She sucked her teeth and turned to fix her hair in the mirror.

The first girl, the lairy one, came out of the loo, and, squeezing past me, indicated to her friend, the big girl with the suede top, to go in next. "Me nah ready yet", she said. I looked at the third girl who, again just sucked her teeth.

"Do you mind if I go in then?" I asked. "I'm dying to go".

"Look anudder toilet dere" said Lairy, indicating the other one. "Wha' wrang wid dat one?"

"I thought there was someone in there. The door is shut, and no-one has come out yet?"

"Is outta arder", said the third girl, breaking her vow of silence. Fed up now, she added "Le' de gyal piss nah or go an' piss yuself. Cho' me tired waitin' in ya so".

"Gwan," said Big Gyal, beckoning me towards the cubicle, "me nah wan piss neider". I went into the loo and, with great relief, did what I went in there for. Hopefully they would go, but no. A conversation started between them.

"Why yu a gi de white gyal problem?" said Quiet One, seemingly speaking up for me.

"Me? Gi de white gyal problem? Yu Joke! Is dem a gi' me problem! Yu nah see she fren a dance wi Tempo? All night dem a 'crub an' 'crub like breeze cyan pass 'tween dem! Me a go bus' one a dem, mek me a tell yu" Big Gyal sucked her teeth and I could hear Lairy grunt "Hee" in agreement.

Shit, I thought. Liz is for it. Big Gyal must be his woman and not best pleased to see her man dancing all night with Liz. I decided to get brave. I flushed the loo and opened the door. They all turned and looked at me. Lairy and the Quiet One were now sitting on the counter and Big Gyal was by the door. Shit, I thought, and shit again, as I wanted to wash my hands and doing so without splashing water on either of them would have been hard. I decided to take the bull by the horns.

"It seems you are vex' that my friend is dancing with Tempo. She just dances with him. They don't see each other or anything. She wouldn't dance with him if she knew you was here."

Big Gyal was not impressed. "I will tell her not to dance with him anymore." I went on, hoping I was being diplomatic enough now to ask them to excuse me so I could wash my hands. "Scuse, can I just wash my hands please?"

"Cho", said the Quiet One, "jus' leave de gyal alone, nah?" Indicating the sink and making space for me, she went on "Gwan, washup yu 'ands" Then to her friend. "It's not har business wha' she fren do and is Tempo fault. I dun tell yu a'ready 'im no good. Leff 'im and go 'bout yu business".

Just then Liz came in. "Ah, fock dis, man" said the Lairy one sensing there could now be big trouble. It was crowded in there now with five of us. Lairy turned to leave. "Me nah come 'ere fe no aggravashun – me wan' dance, man. Cho!" The door squeaked shut behind her. Big Gyal went to sit on the counter

"You alright, Jenifer?" Liz asked, "You've been ages. I'm dying to go loo". Little did she know what she had walked into. "Tempo said he had to go, so you've got me back now".

"Good to hear it," I said trying to catch her gaze and get her to see something was wrong. I hoped she would not say anything more about Tempo. Big Gyal got up from the counter and moved towards Liz. Here we go, I thought.

"So, yu dun rub up on my man? Yu get 'im number? Yu bitch! Why unno cyan lef people man alone?"

Liz now realized what she had walked into. "Right," she began "I danced with him yes, but I don't have his number, he doesn't have mine. We just dance together when I come here. So, don't start anything with me. I ain't after your man. He's gone now – so why was that? He must know you're here."

Big Gyal looked like she was considering landing Liz a thump; she was in a corner and had to retain her stance even if she did believe Liz. Quiet One chimed in.

'Leff it, nah. Seriously Bev. 'Im nah good, me keep tellin' yu. Yu mus tun 'im loose. Daag!" She sucked her teeth. Tears began to flow from Bev's eyes. I felt sorry for her, so did Liz.

"I'm sorry," said Liz. "I wouldn't knowingly take someone else's man. I only know Tempo to dance with and I'm sorry if I've spoiled your night".

 Seizing the moment, I grabbed some loo roll and handed it to Bev whose tears had washed her mascara down her face. Quiet One took it and wiped away the running make-up.

"I's all right now. It nah dem fault. Is Tempo. Yu cyan trus 'im."

Just then the door pushed open. Oh no. It was Marvalette - a parent from the nursery where I worked. Oh gosh, this could get awkward. I imagined the whole story getting around the nursery Mums – and then what if Matron found out?

"Hi Jenifer – you all right? Hi Bev. Hi Marcia. Sorry I don't know your name" she said facing Liz, "but hi anyway! God. It's pack up in there. Wha's up Bev, darlin'?"

Crikey, she knows them too! I thought. Blimey, she knows everyone!!

"Blasted man," muttered Bev.

"Bev fin' Tempo dancin' wid de gyal 'ere and we was jus' discussin'" explained the Quiet One, whose name, it now appeared, was Jemma.

"Yeah," I added in quickly, "he was dancing with Liz and she didn't know he was Bev's man and we were just sorting it out."

"Well, I saw him leave as I was coming in," said Marvalette, "and I'm telling you Bev, dis raw, fe tru, sis, I saw him meet up this woman and get in a cab wiv 'er and go off."

At this point the reality of the situation sank home to Bev. It wasn't Liz who was a threat to her relationship with Tempo, but Tempo himself who clearly had a prior arrangement to meet another woman outside the club.

She snuffled a few stifled sobs and turned to look at Liz and me. "Me sarry love; it nah yo fault fe tru. De man is a bastard. Me gi' 'im money, me gi' im me 'ome, me buy 'im clothes and everyt'ing. An' him carry on so. Cho! Enough now! Le' we go enjoy all weself and fock dese men!" With that she blew her nose, wiped her eyes, slipped down off the counter, fixed her clothes and her hair, held her head up high and she and Jemma walked out.

Marvalette looked at me. "So, you two enjoying yourselves tonight? Looks like you get plenty excitement already! Come, let's go get a drink."

We were glad enough for that! The club was packed now and we edged our way to the bar. Bev and Marcia and the Lairy one were nearby, clearly telling Lairy the story. Lairy was nodding. They made their way through to where Liz and I were standing with Marvalette and her friend Lara, another Mum from the nursery.

"Look like is pack-up in 'ere tonight" said Lairy in my ears, "Sarry 'bout earlier, but me fren was upset, yu know. Nah feel no way".

I said it was ok and that I understood. Lairy then replied that it was cool and said her name was Jemma. Bev passed me a spliff and Marvalette handed me a bottle of Coke and one for Liz. A Phyllis Dillon tune came on. 'Perfidia'. Suddenly we were all singing the lyrics together.

'And now, I know my love was not for you
And so I'll take it back with a sigh
Perfidious one, Goodbye'[ii].

Me and Liz often saw Bev, Jemma and Marcia in the club after that night and we always said hello. Marvalette and Lara were cool and did not tell anyone at work about what happened. I became good friends with Marvalette in the end. Bev put Tempo's stuff out in the road for him to collect. Liz never danced with him again.

2   The Party

Three months had passed and Liz and I were now sharing a flat in Malvern Road. Life was going pretty smoothly and I was learning to dance from the great maestro herself and was becoming more confident. We had stopped going to Hot Forties and used to frequent a little basement dive off Kilburn High Road. The music was good and the guys were more like your regular young black man who liked to work all week and enjoy themselves at the weekend. Liz had forgotten all about fancying Tempo and was now going out with Gregory. She liked tall, light skinned men and he was no exception. There was something about him I didn't like and I kept telling her that. Most of the time she just laughed me off and said he was fine. He drove a black BMW and always looked 'cris'', yet he didn't seem to work. He was in the West End clubs every night and as Liz put it, 'lazed about all day'. I asked her what he did for a living. She said he was a Hustler.

"But what does that actually mean?" I asked her, probing for more information. She said he did private business and never talked about it.

"Doesn't that matter to you? I mean, he could be doing anything – a big time criminal or something and you could get caught up in stuff." Liz just laughed and said I was paranoid.

"Marvalette has invited us to a party tonight. It's in the Grove somewhere, round near Lancaster Road, I think. It's a twenty first – her cousin's wife, I believe. Duke Tam is playing and he's a good sound system, so it's gonna be good. I'm just going up the market to find a dress or one of those cat suits to wear."

"Oh, so have you got money then? I thought you were broke." Liz liked prying into my money business; truth was I had kept quiet about some money that I had stashed away. Our flat was a basement – damp, cold, rather dowdy and, rumour had it, up for demolition to make way for modern flats. But it was our pad and we kitted it up with some drapes and cushions, and when the lamps with the red light bulbs were on in our living room it looked quite cosy. We shared a little record player and took it in turns to buy one record each week so we had a nice little collection. Delroy Wilson, The Melodians, Jackie Mittoo, Pat Kelly and Alton Ellis. We were dancing to the latest track by the Cables – 'Baby Why?' - and singing along.

'Baby, baby why oh why
Why did you leave me for another guy, girl?
Baby, baby why oh why?
Why did you leave me and now you come back crying?'[iii]

"So, will you be bringing Gregory later?"

Liz laughed. "No, he will be out seeing to his business. I will see him back here about five".

That meant in the morning, so they would be in bed all day and not getting up til three in the afternoon on Sunday and I would be creeping about trying not to disturb them and pretending not to hear the sounds coming from her bedroom. I really needed to find my own man, then I could be in bed all afternoon 'doing t'ings' as well!

"What's the point in having a boyfriend and not going out with him?" I asked naively, knowing that she would just say that this was how Hustlers operated and that it was Ok because he came home to her. And he gave her money to buy clothes. I was jealous of Liz's growing wardrobe and could have done with a wardrobe man myself.

Anyway, that afternoon I went up to Church Street market and paid for my own dress, bought some new tights and some new eyelashes and looked forward to meeting up with Marvalette. When I got back, Liz's bedroom door was closed, and I noticed Gregory's shoes and long leather coat in the passageway. I resigned myself to eating alone, after which I popped out to the corner to call Marvalette from the phone box to arrange to go round to her place before we all went off to the party. "Great", she said, "come early and bring your stuff and we will get ready here and have a T-bird to get us in the mood." Thunderbird, or T-bird, wine was all the rage. It was vile stuff, but I liked a little bit of it, just to taste it.

When I got back, Gregory had gone. I was only ten minutes. I wondered if Greg had seen that as an opportune moment to split, thus avoiding me. He wasn't that impressed that Liz shared the flat with me. "That was quick" I remarked, taking a bit of a poke at Liz, who was just getting out of the bath. She was clearly upset by my comment and I felt bad.

"He had to go and meet someone. He's got his business to see to."

I thought to myself that if that was what you had to put up with to get a wardrobe man then maybe I would rather buy my own clothes.

"I'm gonna have a bath, then I'm taking my stuff up Marvalette's and getting ready there," I announced, glad to be getting out of the way of Liz and her romance. But then I added "You coming?"

"Ok" she replied, seemingly still stoned from her afternoon smoke in bed with Gregory. The bedroom stank – "Christ, open the bloody window. It stinks in here of weed, sex and his aftershave. Jeez, what does he wear?"

"You know, I'm not coming out tonight after all." Liz went to open the window and threw it up so fast it got stuck on the slant because one sash was broken.

"You are pissing me off. You are just jealous because you haven't got a man – not since Benjamin finished with you. You have to get over him sometime, you know." She was struggling with the window now and swearing under her breath.

"Just leave off about Benjamin. You know how I feel about him. He might be at the party tonight. Maybe there's a chance that he might see me in my fab dress and fancy me all over again."

It was wishful thinking and Liz retorted "Oh for heaven's sake. He's been going out with Maggie's sister - that miserable looking chick, whatever her name is - for the last three months. Forget him."

"Yeah, but have you seen her?" I was getting below the belt now. "She looks like Weed in Bill and Ben. I bet I can get him back. Anyway, at least he works and took me out, like a proper boyfriend."

"If you're taking a pop at Greg, don't bother. He loves me and he gives me money. He's out there making more money than your Benjamin, the pathetic postman, ever will. He sees me when he can and we are good together, so lay off me and Greg's business will you? Anyway, he's taking me up his Auntie's tomorrow for dinner. She's going to teach me to cook."

That'll be the day, I thought.

The bath was full now, so I muttered "All right then" and went off to start the getting ready process. While in the bath I reflected on what that would mean if I went up to Marvalette's on my own. She lived on the tenth floor of Treetop House.

I had a fear of going up in the lift on my own. It stunk of piss and a woman had been mugged there a few weeks back. I don't know how Marvalette did it every day, but she did. She said she was used to it by now. Anyway, I wasn't used to it and wondered if I could persuade Liz to come with me.

Music was playing in the sitting room, so, with my towel wrapped round me, I popped my head round the door. "Sorree," I said, in a silly sort of voice, "Let's both go out like we planned. I didn't mean to be horrible."

"Do I look like I'm staying in?" said Liz, grinning at me, wearing a new Biba dress. "I can't let my latest sit on a hanger all night, can I?" She looked stunning and I suddenly felt conscious of my little cheap dress from the market. Still it looked good enough and I had my new shoes from Ravel that I bought last week. I laughed and went to get my jeans to wear round to Marvalette's.

"Why don't we give Marvalette and her cousin's party a miss? We could go down the West End, have a drink in the Tinker Tailor and then go to Hot Forties. We haven't been there in ages. We might see some of our old flames!"

"What, like Tempo?"

"Huh – don't put me in a bad mood. I don't want to hear his name" She laughed and pulled a face.

"I'm not sure. First, I promised Marvalette and she is expecting us, and two, you know Gregory does not like you to go there. Even though he met you there."

"Well, first, I don't fancy some silly party and second, Greg can't tell me where to go or not go."

There's big talk, I thought. There must be a reason why he does not want her to go there, but I said nothing.

"Tell you what then. Why don't we go to Marvalette's cousin's wife's do and if it's crap, we can go down the West End on the last train? Don't forget Duke Tam is playing and his sounds are always good and he has a good crowd following." I was banking on the party sounding good enough to hold her interest. I was wrong.

"You're joking. It will probably be full of old grannies and old men who have had too much to drink and want to pester you. Anyway – I've got cab money, drink money and entry money for both of us!" Liz waved two ten pound notes at me. We didn't even bring home two ten pound notes in our wages, so it looked like a fortune.

"Save your money and let's just check out the party. If it's no good, we will go up West in a cab, OK?"

"Good" she said. We collected up our stuff and got ready to head off for Marvalette's. "Let's call a cab rather than walking if we've got all this stuff to take."

"Are you paying then?" I asked.

"Sure," she replied with the confident air of one with two ten pound notes in her purse. She went upstairs to ask Old Nosey Parker to use the phone and left her fourpence for the call.

Within ten minutes the cab arrived and we, (me still in my curlers), our gear and Liz's ten pound notes got in the car. My fear of going up in the lift went as we giggled along the way.

We got to Marvalette's about half past ten. No problems befell us in the lift and we rang on the doorbell, which Norman, Marvalette's man, answered. Norman was lovely. He worked on the railways and they had been together for six years, since Marvalette was sixteen. They had a little boy, Aaron, who I had looked after in the nursery and was now in school. It wasn't really allowed to socialise with the nursery parents but as he was no longer at our nursery, it was alright for me to be friends with Marvalette. Aaron was still up and rushed to the door to greet me. It was so good that he remembered me and seemed fond of me still. "Hello, Aunty Jenifer," he said, "I'm at big school now and it's really good."

"Come Aaron. Bedtime", said Norman and I kissed Aaron goodnight, promising to come round one day to take him to the park. "Go t'rough to de sittin' room," said Norman, opening the door whereupon Marvalette got up and came over to greet us.

"We was givin' you two up for lost! Come, take a glass of T-bird. This is Lara, well you know her already, my Aunty Cora, who's babysittin' Aaron, my friends from up Stokey – Justine and Mary and...last but not least, my cousin, Leroy".

I greeted each one in turn with a "Goodnight, how are you, nice to meet you' in the traditional West Indian way to be respectful. Liz just said 'Hi' and went to sit in a chair. Meanwhile, I was picking myself up from the floor – not literally of course, but one look at Leroy had made my legs go weak! I tried to think of something to say but failed. In embarrassment I said to Marvalette – "I've got my stuff to get ready, can I go upstairs?"

"Yeah, let's go up to my room and we can get glammed up, bring your drink. Liz, you coming?" Marvalette, me, Liz, Justine and Mary all went up to Marvalette's room to get ready. After an hour or so, we emerged, hair pressed or unrolled, make-up on, dresses on and looking good. It was fun and we liked being together comparing and laughing at the different ways we attended to our beautifying. I noticed that Leroy seemed not to take his eyes off me when I re-entered the room in my transformed state, and I liked that. He was very handsome and I looked forward to being in the party where, maybe, he might ask me to dance. Liz was pissed off; she could see that Leroy was interested in me and that might mean she would be gooseberrying.

There was seven of us between two cars. Marvalette, Justine and Mary went with Norman, with our bag of stuff in the boot, while me and Liz went in Leroy's car – I sat in the front seat, of course, next to Leroy. He played some music in the car and asked if we smoked. I said we did, but we would wait 'til we got in the party.

Grace was Marvalette's cousin's wife, her husband being Winny, Leroy's brother. They lived in Lancaster Road, in a newly converted flat owned by the Housing Association. She had only lived there for a few months, so her twenty first was also a housewarming party. They had two kids, both under four, who were still running around at nearly midnight.

"Why you didn't bring them by me?" asked Marvalette, "Aunty Cora is minding Aaron already, two more wouldn't fuss her."

Grace declined the offer, saying she wanted the kids to enjoy the party and then go and sleep upstairs with the neighbour. It was easier that way in the morning. It was twelve o'clock and there were just a few people there. Grace's Mum, Rose, was in the kitchen, with her Aunty Noraleen and the lady from nextdoor. That was the thing. You could get away with all night house parties because half the neighbours would be in there with you. It was not as sophisticated as a club, but there were so few clubs where reggae was played and many were just shebeens, so house parties were popular. I knew Grace vaguely; her kids went to the nursery up at Kensal Rise and her Mum, Rose, was a cleaner at the nursery where I worked. I went in to say hello and was greeted with a massive hug.

"Hello, hello Jenifer, darlin'. Yu come out to enjoy youself tonight, eh? You want a drink? And what about yu fren? Darlin', what you drinkin'?"

At last Liz lost that bored look and answered, "Coke please?" We still only drank soft drinks when we went out, preferring a little smoke if it was going around.

"You wan' some food?" asked Rose, taking competent charge of all things kitchen. The big pots were on the stove and the aroma of curry goat and rice, pig foot souse and fry dumplin' with saltfish fritters greeted us, making us feel hungry. Given there were so few people dancing in the front room we hung out in the kitchen with the women. I was dying for some curry goat, but the last time I ate it off a paper plate in the dark, I held the plate wrong and the sauce dripped down my pink dress. This time I would go gravy free and have the fritters and the dumplings with a bit of salad. It was delicious and no fiddling about sucking bones, ruining my makeup and my clothes.

Duke Tam was playing some old school type of music, lots of Ska and even some Jim Reeves. Liz was not impressed.

"Music's crap" she whispered, "I'm ready to go when you are." I was not ready to go and said that he was just playing for the older crowd to warm up the dance. I was right, and as soon the music changed Liz went off to dance in the front room. A younger crowd was gathering now and I followed behind her. We moved to the corner. Leroy was on the other side of the room. He was quite dark skinned and

14

his hair was in small plaits. He wore blue velvet jeans and a loose African style Dashiki top with some Clark's shoes. In his left ear he wore an earing. He was sort of alternative, hippyish looking and I liked that. He came across to our corner of the room and held out his hand, gently touching me on the arm to invite me to dance with him. I turned slowly and rolled myself round into his arms. Yep, he could dance, one two steps on the right foot and then a long slow move on the left, dropping me down onto his leg to sway me and bring me up again. He passed me the spliff. I took a small drag and passed it back. He laughed.

"So, yu's not a real smoker, jus' a joker smoker?" I smiled inanely. "Seen", he replied, getting back into the dance. One tune after another we danced until he went to get me a drink.

"I see you've come up for air at last,' said Liz, pissed off as she was bored that only lesser guys (lesser than Gregory she meant) were asking her to dance and mostly she was refusing them. "Let's go in half an hour" she urged.

"I'm OK here" I replied.

"Oh. Just 'cos you've struck lucky! Why don't you ask him to come to the club with us?"

"OK" I said, happy to be anywhere where Leroy was. He came back, bearing Cokes and birthday cake. "From Grace" he said. I felt comfortable here, with friends, like being part of the family. Marvalette and Norman were dancing, as was the birthday girl, Grace, and her husband, Winny. The room was dark now and full of bodies moving and swaying to the music. The acrid smell of weed filled the air. We started to dance again.

"Liz wants to go down to the West End" I said. "Would you like to come"

"Where to?" he asked.

"Probably Hot Forties", I replied.

"Nah," he replied. "Too much bad man inna dem place dere. So, you like bad man?"

"No No," I replied hurriedly. "It's just that Liz likes it there and Count Coxy does play good music." Leroy laughed with that kind of laugh of a man who knows all there is to know about a subject, such as reggae music.

"So yu tink Coxy better dan Tam?"

"Actually," I replied, opting for the diplomatic route, "I am really liking it right here. The music is good, the food is good and I am enjoying the company."

"Oh, so yu like me company?" I fell fair and square into that one.

"Yes, but I meant generally, with Marvalette and everyone."

15

Leroy gathered me in closer. "Dat's nice" he said and we settled into another dance. A Tamlins' tune – 'Ting a Ling a Ling. I called you on the phone'. We started singing the chorus together. He laughed.

"Me like yu, yu know." I smiled, put my arms round his neck and slid snakily down his leg and back again. "Bwooooy" I heard him say. I'd pulled and I was happy.

Leroy excused himself again for a few minutes. I had come up for air, as Liz had put it, and she pulled me over and said "Look, Benjamin is here".

"Oh shit."

"Don't worry. He is with that miserable looking girl. I can't stand her. You are much better looking. He must have been mad."

"I don't care," I replied in that slow drawl of someone quite stoned, "I'm happy dancing with Leroy."

I didn't even want Benjamin to know I was there. I stayed in the dark corner, like a spider, waiting for my prey to return. He came back this time with a plate of curry.

"No thanks" I said.

"Eat!" he said, pushing the plate at me. I took the plate and carefully folded it in my hand to hold the food in. It was nice but sorting out the boney bits from the meat and the gristle in the dark was a matter of trial and error. I ate some, enjoying what I managed to get and finished all the rice. Leroy saw I was not managing the bones.

"Yu nah eat bone? Gimme." He took what I had barely touched and sucked the living daylights out of the bones, then crunched them up, leaving a pile of chewed up bone on the side. He put our two plates on the top of the speaker, wiped his face and fingers and said, "Soon come." He came back with more drinks for everyone. I was beginning to warm to him more and more.

I suddenly realized Liz had her jacket on. "I'm going. Are you coming?"

"No," I replied.

"OK, see you later then."

"Liz, Liz, wait." I tugged on her arm. She turned back to face me.

"Look,' she said, "I'm bored here and you're doing OK. I want to go down the West End, to Hot Forties. I just feel it's going to be good. It's fine if you stay. I will be OK; I have money for cabs. I'll see you tomorrow at home. Don't forget my stuff is with yours in Norman's boot."

16

I didn't like letting her go off on her own, but she was stubborn. She said her goodbyes to Marvalette and Grace and left. Meanwhile I was back in Leroy's arms without a care in the world. However, two Cokes on, I was needing to pee, so I told Leroy I was off to the loo, edging my way through the crowd and down the passage to the bathroom. There was a crowd standing in the passage, including Benjamin. I tried to slip in quick before he saw me, but no such luck.

"Hi! Long time! How you doin'?"

"Fine", I said "and you?" I hardly gave him time to reply when it was my turn to go into the loo. I hoped he would be gone when I came out, but it was like he was waiting for me.

"I saw you dancing with Leroy earlier. I didn't want to interrupt you. Do you know him? Is he your new man?"

I didn't like being asked these questions, so I just shrugged "Just dancing, that's all."

"Be careful of him. Not for nothing they call him Crab-I. I don't want you getting hurt. I miss you, you know."

I didn't know what he meant by Crab-I. I took it to mean 'crabby' in that Leroy could be grumpy. Most of all I took it to mean he was being jealous, but I didn't believe he missed me. If so, why hadn't he come to find me?

"I've got to get back. Nice to see you." I said walking away, and back to Leroy.

When I got back Leroy was looking agitated. "Yu took long," he said.

"Sorry, there was a queue."

"Who dat man me see yu a talk to?"

"No-one", I lied, "He was just waiting for his girlfriend and was asking me if I was enjoying myself."

"Seen," said Leroy, although I guessed he did not believe me. We got back into our dance. Damn that Benjamin, I thought.

About an hour later Leroy said, "You wan' me drop yu 'ome?" I was feeling tired now and I did want a lift, so I accepted and we said our goodbyes and left. We got mine and Liz's stuff from Norman's boot – to his inconvenience as he was enjoying a dance with Marvalette. The chilly night air hit me, even with my jacket on, and Leroy saw I was cold and put his arm around me.

"I 'ope yu fren is a'right by sheself inna de Wes' End."

"She can look after herself" I replied, not wanting to talk about Liz right now. We got to the car and drove off, back to South Kilburn to our flat. I asked Leroy if he wanted to come in.

"Is who live 'ere? Is jus yu or yu live wid a man?" I laughed.

"Would I invite you in if I was living with a man? No, I share with Liz and looks like she is not in yet. I expect she met her man up West and they are late night clubbing."

"Cool," Leroy replied. We went in the flat and into the front room together. He looked a bit uncomfortable. I asked him if he wanted a hot drink, and he asked what we had, I listed out the choices and he said he would like a Horlicks, three sugars. I went to the kitchen and came back with two cups of Horlicks, one with three sugars. Leroy had found our records and selected a Pat Kelly album; he put it on and turned it down low and was lying stretched out on the sofa. We drank our Horlicks, chatting about what we did for a living – he was a painter and decorator (no wardrobe man then) and lived alone (so he said).

"Come," he said pulling me to him gently, and slowly he began to kiss me. Mmmm! It felt good and very soon I was leading him off towards the bedroom.

It was a night of pleasure and passion indeed. He left about 11 am. Early, I thought, as we had not gone to bed til five o'clock. I had made him some toast for breakfast and sweet tea and he kissed me and left, leaving me his number to call him. If only we could afford to have a phone installed. It was then I heard muffled voice coming from Liz's room. No man shoes in the hall, so I figured Gregory was not there and went in.

I began to ask her if she wanted tea and then stopped in my tracks, in horror. Her face was a mass of bruises. She lifted her nightdress and there were more bruises. They were everywhere. Her mouth was so swollen she could hardly speak.

"Who did this?" I asked, "Was it Greg, or were you attacked or something?" I looked around the room, and I realized she had been beaten up here, in her bedroom; there was blood on the sheets and stuff had been knocked over and on to the floor. Her dresses were all ripped up. Stuff was smashed. She could not stop sobbing. "Was it Greg?" She nodded. It must have happened before I came home with Leroy and she had stayed quietly in her room all this time. I suppose not wanting him to see her in this way.

She was not in a fit state to talk, so I asked her to nod if she wanted to go to the hospital. She nodded. I asked her to stand so I could put something round her but she could barely walk. I called upstairs to ask if I could use their phone to call an ambulance. Mrs. Cameron (the landlady who lived on the floor above us - Old Nosey Parker) came down. She must have heard what went on but lied and said she had not and then was a paragon of sympathy. So false. The ambulance came and we went down to Paddington Hospital, to the A and E. It took ages waiting, so, bit by bit, Liz told me what had happened.

She had taken a cab from the party straight down to the Hot Forties and had gone inside. It was packed in there but as she made her way to the bar, she saw Gregory. She ducked out of the light and stood where he could not see her and watched him. There he was dancing with a woman. Ok, she had been dancing with a man, but if he wanted to dance, why hadn't he taken her out and danced with her? Then she saw the woman reach into her bag, give him something which looked like money and then he kissed her. The light on the glitter ball flickered on the woman's face. She was no oil painting. A 'state' Liz said, old looking and rough. White, with her hair dragged back into a ponytail, showing how rough she looked. Liz had riled up with anger – how dare he do this to her. She now realized what his business was – or at least one aspect of it. She pushed her way through until she was facing both of them. She took her drink and threw it over them.

"Wha' de fock?" said Gregory almost blazing, but then cooling down. "Go!" he said to the woman. She looked at Liz and then looked at Greg.

'So, is this the woman you've been seeing?"

"Go! Now!" glared Gregory and obediently the woman backed away into the crowd.

"So?" said Liz.

"Come," said Gregory, le' we talk outside." By the cloakroom, he pulled her arm and said, "Get your coat. Is col' outside."

"But we are coming back in?" Liz had asked, to which Greg had nodded. Once outside, Greg grabbed her arm and marched her off to the car. Liz could sense his anger and stayed quiet. He pushed her inside and came round to the driver's side. Then he drove off. "I thought we were going to talk" Liz ventured after a while. Gregory sucked his teeth and carried on driving. Liz resumed her silence. When they got in the house, he dragged her into the bedroom.

"Right," he said, "Yu wan' talk?" and with that he boxed her right in the face four times. "I t'ought me a tell yu nah come a 'ot Forties. One t'ing, is all me hask in return fe all me a do fe yu."

Bam! Another punch hit her in the stomach, followed by more blows all over her body.

"Never disobey me! Yu hear? An' never, never come face up any of my girls. Is dem money a pay fe all de tings me a gi yu. An' you wan' make fuss wid me in de blood claart place!'

More blows fell on Liz; too shocked to speak, she muttered, "I'm sorry Gregory." By now Greg had thrown the stuff from off the dressing table and was making for the wardrobe, pulling out Liz's dresses and ripping them apart.

'No!" cried Liz, to which Gregory responded with more blows. And then the worst horror of all happened. After all the beating, Gregory undid his trousers, threw himself on top of Liz and raped her. Hitting her again if she protested. When he had finished, he seemed unnaturally calm.

"Yu bring dis 'pon yuself. Yu was my good girl. Me wan' keep yu away from nastiness like dat place dere. T'ings I ha' fe do fe make money is my business and me nah like yu a dig up inna it. Me nah like dem kinda behaviours yu get along wid tonite, so yu ha fe learn de 'ard way. Me learn de 'ard way. Me tough. Me smart. Yu cyan fool me wid yu nicey nicey ways. Yu is jus' de same, jus wan' black man for one t'ing; tek we fe fool. I coulda put yu pon de streets fe me too, yu know, but me a seh, nah bodder wid dat. Dis a nice gyal, man. Treat she nice and good and everyt'ing cool. Yu 'pwoil up de 'ole t'ing, Liz. Me nah want yu again." And with that, he turned and walked out of the door, cool, like nothing had happened.

It had taken a while for Liz to tell me the story, her mouth was so swollen, but it took up the waiting time. Now the doctor came into the cubicle to see her. He examined her, then ordered the nurse to take her off for an x-ray and other tests. Three broken ribs, a broken nose and substantial bruising with possible internal damage. Whatever that meant. They would have to keep her in, under observation for a day or so. Did she want to call the police, press charges? There were no witnesses. What could she do? Plus, the police interrogation would be a nightmare. They hated white girls like us. I cried to see her like that. Why didn't she just stay at the party? I'd had such a nice time with Leroy.

I said good night to her and went home to bed to dream about him. I would tidy Liz's room for her in the morning. I got undressed to get into bed. Something was tickling my pubic hair. I scratched it, but there it was again. "I bet this bloody place has fleas," I thought to myself, taking the mirror to have a look and there, to my horror, were these things, these little mites, crawling in my pubic hair. Then I remembered what Benjamin had said. "They don't call him Crab-I for nothing." This was crab lice. Leroy had given me crab lice. What a fool I had been, sleeping with him so soon. I put a shilling in the meter and ran a bath with loads of Dettol and shaved off all my hair down there. I don't know what caused me to itch more – the crabs or the shaved pubes. Monday would be the Doctor's for me, then.

I turned out the light and went to sleep.

3   The Cinic

I was first in the queue to see Doctor Samuels at 8.30 on Monday morning. No appointments - just first come first served. After me, soon came women with their runny nosed children, squabbling as they waited, bored in the queue. "Be-have!" yelled a West Indian mother to her two children scrapping on the pavement, "or is licks fe bot' o' yu." They were quiet for a moment. An Irish woman with a baby in a bashed-out pram, sobbed uncontrollably. No-one took any notice, not even me. I was too wrapped up in contemplating the dramas in my own life. An old man arrived, coughing and spluttering, followed by his wife. "Bleedin' freezing, innit?" she said to the Irish lady. 'Wha's up? He been 'ittin' yer again? Yu wanna tell him where to get off, lovie."

The door to the surgery opened and I led the way in, making sure I was first to register with the dour looking receptionist. The waiting room was filling fast, but at least I would be first to go in. 9am sharp, Dr. Samuels opened the door. 'Jenifer MacKay," he called. That's me then, I thought as I went in. He was a pleasant enough old guy, straight to the point, not exactly a bedside manner, but OK in his own way. I liked him. I thought I could be big and brave enough, like I was when I asked to go on the pill, which my previous doctor had given me, albeit reluctantly. I tried to begin…

"I think I've got…………………"

"Go on," he said kindly.

"Crabs" I blurted out and then burst into tears.

"First of all young lady," he began, "I don't treat Venereal Diseases here. If indeed you have crab lice, like you suspect, then you may have contracted another venereal disease at the same time, so you must go to the VD Clinic in Praed Street. You won't need an appointment. Just go along and they do all the tests. It's quite confidential, but you will have to get your boyfriend tested too."

I was too shocked to say anymore and was doing my best to hold off the tears. What had I come to? Venereal Disease? Was that like syphilis or the clap, whatever that was? I felt small, foolish, stupid and terribly ashamed.

"He's not even my boyfriend……I just met him and…."

"Jenifer, now, now," he said kindly. "I am an old-fashioned man and believe that sex should take place within marriage. Sex is something that a woman should only have with one man who loves her and protects her. When you young girls go on the pill, you think that it's a green light to have fun. But this is the outcome. If you don't have a regular boyfriend Jenifer, I may decide to refuse you any further prescriptions for the pill until you are in a stable relationship with someone whom you intend to marry."

He wrote out a referral letter and handed me a leaflet with the address of the clinic on. I muttered thank you and felt too confused to respond to his little homily about sex. I was a modern woman, and clearly, he was old fashioned and did not understand how it was these days.

I went home and made myself a cup of tea and some toast. I prepared myself to go down to That Place, wishing Liz was here to go with me. I had phoned my workplace on the way back from the doctor's and told Matron I had bad period pain and a headache. She was not pleased as another staff was on leave, but at that moment I did not care about anything but the agonizing thought I may have a venereal disease. How did I get into this mess?

At least the clinic was in the hospital where Liz was, so I could go and see her after my ordeal. When I got there, I tried to follow the directions on the leaflet. "Department of Genito-Urinary Medicine" the sign read. I equated that with what was on the leaflet and that this must be the new term for what my elderly Doctor called the VD Clinic. I went down the staircase and found I was in the basement of the hospital. A painted pathway was set out on the floor with arrows for me to follow. I passed porters with trolleys of washing and other stuff in big waste containers. I felt embarrassed. They must know where I am going, I thought, holding my head down and wishing I was wearing a headscarf and dark glasses or something to disguise me. There were the signs – Men, Women. I had to pass the Men's Clinic before I got to the Women's Clinic. The door was open. Oh no, that meant someone might see me. I could see there were three white guys in there and two black guys. I rushed past and into the Women's Clinic, where, thankfully, the door was shut. I went up to the reception and handed her my Doctor's letter. She took me into a room to fill out basic details and gave me card with a number on it and the opening times of the clinic and a phone number.

"Bring this with you on every visit" she said, "the Doctor will call you by this number. Don't worry, it will be fine. They are all very nice here. What they do is take some swabs and you come back here and wait for the results. Then you go back in and get treated if you need to. If you do have anything wrong, we have a Social Worker for you to talk to. You may be asked to come back for a further check up. Is that OK?"

I nodded sheepishly. I was hoping I would wake up and this was all a dream. I waited on the chair behind the door so, if someone came in, I could not be seen through the open door. I read the magazines and avoided the gaze of the other three women there, all white and much older than me. I immediately thought of the woman Liz had seen with Gregory and imagined them all to be like her. I was different, I hoped the Doctor would be able to see that. I was not a prostitute like I imagined they were. Eventually it was my turn.

"Come in and take a seat" said a cheery young male doctor. I groaned inside. How embarrassing was this? He read the letter. "Ah let's see. OK. Your GP says you found some crab lice – annoying little devils, aren't they? And he wants us to give you a check over just to make sure nothing else is wrong. Sensible GP. Seems like he's looking out for you!"

I felt at ease with his cheery matter of fact manner and just thought to myself I was an adult now and I just had to deal with it in a matter of fact way like him. He asked me routine questions, like when my last period was, when I last had sex and was it with a new partner and when my last partner was before that. I explained how I had seen the lice and what I had done about it. I also said I felt sore and itchy down there, that I had just noticed that this morning. Then he asked me to wait outside again. A few minutes later, a nurse called my number and beckoned me to follow her to a cubicle. There was a doctor's couch, but it had these stirrup things at the end. There was a trolley with weird looking instruments on and tubes of stuff.

"If you'd like to remove your pants and tights and sit up on the end here. While we wait for Doctor Hanson, I will take some blood tests and, after he's seen you, I would like you to pass some urine in here please."

She handed me a kidney shaped tray with a pot in it with my number on. There were so many questions that I wanted to ask but I could not bring myself to even open my mouth. I just did as I was bid. I was afraid of the couch with the stirrup things. Just what was he going to do to me? I would soon find out. I sat up as she directed while she took some blood. "This is to test for Syphilis" she said. I bust into tears. "Don't worry. It's just routine. Syphilis is rare these days but we have to test everyone anyway. That's great. Now just hold that cotton wool in place for a few minutes and then I will give you a plaster. There you go. Lovely! Now let's have you ready for the Doctor. Just swivel round here and lay back. Put your legs in here, wriggle down a bit. That's it. Perfect. He will be here in a minute."

Perfect? Was she joking? It did not feel like 'perfect' to me. I was uncomfortable and I felt vulnerable. I was trying not to cry. Anyway, the handsome Doctor Hanson came in. God, this was embarrassing. He lifted my skirt and I was fully exposed. How could he do this job all day, I wondered. He looked around the outside for the lice.

"Can't see any lice Jenifer, you must have shaved them all off, but there could still be the odd egg lying around so we will treat you and give to some stuff to use at home OK?"

I nodded and made to get off the couch. "Whoa there!" he said, I'm afraid there's more to come!" I resumed the supine position. He parted my vaginal lips. "Yes, you are looking a bit red. It's early days though and we may just have to grow a sample swab as the culprit bug may not show up today. Ok. Just relax. This one stings a bit. There we go. Just taking a little swab from your urethra"

I nearly shot off the couch. The nurse held my hand. "It's OK love, just try to relax. It will all be over in a minute".

Relax!! Ha!! That was a joke. Oh my God! The next thing I felt was something cold pushing into my vagina. I squirmed in pain. I was terrified.

"It's Ok, Jenifer. Just opening you up a little to have a look inside. That's it. Ooh, Yes. I can see you are growing some little buggies in here. Don't worry we will soon get rid of them."

I could not help the tears now. I hated that Leroy with all my might. If only I knew someone to beat him up – but how could I tell anyone, except Liz, about what had happened?

23

"Ok, Ok," I heard the nurse say handing me some tissue." All done now. Just wipe that gel away and then go and do me that urine sample. Pee, stop and then pee into the pot, then leave it in the dish in the little hatch. Then go and sit in the waiting room until Doctor calls you for the results."

I felt dazed, sore and ashamed. I did as she bid and sat in the waiting room. No-one else was crying, so I held back and did my best to compose myself. The wait seemed like ages. I shuffled in my seat, not wanting to pick up the magazines in case I caught something off them. I scrabbled through my bag and turned out lots of bus tickets and sweet wrappers. I checked my purse and counted the money. At last, the Doctor called my number and I went into his little consulting room.

"Well Jenifer. We found some little bugs and, yes, you do have an infection. Have you heard of Gonorrhea? Well we found some of those growing. But don't worry. It's easy to treat and soon you will be OK. I will need you to come back in ten days and no sex until you are clear, OK?" I nodded. A million questions went round in my mind, but I was too numb to speak.

"After you have seen the nurse again, we can fit you in to see the Health Social Worker."

"Why?" I asked.

"Just so she can answer any questions you may have and we need to trace that partner of yours"

"But." I began, but he was already ushering me to the nurse and that couch again.

"Don't worry," she said, "the worst is over. I am going to treat the lice with this solution, just dabbing it around and then I am going to give you some anti-biotics as an injection in your bum."

I looked horrified. What an undignified ordeal. I wanted my Mum, but how could I tell her about this? I removed my tights and pants again, sat up on the couch, laid back, legs in the stirrups, while she applied the lotion. She chatted away to me, but my mind was elsewhere, wondering how Liz was. I wanted to see her so badly. When the nurse had done, she got me out of the stirrups and asked me to roll on my side away from her. Then I felt this sharp jab in my bum. The final indignity. Tears streamed down my face. But she did not see.

"OK get dressed now. All done. Just wait in the waiting room. The Social Worker will see you in about ten minutes."

I must have taken ages getting my pants, tights, shoes and coat back on. I fixed my face and brushed my hair and went out and sat back in the waiting room. I was so in my own world I hardly heard the Social Worker call my number. She led me into her office at the back of the clinic. There were two chairs, a coffee table, kettle and a small fridge.

24

"Hi Jenifer. My name is Sally Graham and I am the Health Social Worker. Before we start, would you like some tea? I have some biscuits too. Nothing exciting, I'm afraid, just good old NHS digestives".

I was glad of anything, suddenly feeling hungry. It was 1.30pm and I had been in there for two hours already.

"Ok," she said gently, "It looks like your boyfriend has given you some sexually transmitted infections."

"V.D. you mean?" I asked.

"Well, we don't use that term these days, but, yes, if you like. The tests have found Gonorrhea and you have also been treated for Crab Lice, although we did not find any today. We will need to contact your boyfriend."

I had tried to call Leroy three times but there had been no answer. She handed me the phone.

"Would you like to try from here?" I rang the number I had on a piece of paper that he had written for me. It rang a few times and then someone answered it. It was not Leroy, but a man with an Irish sounding voice.

"Can I speak to Leroy please?" I asked.

"This is a phone box, love. I was just passing and heard it ring. You have the wrong number, sure you do."

I put the phone down without as much as thanking the man. Leroy must have known he had given me a bogus number, so he had not wanted to see me again after all. I felt so used. I told the Social Worker the whole story. I then realized what a fool I had been, getting so carried away with all the romantic dancing. I didn't even know his last name, where he lived, only that he was a painter and decorator. She could not even trace the hospital records as there was so little to go on. We talked for ages and I told her about Liz. She said we needed to do some thinking about our lives and whether we were making positive choices for ourselves. She gave me a card with her phone number on, saying I could call her if I needed to come in to see her again. She said Liz should have a check up too and she would be happy to talk to her if she came in. She was so kind and I thanked her. She also have me a contact slip just in case Leroy got in touch again. She wished me well and I left there feeling a bit more sorted out at least.

I went back up the hospital staircase and out to the main entrance and who should I see walking in but Tempo. Oh Shit! I was glad I was in the main entrance and not in the basement – that would have been a dead giveaway. However, Tempo did not see me, or at least pretended not to, but I saw him and he was going down the stairs to the Department of Genito Urinary Medicine. I thought of Bev and that night some months back and how she was best shot of him. I looked up the directions to Ward 9, where Liz was, and went up to see her. It was half past two now and visiting time was until half past three, so we had some time together. I got to her bed and she looked even worse. All the bruising had come out now.

"Hi Liz. How are you?" I said barely able to hold back the tears. What we were both going through was just terrible; at least mine did not show, but it was just as much abuse, exacted more sneakily, with me as a 'willing' participant. However, it was not to the extent of what Liz had suffered. Poor Liz. My heart went out to her.

'What did the Doc say? I sat beside her. She was able to talk to me a bit better today.

"The Doc said everything was Ok, but Jen, they did a pregnancy test and they say I am pregnant – about 2 months. Of course, it will be Greg's but I don't want it. What am I going to do?"

With a bit of luck, you might lose it, I thought to myself, but I could hardly say that. "I don't know," I answered vaguely, wondering why she had not been taking the pill.

"Not only that. The Hospital called the Police because they said I had been assaulted. I told the Doctor that I had just got out of my boyfriend's car and after he drove off, this man came up and asked if he could use our loo, so I said "No" but as I opened he door, he pushed me into the flat and into the bedroom and did this. I think they believed me. I said I did not want the Police involved but they said they had to anyway. Report it, I mean; so, two big coppers came to see me this morning. They didn't believe me and they knew I was covering up. Apparently, they had already been to the house and spoken to Old Nosey Parker upstairs who told them it was my boyfriend. I said he had just dropped me off, but she said she saw him come in and then leave the flat after half an hour or so, and that she had heard 'a kerfuffal' but had done nothing because it was not her business. I insisted to them it was not my boyfriend, but still they said they wanted to speak to him. Jen, I don't even know where the man lives, I just have his Auntie's phone number and wait for him to come round. You know how it is with these guys. Anyway, the copper almost threatened to do me if I kept lying, so I told them everything. Jen, I am so scared. They say they know him and he is someone to steer clear of. He's dangerous. Of course, they wouldn't say more than that about him. Jen, we have to move. I still said I would not press charges, but they want me to and I can't. It's his word against mine and the woman upstairs can't actually say it was him who did this, she is still just assuming. I am so scared. What's your news anyway – You look like you've been crying?"

I told Liz the whole story, including the bit about me seeing Tempo, and she listened as shocked as I was. What were we doing? What were we thinking of? We were so out of our depth involved in a world of criminals, pimps and God knows what, and that was where the music had led us. Liz said she hated black men and from now on no more - ever. I said it was not all black men – look at Norman and Winny, even Benjamin and others that we knew from before we started going down the West End. They were nice guys. They worked hard, supported their

26

families, loved their women and did not do anything bad. "Yeah but they're boring." I couldn't believe she said that. I was beginning to see another side to Liz, one that I did not like. However, seeing her in that state I wasn't going to take issue with her about anything.

I kissed her goodbye. "I tell you what I'm going to do tonight. I'm going to go back to the flat and clear up your room so it's all nice when you come home in a couple of days."

"Thanks," said Liz vaguely. Then, more adamantly. "I've been thinking. Let's move. Yeah, I know it will take a few days or weeks and that, but we can do it and, in the meantime, can we swap bedrooms? I can't face the thought of sleeping in that room ever again."

"OK, I will swap the rooms around, but I don't know about moving. I am broke – as per."

Liz got a wicked look on her face. "Gregory might have beat me, yeah, and tear up all my clothes, and that, but there's one thing he forgot."

"What?" I asked, curious to know what she had up her sleeve.

"You know that twenty quid I had the other night? Well I only spent about £2; plus, I had some more stashed away that he gave me from before. I reckon I have got about a ton tucked away. It's in the tin under the mattress."

"Wow!" A hundred quid was a lot of money.

Liz looked at me and managed a cheeky smile. "Game, set and match!"

4   **The Visitation**

I got back to the flat, made some tea, picked off the plaster from the blood test and thought about the events of the day. I put together a fry up – there was nothing else quick to eat -and then I put some music on and set to clearing up the mess in Liz's room. I got two black plastic rubbish sacks and started with all the ripped clothes – even that lovely Biba dress. What a shame. I looked to see if I could mend any of them, but I thought Liz certainly would not want to wear them ever again, neither me, come to that. I shoveled them all in to sacks and then carefully picked up all the bottles from the floor, putting the broken ones into the sack, then I got the broom (we didn't own a hoover) and swept up the glass as best I could. The light was bad and I couldn't see if I had got all the little shards. I just hope for the best. I stripped the bed and put the sheets into the bagwash bag and put it in the passage. It was starting to look a bit improved. Then I took all the rest of her stuff and took it into my room and put it on my bed. Soon her room was empty. Then I set to having a good thorough clean. I had to open the window, so pungent was the smell of the perfume that had spilled. Tabu, she wore. I put the furniture on the top of her bed and had another good sweep, then I got a rag, a brush and a bucket of water and gave everything good scrub, even the floor. I put the furniture back and gave it all a polish. I went to get some of my clean sheets and made the bed up and then went and got all my stuff. It was now 9pm and I was tired after my mammoth going over. I took the overflowing rubbish bag to the bin outside.

"Jenifer. Jenifer. Is that you? I wanna word wiv you. Where's my Lizzie?' I knew that rough Cockney voice anywhere. It was Jean, Liz's Mum. (She hated being called Lizzie).

"Oh, Hi Jean," I said and was about to invite her in. Good job the front room was clean and tidy.

"Right." said Jean, "I'm not standing here talking on the doorstep, it's raining for one and I don't want the neighbours earwigging and poking their noses in. Especially round here". She marched past me and went into the front room.

"Do you want some tea, Jean?"

"This is not a social call Jenifer, so no ta, I won't bother to take tea with you."

Take tea indeed. I stifled a laugh. She perched herself on the edge of our black imitation leather sofa and looked around. "I see my Lizzie keeps it clean then."

"We both do." I answered rapidly. What does she think I am?

"That's as may be. Now. To get to the point. Where is Lizzie? No Lies now. I've heard she's been beaten up."

How on earth could Jean have known that? There was no point in lying. I don't think I could have made it up if I had tried. "Yes, badly." I said. She's in the Paddington Hospital in Praed Street."

"My days!" exclaimed Jean. "My girl, my pet, Oh, Oh." She started to cry. I went and got her a tissue and some water.

"I will tell you all what happened. There's no point in keeping anything from you as you will find out anyway."

I sat down and told Jean all what had happened, about Gregory and everything. She seemed grateful, thanking me for being so honest. I then told her how Liz had asked me to swap rooms and how I had just finished cleaning her room and moved my stuff in there and would do mine for her tomorrow. Her face turned back to thunder.

"What? You stupid girl! What did you do that for? You have destroyed the evidence for the police. They need to get fingerprints and everything to nail this guy."

28

I told her Liz did not want to press charges. She just wanted to move away and forget all about it. She was scared of Gregory and I was too. Jean then accused me of deliberately destroying the evidence and covering up for Gregory.

"Are you sleeping wiv him too?" I could not believe how callous this woman was.

"Of course not. Not even if you paid me." That was the wrong thing to say, given the circumstances.

"So, who does pay you then? Do you sleep with blokes for money?" I denied this strenuously and burst into tears.

"Sorry dear," she said after letting me howl for a bit. "This is all a bit much for me and I dunno what to fink. I 'specs you've 'ad a bit of a shock too. Why don't we 'ave that nice cuppa you mentioned before and start again at the beginnin' of all the 'ole story."

I could have done with just going to bed, but a cuppa seemed like a good idea and as much as I wanted Jean to go, I didn't want her to leave believing heaven knows what about me.

"Coo, you makes a good brew don't you, dear?"

Oh well, I thought, at least I am her 'dear' now.

"Right then; let me 'ear all about ya. I've only met ya the once, with Lizzie, like, but I don't know nuffin' abaht ya."

I told her how I had met Liz while I was at college. She was doing hairdressing and I was doing nursery nursing. We started hanging out together and had a group of black and white friends who were into the soul and rock steady scene. We had all started going to clubs together, but they were mainly from South London and it was hard getting back from there at night. I told Jean how we met Benjamin and Tony, also at our college and they were nice young black boys, learning trades, and we went out with them and that's how we found out about the clubs. I had a romance with Benjamin (I didn't go into the details), but Liz never really liked Tony in that way and he got fed up pursuing her. While I was dating Benjamin, she was hanging out with some other girls and then she started going down to the Hot Forties. When my romance ended, I started going down Hot Forties with her. I was still living at home, but my Mum and I argued over everything – the music, my friends, Benjamin.

"I can't say as I blame her," muttered Jean.

I ignored her and went on to say how I had left home and went to stay at Liz's old bedsit and one day she suggested we get a flat together and I had agreed. That's how we ended up in this one in Malvern Road.

29

"I don't understand it. Two nice girls like you, grew up in nice suburbs an' all, got education and you want to be in this dump chasing those coloured boys. None of 'em are any good. None of 'em."

I thought to myself that this was rich seeing how Liz's brothers had both been in trouble with the law and their Dad, Frankie was a known bent ex-cop. At least no-one in my family was a villain. I said nothing in response to her comment. Liz had told me how her whole family were racist and she didn't want anything to do with them. I suppose it was this that drew us together. My Dad had called me a 'nigger lover' and virtually thrown me out of the house. Liz and I often said that we'd left them behind in their suburban ways and their suburban values and they could stuff themselves. We used to laugh.

"We are each other's family now," she used to say and I used to agree. Indeed, we were like sisters.

"I s'pose you wanna know 'ow I got wind that somefin' was up." I had not asked, but as she was going to tell me anyway, I let her continue.

"It was Frankie. My 'usband. He was a copper and well known in the West End. He used to watch the gambling clubs. Illegal of course, but they was all for the posh lot, so it was difficult to close them. High up connections like. I was workin' in one, on the Roulette tables. That's 'ow I met Frankie. Anyway. He 'ad a mate called Big Dave. Frankie retired and we moved to Watford and we went into the pub trade. Big Dave, he's not like Frankie. He liked the ol' duckin' and divin' lark too much. It was all 'e knew. No ambition. Anyway. He bought a club near Carnaby Street. That dive yous two go to." My eyes were popping out.

"Does Liz know this?"

"Nah. Not to my knowledge anyroad. Now, the story goes like this. Big Dave has to keep the Old Bill sweet, know what I mean?" I didn't, but I let her think I did.

"Right," she went on, "Big Dave has got a few Old Bill on side. Top brass, not plods. One of them is a mate of Frankie's. Good mate an' all. Now for years Big Dave was a friend of the family and he knows all my kids. He seen Liz at that dive, yeah, that one, Hot Forties, and 'e's told this copper, what's Frankie's mate, that he seen yous two in the dive."

I was tired and could hardly stay awake but this was interesting. I let her continue.

"One night, Big Dave saw out of the office window that Liz was wrapped round that black bastard's neck. 'E's told him 'e never wants to see him talk to 'er again. Threatens 'im like."

"Oh." I said putting the puzzle together in my own mind, "is that why Gregory said he never wanted her to go there again?"

"Yeah, must be - that and to hide his dirty business. He's a bastard, Jen, make no mistake. A fuckin' black bastard."

I nearly asked her if she called white villains fuckin' white bastards, but I didn't want her to get sidetracked. It would only be some racist ranting, so I let her carry on with the story.

"Now," she continued, "Saturday gone, the girl on cloaks saw Liz coming in on her own and she knew 'our friend' was there, so she phones Big Dave to come down. Anyway, b'time 'e's got there, Liz and 'our friend' 'ave gone. He's thought nuffin' of it at the time, like. Then Paddington Hospital calls Paddington Green nick and the boss recognizes Liz's name and clocks it that she's Frankie's daughter, so 'e sends two plods out to see wha's 'appened. When they report back, 'e phones up Frankie's mate in the West End nick and they pay Big Dave a visit and get the story from him. So, we know all about what happened, how Liz went there on her own about half one in the morning, finds that black cunt with a girl - one of his prozzies - Yeah, don't look so shocked Jen, you must have known."

So, Jean knew all along that Liz was in hospital. Maybe she was just seeing if I would tell her the truth. I said that I didn't exactly know what he got up to, but I had suspected he was dodgy.

"Dodgy ain't the word for it. Prozzies all over, beats 'em up, to a pulp, and sends 'em out again. He's a psycho and wants lockin' up. Anyway, the barman saw Lizzie throw a drink over 'im an' that 'ooker, an 'ow he leaves with our Lizzie, all calm like nothin's goin' on. Jen, I want that bastard putting away for what 'e done to my girl and now you, ya daft cow, you've destroyed the bleedin' evidence!!"

"I'm so sorry. I wasn't to know," I cried. "This is all so awful." Jean put her arm around me and gave me a tissue.

"Not to worry. Like you say. You weren't to know all these ins and outs. But we will get 'im. 'ook or by crook, probably crook now the 'ook's gone." She laughed a moment at her own joke.

"I wish I was at home with my Mum, listening to her nagging. I just don't feel safe. Jean, please will you stay here tonight?" Jean hummed and harred but went upstairs to phone Frankie. Mrs. Cameron was not pleased at being disturbed so late, but I said it was an emergency.

I lent Jean one of Liz's nightdresses. "Bit short," she noted, but we were both so tired we got into Liz's bed that I had remade with my clean sheets. Still neither of us slept that well, this being the room, and the very bed, in which Liz, my friend, Jean's daughter, had been so badly beaten up and raped.

I was glad when it was morning. I got washed and dressed and showed Jean our moldy bathroom. She turned her nose up, but still used the facilities to freshen up. I made us both tea and toast. We sat on our sofa silently eating until she spoke.

"You goin' t'work today? She asked me, mouth full of toast.

I was feeling awful.

"I don't think so", I replied, still thinking it through. "No actually I will phone in sick. I feel awful and need to clean out the other room for Liz. She should be coming home today or tomorrow."

"The only 'ome Liz is going to is 'ome with me. She will need looking after and you can't do that, Jen. You're workin'. And she needs to be out o' this dump. I will ask Frankie to pay both of you's rent to the end of the month which will give you time to get another sharer in or move out y'self." Her mind was made up, I could see, so there was no point telling her about our plans, nor about the £100 that lay in the tin under the mattress, right where she had been lying!

I decided to go to the hospital with Jean to see Liz. She didn't know the way for one and hated South Kilburn. "Too many blacks" she complained. Oh, shut up, I thought.

When we got to the hospital, Liz was sitting up, looking brighter but still awful. Her Mum nearly fainted when she saw her and she nearly fainted when she saw her Mum, coming in with yours truly. I sat back while Jean took charge and in no time, she had Liz eating out of her hands. Just the thought of the security of Mum and Dad felt good, even worth putting up with the nagging and all that racism, but to my surprise, and horror, there was Liz joining in with all the black bastard and black cunt talk. Even referring to one of the nurses as 'that Nig Nog'. Now is not the time to say anything, I thought to myself. But I had a plan. When Jean went to the loo I said,

"Liz, I cleared out your room last night and I checked under the mattress. The tin is not there!"

"What?" she exclaimed. "He couldn't have done – could he?"

"Well it's gone, unless old Nosey Parker upstairs used her landlady keys and found it, or unless he took it when he came over Saturday afternoon, it's gone. And you know I wouldn't take it."

"Fuck!" said Liz and then again "Fuck! Are you sure?"

"Yep," I replied with the confidence of one who has searched and searched and done a real thorough job. "But I haven't told your Mum. Nor about the baby."

This nicely deflected her attention towards the worst thing that she could tell her Mum – that she was expecting that 'black bastard's' baby.

Jean came back carrying paper cups of machine tea and three Kit Kats. I sat for a bit while Jean told Liz everything. "You crafty buggers!" was all Liz could manage to come up with, "but all your noseying didn't stop 'im though, did it?"

32

"We was just keepin' an eye out for ya. Anyway, I told Jen, Dad will pay your rent to the end of the monf. I don't want you going back there, Lizzie. Come 'ome wiv us and we will look after ya."

"OK Mum. I'd love to. I was gettin' fed up with South Kilburn. Too many blacks – though Jen likes them, don't you Jen?"

"Yes!" I said, "I do actually. People like Marvalette and Norman, Grace and Winny, the Mums at the nursery where I worked, Rosie, even Bev and her crew, or Benjamin and Tony. They are all nice people. But you didn't seem to want to know them. You always went after the villains and look where it got you."

Liz burst into tears and Jean said she thought I'd better go back to 'my blackies' and leave Liz alone.

"Fine," I said. Thinking 'you wait 'til you find out about the baby'. I felt chuffed that I was about to rip Liz off for her £100 as I thought she deserved it. I was safe knowing that she could not and would not mention that to her Mum – about the money he had given her. I went back to the flat and started packing my stuff. I found the tin with the money. It also had a stash of weed. Crafty cow, I thought. She's saved that up too! I had to take it somewhere fast to make sure old Jeanie did not come for it. She had phoned and told Mrs. Cameron to tell me that she was taking Liz home that day and would send Frankie and Liz's brother for her stuff tomorrow evening– and I'll be gone already. I thought to myself. Oh, and she also said that Liz had said I could take all the records.

I decided to pay the money into the bank there and then – if I ran, I could catch it before closing. Having deposited my stash, I got the bus and went to Marvalette's getting there about four o'clock. It was on the off chance that she might be home from work. Norman opened the door. He was on shift work, so he was home. What a relief. For the first time since this whole nightmare started, I burst into tears and told him the whole lot – except about Leroy and the VD. Norman was a calm kind of guy. He didn't hug me when I cried, but just made me some tea and sat and listened.

"A so it go. Y'know Jen. I never like dat Liz. I coulda tell she was prejudice y'know. She jus' never seem genuine, not like you. You's a very nice girl and Marvalette always talk about how you do dis and dat for Aaron and a lot of the coloured, or black, parents say 'ow good you is wid deir kids while some of dose others don' give a shit. So, if we can 'elp you, we will. But before I say anything, we mus' wait for Marvalette to come in and we can discuss. Now go an' get some res' on the sofa. Dat is, if Aaron will let you."

I went in the front room where Aaron was watching TV and sat on the sofa. Within minutes I was asleep.

I woke up to the sound of Marvalette's cheerful voice. I could hear her talking with Norman in the kitchen. They both appeared at the doorway.

33

"We 'ave been talkin' 'bout your situation. Jen, you can't stay in that flat. Norman will run you over and you can pick your stuffs and bring dem back 'ere. We 'ave a spare bed in Aaron's room and you can have that. Stay wid us til you get yourself sorted". I said I could pay them and I even confessed to her about the money. Marvalette laughed.

"Serve her blasted arse right!"

"And I've got her stash of weed too!" I added.

"Now you're talkin! Show it to Norman." I did. He confirmed it was indeed top Sensi and that we could all have a little smoke later!

I felt so relieved to know I had such good friends. I knew I would never see Liz again and felt, at the age of nineteen, that I was starting a new life. Norman came with me and we quickly gathered my stuff that I had packed, including the records.

"Bwoy" You two 'ave some good music 'ere!" chimed Norman appreciatively.

"Never mind about that now", I said. "I want to get out of here in case the Watford mob get come tonight instead of tomorrow. Let's go."

With the last plastic sack and box of my stuff loaded into Norman's car we drove off. I left the keys with Mrs. Cameron and said my goodbyes. Now I had really given Old Nosey Parker something to gossip about as I drove off with Norman and all my stuff. Ace!!

By the time we got back to Marvalette's she had made up the bed for me and sorted me out some cupboard space for my things. My boxes of household stuff – towels, sheets, cutlery, plates and a few pots, went in the cupboard under the stairs and my clothes fitted well into the space she had made. The records sat next to her and Norman's pile, waiting for some good selections later on. Dinner was on the stove and a lovely smell of West Indian stew chicken and rice beckoned us four to the kitchen where we had our first of many family meals together.

"You mus' teach Jen to cook," joked Norman to Marvalette.

"You bet!" she replied "Yu t'ink is me doin' all de work in dis 'ouse!"

We laughed, and after the dishes were washed up and Aaron was in bed – I was now number one bedtime story reader- the three of us settled down and Norman selected tunes from my box and we listened to rock steady, smoking a couple of spliffs until it was time for bed. I felt safe and happy, welcomed and like I belonged. No-one could be more genuinely nicer than these two. Best of all I was walking distance from work. Next day, I arrived at 8am for my shift, happily starting my new life. I would probably have to tell Marvalette at some point about what happened with Leroy, but not yet. Plenty of time for that!

5   The New Life

My New Life settled into a cosy routine. I didn't go out at all for a good six months and was happy to stay in and babysit while Marvalette and Norman went out to parties. I had been in my job a whole year and had got a pay increase, plus extra London Weighting. I brought home £15.65p a week (we had gone over to the new money about a year ago) and I gave Marvalette £3 a week for everything. She wouldn't take more. I saved a fiver too and had plenty left for records and clothes. Norman and I would have little competitions about the latest white label single. I used to go to Hawkeye Records in Harlesden – Benjamin had taken me there over a year back and introduced me to the guy in the shop. When we split up, I still used to go there and had introduced Liz to the joy of buying records. Norman used to go to some people on Askew Road and we bought a couple of records every week, or sometimes an LP. Marvalette used to laugh and say,

"You two should start a sound system. Y'ave plenty good music!"

I liked Norman. I felt I could trust him. He never made a move towards me and Marvalette trusted me around her husband, so the home atmosphere was relaxed and comfortable. One Saturday afternoon, Norman was tired, but Marvalette was itching to go out that evening. She had promised Bev and Jemma she would come to the house dance in Powis Square – more Duke Tam. Marvalette begged me to go with her.

"Oh, c'mon Jen. You can't live like a Nun for the rest of your days. It will be good."

I had a choice of new clothes that I had not even worn and I sort of wanted to go so that I could at least wear a snazzy outfit. But Duke Tam? – Leroy might be there. I had never told Marvalette what had happened. I felt too foolish and ashamed, for one, and did not want her to think less of me because of it. The only person who knew was Liz and we were no longer in contact with each other. But I had to face the world and its idiots at some time, I thought, and nothing could be a worse ordeal than the Clinic, so I steeled myself to handle the prospect of bumping into Leroy.

"Ok," I replied, "You're on. Let's go out!" She put some music on and started to dance.

> 'People get ready to do do rocksteady
> People get ready to do do rocksteady
> Out in the moonlight we will dance
> Out in the moonlight, hands in hands
> I'm just a lonely boy looking for someone
> To love me the way that I love you.'[iv]

"I love that sax in the middle playing 'Blue Moon'" I said as we swept our hips around the room, before we both came in with the chorus line in perfect harmony, pretending to sing into a microphone. Then we fell about laughing.

Marvalette went to phone Bev to say she was bringing me and that Norman was staying in. The conversation began to sound a bit – well, uncomfortable, is the only way to say it really. From what I could hear from Marvalette and the expression on her face, it seemed I was not welcome.

"But she's my good fren'," I heard Marvalette say, "No matter she white or black, she's me fren and dat's dat. .... Well, she's comin' and I don't give a hoot what Jemma seh jus' because turn she self Black Power. Blouse and skirts! We is all human, Bev, man."

Black Power was becoming strong in the community. Developments – and events - in America, had begun to influence and grow a whole political scene here. I had heard of Martin Luther King and the Civil Rights Movement and learning about that in social studies in college had helped shape my views and awareness about race issues and the stand I had taken with my parents. But this was very different and sometimes Norman would pick up a leaflet from the counter in the record shop about a meeting for this or that. People were talking about a guy called Malcom X, and there had been a big trial in America of the Chicago Seven in 1968, where seven young men had been accused of causing a riot. There was an eighth man, Bobby Seale – they had broadcasted his trial a while ago and it showed how the police had really conspired against him. A total fit-up, as we would say. He had been a founder member of the Black Panther Party in America and it seemed that one similar was starting here, The Pumas. I was interested and would read some of Norman's pamphlets, but he didn't always leave them around. Maybe he thought of them as private or maybe he didn't want to offend or upset me.

"Don' worry yuself wid all dat, Jen," he would say.

Anyway, there was going to be a march against police brutality next week in North Kensington and Norman was going to go. Marvalette was unsure. She supported the cause – her brother had recently been stopped and searched in an unpleasant way and she knew of many young men, as did Norman, who were 'taking pressure' as she put it. But she was afraid for Norman. She did not want him to have to "face up no police brutality at all!"

When she came off the phone, I asked Marvalette what was wrong. It wasn't Bev who was the problem, she told me. In fact, I knew that Bev quite liked me after she got over that awful night with Tempo and Liz. She thought I had been 'cool' in how I had handled it and she liked me for that. Plus, she had a baby now who was in my nursery, so I saw her quite often when she brought her in and collected her and a few times we had chatted. No, it wasn't Bev, but Jemma. She had 'gone Black Power"; that meant, according to Marvalette, she had given herself a big Angela Davis Afro hairdo, wore jeans and no make-up and 'read books an' t'ing', She had been going to meetings of the newly formed Black Puma Party and was helping to organize the demonstration. I had to wonder what me going to a dance and police brutality had in common. I asked Marvalette that very question. She shrugged. "Search me," she replied.

At the heart of the matter were some very serious issues about racism in our society that I was beginning to be more and more aware of, especially since I had been living at Marvalette's. I had been thrown into a rude awakening by the reactions of my family at the thought of me even mixing with black people at college, let alone socializing or, God forbid, going out with a black boy. I had grown up in Oxey, not far from Watford where Liz was from, and we had ended up at the college in Willesden because the college in Harrow was oversubscribed for the courses we wanted to do. Some things are just meant to be, and regardless of my parents' fears, this did me lots of good as it was an education in itself to go to a very mixed college, have my placement in a nursery in Harlesden, and to learn to mix with people who were very different from me in terms of background and culture. My parents thought it was dreadful and for a while they fought to get me back into the college in Harrow, but I would not have changed even if they had succeeded. Sure, the area was no leafy suburb, and I never realized until now that people lived in houses with all the rooms rented out, even sharing just one bathroom and a cooker on the landing. Many of the parents, both black and white, that I met through my work had real housing problems – lack of space, damp, outside toilets, no bathroom, and that sort of thing, and I had grown up taking those things for granted. My Mum said,

"Jenifer, dear, before we moved out here, I grew up in Dollis Hill. We were bombed out of our house during the war and lived wherever we could find rooms as my Dad worked as a milkman and it was hard to get transferred out. Eventually, he got a transfer to Stanmore and we moved up this way. I can't tell you how pleased we were. And now, here's you, wanting to go back to the slums and thinking it's all exciting and different to the boring old 'burbs. But I tell you, my girl, living in a slum is not fun and exciting and you meet real low class people, like all these blacks you are associating with. Do you know where they come from? God knows what they are used to in their own countries. They have diseases and all sorts they are bringing here. Their way of life is different and they are not like us. They haven't had the education or the moral upbringing that we have. You will come to regret it, my girl, and I just hope and pray nothing happens to you before you come to your senses."

That was the mild version of my parents' racist views. They were steeped in mindless prejudice and my Dad wanted them all "sent back to where they came from – every bleedin' last one of 'em." When I told them I had met this really nice coloured boy at college who was training to be a postman, my Dad hit the roof. "You better just stop seeing him or you are no daughter of mine!" he had shouted at me. Mum said to leave me, that I was sensible and would soon come to my senses, but he was adamant that if I continued to see Benjamin, he would "throw me out on my ear."

Which he did. When my Dad had to face the fact that not only was I dating Benjamin, but we were also sleeping together, out on my ear I was thrown! I went to my sister's place for a few days, but she was as bad and her husband walked out of the room whenever I walked into it. Hence me ending up at Liz's little bedsit and from there we got a flat together and, as I just found a job in a nursery near Ladbroke Grove, it was perfect.

I had met Benjamin at college, but as I was so tied up with my course homework and studying for my exams, I wasn't dating him then, but we were friends. It was at the graduation dance at the college when we got a bit closer and decided to date. Nothing happened for a couple of months but one night we had been to a blues party – my first one – in South London and we missed a lift back so we walked to Brixton where his sister, Doreen, lived, banged on her door at three in the morning and, to my surprise, she welcomed us in with open arms. She was lovely, his sister, and she had been like a mother to him when he arrived from Jamaica aged six years old. I will never forget her house. It was the first West Indian house I had been in, other than party where everything was moved from the rooms. She has a spare room, where we went after having a hot drink in the kitchen.

'Toilet's outside' she said 'and the torch is by the back door. Mind how you go.'

That was another first for me. I'd heard of the outside lav as my Dad called it, but couldn't imagine what a palava it must have been in the winter. Still it was a full moon and Benjamin had taken my hand in the yard, kissing me under the moonlight – before we went to the loo. How romantic! We stayed the night there together in Doreen's spare room on a creaky old double bed with Candlewick bedspreads for bottom and top sheets. Benjamin explained to me how when people came from the West Indies the houses in winter were cold and they could not sleep on the cotton sheets. It seemed odd, but it was soft and comfortable. That's when we first made love. But that is another story, and I digress.

I was by now familiar with what race prejudice was like in terms of what I had experienced, but I was also beginning to find out what it was like in terms of what black people experienced. To be honest, I had wondered, when I encountered people like Tempo, Gregory and Leroy, whether my Mum had a point. But then I thought of Liz's family and what dodgy crooks they were, hidden under a veneer of respectability and affluence. I came to the conclusion that there was good and bad in all races and I just had to look around at all the great friends I had made to realise that I just needed to choose people who were right for me to be friends with and to reject those who I knew were no good, regardless of what colour they were.

I began to see a different side of how race affected my job in the nursery. There was black member of staff there, Gabriella, – we were not friends in that we met outside of work, but we managed the odd chat in the staff room when it was just us on late break or sometimes, we popped out in our lunch break and went round the market together. Norman had brought home a small book by a teacher called Bernard Coard entitled 'How the West Indian Child is Made Educationally Sub-normal in the English School System'. He and Marvalette were concerned about the education that their son, Aaron, would be receiving at the local school, and they had spoken about what had happened to many West Indian children when they first arrived in the UK and started to go to school here. Norman had come here as an adult but Marvalette had had an awful time as a child arriving from Jamaica when she was seven, and I hope to share that story another day. For now, I want to share what happened in my workplace one day.

I went for a walk one lunch time with Gabriella and told her about this book I had read. She sounded surprised that I would have even heard of it, let alone read or understood it. Anyway, it turned out that her ex-husband knew Mr. Coard and had gone to meetings where he had spoken.

"You know it all starts with us, though, don't you, right here in the nursery."

"How?" I asked, not sure what she meant.

"Well, have you ever noticed how some white staff talk about the black parents and how they act with the black children?"

"Oh." I said, nodding. "Like Carol Clarke in your room?"

Gabrielle laughed. "Got it in one. That girl makes some of those babies' life a hell. If a white baby cries, she runs to pick them up. If a black baby cries, she ignores them for as long as she can before she moves her butt towards them. If you hear her go on about Samuels' willie – how he's a big boy and is going to be a 'king dick' – yeah, believe me, that's what she said, and how he will have women all over London. Makes me sick she does. She moans about Nanita's Mum, criticizing her for going to work, yet moaning about Lashley's Mum that she's got a free place for staying at home all day. Can you imagine what it's like for me, listening to that crap day in, day out? Let alone how that mood of hers, and her attitude, comes through to the babies and how it must affect them."

I didn't know what to say. I knew Carol had attitudes a bit like my sister, but I never really thought she would actually let that seep through to the children in that way.

'That's very unprofessional," I said, meekly, lost for words. "I don't know what to say, Gabriella, I didn't know it was that bad. Have you told Matron?"

"What do you think that daft old dear is going to do? Do you know she is nearly seventy – seventy, I tell you - and the borough have been trying to get her to retire for years. She's worked for them since the war, - which one I don't know! No, you can't tell her anything. She thinks she is doing the council a favour by not spending all the budget they allow us, so every year we get less money. Have you noticed we have absolutely nothing as equipment? I buy baby toys out of my own money."

"How long have you worked there, Gabriella?" I asked, wondering why she put up with it. "Six years, and would you believe I am the room senior?" she replied. "It's not easy to speak up when you are on your own. I am the only black staff there and I just keep my head down. You are the only person I have talked to about all this. You won't tell the others, will you? I don't trust any of them."

"It's between you and me," I reassured her. "We will talk again and see what we can do, now we have joined forces, so to speak!" Gabriella laughed and I felt we had ended on a good note.

I had told Marvalette, and she told Norman, about my conversation with Gabriella. She just said it didn't surprise her and left it there. It was as if it had touched a nerve and had hit on a memory that she did not want to speak about. So, coming back to the night when Bev had told Marvalette that Jemma did not really want any white girls coming to the house dance (not that it was her house dance!) because she was all for Black Power these days, I kind of had an inkling of what lay below that seemingly hostile response. I was kind of curious to know more about where she was coming from. Surely, we should all be joining forces to fight to build a world where everyone was treated with the same respect? Where we were equal? I thought of Martin Luther King's speech 'I have a dream' and interpreted it to my own version of that dream, here in West London. But perhaps the 'dream' meant different things to different people – black and white people.

Marvalette relayed back to Norman what Jemma had said to Bev.

"An' I says to 'er, I says, 'Bev, no-one cyan tell me who to fren' and who not to fren'. Cho! Norman, is this 'ow dis Back Power business gwine play out? Don't it soun' like more prejudice to you?"

Marvalette's speech oscillated between Jamaican English, standard London Cockney-ish English, and her 'work voice', depending on what her mood was, who she was taking to or how she felt about what she was saying.

Norman muttered that us ladies needed to sit down and discuss and try to sort it out and come to a conclusion that was agreeable to all, including me. That was Norman's approach to most things in life and was why he was such a rock of stability to Marvalette. If there was any problem between them, Norman would say "Marv'lette, le' we wait 'til Aaron in bed an' den we can sit down an' discoss." And they always did, and sure enough they found solutions and they truly believed in never going to bed on a quarrel.

"Norman - is right yu right. We ladies can discuss later. Jemma live right by where de dance keepin' so we can pass by her and fin' out wha' she gettin' on wid. Right Jen?"

"Yeah, yeah. Fine with me. I would be glad to hear how she sees things. I think there is a lot that I need to learn and I am interested to know why she is saying these things. Plus I don't like the feeling of you having to defend me. It feels like when I had to defend Benjamin to my parents. I don't want you to be in that position, Marvalette."

"No worries. Anyway. Bev says to pass by her at ten tonight. Norman, can you give us a drops, please darlin'?" Norman grunted yes. He would do anything for her, and she him too. He never fussed when she went out. He trusted her. And she always let him have his space too. I believed that nothing could ever come between these two. This was the kind of marriage I wanted. Not like my parents, who were always carping at each other.

It was 7.30pm and we aimed to leave the house at 9.30 to get to Bev's by 10pm. That left me two hours to get ready. Bath, hairwash, dry and style hair, press clothes – what to wear that did not look too flirty, yet looked stylish and sophisticated? I chose my black cat suit – yes, I got one eventually. It was an Ossie Clarke one in black crepe and I had some platform sandals, not very high platforms I hasten to add, but they were silver and looked swish. I wore a silver chain belt and with my slim figure, (but no behind, as Marvalette always said), I looked really good. I had ditched the green false eyelashes by now and preferred a more natural look with not too much make up. Foundation and powder, I had discovered, was not much good in a hot sweaty dance. It would all cake up, mascara would run into it and if you were lucky enough to dance cheek to cheek with a man, he would end up with Natural Beige Max Factor all down one side of his face. Not very attractive on a black man! So I had ditched that as well and opted for a small bit of blusher, eye shadow and liner and some waterproof – i.e sweat proof - mascara. I had some fake silver hoop earrings, and with my blonde curls behind my ears, they looked fab.

"Very nice," said Norman as I appeared, then to his wife, "Superb, my Black Queen!" He always gave her the greater compliment to show her that he loved her and saw her beauty above all others. She was wearing wide blue satin trousers – bell bottoms – and a short tie top, showing off the fact that she, indeed, did possess a behind! She had recently stopped pressing her hair as the fashion was coming in for black women to 'go natural' and she had her hair styled in a neat Afro. With little make up, but real gold hoop earrings (present from Norman) she looked indeed like a Black Queen.

"Heee! Unno look too good!" Marvalette said to me jokingly. "Yu gwine tief all de black man dere an' lef' none fe we fren' Jemma!"

"Is that what her problem with me is all about?" I asked.

"Look so," Mumbled Norman as he went to get his car keys and his jacket. "Come Aaron, man. We needs to hescort dese fine ladies to dere des-tin-a-shun!"

"Wow, Mummy, Aunti Jen, you look nice nice!"

"Don't be flirty young man" said Marvalette, half jokingly as we all left the flat to descend the pissy lift down to the car park where Norman's car was waiting. It was a warm enough night and we just took light jackets rather than big coats and small shoulder bags. We got in the back and Aaron sat up in front next to his Dad. We were all in good moods and Norman was whistling a tune as he drove.

41

We turned the corner onto Carlton Vale and had not gone very far when we heard the sound of a police car behind us. Marvalette looked round.

"Dey flashing you, Norman? Yu 'ave anyt'ing on yu? Jen?"

"Nutting, man. Jus' be cool."

"Neither me." I answered hurriedly. I was a bit worried though as I knew what the police could be like. I never took weed outside of the house and Norman always hid it well and sprayed liberal amounts of air freshener because people said the smell filtered up the air vents into other flats in the block. Norman pulled over.

A burly Plod came up to the window and Norman wound it down.

'Evening, sir," said Plod number one. His partner waited behind him, looking the car over, seeing if there was anything he could do Norman for, like broken lights or flat tyres. But Norman was meticulous about his car; always cleaning or fixing it, so it was ever perfect.

"Step outside the car please, sir."

Norman was nervous and it made him sound a bit surly. "Is why yu wan me get out me car? Me ent do nuttin'?"

"Just do wha' 'im sey and don't fuss dem," whispered Marvalette from behind him in the back seat. Norman got out.

"Is this your car, sir?" Norman nodded. Plod Two looked at his tax disc. All in order there. "Do you have a driving licence, sir?"

"Of course me do." Norman was sounding agitated.

"Where is it?"

"At home."

"Where is that then?" said Plod One. "Dere so." Norman pointed in the vague direction of Treetops House. "What's your name and address, sir?"

Norman gave his name and address. "Who is in the car with you, sir?"

"Me son, me wife and she fren'."

"Ask them to get out of the car will you, sir?"

We all got out. I had that feeling in the pit of my stomach that something awful was going to happen. But I remembered what Norman had said about being cool, even though he himself was finding it hard to hold his anger down. It was utter humiliation in front of his family, but he held it down and I could see Marvalette too was keeping her tongue in check and I was resigned to being as polite as I could be if they asked me anything.

"Ah, what have we here?" said Plod Two, looking at me suspiciously. "Where are you four going?"

"Ah was jus' droppin' me wife and she fren' over to anudder fren' house fe dem fe go out."

"So, you and your son are dropping your wife and her friend to go out while you go home and look after your boy here? Is that correct?"

"Yes, dat is correc'." confirmed Norman.

"Which one of you ladies is the wife?"

"Me," answered Marvalette, "an dis is my fren'." To which I nodded.

Plod Two came over and tapped me on the shoulder and led me over to where he had been standing, a little way away from the others.

"So, these people are your friends? Don't you have any white friends to go out with?"

"Yes, they are my friends. I live with them. I share a room with their son. They are good, honest people?"

"So, you say you live with them. Do you give them money?"

"Well, I pay for my keep and I help out with babysitting and the cleaning."

"How much? How much money do you give them?"

"Three pounds a week" I answered, wondering where these questions were leading. Then to pre-empt his next question, "I work in Grove Park Nursery by Ladbroke Grove and its really easy for me to get to work. I have known them ages and they are a lovely family."

I realised Plod Two was not in the slightest bit interested. He had just wanted to draw me away from what Plod One was up to. I looked around and could see Plod One looking through the car. Marvalette was holding on to Norman and Aaron. They seemed to have found nothing in the car and then they went to check the boot. Just then a call came in from their walkie talkie telling them to get somewhere or other sharpish – so it sounded. They forgot about the boot.

"Thank you, sir. You and your family and your wife's friend can all get back in the car now." Plod One opened the car door for Marvalette and Plod Two helped Aaron into the front seat. As I opened the door on my side he muttered

"You might like 'em, but I don't think much of your choice of friends, nigger lover."

I went cold with fear, then hot with anger, but I got into that car seat, relieved that we, and they, would be on our way. Norman drove off slowly and when they were out of sight he pulled over. "Jus' gimme a minute," he said and just sat with his head in his hands for a moment or two. Then, to everyone's surprise, he burst out laughing with such intensity, that we all joined in, even though none of us knew what was so funny. Then Norman said,

"Damn fool Babylon! Dem never look in me boot, sah!" he laughed aloud again, "I have t'ree box o' leaflet 'bout de march nex' week. Imagine if dem a fin' dat. So we have to t'ank some big criminal fe tek dem off we case. Imagine if dem a fin' dat! We lucky, bwoy, we lucky."

We all laughed even more, but Aaron seemed perplexed and was asking why the police stopped them. His Dad's laughter had taken his mind off the question, but I knew Norman would be sitting down and 'discossin' the whole thing with him when they got home – or at least in the morning.

Then we drove off to Bev's, a little shaken, but otherwise none the worse for our ordeal. I asked Marvalette what Plod One had said to them. Apparently he asked what I was doing in the car with them, why were we going out and Norman staying home and were we going out to make money for him. Jeez. How they held it down I don't know. Norman had said he worked for British Rail and that his wife was a clerk for the Gas Board and that I worked locally too. I told Marvalette what Plod Two had said to me and she sucked her teeth.

"Bumber claart Babylon. So now yu see how police is racis' and why we a march nex' week."

"So, all yu marchin wid us nex week den?" asked Norman.

"Oh yes! Oh yes, me 'usban'! Me a march right along side o' yu. Me min' made up!"

"Can I come too? Or would you rather me stay home with Aaron?" I asked, absolutely incensed by what I had witnessed and experienced and wanting to express my outrage by demonstrating too.

'Le' we t'ink about it and we will sit down an' discoss tomorrow an' see what is what and what is bes' fe do," replied Norman in his usual wise way.

We arrived at Bev's about half past ten. She was a bit vexed that we were so late, but Marvalette just said:

"Babylon gi' we problem, Bev. But we a'right and we 'ere now."

"Wha' 'appen, wha' 'appen?" asked Bev, genuinely wanting to know. Norman said he did not want to go into the whole story again in front of Aaron and did we want him to drop us all off at Jemma's and we could tell Bev and Jemma together, while he went home with Aaron who was by this time half falling asleep.

"Mummy, will you and Auntie Jen be alright without Daddy and me?" Norman and Marvalette shot each other a look as if to say they recognized the impact this had had on such a small boy. His first real encounter with racial harassment from the police. This would be something else that Norman and Marvalette would need to 'sit down an' discoss", but for now, Marvalette just answered

"Me? Who gwine trouble me or Aunty Jen? Go home an' sleep and yu will see Mommy in de marnin'!" She, then I, kissed Aaron and they drove off as the three of us walked up the steps to Jemma's front door.

6   The reasoning.

Norman dropped us off at Jemma's about half ten. She lived in a top floor flat in one of those big old houses in Powis Square. The house dance was next door and you could hear the muffled sound of the bass thudding through the building, stopping and starting as they set up the system.

"Dem nah ready yet fe start de party. Tam late – im get 'ol' up by Babylon near Hedgware Road. Search de van and everyt'ing. Is like Sout' Africa inna dis place 'ere. A-par-theid me a tell yu'" Jemma spat out the word 'apartheid' and looked at me long and hard, then she sucked her teeth and went into the front room. We three followed behind her. Marvalette squeezed my hand for a moment.

"Don' tek she on, know what I mean Jen?" I nodded. I wanted to listen to what Jemma had to say. Not take her on. But Marvalette meant more than that. She didn't want me to be hurt or take personally Jemma's outpourings of anger against white people. "Is she pain talkin'. Me know."

"Sisters, wha' kep' yu? Why all yu so late? Yu on BPT or what?" BPT stood for Black People's Time - a kind of joke in the community about how black people always managed to be late, no matter the occasion.

"Hactually," began Bev "dem get stop by police inna Carlton Vale. Tell she Marvalette."

Marvalette began to tell them about how they drove up alongside Norman and told him to pull over, got us all out of the car and were about to search the whole vehicle, 'til they were called off somewhere else, and how they missed finding the boxes of leaflets about the march.

"Mos' probably call' away fe go hol' up Tam, "interjected Jemma. "So yu survive de ordeal, Missie? She was looking at me. I looked back at her and answered.

"It was frightening for all of us. They called me a 'nigger lover' and gave me awful looks. Almost accused me of being a prozzie and giving Norman money. I think Aaron must have been very afraid. I can understand now why you all want to march against police brutality and harassment. You should not have to live your life under these conditions."

"So, yu start see what shit we does ha' fe deal wid on a day to day. Is not all 'bout fun an' clubbin' and wine up yuself on black man, hee?"

"No Jemma, I know it's not. I've been through stuff too this last year with my family and I am beginning to find out what racism is. I never knew white people could be so..so..well, cruel, I suppose. I want to do my best to support the fight afor freedom and equality. Just tell me what I can do to help, and I will."

"Yu wan' 'elp we, Missie?" I nodded. "Den lay off black man fe a start!" She sucked her teeth and looked at Bev and Marvalette. "Yu no see 'ow de brudders dem a mock we, run up after Missie an' co, cos dem skin so white, an' dem hair so straight? Then all yu turn dem fool, like dis poor brudder 'ere so."

She handed me a leaflet. There was a photo of a man, all beaten and bruised. Underneath it said "Support Emmett Jonson. No to Police Brutality." It went on in smaller print, "Six weeks ago Bro' Emmett was stopped by the police on the trumped up charges of assaulting and raping a white woman in her flat in South Kilburn. He was beaten to an inch of his life. Come to the Old Bailey on 27th August and demonstrate in support of him. Free Bro' Emmett."

I thought I was going to be sick. I ran to the loo. I was rushing hot and cold. The man in the picture was Gregory. I looked again in the bright light of Jemma's bathroom. Definitely him, despite the bruising, I could still recognize his face as clear as day. What was going on? I went back in and joined the others.

Jemma had gone to the kitchen to get cold drinks for us.

"Are you Ok, Jen?" asked Marvalette. She could see I was in shock and still shaking. "What's wrong? Tell me?"

"It's...it's Gregory!" I spluttered, taking the glass from Jemma and muttering a thank you.

"Is who?" said Marvalette.

"Yeah, what you sayin'? Is wha' yu call im? Yu know 'im?" added Jemma.

"His name's Gregory – or at least that's the name I know him by."

"True," put in Bev, quiet until now. "'im is a Wes' End 'ustler. Yu mus' recognize 'im Jem. From Hot Forties and de Baggo."

"Me no know 'im." Jemma looked confused. "Ok, Ok, Missie. So wha' yu ha' fe tell we bout dis ya man, so? Bev, is wha' unno know – yu seh 'im a 'ustler, but dis ya paper seh 'im a haccountant?"

I looked at Marvalette. I was almost too afraid to speak. Clearly something had happened with the police and Gregory as Liz's Dad was out to get him, but this was indeed a turn up for the book. Marvalette knew the whole story about what had happened that night. I looked at her. What should I say? Would Jemma believe me or just write me off as being part of the conspiracy to condemn this man, a black man? Marvalette must have read my expression.

"Jem, this is very serious an' you need to listen good. Jen knows something about this case, but you, and you Bev, must promise, promise on your baby life, never to tell anyone. Jen's life could be in danger if you do." Marvalette spoke in her 'work voice' as she put it, dropping the Jamaican talk for a moment. This meant she was serious. Jem stopped for a moment, but unsure of what to make of it, she retorted,

"So what now? Emmett, or as yu call 'im, Gregory, 'im life nah in danger? Is who side yu on Marvalette? Miss white Missie 'ere or yu black brudder man?"

I burst into tears. "Please, please," I said "I don't want any of my friends to feel that they have to choose between me, as a white girl, or a black brother. That is not fair. I will tell you the truth as I know it and you can judge for yourselves, but please don't let all this stuff about racial discrimination stand in the way of recognizing the truth."

That was a bit unfair actually, as I could see it riled Jemma, but Bev knew what I meant, and she shut her up.

'Jem, hush nah! An' stop callin' her Missie – she name Jenifer. I trus' her. She look after Mason and she look after Aaron before dat, and she live good. Dis man 'ere, me KNOW 'im nah good. So don' harassin' de girl and le' she talk."

I was heartened by Bev's defence of me and thought back of that night when she had to get real about Tempo and about how it was Jemma who intervened to stop a potentially nasty situation developing there. I knew Jemma had a different side to her and I waited for it to emerge.

"Ok, let's reason," she said calmly. "Bev, roll up. Le' we smoke a spliff an' calm down fe' tru. Sorry Jen. It was wrong to call you Missie. I want to hear what you have to say." All of a sudden, Jemma was using her 'work voice' too. It was calm and considered. I felt I could trust her.

"You do promise to tell no-one?" I pleaded.

"Jen, I am not a fool. I know what goes on and I know about that West End scene, so I can see that maybe, someone is playing us all for fools here and that sometimes brothers can get carried away defending each other while we women know another side. So talk. Your story won't go beyond these walls."

47

"At las' unno see sense," muttered Marvalette. She took my hand and I gathered the courage to speak.

I told them how Liz had been seeing Gregory for a couple of months, how he gave her money and bought her stuff and even though she knew he was a 'hustler', she didn't seem to want to know how he really made his money and just seemed to like the excitement of the whole affair. I recounted how we had gone to Grace's party and that because I was dancing with Leroy, Liz went off down the West End to Hot Forties, hoping to meet up with Gregory, even though Gregory had told her not to go there. I told them how she said she had seen him with a white woman who was giving him money and that she had confronted them and how he had marched her out of the club, driven her home and then beaten her up and raped her and how I had found her in the morning. Jemma questioned me a bit and I filled in details - I wanted to avoid the bit about Leroy staying the night but they did not seem interested in that part. I told them about the injuries, that she was pregnant for him and that he had torn her clothes and half wrecked the place. I skipped the part of me going to the Clinic but told them how I went to Paddington Hospital to see her and promised to clean the flat up for when she came home and how we were swapping rooms over and planning to move.

"'Im seh 'ow police mussa get de place clear up to destroy evidence of who did this to Liz, so they could frame him. But it was you! You was 'elpin Babylon?"

"Oh no, nothing like that," I was sobbing. I was afraid of telling the next part, but Marvalette urged me to go on with the part where Jean had turned up and the whole story of Frankie and Big Dave and how Jean was angry with me that I had cleaned the room, thus destroying evidence that would have nailed Gregory.

"I'm sure the police were out to get him for Frankie's sake and all those favours that they all call-in in these kinds of situations. So it is probably true that they did beat him up, that they did make up evidence and that they are definitely out to get him. But it's not true that he is innocent. He really did beat up Liz, very badly and he did rape her."

"Psycho," muttered Bev, "fancy 'im usin' all the Stop Police Brutality campaign in this way.

Jemma was thinking. "An 'im t'ink people nah fin' out de trut'. Cho! Me sick o' dese men. However," back to her 'work voice' she added, "There are some issues here and we have to tread carefully.

"First of all under the name of Emmett, our Mr Gregory has managed to create a Campaign around his story and get people flustered about the injustice he is facing and the Campaign group is using this as a flagship case. So he is using the Campaign as a smokescreen to cover up his guilt. This is wrong.

"Second. While our Mr Gregory may be guilty as charged, what the police have done is clearly wrong and attests to the racist behaviour of the police, seen? That is the hub of the Campaign – to protest against police brutality- and we clearly have a very nasty case of that here."

"So what to do? asked Marvalette.

"Hmph. Me no know." Jemma was thinking, as she curled up on her sofa and rolled another spliff.

"You are right." I said, "but I can see the predicament this puts you, as the Campaign, in but there is also the predicament it puts women in. Do we support a man who has committed violent and criminal acts against a woman, albeit a white woman, because the police indulged in criminal means to nail him? In which case we run the risk of the guilty man going free. And I must add, from what Jean said the police knew about him, Liz was not the first woman he had beaten to within an inch of their lives, and I doubt they were all white, plus he made his living out of brutal exploitation of them. From a woman's point of view, any woman, white or black – are we safer with him behind bars? Can we run the risk of him being found not guilty just on technicalities over evidence and the fact that the police battered him?"

"Me ha' somet'ing fe add," said Bev, quietly and slowly. "He has done this to black women too."

"Is 'ow yu know dat? Who?" demanded Jemma.

"'im batter Marcia. Don' seh nuttin'. Me promise ar me nah fe tell. Oh Lord. What on eart' can we do?"

Jeez. You could feel the shock of this resounding in our hearts around the room. No-one knew what to say. Last thing I had heard about Marcia, was a short conversation with Bev that she had 'gone off'. That meant gone off her head – had a breakdown – and had been in a mental hospital. The penny was dropping fast and Bev went on to add that Marcia had had a breakdown following this incident where she had apparently met Gregory in a bar in Notting Hill and, rejecting his unwanted advances, she had 'cussed him out'. He had then followed her home, pushed his way into her flat, raped her and beat her badly. No, she had not gone to the police, one because she was afraid of him coming after her, and two, because she just could not face the whole ordeal of the interrogation by the police. It was hard for a woman, let alone a black woman, to be taken seriously about rape. The police usually made the victim feel like the guilty one for 'leading him on', or some other such nonsense. There had been an article in the Guardian about it a while back.

"In one way, if Marcia came forward and reported this, it would give the police more evidence to get him sent down. But can you imagine what Marcia would have to face down from the community if she told the police now, as it would undermine the whole Campaign. Plus what evidence would she have to prove it was him?" I was thinking out loud.

"I think is bes' we leave Marcia outta it. She been t'rough enough a'ready and she cyan 'andle no more," added Bev.

Jemma was still thinking. Then she sat bolt upright.

"Ok. Me have a plan. We need to be a bit under cover here with a strategy. We kinda have to find a way to undermine the Emmett Campaign from within, without the brothers findin' out – especially Mr Gregory. Now. We have the March on Saturday, yeah? They did plan to give out the leaflets about 'Emmett' on the March and it's my job to distribute them. The point is to get publicity to then try to rope in as many people as possible to demo outside the Court when his case comes up. Now, the first sabotage is to get the leaflets and destroy them. I can do that. It may cost me my reputation as reliable, but I can live with that. I will think of something. But I will go into the Campaign room on Monday, pick up the boxes of leaflets, stick them in the car boot and get rid somehow."

"Good thinking," said Marvalette. I kept quiet here as it really was their job to make the decisions. I agreed anyway and thought how amazing Jemma was!

"The next part is that I am banking on is the unpleasant outcome that the police will make trouble on our March. There will be arrests and there will be police brutality, mek no mistake sistas, plain for the public to see. This is the real campaign case, not Emmett or Gregory and his blasted self-centered using of our legitimate claims on behalf of law abiding black brothers and sisters like your Norman, Marvalette, and Tam. We will have to mobilise in the defence of demonstrators and that will become our key platform and thus the whole focus on Emmett will fade away."

We all looked at Jemma in awe. Strategy or what?

"However, Jenifer, I will have to share this with one brother on the Campaign. It is Bro Kwame, the one who chairs our committee driving the Campaign. He is a good friend and I trust him and I know he will be as angry as us at how Emmett is manipulating us to cover his own guilt. Can you come round here next week Tuesday please? Kwame will be here to meet with me about Saturday – I am typing his speech – so we will discuss then."

"Ok. I can be here around half six, after work as I am on lates that day." I no longer felt afraid. We had all 'touched base' that evening, realised what was important, and that the struggle was complex, with many dimensions.

"Yu wan' Norman to pick yu up after and bring yu home?" asked Marvalette caringly.

"Ok," I said, "thanks. Now can I make a suggestion? Can we forget about this now and just go next door to the party and get some good music in our bones?"

"Yeah. Sound like Tam well into 'im session now, an' we missin' out!" added Bev.

There was a resounding agreement that we should get up and go out; after fixing our hair and make-up and getting our stuff together, we all filed out of Jemma's flat.

"Jenifer," called Jemma, quietly, "a moment." She beckoned me back into her hallway.

"I'm sorry if I was hard on you. At the end of the day, brothers and sisters are taking pressure here and sometimes I am so angry with white people, and I know not all whites are racist and that you are doing your best to understand and be helpful. I just get so angry sometimes, that's all. I am sure there will be times when we can talk more. Hanyway, come, le' we go rave!"

I just smiled. No more words were needed.

We all went downstairs and into the house next door. Three floors of the house were being used for the party incorporating two flats. Ground and basement wired up with the speakers for dancing and upstairs on the first floor for food and chill out. I don't know about the people in the flats above – I assumed they would be at the party. I parked all the events of the evening thus far in the back of my mind and went into the house.

Oh shit. I thought. There's Leroy. I blanked him and walked past him. Marvalette noticed.

"Wha' 'appen to Leroy? Yu an' 'im nah fren' again?"

"Long story," I replied.

"Seen," Marvalette nodded. "We go haffe wait 'til Norman 'pon night shiff, den you an' me go sit down an' discoss!"

I laughed and said "Sure."

We had a nice time that night in the end. Tam played some great music and I danced, mainly by myself, but also with a couple of guys, nothing too romantic or suggestive and a guy called Delroy gave me his number. I knew I wouldn't call him. I was still wary after Leroy and wanted to take my time. But it was a good night, and by the time Marvalette and I had dropped off Bev in a cab, then gone on home, we were more than ready to pull our shoes off our aching feet and get ourselves to bed.

7   The Incident Record

"Good morning Jenifer. Today is a good day!"

It was Gabriella, sounding cheery for some reason. I had just walked into the nursery for my shift. We both had the same shift patterns so saw each other for a

51

brief exchange before starting work and on our breaks. She always had to rush at the end of the day as she had to pick up her ten year old daughter from her Mum's. Gabriella had married young- at nineteen. Her husband, Kenneth, was a teacher at a primary school where she was doing her Nursery Nursing training placement. They dated for some months, became lovers, had a baby and then got married. Baby Sharlette was just 6 months old. They had combined their wedding with a Christening and it had been a wonderful family occasion with people coming from far and wide to celebrate with them. She always spoke of this day with fond memories. When Sharlette was three, he left her for someone else, leaving her devastated. But she had a great flat from the Housing Trust, just doors away from her Mum, who looked after Sharlette after school and whenever she was working. This was a great help and saved her fortunes on childcare, allowing her to save a fair bit each month. She was hoping to buy her own place one day and had it in mind to also train as a teacher.

"Why so?" I enquired, interested in what had her so animated. Usually she was quite reserved and quiet.

"Two things! First of all, I got confirmation that I have a place on a teacher training course to start in September and I will get a full grant. Doing that Maths "O" Level last year – all that struggle – has paid off and I'm in!! It will be three years for the Cert Ed and I can add an extra year to do the degree. It will be worth it. At least I can have so much better career opportunities. I will train in Primary, specialising in Nursery. My focus academic subject will be Sociology of Education. Then I can really get into some study on how to improve educational opportunities for children – especially black children. Our community needs to have more black teachers and I am stepping up to the plate!"

"Congratulations!" I said with heartfelt joy for her, wondering why I was not embarking on a similar journey as Nursery Nursing in a Social Services Nursery had its limitations. Notwithstanding having to put up with the Carol Clarkes of this world.

"I am so pleased for you. You will be a great teacher, but you are also so brilliant with the babies. They will miss you. But what's your second piece of news."

"Carol Clarke is leaving! It was announced on Friday, but you were on Annual Leave. I have been dying to tell you!"

Jubilant to hear it, I almost jumped for joy.

"That means there is a vacancy in baby room – will you ask for a transfer? I think we can really do some good work in that room."
"I will do it right away. I will go into Matron this morning and ask her."

The thing with Matron was, even though she was as daft as a bat, she was cunning and often did not like putting nursery officers who were friends in the same room. You had to get round her, say like it was for your career and hope she would not twig. I nipped round to Matron's office. The protocol was simple. There was door with 'Matron' emblazoned across it on a shiny plaque (and she made sure it was polished); if the door was closed it meant she was busy, not to knock unless it was an emergency, and if it was open, knock and go in.

Her door was open.

"Good morning Matron. Lovely day isn't it? I heard that Carol is leaving. You will miss her, won't you? She is a very reliable staff member and I am sure you will find it hard to replace her."

God was I lying through my teeth and felt a stab of guilt at how two faced I was being. The truth was Carol was reliable, in that she was bang on time every day, and was rarely off sick; but she could also sweet talk Matron and, after eleven years working in that nursery, she knew how to make herself look good in Matron's eyes. That was all Matron cared about. She did not see the Carol that was a trouble-maker, cruel, even, sometimes and blatantly racist.

"Good morning Jenifer. Yes it is a lovely day. I see you have heard about Carol. Yes I shall miss her as will the children and the families here. She's so good with the children, don't you agree? Now what can I do for you?"

I ignored the bit about being good with the children and went into my question.

"I wondered if this might be a convenient time to ask you if I can move into the baby room. I have not worked with the Under Twos since my training and would love to get some more experience with that age group. Plus you will be a staff down in there and rather than get a temp in to cover, it might be better for the babies to have someone familiar going in there and staying there."

Matron would never give you an answer then and there. She always made you wait, and then came up with a proposal that had a subtle twist to what you asked, so she wasn't directly ceding to your request but making it look like she had thought of it all along.

"Thank you for putting in your request. I will certainly bear it in mind and let you know."

"Thank you Matron." I left the office and went to my room to set up, having to hurry now as children would be out of breakfast in ten minutes. As Nursery Nurses we were glorifies skivvies. The 'earlies' (early shift from eight o'clock) set up breakfast for the early children – these were the ones of working parents, especially the single Mums, who came in around eight o'clock. 'Middles', that was me today, on at nine, set up the rooms and 'lates', on at ten, who came in and relieved the early shift to go on breakfast break. That would last half an hour, then middles would get a fifteen-minute break, so from ten fifteen, the rooms would be fully staffed until lunch time. The early staff went for their lunch at twelve while we fed the kids, washed and changed them for sleep time, put them down for their sleep at one and went on our break. Middles and Lates had lunch from one to two pm and got lunch served by Matron in the staff room, while the Earlies 'sat in' the rooms while the children slept or finished the after-lunch bathroom cleaning. And all children had to sleep, even the four-year olds. The rooms were fully staffed again from two to three in the afternoon. Then it was time for Earlies to have a 15 min tea break, followed by Middles, after which tea was served for the children. Lates went for a half hour break, coming back at four when the earlies went home. Then Middles cleaned the rooms, washed the floors and cleaned the toilets, until they went at five, while the late shift set up the communal area until six pm. Basically children were herded throughout the day according to our breaks and everything had to be put away at the end of the day so we could have a clear floor to clean.

I was in Red Group. A mixed age group from two to five, and often from 18 months as there was such a demand for baby places that Matron often moved a baby up early. That was a nightmare as these little ones could barely keep up the pace. There were 15 children in our room and three of us staff. I worked with Jaqui, a bright and ambitious Nursery Nurse, but who, like me, came from out of the area and had no particular interest in working in a mixed community and then Big Mary, who had worked there for yonks and who was a rather unpleasant character.

Big Mary was like Carol Clarke in many ways. She did not like black children, unless they were wide eyed and cute.
"Some of 'em can be lovely at this age, but it's when they grow up they get to be trouble," she would say, amongst other things.
 She would have no patience with the quiet, passive child, white or black, who actually froze in terror when she called their name, often prefixed with 'dozy'.
"Come on, dozy Annie," she would say to Annie or another child slow at eating or who did not understand her.

There was a white Mum who had two mixed race children, both by different fathers. Hers was a sad story, but she was trying really hard. Nevertheless Big Mary used to go on about her having had these two children by two different men – even though the Mum – Kate, now lived with the Dad of her second child. Kate had grown up in care but, despite all that, she was doing really well. But Big Mary would go on about her, and her children, in the most unfair and prejudiced way.

One of our domestic staff's grandsons, Anthony, was in our group. Granny Simmit would often pop her head round the door to say "Hi" to Anthony and give him a big kiss. It was as if she was keeping an eye and Big Mary kind of felt it – and would go on about that too and how Matron let the domestics get away with anything – meanwhile Big Mary was filching toilet rolls from the store cupboard and anything else she could get her hands on. I disliked her intensely, but did my best to get along, as we could not make a bad atmosphere in the room for the children's sake. One good thing was that she was a hard worker and never slacked on the job, so she pulled her weight, especially with our arduous cleaning duties.

Because of all the shifts patterns and all the breaks creating this constant coming and going, nothing ever really got planned and what the children were offered was down to who set up, what they felt like, or whether we were going to just set up outside play and get the kids going round and round on the bikes outside, while they sat behind the sliding doors watching. There was a loo roll for wiping noses – which was frequently needed when children had colds, dripping what we called 'candlesticks' from their noses. Staff would take it in turns to go out to wipe a child's nose and shove the slimy tissue down the centr tube, popping them all out down the sluice later when the children were all inside again. There was not enough in the way of play materials and staff did not bother with sand, water or paint (too much palaver to get out and clear up), nor project work (the little ones can't keep up and ruin what the older children are doing) and so the excuses for an easy life went on. There were no books as staff used to say 'these children don't know how to use books' and basically everything I and, to some extent Jaqui, suggested got scotched by Big Mary, who was our senior and who never stopped moaning about the staff, the Council, the families and the community.

Gabriella and I had discussed how we couldn't stand these two, Carol Clarke and Big Mary, and how awful they were with the children. We decided we had to do something and so we started making a record of each and every incident in a notebook which we kept at our homes.

"But what are we going to do with all this?" I asked Gabriella later when we were on middle tea break.

"I'm not sure yet, but I will ask Kenneth. Him and some other black teachers have set up a support and action group for black teachers to discuss race issues– both what they experience and what they see black kids going through at the hands of white teachers who are clearly hostile to them and their parents."

"Why doesn't he just go through the NUT? They seem more on the ball than our Union."

"He has tried and they don't want to know. At the end of the day, the NUT is just about looking after teachers and sod everyone else. Look at how they treat Nursery Assistants in schools – I know places where the they and the Welfare Assistants can't even use the staff room as they say it's just for teachers. I will make sure I am never like that when I am a teacher. Anyway, getting back to the point, I will ask Kenneth later – he is meeting me from work and we are taking Sharlette to see his sister's new baby."

"Well, that would be good – especially as that Carol is leaving and you have all those pages of notes about her written up."

It was Kenneth that explained to her, then she explained to me some weeks later, how to keep these 'Incident Records' as we called them, but we did not yet have a plan as to what to do with these records we had collected so carefully.

Just then, there was a sound of shouting in the hallway. Big Mary was being yelled at by Anthony's mother, Mabel. Granny Simmit just stood watching as her daughter gave Big Mary a verbal dressing down. Matron slipped into the office and rang the Town Hall for her manager to come right away but was told to call the Police which she did, although they did not come.

"Big Mary. Yu stink like ol' daag! Yu mout' too big an' fanciful, tellin' Sandra me never sen' Anthony nappy into nursery an' 'ow im clothes too smaall. Cho! Me bring de nappy dem, look!" She shoved a bag of Paddi-pads at Big Mary. Sandra was Ryan's Mum who was also in Red Group and friends with Mabel. Big Mary apparently had said these things to Sandra when Sandra had asked if Anthony had nursery clothes on as they were looking a bit on the small side. Big Mary had said more than she should have done about Mabel and Sandra went straight back to her and Granny Simmit, telling them what Big Mary had said. Granny Simmit added a few more things to fuel the fire and boof, up went Mabel. Gabriella and I looked at each other and winked! Both of us secretly glad that Big Mary was getting some come-uppance at last.

Big Mary complained to Matron that parents should not be able to get away with it and that Granny Simmit got away with far too much and how she always brought tea round late and whatever else she could find to moan about. Carol Clarke came out to stick up for her and, as they were both on late tea break, they went off to commiserate together and moan about how rude the black parents were and how Matron was too weak to stop it and it would be a fine day for the nursery when she retired and this was why Carol was leaving anyway.

Big Mary came back into the room, full of self satisfaction that she had written up a report of it to Matron and how she was going to make sure Granny Simmit was up on a disciplinary and even lose her job, what with all what she had on her, and that Mabel would lose her nursery place.

"The bloody coloureds think they own the place. God, how this area has gone to the dogs since they moved in. Bloody ten in a room, the cooking smells and the bleedin' parties going on all night. You go down the market and can't get a thing to buy because all the stalls just sell their stuff- stinking stinking stalls. And they smell. And none of them work – look how they all have free places here, but you see them in the market buying, buying and their kids all have new stuff every week, while hard working English people get nothing!"

"So how come you are complaining about Anthony not having nappies and proper clothes if all 'they' do is buy their kids new clothes every week?" Oops! I couldn't resist a dig.

'That's not what I said. Who's side are you on anyway? Trust you! I know you like a bit of the old black, so I expect you will stick up for them. Dirty Niggers."

She muttered the last two words under her breath, but I heard them all right. Of course she knew it was wrong to use language like that in the workplace – even at that time, the Council had some standards- but it was if the words were there and she just had to let them manifest in speech, albeit quietly.

"I heard that Mary and I'm going to Matron about it," I answered quietly, but seething inside. I had to get out of that room. "I have been making notes about all the prejudiced things you say to and about the children and their parents and, after what you have just said, I am going to report you."

"Yeah, I bet. Anyway, you can't leave the room. You have the cleaning to do"

"I am leaving the room and I will clean later, after my shift has finished if I have to."

I went off to Matron's office. The door was closed, but I didn't care. I knocked and walked in. There was Matron, packing two flowery shopping bags full of catering packs of groceries. On her desk was a glass of red wine. I was aghast. And Matron, looking like she knew she had been caught out, summing up the words to dismiss me from the office, but I got in first.

"I don't care what you get up to Matron, but I am coming to tell you the truth about Big Mary. There has just been another incident and she referred to black staff and parents as 'dirty niggers' and has insulted me in a racial way too."

"Jenifer," said Matron in her daft, but cunning little voice, "I have really had quite a shock to my system today and I expect Mary has too. Perhaps she is a little overwrought with all the unpleasantness that went on and she was rather shaken up after her ordeal. I am sure she will apologise in the morning when she has calmed down. What you see in my glass is nerve tonic and what you see in these bags is additional groceries that won't fit into the larder, so they are in these bags, ready to go in the additional space in my cupboard over there."

I told you she was cunning and could turn everything around to suit her. Not to be daunted I went on.

"Matron, I have a record of 17 incidents, not including this one, that have occurred over the last 3 months."

"Witnesses?"

"Jacqui." I was not sure if she would back me; although she had been in the room when things had happened, I had not told her I had recorded stuff.

"This is very unkind of both of you, I think, to gang up on poor Mary like this. I am going to speak with both of you tomorrow, be in my office at eight thirty please. Now go back to the room as you have left Mary on her own. This puts a very different light on me agreeing to your transfer."

"Matron, I am not ganging up with Jacqui. She knows nothing about the records I have kept. But I will be here in the morning. Good afternoon."

I left Matron with her 'nerve tonic' and her bags of council bought groceries, not believing her story for a minute. I said that she was crafty and look how she was already twisting this around to save herself. I went back to the room.

"Got it off your chest then with Matron? Fat lot of good that will do you. You can't touch me, Jenifer and that's that."

"Bathroom," I said, ignoring her, "just going to do the cleaning, then I'm off."

Just then Matron made one of her rare appearances in the room. "Oh and Jenifer, I have said that Mary can go early on account of the shock she has had this afternoon and you will be staying in til six. You can claim the time back."

Game, set and match to Matron and Mary. I realised I had acted in haste, in anger and had not been, as Gabriella put it, 'strategic'. I thought about this as I scoured and bleached, feeling snared, feeling a fool and feeling worried that I had blown Gabriella's strategy, even if she did not yet have one. I had let her down even though I had not mentioned her teaching me to keep the records, nor that she was keeping some herself. I would have taken away the impact of her making a case about racial prejudice by staff in the nursery to the management in a way that would make them listen and clearly no-one was going to take notice of my outburst. I would just say I had made up the bit about me keeping records on Big Mary, take the flak and play the whole thing down. I had messed up and felt I had let down Gabriella.

I had her number, and even though I rarely called, I did ring her later that night to tell her what had happened. To my utter surprise, she laughed. First at the picture of Matron with the wine and the shopping and secondly at my audacity to report Big Mary.

"I wouldn't have had the nerve," she said. "If it had been me, she would have suspended my black arse out of there. You can get away with things in ways that I can't as a black woman."

"Maybe it's just that I don't hold the same fear as you do about speaking out."

"Perhaps" said Gabriella, "but at the same time, it will come back on you because they will gang up, but in another way, you have broken the silence. Maybe there is no perfect strategy after all. You 'seized the time', like Bobby Seale says, and now we wait to see what happens next. Good for you! Kenneth is here, just saying good night to Sharlette and I will have a chat with him and see what he says we should do next."

"We?"

"Yes, we! Maybe it's time for me to speak out too, and this will back you up. We are backing up each other. I am leaving to go to teacher training, so what have I to lose?"

"Thank you, thank you," I replied, so grateful that she had not been angry with me. "You know what? Maybe I will apply for teacher training too. I admire you for taking the plunge. At least as a teacher there is the opportunity to make a difference, far more than cleaning bathrooms and being under that daft old bat!"

"Yes, great. Why don't you check it out? But back to the business in hand, Kenneth is here now and I will tell him all and get back to you later."

"Ok, but not after ten, though, as Marvalette doesn't like the phone going so late."

"Alright then, bye for now."

It was already nine and I didn't expect Gabriella to call back and she didn't. Neither was she at work the next day. So I decided to face the music alone and retract my allegations against Big Mary. I was given a verbal warning for unprofessional behavior and Big Mary got off scott free.

"A so it go," said Norman, when I told him and Marvalette about it, summing it up in four words and so it went indeed.

8   The meeting.

I tried calling Gabriella from the phone box as I came out of work. The phone just rang and rang; I put the phone down and walked round to Powis Square to where Jemma lived. I rang the bell. I heard a window go up and a voice yelled down:

"Is 'o dat, ring me bell ya so?" It was Jemma. "Oh. Is yu. Catch de keys dem!" She let go of the keys she was waving, and I ducked out of the way, in case they might hit me. I followed them to where they fell on the pavement, picked them up and tried them in the lock 'til I got the right one and then began my way to the top floor. Fourth floor to be precise. When I got to Jemma's flat, the door was open, but I knocked anyway.

"Good evening Jemma. How are you?"

"Me a'right, t'anks. An' more to de point, how is yu?"

"Could be better," I responded sinking into her sofa. She went to get me a cold drink. In the daylight the flat looked really nice. She had some lovely African paintings, sculptures and that sort of thing. Shelves with books and walls painted white. It looked clean, arty and well, interesting. I looked at the titles of the books on her shelf. 'Seize the Time" by Bobby Seale, 'SoleDad Brother' by George Jackson, "If They Come in the Morning' by Angela Davis, 'Lonely Londoners' by Sam Selvon and lots more; lots of books about African Art. And then there was her music. I could see she liked Jazz. A Pharoah Saunders album cover was looking up at me from the floor.

Jemma came back into the room and I averted my gaze from her stuff.

"Yu checkin' me out? Books and t'ing? Is what yu make o' dem, den?"

"Really interesting." I answered enthusiastically.

"Maybe yu might borrow one or two." Then adding quickly, "yu does gi people dey t'ings back?"

"Oh, yes, yes. Definitely."

The door bell rang.

"That will be Kwame". She had gone all work voiced. "Not me and those stairs, girl," she added, doing the same routine with the keys for Kwame to let himself in with.

"Greetings sister Jemma," a deep voice calm and smooth greeted her at the top of the stairs. "I hope you had a good day at the studio. I have been at the Campaign office all day. I need to talk to you later about some ideas that the brothers and I have been discussing. Anyway, is our young friend here?"

Kwame's voice sounded educated and calm, Jemma had gone into her officey way of speaking and I could hear that she was naturally well spoken. I wondered about her Jamaican talk – was that because she grew up speaking that way, or had she learned it later and used it to 'fit in'. Anyway it was not my business. I heard some whispered sharing of matters that I was obviously not meant to hear.

Then Jemma walked into the room, with a tall, slightly rotund, black man behind her. I recognized him immediately. It was Kenneth. What is going on, I wondered? Kenneth/Kwame recognized me straight away.

"Good evening Jenifer. You are the young lady who works in the nursery with Gabriella, are you not?"

"Yes, and by the way, how is Gabriella? I was worried about her. She called in sick today and is not answering her phone." I knew he had had a hand in that somewhere, so I was putting it out there for him to acknowledge and to see what he would say.

'Gabriella is fine and she will be back at work next week. She has a bit of a bug and does not want to talk to anyone at the moment. However, she told me what went on at work yesterday and I need to put you straight on one or two things as far as that little matter goes. However, for now, we will address the more important question in hand. Jemma has given me an outline and we all know this is very serious as the whole credibility of our Campaign is poised upon what action we decide to take. Just so I can be absolutely clear, can you tell me the whole story again, and don't leave any detail out."

60

"Ok," I said and went on to give my account of everything I knew. I had even gone as far as to check the dates in my diary so I had everything right. I didn't know what he was going to do with this information, but I trusted Jemma and she seemed to know what she was doing. However, I was a little wary. He was a clever man, I could see, but I also had an impression that he manipulated Gabriella and I felt sure it was not quite the full picture he was giving me about her absence from work. Still, he said he would come to that after this discussion. I did not go on to discuss what Jemma had said about getting rid of the leaflets, just in case that would get her in trouble.

Jemma was perched on her bar stool, over by the window. She was flicking through a copy of Ebony and kissing her teeth quietly, I presumed, at the adverts for hair straightening stuff and skin lightening creams that were on every other page.

"So you are saying that Emmett, whom you know as Gregory, violently assaulted your friend and raped her. You found her, took her to the hospital and from there you went home and it was you who cleaned the flat, thus destroying vital evidence that would have proved this case one way or the other?"

"Yes, that's correct."

"I have to ask you again how you are sure that it was Emmett who assaulted your friend. You say she had said to the hospital staff and the police that it was a man that she did not know who pushed his way into the flat. How can you be sure that this was not what really happened and that she then went on to accuse Emmett because she was angry and jealous and wanted to get him into trouble."

"I found her and the clothes that were ripped up were things he had bought her and the perfume thrown on the floor, Tabu it was, was also what he had bought her. Surely a stranger could not be so selective? Plus I think it is important to bear in mind what Liz's Mum and Dad said about him, and about Big Dave, who owns the club, what he knew about him."

"An' 'im rape an' beat sista Marcia in de same kinda merciless way." added Jemma.

"Jemma, I hear you, but, for now, that is another matter and for the moment can we just leave it to one side. The thing is," he went on, turning back to me, "our historic experience as black men is replete with instances where white women cry rape against a brother and the next minute he has been on trial and found guilty on very flimsy evidence. Our brothers in the American South have suffered in this way for centuries. A white woman has only to say that black man looked at her 'in the wrong way' and it's enough to get him lynched, or hung, or she has an affair and gets worried her husband or even father, finds out and then accuses him. Do you know how many black U.S. service men were hanged in Shepton Mallet goal right here in England, during the last war because of such false accusations? So this could be something even her parents persuaded her to do – to lie, just so they could wreak vengeance for him simply sleeping with their daughter."

When you think about it, Frankie and Jean would not take much persuading to do such a thing, but the timing was wrong. I told Kenneth/Kwame that and he nodded as if to show he agreed with my logic.

"The thing is, as you know, and as you have already discovered yourself – yes, I know about what happened to you all on Saturday- the police make life very hard for us. There are hard-core racists within the force who stop at nothing to harass and intimidate black people; our youth in particular have a very hard time. We have to organize and take a stand against that. You know about the March that we are organizing to protest and to publicise our cause. We need a high-profile case to highlight the ill treatment blacks receive at the hands of the police and Emmett came to us for help. As a community we felt we had to back him up. He was beaten very badly in custody. He too has broken ribs and a broken jaw as well as sustaining other injuries. They stubbed their cigarettes out on his body – we have seen the scars. So while you want to defend your friend, we want to defend our friend and if your friend gets hurt in the meantime because he gets off the charge, what is that to us? Brothers and sisters care more for their brother than they do about a white girl; it's what they call in war 'collateral damage' – sort of like not being able to bake a cake without breaking eggs. Do you see what I am saying Jennifer?"

"I do, in a way. But even though what the police did to him is wrong, they are doing so for Frankie. It's his daughter and he will do anything to get revenge for what Gregory did to her, especially after I unknowingly destroyed the evidence. He is a father, like you, if someone treated your daughter like that, wouldn't you want him sent down, by any means possible?"

"By any means necessary," interjected Jemma, climbing off her stool and looking like she meant business. "What about Marcia? Is she 'collateral damage', as you put it, too? She mus' keep quiet then, so you all can have your day, playing big lawyer man in court? This man is dangerous, Kwame, everyone knows it except you? Wha'appen – you 'fraid o' he too? Everyday good honest decent black people, like Norman and Marvalette are getting harassed and intimidated by the police dem. Our youth can't do 'so', without they get their collars felt. This is what is wrong and if we use Emmett or Gregory, or whatever his blasted name is, as our headline case, knowing that the police **know** he is guilty, we just make ourselves look like damn fools or the crooks they say we all are. Forget Emmett, for raas sake, Kwame. This case brings no value to our cause. Please. And no woman can be 'collateral damage' as far as I'm concerned, neither black nor white. It's Justice we're seeking, for all, an end to racial oppression, not another kind of oppression in its place."

One thing I noticed that Jemma was not doing in front of Kenneth/Kwame was rolling a spliff and I could see she was like she could really do with one. She went off to the kitchen to calm down and came back with a pot of tea and three mugs, a bag of sugar and a tin of Carnation milk. I hated that in tea, but I was sort of getting used to it at Marvalette's, and I was dying for a cuppa to take off some of the stress. I was hungry too, having not eaten since leaving work.

62

"Ok, Ok." Kenneth/Kwame took a deep breath and looked at me. "I am sorry. You and Jemma are right. We do indeed have to drop our campaign for Emmett. I too have heard other reports about him. I just needed to push Jenifer to satisfy my own mind that she is telling the truth and I do in fact believe her. I conclude from this that the Principle of Justice for all is primary to our cause and that principle is not best served in supporting Emmett."

Jemma took a deep breath and stood up. "The first Principle of Justice for us is that of supporting women, black women. Always going on about your sisters and yet look how much persuading you have needed tonight. All through history, in slavery that is, we have been raped and abused and that time there was nothing our brothers could do to help us. This is as important as the unjust lynching of black men. The rape of sisters by other black men is as important to our cause as police brutality and you can't hide that away and only look at what white men did to us. Any black man who rapes and beats a white woman would do just the same to a black woman and we have the proof here. Anyway, as you say, we now agree that the campaign must drop its defense of Emmett or Gregory or whatever his blasted name is."

"Sister, I understand what you're saying. We will talk more about how we will proceed later, when our young friend has gone. Meanwhile, is anyone hungry?" Jemma and I both nodded. "I didn't cook yet," said Jemma. "Never mind," went on Kenneth/Kwame "can you make a call to the Roti man to send up three chicken rotis and some carrot juice?"

Jemma, I felt, was somewhat pleased that she did not have to cook now and went to make the call. Kenneth/Kwame took some notes from his pocket and gave it to her.

"Eh? Me nah run up an' downstairs fe fetch rotis fe unno and me nah drop key fe no delivery bwoy. So is one outta you two haffe make de stair trip when him come. Seen?"

"I'll go", I said.

"It's Ok," said Kenneth/Kwame. "I'll go."

While we were waiting Jemma put on some music - her lovely jazz that I could feel myself beginning to really like. It was Miles Davis' 'Sketches of Spain'. Feeling at once more relaxed, I turned to Kenneth/Kwame.

'Do you mind if I ask you what name do you prefer to be called by? Is it Kenneth or Kwame?"

"Ah. Good question. Just to confuse you even more – either will do. They are both my names. I am Ghanaian. In Ghana, as indeed much of West Africa, the legacy of the colonials and the missionaries meant we all came to be given 'Christian' names, plus a tribal or ethnic, name as well as our family name. So my parents named me Kenneth Kwame Osei. I was sent here as a child and was fostered by a white couple in Kent. I am sure you know the story Jenifer and have seen the ads week after week in Nursery World from West African parents looking for foster families for their children while they work or study. They think they are also doing them a favour by ensuring they will grow up speaking 'proper English' and getting a good English education. If only that were the case. Anyway. My parents came here in 1949 – I was seven years old at the time. My Dad was studying law and my mother was a nurse. Like I say I was fostered by a white family in Kent. They had been in the colonial administration in Ghana and knew my father's parents. The wife had no children, she could not conceive, and so they agreed to foster me and then my brother, while my parents studied and worked. We were due to return when my mother died. I was about eleven then and my brother was eight. My father agreed with the family that they could continue to care for us until he found a new wife, but when he did, she did not really want us and we continued to be cared for by our foster carers. There was never any talk of adoption. Our father was always our father and he would write and we went to Ghana, but I hated all things African then and wanted to be English and white! I was sent to a good school and went to university, so in a way I have had a very privileged time. Coming to UCL in the early sixties during the time of growing Pan Africanismn among African and Caribbean students, I was put in touch with my roots again. Most English people call me Kenneth, in the Party and among the circle of African friends I am known as Kwame, but more and more that is what most people call me. Gabriella knows me from when I was called Kenneth, so she prefers to call me that. So it's up to you."

"Probably Kwame if I see you with Jemma and Kenneth if I am around Gabriella!"

"That's fine. Now that sounds like the doorbell and I need to do my sprint." He disappeared and came back with three chicken rotis, a carrot juice and two pine (pineapple) juices. I took my carrot juice and a hot wrapped up roti from out of the carrier bag. It smelled delicious.

"Now, young Jenifer," he said munching away at his roti, the juice trickling into his beard, "we need to talk about what happened at the nursery." He reached for a tissue and wiped his face. He went on to tell me about how Gabriella had talked to him about the kinds of things she saw in her day to day work at the nursery, the treatment of the black parents by some of the white staff, the differential and preferential treatment of children – both black and white – and Matron's hopeless management of the staff.

"We have to take a strategic approach with this situation. I know how the council operates. They will deny and cover up. If we just hit them with accusations we are not going to get anywhere. Gabriella told me you have read Bernard's book and she has also been made aware of how the system works against the black child. What she can see clearly is how that process of undermining the educational and personal development of the black child starts within the nursery setting. As a nursery nurse you would tell me that the first five years of a child's life are the most important; their brains are growing, their language skills are developing, important for thinking and learning to read, plus the all-important aspect of the

64

development of their identity. Positive identity, knowing who they are, being proud of who they are, is critical to all these processes."

I nodded in agreement. "So when black children are faced with staff who are supposed to be caring for them and loving them, but who mock them and don't even like them and where the general provision is poor, then that puts black children at a disadvantage."

"Yes", went on Kwame, "Not only our children, but you have to think of all children. What negative messages are white children picking up? How does the poor provision of resources and lack of real care undermine their progress too?"

He went on to say that he had shown Gabriella how to keep the "Incident Records" – date, time, who did or said what and to whom and who saw or heard it and what she may have said or done at the time. He said that this was the first step in the strategy and was glad I was on board. The next step was to work behind scenes, as he put it with a Councillor he knew was on side, some of the Union reps and a couple of staff based in the Town Hall. Like getting a football side together – you can't play the game without a good team – and a strategy.

"Gabriella told me about the records and she showed me as well how to keep them and I have been doing so – especially about that Big Mary – I am in the same room as her, and I know Gabriella has a lot of stuff recorded about Carol Clarke – the one who's leaving. I had asked Matron to go into baby room with Gabriella so we could team up and create the right kind of environment where all the children can flourish."

"Ah, yes. I am coming to that. Now, yesterday afternoon there was a big incident with Mabel and Big Mary. You rang Gabriella and told her what had happened. You said you had blurted out that you were keeping records on Big Mary and made other accusations against her and were due to go into see Matron and the Head of Service today."

"Yes, and I thought I had blown it by doing so, but Gabriella said no, it was good, it had to come out at some time and this was just sooner. She said she would be in today to back me up and then did not turn up for work and has not been answering her phone."

"So, what happened?" went on Kwame, leaving Gabriella out of it for now. "Did you bring in your book? Did you expose all? Did you mention Gabriella at all?"

"No, it did not go like that. I felt all along that I had blown it by saying all that to Matron. It was because I hated Big Mary with all my might at that moment and I was not thinking of the main plan, The Strategy. Even though Gabriella said it was fine, when she did not come in I knew I was right, that it was not fine, so I denied what I had said, withdrew my allegations and left Gabriella out of it."

"Yu smart to raas," muttered Jemma, sucking on a chicken bone.

"I ended up getting a verbal warning."

Kwame looked at me. "You sure that is the truth?"

"Yep." I showed him the confirmatory letter which was crumpled in my bag.

"I see they've wasted no time with this. Thank you. This has saved the day. You see, Gabriella cannot afford to get into this disciplinary business or get a reputation for being a troublemaker. She wants to go to teacher training and all that kind of stuff follows you on your records. Believe me, I have seen it happen."

"So, is that why she is off?"

"Yes. But this does not mean your efforts are in vain. We are not planning to be openly confrontational coming up from the ranks of the Nursery Nurses. Now this must not go beyond these walls, what I am going to tell you. Ok?"

I nodded and shook my head at the same time, meaning yes I understood and no I would not breathe a word.

"Through a good local Councillor and one of the Union representatives, we have been able to get funding for an Under Fives Research project. We will work in conjunction with the local Community Relations Council and there will be a researcher from UCL, my old university, and a team of assistants going round four Inner London boroughs, spending time in different under fives projects, nurseries, childminders and playgroups – everything – looking at how services meet the needs of children generally in the community and at the heart of that, will be the needs of the black child. We will be backed by a team of psychologists and black educationalists and we will hope to prove that our present services are not doing the job well enough and we will make recommendations to improve. We are heading for a new day here and we can't scupper it by these confrontations with managers. So please, you must learn to control your urge to anger and speaking your mind. But be assured, your evidence will not be ignored and will be fed into the process,"

Kwame went on a bit more, but I was getting too tired to take it all in. However, he did say that Matron might further punish me by not agreeing to my transfer to baby room, so all our plans to improve the care of babies would be undermined. I said I was sorry and would do my best to rectify things at work. I asked if I could make a call to Norman to come and pick me up. Kwame looked surprised.

"You know Norman. Always the gentleman," Jemma said to Kwame who chuckled. "Good people, those two. I know they look out for you. Don't let them down will you?"

I didn't know what he meant but I said I wouldn't. I thanked him for the roti and got up and took the plates in the kitchen and washed them up.

"Yu bes' rinse dem off. No Hinglish washin' hup please?" called out Jemma.

"Don't worry. Marvalette has trained me well. And I can make a mean corned beef and rice now!"

Jemma laughed. "Nex' time yu come 'ere yo can cook fe me n Kwame den!"

"Sure will!" I replied.

What a day. Norman came and collected me. I told him a bit about what happened.

"A so it go," he answered softly. "Marvalette ha' some news fe yu. 'bout yu fren Liz."

"It will have to wait til morning. I am too tired for anything else today."

"Seen" said Norman as he pressed the button to call the smelly lift.

"Goodnight Marvalette," I called as I went in.

"Ooooh! Me ha' news fe yu 'bout yu fren Liz. 'ere is she number. She gi 'it me, seh yu fe call har."

"Thanks Marvalette. Can you tell me in the morning please? I just want to go to bed."

"Ok. Sleep good."

"You too."

9. The phone call.

After the furor at the beginning of the week at work, things settled much into the pattern that I had anticipated. Matron offered the job in the baby room to Big Mary – of all people! It was her way of saying how much she valued her and not to worry about those other nasty people who were being horrid to her – as in me! Big Mary did not want to go back into the same room and have to face Mabel and co. Gabriella dreaded the thought of her coming to babies. Big Mary was Carol Clarke in another guise and as Big Mary was also a room senior, it made Gabriella worried about her role- like, exactly who was who in Baby Room now? She was a bit off with me when she returned to work and heard about Matron's plan. Then Big Mary went off sick with stress; the doctor signed her off for a month. I thought this was Big Mary buying herself some time and I predicted to Gabriella that she would be using the time to look for another job and then announce she was handing in her notice. I doubted that we would see her back in work. Matron flapped about, asking everyone else if they wanted to be transferred to babies, but they said no. In the end she had to give in and offer it to me.

"Not that I necessarily think this is best for the nursery, or that you have the right temperament, but under the circumstances I will agree as I don't really want a temp in there."

I was thrilled, but Gabriella took the news rather coolly. I knew it was about what happened and that she felt she could not trust me. I expect Kenneth/Kwame had undermined her own sense of judgment and perhaps she was projecting that on to me? I thought of asking her outright, but then something told me that was not the way to approach her. It would be better to rebuild the trust between us by actions – through showing her I could be a reliable teammate. The only thing I asked her was whether we should still keep our 'incident records'.

"It's up to you, if you want to, but I am not prepared to discuss them until it's the right time."

"Ok," I said, not taking it any further. I would continue anyway but keep quiet about it. What we did discuss was how to improve the provision in baby room. She was actually the room senior, but had been unable to move Carol Clark in the direction she wanted to go in. Our other co-worker was Vicky, previously blowing in the direction of Carol's wind. Without Carol to follow, nor Big Mary as it transpired, Vicky settled into going along with suggestions that Gabriella came up with. I gave her the support she needed to get into her role as a room leader, setting a new standard. We had to be careful not to be too radical as Vicky might have undermined us by gossiping with the others and Matron might have moved me out of the room.

It was beginning to feel good and by the middle of the following week I recalled that in my purse still was the piece of paper that Marvalette had given me with Liz's phone number. It was definitely her home number, so I figured she was back at home.

"Marvalette. Do you think I should call her? I can't decide. It's like I am curious to know what she wants and I would like to know that she is OK and has got over her ordeal, but I don't actually want to make back friends with her."

Aaron was in bed and Norman was on late shift. We were just finishing clearing up the kitchen and I was seasoning some lamb for the next day's dinner.

"Well, you know me go seh is up to you. When I did see she, me never tell har dat yu livin' wid us. I jus said dat if I see you, I will pass de paper to you. So me lef' it kinda vaguey like."

"Thanks for that. I don't really want that girl knowing my business or calling me here. But what haunts me is what her family or the police might know anyway. But cho, that sounds paranoid. I was wondering why, if the police want to press charges against Gregory that they might have wanted to take a statement from me – I did find her after all."

"Yeah, an' clean up de evidence! Maybe dem want you out de picture so dem can trump up dem own version o' de story. Yu neva can tell what dem crafty minds a t'ink bout."

"I feel like I am in too far as it is, Marvalette and I am worried, if I see her, what the outcome might be as far as the case goes. On the other hand, maybe they don't want me involved at all. Surely they would have come after me before now."

"Only one way fe fin' out! Call she!"

"Yeah, true. But I don't want to call from your phone in case they trace back to number."

"This isn't no James Bond movie you know! I t'ink you readin' too much into t'ings. Go get de phone an' plug it in 'ere an' call har. Go on. Do it now an' get it out the blasted way."

I reckoned Marvalette was right. I was seeing too many conspiratorial ramifications. At the end of the day though, there was a conspiracy against Gregory, for good or bad, and I was a key witness - for either side. I was beginning to feel like I was in the middle of it all and this scared me a bit. Either side could come after me if they decided my action was against their case. But the question still remained why the police had not already tried to find me and why had Liz waited all these months to contact me and the family had put her up to it. Or maybe she wanted to warn me – or warn me off. It had occurred to me that the police would watch people like Kwame and Jemma and the Pumas, so my connections to them may already be known.

"Well - jus' phone har! Den you will know wha' she wan'."

I went to get the phone and plugged it in. If it wasn't for the fact that it was dark out and that I would have to negotiate the smelly lift, twice, and that it was likely that the phone in the phone box would be out of order, I would have kept to my preference for not calling her from Marvalette's phone. I found the paper and dialed the number. Shit! What if her Mum answered, or worse, her Dad? I'd put the phone down, that's what I'd do. Say it was a wrong number.

"Hello," a voice answered. It was Liz!

"Hello. It's me, Jenifer. How are you?"

"You took your time to call me back."

"Well, I only saw Marvalette today in the street and she gave me the number and I have called you as soon as I could."

'Liar. I know you live with them lot. Leroy told me."

"You've seen Leroy? What did he say?"

69

"Well, obviously he said where you were living, so I hung around hoping to catch you, but I saw Marvalette instead and gave you my number. Why did you take so long to call back?"

"Life's been hectic and Marvalette only remembered today to give me the number. So why do you want to speak to me?"

"Why d'ya bleedin' fink? I'm goin' a court in two weeks to nail that cunt and I wanna know where you are? You are s'posed to be a mate – ain't you interested? The case is just going to Magistrates – for committal. He will mos' prob'ly plead not guilty and then it'll go to Crown Court, but that will take ages. Meanwhile that cunt is scott free and probably doing more of the same."

"Is he?" I got that sinking feeling. I decided to play as dumb as possible. "I didn't know you wanted me to be there. I would have been a witness if the police had got in touch with me to make a statement or something. I didn't even know you had pressed charges."

"Jen. I just wanna forget the whole thing, but my Dad and his bleeding cronies pushed me to it, but in a way it's right. He does need lockin' up. Now Dad says them bleedin' black idiots wanna defend 'im.

She's fishing, I thought. Marvalette was listening and shook her head, making a gesture of zipping her lips up. That meant for me to say as little as possible.

"So do you want me to be a witness – or do the police want me to be a witness even – or what? Look. I am truly sorry for what happened to you. I can't think of anything worse and I can understand how you feel, but to me it wasn't necessary to make that an excuse to indulge in the kind of racist crap your family get on with. I thought you wanted to get away from all that. We both did. But this turned you back into being more National Front than your Dad and that's why I haven't been in touch."

"I ain't no racist. I just 'ate that black cunt for what he done. My Dad and all, they are the ones who's racist. They are using all the means they can to get him sent down and believe me, they will stop at nuffin'."

"So why don't they want to talk to me? I found you and took you to hospital."

"But you destroyed the evidence. Why? Was you coverin' up for 'im? My Mum says you must be because the money went as well and only you knew about that."

"Yeah, she almost accused me of having an affair with him. As if! Liz, if you remember, when I came to the hospital you had said you couldn't go back to the flat in that state and we agreed we'd swap rooms over. I was trying to do you a favour, so you could come home and it'd all be nice and clean and no reminder of what happened. It never occurred to me that it was evidence that I was destroying. What do I know about police investigations?"

"Oh what? Like you never watched Z Cars when you was a kid? We used to watch Columbo together, so you know police are all over the scene of the crime when one is committed, so don't give me all that."

"Liz, I was stupid, I know, really stupid and I know that now. But at the time nothing like that went through my head and I am sorry. At the time, if you remember, you didn't even want to talk to the police, let alone think about them investigating. I am not covering up for Gregory at all. I loathe what he did and I loathe him for doing it. Yes, I would like to see him locked up too. He is dangerous. But I don't believe you have to resort to the same isms and schisms in order to seek justice. That's all. So, what do you want me to do?"

"Well I might believe you, if it weren't for the money. That's the bit I don't understand as he definitely did not take it?"

"How can you be so sure?"

"Before I put the tin back under the mattress I left it in the drawer of the dressing table. He did not find it, but when he left, the one thing I did was take it out of there and put it under the mattress. So, I know it wasn't him. It was you, weren't it?"

Should I continue to blame Old Nosey Parker? She had a key after all. I decided to opt for that tack. But then I wondered what she would have done about the weed. She was no smoker and that was for sure and she may have been the sort to have reported it to the police. So I changed my mind and confessed.

"It was me. I took it to get back at you for being so racist; for talking about the nurses in the way you did, who were there to look after you, and for calling people like Marvalette or Benjamin black this and that. I took your money – and whatever was in the tin to get back at you. OK."

"Fine friend you turned out to be."

"Likewise." I suppose I ought to offer the money back. It was in the bank, part of my savings. I waited for her to suggest that – or even demand it back.

"When I went home my Dad gave me a one-er so you can keep it. I don't want it back. At least you told the truth at last. You know if you take the stand at the witness box both sides are gonna make mincemeat of you. My Dad says you'll go where the wind blows and will be a liability. That's why we haven't called you."

"But don't you have to? I mean if I was a witness?"

"Who said you were there? As far as they think that 'man' (so as not to be racist) sent someone to clean up – and they took the money. I ain't arguing. I don't want you mixed up in it. You don't know those plods, rather the top brass, especially the West End lot. They make it up as they go along and as long as they get a

71

conviction that's all they care. So no, we don't want you, and no, I don't want the money back."

"Right," I said not wanting to comment further. "Liz are you well? I mean what happened about the baby? Your injuries? Have you recovered?"

"Nope. I can't walk prop'ly. Breathing is still painful. My face looks like a bomb site and I lost the baby. It ran away. Hahaha. Down my legs. Thanks to fuck. Imagine having that bastard's kid? I would have drowned it at birth. So, is that what you wanted to hear? Does that all serve me right 'cos I'm a racist, as you put it? Jen, you are so up your own backside, your nose is coming out the other end."

"I'm sorry to hear all that. You did not deserve to suffer in this or any other way and I never said it was your fault for being racist. I never thought you were, til I heard you talking to your Mum in that way. I know it must have been awful for them too, to see what happened to you. I understand why they are doing what they are doing and I hope with all my being that he gets sent down."

"Yeah? I know different."

"No you don't," I said emphatically. She had given the game away. The police must know about my links with Kwame and co. and that had been relayed back, in whatever way. However they didn't know what we had talked about and how I never betrayed her and how I had persuaded them that he was guilty as charged and not to mention what happened to Marcia. I decided to keep quiet and not go further. "I think we have said all we have to say to each other. By the way though, when did you see Leroy?"

"I seen him last week, week before and before that. I'm going out with him."

She loved a game, set and match, Liz did, and this was her triumph. I didn't care though, but I knew then that this was where she was getting her info from. I bet Leroy did not know what she really thought of black men.

"Oh. Does your Mum know? Mind how you go with him. Not for nothing do they call him Crab-I"

"He said it was you give him".

"Keep believing that and take care. Bye." I put the phone down.

Marvalette had a look of shock on her face at all that she had heard. She was getting the kettle on. It was time to 'sit down and discoss!'

10   The story

I finished off seasoning tomorrow's meat and put it in the fridge. Marvalette finished off cleaning the kitchen. We were both rather quiet; for one, I was livid with Liz and saw her as scheming, crafty and untrustworthy. What would she stoop to next? Marvalette was angry too, but she held it in – we both did – waiting to finish our chores first and gathering our thoughts meanwhile. Marvalette made two cups of tea and I rolled us a spliff. We head off to the living room, armed with the jasmine and lemon air freshener and settled down to discuss the latest developments.

"Well! What a turn up for de ol' book dat was. Me never hear everyt'ing dat Liz seh, so le' we start with de whole t'ing – chapter, verse and full stop."

I told Marvalette the whole conversation and how I was actually frightened of Liz's Dad and his cronies. How strange it was that I had been a witness to the aftermath of what happened to Liz, yet I had not been called to make a statement. Why was that?

"T'ink about it dis way," said Marvalette, "Yu neva hactually saw what 'appen to de girl, is it? I mean, yu neva saw Gregory bring har 'ome an' beat she, nar rape she, is it? So yu nah hactually much use - seen? Is wha' dem call 'circumstantial evidence', ok? Plus, you destroy de evidence an' dem wan' pin dat pon Gregory, so no way does dey want you inna de picture, yeah?"

"So why was she almost asking for me to be there, accusing me of not caring, yet telling me that they don't want me as a witness. None of what she said made sense. In fact she sounded contradictory at times. Anyway, so far, I've not been called as a witness and need to be grateful for that. But what worries me Marvalette is that the other side – that is Gregory and his solicitors – may want to call me. Do they know I found her and destroyed the evidence? If not he must never find out, because if am on that stand, the police will not be happy and if I don't do it Gregory will not be happy and I don't know who I am most afraid of."

"Jus' lay low Jen and if dem come fe yu, go along. If not, keep quiet. But wha' me wants to know now is where Leroy come into all dis. Some conversation go on dere which is de firs' time me hear. Yu t'ink Liz and he goin' out fe tru?"

"I don't believe it, unless it's her way of keeping an eye on me, finding out where I am living etc."

"An' is me tell Leroy you live 'ere so, me neva t'ink nuttin' of it. Me jus' t'ink is cos 'im like you dat 'im haks after yu."

"Well, after how she and her family get on about black people, I can't see her going out with him. I think she met him up, asked him a few questions, found out what she needed to know and we know how it goes from there. She knows what Leroy did to me wasn't nice and that was just to rub salt."
"So wha' im do, in trut'. Yu neva tell me de story, but me notice 'ow yu an' 'im was getting' on good one minute and den it's no more Leroy. Me neva want to haks yu 'bout yu business, so me jus' let it drop. Tell me, wha' appen? An' wha' she mean 'bout Crab-I? Me neva know is dat dey call 'im."

"It was what Benjamin said. Remember the night at the party? Benjamin was there. I went to the loo and he chatted to me, asked me about Leroy, if I was going out with him. I told Benjamin that I was just dancing with him and he said to be careful and that he is known as Crab-I. I didn't have a clue what that meant so I ignored it."

"So why dem call 'im dat den?" Marvalette wanted to know.

"I found out in the end. That night, Leroy took me back to the flat. We had Horlicks and stuff, played music, got cosy on the sofa and ended up in bed. Marvalette, I really liked him and thought he felt the same way. I regret going to bed with him so soon. He was just using me. What happened was he gave me crab lice – that's why they call him Crab-I, even though I don't know the story of how that came to be. I think he knows he has them and gives them to women on purpose. He also gave me a disease. He gave me gonorrhea. It all got cleared up quickly as I got it treated the next day. I couldn't get in touch with him because he gave me a false number. It was for a phone box! Can you believe?"

"Well, what is dis me a 'ear right now?" Marvalette kissed her teeth. She was shocked. And, by the look on her face, disgusted. For a minute I thought she was going to blame me, be disgusted with me. She re-lit the spliff and took a long drag on it, blew the smoke out and then spoke.

"To be hones' Jen, me surprise dat you go off sleep wid 'im so. Yu mus' get to know man firs', ca' yu need to know if dem is in yu carna. But yu wasn't to know. Yu nah carry on like dat since, so me figure you learn yu lesson, de 'ard way. Nah, me na angry with yu. Is dat daag Leroy. Me t'ought im get 'imself a bit sorted out an' stop 'im carry ons. Me vex, car is t'rough me, dat 'im get fe know yu and me is family to 'im. Jen, me nah know wha' fe seh to yu, fe tru'. Is like yu go t'rough so much a'ready and yu so young. Is not right yu get treat so."

"Please don't tell Norman will you? This is woman to woman, yeah?"

"Jen, is no shame. Me an' Norman have no secrets, Jen and you can trus' 'im 100%. But me might jus' forget to mention it."

We were both quiet for a minute.

"Yu know," began Marvalette, "dere is a sad story attach to Leroy. 'im did 'ave an 'ard time as a yout'. I will tell you what happen."

I went to get a glass of water and got a bunch of grapes that I had bought in the market that lunch time. We had let them chill in the fridge and now, with feeling like we had the munchies, tucking into the chilled, sweet red grapes was perfect. I was sitting on the cushions on the floor and Marvalette was on the sofa with her feet up on a stool. She began the story of Leroy.

Leroy had grown up in St Anne's in Jamaica. Winny, his brother was six years older than him. As I knew Winny was five years older than his wife, Grace, who was twenty-one, that meant he was twenty six, same age as Marvalette, and doing the maths I deduced that Leroy was only nineteen. Just a year older than me, bit less even. It occurred to me that we had not even spoken about our ages when we met. As a painter and decorator and driving a reasonable little car, he did not seem to be doing too badly for one so young. I interrupted Marvalette for a moment to make this observation.

"Yu wan' hear dis, or sit n do sums?"

"Sorry. Carry on."

Marvalette went on to explain the complexity of their cousin relationship. I confess to being a bit too stoned to take that part in, however what I did understand clearly was that Leroy and Winny's Dad left them when they were small boys and how it was Marvalette's parents who used to help their Mum out with a bit of money, even after her Dad died. The Mum never re-married, as she had loved only their Dad, or so they say, as Marvalette hinted that there were other stories about her. When Marvalette's Mum came to this country she still used to send her some money until she remarried. I never knew any of this about her and her family story – she didn't know about mine either, for that matter.

The money stopped. Winny was about fourteen and Leroy was just eight at the time. There was another uncle over here and he sent for Winny when he was fifteen. At that time, you could leave school at fifteen and get a job. Winny came here determined to work and send money home. He got a job first on the paraffin vans, delivering paraffin to people's homes. As soon as he turned seventeen he learned to drive and got promoted. He sent money home regularly and lived at the uncle's almost for free and saved some too. Everything was going great for a couple of years, when suddenly their Mum died.

Leroy had been badly affected by the death of his Mother and went a bit wild. He stopped going to school and hung out with what Marvalette called 'de rude bwoy dem', smoking and doing petty hustling. Winny went to Jamaica to find out what was going on and he brought Leroy back up with him to his uncle's place. They lived there for a couple of months, got Leroy into secondary school and then the council gave them a flat. Winny was eighteen and there was no-one going to look after his baby brother but him, so the Social Services let him.

Marvalette stopped talking for a moment. I could see she had tears in her eyes. "Jen, when me t'ink 'bout what dat man do fe Leroy, it touch me 'eart, yu' know? From 'im eighteen, 'im tek on a fader role, and Leroy is no saint. 'im bunk off school, 'im tief, 'im smoke an' de Social almos' put 'im in care. Winny nah put up wid all o' dat. "'im tell Leroy fe de las' time 'ow is 'im work since he was fifteen support all o' dem an' 'ow he nah let Leroy fall to de wayside. Leroy jus a bawl dat 'im miss 'im mudder, an' Winny jus' 'ug 'im an' hol' 'im all night while de bwoy a bawl. 'im seh is de firs' time 'im really show 'im grief an' 'im an' Winny bawl til neider dem cyan bawl na more. From dat day, Leroy a go to school, good good and is behave 'im behave."

"Winny is a very kind man, then. It's not many teenage boys who would take on that kind of responsibility. What an amazing story. But what happened from there then?"

"Ha! Leroy a go school ev'ry day. "'im nyam 'im school dinner, 'im do 'im P.E. an' football an' t'ing; 'im do 'im woodwork an' metal work an' get on good good. 'im do art and 'im do 'im maths, but only so far. De main t'ing was, yu t'ink anyone coulda mek dat bwoy read? Leroy nah learn fe read. Not even in Jamaica, car 'im 'ardly go a school, car de Mum a need 'im 'ome, look after she. Leroy lookin' forward fe leave school and go a work, like him bredda, but de gov'ment raise de school age and Winny nah realise. When 'im did, Leroy vex and de trouble a start up again. "'im nah go a school, but 'im na go work, so 'im jussa loaf about, start smoke an' ting. When Winny fin' out, 'im vex. But 'im neva know Leroy cyan read. Leroy 'ide it. It was shame 'im feel shame. So Winny have a fren' – dis same one Kennet' – and Kennet' meet Leroy, sen' 'im back go school an' ev'ry day 'im come to de 'ouse and teach Leroy fe read."

I couldn't help feeling sad for Leroy, to lose his Dad – who never contacted the family again after he left and apparently went to America – and then his mother. I was amazed at Winny's sense of responsibility and loyalty for his younger brother and the fact that he was prepared to go to such effort to make sure Leroy stayed on track. But there was more.

Marvalette then went on to explain how Leroy then stayed on at school until he was sixteen and how it was through Kenneth (the same Kenneth/Kwame it turned out) that Leroy learned to read and that he even managed to get three CSE's in Art, Woodwork and P.E. When he left school, he got an apprenticeship as a carpenter, but the boss was white, and all the guys in the workshop were too. Leroy found entering the world of work and facing the day to day racial carping in his workplace too much to cope with. He rowed with the manager and got sacked. Being young he could not handle what happened, started smoking again and just hanging around in the day, not looking for work. Again Winny and Kenneth talked him round and found him a job with some painters and decorators. It was a pair of them. One Jamaican and one Irish guy. They taught him the trade and then Leroy went out on his own. Bought himself a little van, then a car, then got himself a small flat and seemed to be going Ok. Then he met a girl. A white girl and was besotted with her. But she was no good and was sleeping around behind his back. She gave him some 'problem', but Marvalette had not known what that was but now the penny dropped to both of us.

"She must have given him crab lice and to get his own back, he never got them treated but just gave them to other girls instead. Like me. Too stupid to get to know him, but just jumped in bed with him without thinking, falling for all the charm and then getting caught. But he must have got the other thing recently. Yuk. What a mess and how stupid. Idiot."

"Blood clart!" exclaimed Marvalette, 'but is 'ow 'im could nasty so?" It was not often she used Jamaican swearing, so she really was mad at his foolishness. "It seem like ev'ry time dat bwoy face pressure 'im haffe tek it out on people so. Is like 'im wan' get attention, or what?"

"I wonder what he makes of our Liz then? Hardly virtuous - and racist through and through. I can't believe he would go out with her – unless it was to mess her up in some way. I don't know if he knows what happened to her but wait! He was in the house that night. Supposing they are trying to fit him up. Like saying it was him there that night destroying the evidence? If they tested my room, for finger prints, they would have found his. Do you think that could happen?"

Marvalette kissed her teeth. I could see she thought I was getting over-imaginative about possible eventualities.

"Maybe not then. Still, him and Liz in the same sentence is not a good idea; it smells of trouble to me."

"Jen, jus' be cool nah! Go to work, do your job, get on with buildin' your life an' forget 'bout all o' dem. Unless trouble knock 'pon your door, don't go lookin' for it. Now, is tired me tired and me wan' go a me bed."

"I suppose so, but with all this mess through what happened to Liz, I don't know what to make of anything. And I am afraid. But you are right about either imagining or looking for trouble. And, as for getting on with my life, lots of things are happening on that front. I am thinking of applying for teacher training like Gabriella. She brought me in all the information and I am going to give it go. Also, I've saved up a couple of hundred pounds, including Liz's money, since I have been living here and have been looking at what flats are available. I love living here, but I realise I am in Aaron's room and .."

"Yu ain't goin no-where yet. So no hurry fe move out. Aaron love yu bein' here and yu cookin' comin' on good! We have news fe yu! Me and' Norman does save too and we have enough fe a deposit on we own place and we seen a likkle 'ouse up Kensal Rise. It 'ave t'ree bedroom, so yu can have a room of your own and we would be glad of de rent. So t'ink 'bout it. A new chapter could start dis way."

"Wow! Buying a place of your own. That's really great news and well done. It is a good step forward. I would love to rent a room from you if that's what you want. Great. Thank you so much."

11 ♦ The March

> 'Let the power fall on I, Farl
> Let the power fall on I.
> Let the power from Zion fall on I
> Let the power fall on I.'ᵛ

It was Saturday Morning and the morning of the March against Police Brutality. It had been decided that I would stay home with Aaron while Norman and

Marvalette would go and march together, side by side. They felt this was the best way I could support the cause, knowing their son would be safe with me. Both of them knew there was a level of risk involved, as while the police had agreed that the March could take place and had stipulated the details of the route with the organisers, many people felt they were sitting targets should any confrontation ensue.

The other matter, of course, was the campaign to defend Emmett against the 'trumped up' charges of rape and assault. The last I knew was from the conversation last Saturday when Jemma said she was going to get rid of the three boxes of leaflets that were due to be given out on the March and Kenneth/Kwame had agreed the campaign needed to be faded out somehow. Was he going to confront Gregory directly? Would that expose me? Would I be safe if that was the case? Supposing they said nothing to Gregory and he realised they were not supporting him and wanted to know why? Supposing this split the group – the side that believed the white girl and the side that supported the black man regardless? The case would have a different dimension if Marcia came forward. Could Jemma persuade her to bring a case against him? Would Marcia be able to risk the trauma of going to the police as well as risk the possibility of her community turning against her?

It all went round and round in my head. I decided to find a box for all these questions somewhere in the back of my mind and lock them all away in there. Unless someone knocked on my door and demanded I be a witness, it was just not my business. Forget about it Jen, I said to myself repeatedly whenever a question insisted in popping up into my mind. Lord, what a mess! Anyway, with all thoughts of Gregory carefully packed away, I got on with planning what to do with Aaron for the day. I wanted to go out and do something to take both our minds off worrying about his Mum and Dad that day. I suggested we would go to Regents Park Zoo if he wanted to and Norman and Marvalette agreed. For one we would be going away from the direction of the marchers and therefore not likely to get caught up in it. They were both in agreement that would be a great idea and Aaron was over the moon.

So we got ready and left the house before they did. The March was due to start at 1pm, so Aaron and I headed out at midday, walking up to Queens Park Station and boarding the train to Regents Park and, from there, finding our way to the Zoo. It was a lovely sunny April day, crisp and fresh, just right to go explore the zoo, stopping for a lunch of Wimpey and chips, with ice cream to follow. Aaron was excited about the zoo, and was interested in the big cats, the hippos and the elephants most of all. He knew these were all animals from Africa and was interested in knowing more about their African habitats. We bought a book in the gift shop as well as a pencil each for Mum and Dad that said 'Regents Park Zoo' on them. We had a half hour or so left before leaving at 4.30 and we went off to see the monkeys. We sat down and had a Mars bar while we watched them swinging about.

"What's the time, Aunty Jen?"

"Quarter past four. We will leave about half past and get home just after five."

"Will the March be over then? Will Mummy and Daddy be home by then?

"I don't know", I said. "I expect they will come home when they are finished."

"Will they be OK? Do you think the police will trouble them?"

I didn't know the answer to these questions but said that I was sure they would be fine and that they could look after themselves and each other.

"It's important, what they are doing, isn't it? I mean, after the police stopped us that night, and Daddy hadn't done anything, neither Mummy, nor you, but they were being horrid to us. Why? Don't they like coloured people?"

I didn't want to say too much as I knew Norman discussed this with Aaron and had put his mind at rest, but nevertheless he had observed things, had experienced things that reflected the prejudice and stereotyping that he would yet have to face as a black boy growing up in this society.

"I don't know," I replied, "but I think Daddy can explain these things better than me. I do know that Daddy and Mummy are marching to make things better, so that things will be better for you."

"Jack and Tommy at school. They call me names like cocoa puff and chocolate drop. Tommy even called me a nigger. What's that Jen?"

"Nigger is a very rude name to be called. They say these things because they don't know any better. You are better than them, so just ignore them, tell them you don't like being called those names and leave it at that.'

"I just wanted to punch him, Aunty Jen. It did upset me lots."

"I expect it did, Aaron. It would upset me to be called names too. But if we went around hitting people back we would be the ones getting into trouble and so it's best to try to deal with them using words to stand up for yourself. Have you told Daddy, or Mummy or your teacher?"

"No, not really. My teacher wouldn't do nothing anyway. She doesn't like me and I don't want to worry Mummy or Daddy because they've got lots to worry about getting stopped by the police and that."

"Oh, Aaron," I said as I began to see the implications of what this might feel like for a small child, trying to make sense of it, carrying it like a burden at such a young age, working out how to deal with it and not wanting to tell the very people who could support him in case it would be another burden for them.

"I think you should tell Mummy and Daddy. They will believe you and help you. When it comes to you, nothing is too much for them, do you understand?"

79

"OK. I like you Aunty Jen. I like you living with us."

"Right, well, glad to hear it. Now let's go to the station and get on home.

We left the Zoo at quarter to five after all and made our way home. We got out at the station and walked over the bridge, cutting out way through to South Kilburn. We could hear police sirens and ambulance sirens and the distant sound of shouting. It was the demo. I wanted to get Aaron home quickly before he noticed and started to get worried. I chatted inanely about our day to distract his attention and keep his mind engaged. Just then, some youths ran past us, seemingly heading away from the action. I got a bad feeling about it but got to our block and in the smelly lift (I was getting used to it now) and within minutes we were safe indoors.

Marvalette and I had cooked the night before and there was food in the fridge waiting to be warmed up. Aaron and I ate and watched some TV. We had missed the six o'clock news, so now I had to wait until the nine o'clock news on ITV. Thankfully Aaron would be in bed by then. By seven o'clock, Aaron's bedtime, Norman and Marvalette were still not home. He was worried.

"They will be fine, I said. They probably went off with some friends to talk about what happened and have a drink. They will be home soon. Bed time for you, anyway young man, go on – off you go."

I read Aaron a story and he went off to sleep about half past seven.

Eight, nine and ten o'clock came and went. At half past ten, the phone went. I picked it up fast. It was Jemma.

"Hi Jenifer, this is Jemma. Look, to get to the point, Norman and Marvalette got arrested…. No, they are OK… there was a scuffle, but they were not at that part of the march. The police were indiscriminate in singling out people to arrest and they have charged them with riot and affray. They will need bailing out. The bail is £100 each. Would you be prepared to stand bail? Can you get to Paddington Police Station?"

Jemma sounded very stressed, her sentences all jumbling into one. Perhaps she was having to make many similar phone calls. I told her I was babysitting Aaron and could not leave the flat. No, there was no-one I could leave him with, unless Aunty Cora could come over, but look at the time. Also I didn't have cash and it would be Monday before the banks were open. I didn't know that you did not have to pay bail up front, so Jemma explained I would only have to cough up if they skipped bail and as there was little likelihood of that, my money was safe. I decided I would phone Aunty Cora anyway and Jemma left me a number to call her back on, plus the details of the police station. Cora was shocked and said she would come at once, getting Denison to give her a lift over and saying he could also take me up to the police station. Relief. I rang back Jemma and told her. Then I gathered stuff like my birth certificate, bank statements and pay slips to offer as proof of who I was and the funds I had and where from. With half an hour, Cora arrived with Denison. They came in and I explained again what had happened and Denison indicated we should go right away and saying 'Goodbye' to Cora, we left.

We didn't say much, Denison and me, but when we got to the Police Station he asked if I would like him to come in with me. I could see that he was not that keen – neither was I, but I had a job to do.

"It's up to you," I said to him, "personally, I would appreciate you being there. My only connection with the police – ever – has been unpleasant," (I was referring to the time when we had all been pulled over) "and I would feel braver if you were there, not to get involved, but just knowing someone was with me. But it's up to you. I understand if you don't want to go in there."

"Jen." Denison began slowly talking in his Cockney accent. "I don't wanna go in there, but I ain't leaving you to face them on yer own. What you are doin' here is a very 'elpful thing for Marvalette an' Norman. You're good! Let's go."

I thanked him and was sincerely grateful to him. We got out of the car. He locked up and we walked slowly towards the entrance.

"'ere goes, then."

"Yep," I answered, "Here we go." I took a deep breath and we walked in. My heart was thumping, but I was on a mission and I was now focused and determined. We walked in to the main reception. It was slightly less than pandemonium. There were disgruntled demonstrators wanting information about friends and family, solicitors and the press all buzzing in conversation, trying to get some sense out of the desk sergeant and his assistant on the desk. They seemed short staffed and were not coping. You could not see if there was a queue or whether people were just standing because there was nowhere left to sit. The few chairs available (the ones screwed to the floor) were taken up.

I looked around to see if I spotted anyone – like Kenneth/Kwame or Jemma. Stroke of luck! Just then, the main door swung open and in came Jemma along with a white woman and a white man, both carrying briefcases. They look like solicitors I thought – good old Jemma, on the case and looking like she knew what she was doing. Ah! She had spotted me and excused herself from her companions and came over to me.

"Raas! Look at all this confusion. The police don't know what they are doing. They have arrested about 50 people and thought that no-one would flick an eyelid and they are having to face the fact that black people are not going to stand back and do nothing. How are you anyway? I'm glad you are here. Who's this with you?

"Oh, this is Denison. Aunty Cora's husband. She's with Aaron and he drove me here and has come in to give me some support. How are Marvalette and Norman? Have you seen them? I've got every document I could think of bringing. What do I do? Sorry. Denison, this is Jemma. She is one of the organisers and is Marvalette's friend."

The two shook hands and exchanged greetings. A seat became vacant; Jemma quickly indicated to Denison to go and sit down while he waited for us. I felt that at least now I could get done what I came there to do. Jemma led me up to the desk and called the desk sergeant who was in no hurry to come over. We waited.

"Yes?" he said, sauntering towards us, looking as confused as everybody else and not making a very good job of hiding the fact.

" I have come to stand bail for Marvalette and Norman Campbell."

"Oh, have you now." He looked through some papers and found their names. "Ah yes. Well, you've got a long wait."

"Can you tell me what is happening to them?" I asked naively.

"Well. They've been arrested."

Great – that much was obvious.

"Ok. I have been told they have been arrested and that is why I am here. To stand bail for them so they can come home. They have a small son at home. He is worried about his Mum and Dad. His aunt is with him while I am here."

I wasn't making much sense and the sergeant was looking at me like I was stupid.

"Have Mr. and Mrs. Campbell been actually charged yet with any offence?" interjected Jemma.

"Not yet. But they will be. We have a lot of people to get through tonight, so I suggest you find a seat and wait, like everyone else."

"Have they been able to call a solicitor? Asked Jemma, seemingly knowing what to ask about. But the sergeant just shrugged. Jemma looked around for one of the people she brought in with her.

"Barbara, Barbara. Over here."

Barbara came over.

"The sergeant says they have not been charged yet and it could be ages."
Barbara clearly was a solicitor and began to address the sergeant telling him she was there to represent Mr. and Mrs. Campbell and demanding to see them. Jemma told me who she was quietly while Barbara continued with the sergeant.

"That's Barbara Sington-Smith – she a top top brief. Very political. On our side."

"Oh good. Someone needs to be to get through this mess. Are you OK?"

"Yeah – me all right. Glad to see you come help yu fren. Dem Babylon wicked. De whole t'ing was planned. We was all coming down Harrow Road from de Steps– no problems at all, but we turn off down Bravington Road. Me, Kwame, Lenny, Sista Dee, all up in front leading, an' as we turn off, dey let a few of us carry on, 'til it was like they split the whole march in two and then, when we couldn't see wha'appen still to dem on de 'arrow Road, Babylon dem jus' start to cordon off those marchers and trouble flared before we even knew. It all happened so fast, Jen." Jemma sucked her teeth. She looked shocked and exhausted.

"What happened then?" I asked. "Were Marvalette and Norman at the back then? Did you see what happened to them?"

"Slow down, slow down. Me cyan answer all dem question at once!! Yes they were further behind. Norman was stewarding towards the back and Marvalette was giving out leaflets."

Leaflets. For a moment, my face dropped. Jemma knew what had gone through my mind.

"No, no no. Not those leaflets, Nah bodder 'bout dem. Dem gwan a fiyah! I took them round my Aunty Mae's and chucked them on her coal fire!! Bit smokey, but they are no more. To continue. We never saw how the police charged but by that time we were half way down the road until we realised something was amiss and people were running our way to tell us. Cho! Pure madness. When we made our way back up all we could see was cosh here, blood there, people being dragged to the Black Mariah's, screaming, yelling – the lot. It was awful."

Just then, Barbara turned round to Jemma.

"Looks like we're in. I have explained I need to see my clients and find out what's going on. If they can't charge them, they will have to let them go, but they have not even been interviewed yet. I have been able to hurry that up. They believe Norman to be one of the 'leaders' because he was a marshal. The sergeant was talking about sending officers round to search the house. They will take him with them, but they have not yet organized a warrant. It's such a mess. The officers are stretched and not coping. Oh .. looks like I am going in. Wait here."

The sergeant took Barbara through some double doors and Jemma and I went back over by Denison to tell him what was happening. We had a discussion about whether or not he should go. We agreed that I would go with him over to the phone box to call Aunty Cora and let her know what was going on and to say that the police might want to search before they charged them and to expect a visit. Jemma waited behind. I went with Denison just in case there were any police outside who might trouble him – although what help could I be other than witness? The phone call trip passed without event other than Aunty Cora being worried and upset. However she agreed that he should stay with me until we got her niece and her niece's husband out of there.

83

We were dying for a cup of tea and joked about Denison going back to get Aunty Cora to make us up a flask and some sandwiches. It was now half past one in the morning; time being eaten up in the police station. I wondered if there was a tea machine in there. Tea machines were beginning to replace tea ladies and snack kiosks everywhere and everyone moaned about how awful the tea was, but the hot chocolate was bearable. There must be something in the police station, somewhere for refreshment. Asking where and what would be another matter.

We got back inside and looked around for Jemma. She was talking to Kwame who had just been talking to a reporter – from a tabloid not known for its sensitivity towards 'immigrants' of any kind. Sista Dee had called the Guardian – she had a contact there – and they were hoping a reporter from a more sympathetic newspaper would come down. Kwame had been asked why they were 'rioting' by this tabloid reporter, Jemma was saying, and Kwame had been trying to explain why they had been marching and that they were ambushed and attacked by the police. It all seemed to have fallen on deaf ears, but Kwame had kept patient. That was his strength. He was fuming inside but he could maintain calm and be articulate, not getting angry with this fool reporter.

My attention to what they were saying was distracted as I noticed one, no two, people holding what looked like plastic cups, and pulling faces as they drank the unappetizing contents. Denison saw it too.

"Righto. Looks like we can get a cuppa. Hot chocolate Jen? Jemma and your friend – want a cuppa?"

We all nodded and frantically searched our pockets and bags for change for the machine that Denison had spotted over in the far corner. Realising he could not carry four flimsy plastic cups, Kwame went with him, leaving Jemma and I to keep an eye on what was going on. The crowd had settled down a bit and a number of people had now left, supposedly having got their loved ones safely out of there.

"What Kwame has discovered is that four brothers and two sisters have been charged. They have at least twenty brothers and sisters in there. We still don't know about Norman and Marvalette."

"Jemma, I am so worried."

"What for?" said Jemma, leaving me feeling quite taken aback. "Dey cyan kill dem in dere! Soon as dey done question dem, dey out, so don' fret yuself too much!!"

Before I could answer her, Denison and Kwame came back with flimsy plastic cups full of something looking like hot chocolate. Then I remembered I had a couple of Kit Kats in my bag that I had got for Aaron and I when we were at the zoo but we had not eaten them.

"Hang on," I said as I delved into my bag to find the rather sweaty bars, "they are a bit melted, but if you want some we could have half each."

"Yeah – good old Jen," said Kwame, laughing and being uncharacteristically matey with me. I smiled and shared out the Kit Kat fingers wrapped in a bit of silver paper to stop the chocolate from messing up our fingers. All of us looked tired, especially Jemma and Kwame, for whom this had been an exhausting day. I was just about to say, "How much longer?" when the double doors opened and out came Barbara, a police officer and Marvalette. She looked terrible. Stressed and disheveled with a cut on her hand that looked like it needed treating. She had been crying and looked like she was about to cry again.

"I have been able to get them to release Marvalette with no charges, but I am afraid they will be charging Norman with riot and affray. However, they have accepted that he was just marshaling and not a 'leader'. We need to sort out his bail – which one of you was standing bail for him?"

"It's me." I said, handing the rest of my hot chocolate and Kit Kat to Marvalette.

"Ok, let's see if we can get him bailed and then you guys can go home. It looks like I will be here for a while, there are more people in there who have not even been allowed their phone call and who have no one to act for them so it's going to be a busy night for Michael and I."

He was the other solicitor, who was not around at that moment – probably behind the double doors, I thought. We went up to see the same slow desk sergeant who was attempting to drink the unappetizing machine tea. Barbara muttered something sympathetic to him and he managed a smile at least. She spoke to him for a few moments and then he turned to me, handing me some paperwork.

"Fill that lot in," he said, "I usually do it meself, but I've got a lot on. When you've filled it out wait here for me to come back here with all your ID and proof of funds. I 'ope you know what you are doing, young lady. You sure your 'friend' is not going to land you in it by doing a runner?"

"I'm certain he will not do that. May I have a pen?"

The sergeant handed me a pen and I filled out the form as fast as I could, getting all my paperwork ready. The sergeant came back raised his eyebrows a few times here and there as he looked at the documents and started filling out his bit. By now I didn't care what he found to raise his eyebrows over, I just wanted him to get on with it. It was two in the morning and we all wanted to go home. He scuffled about with the paper and Barbara went behind the double doors again. Twenty minutes – yes twenty minutes – later she re-emerged with Norman behind her. He looked exhausted, and a complete mess. Marvalette went up to him and they hugged, and hand in hand went out of the building with Denison and me behind.

"I'm parked over 'ere mate. Looks like they've given you a rough old time alright."

"True dat" answered Norman and that was all he said for the whole journey home. I sat next to Marvalette in the back. She put her finger to her lips indicating to me not to try to talk about it with Norman, nor discuss with her. Denison drove the four of us back to the flat and not another word was said. When we got in, Denison came up to get Aunty Cora who was half snoozing on the sofa. No-one wanted to talk that night. Norman went into the bathroom when they left and ran himself a bath. Marvalette and I made some tea and we just sat there politely exchanging how the day had gone for Aaron. I went to get ready for bed and when Norman came out of the bathroom, he left a bath running for Marvalette. I managed to slip in to pee and clean my teeth and went off to bed, leaving the two of them to wind down a while before they went to bed.

What a night. And of course it was not over as Norman was now facing a criminal charge, that might affect his employment and if he lost his job that would be that with the house plans and with a criminal record finding another job would be hard. I just hoped Barbara what's her name would get him off in court. In addition to those who had been charged, I thought of people like Kenneth/Kwame, Sista Dee, Lenny and of course Jemma, all active members of the Pumas who were not arrested but whom the police would be interested in. It's not over yet, I thought to myself as I settled down into a deep sleep.

12   The day of reckoning

'Cause a pressure drop, oh pressure
Oh yeah, pressure drop a drop on you.
I say a pressure drop, oh pressure
Oh yeah, pressure drop a drop on you.[vi]

After the long night, we had all got to bed late. I woke, hearing the phone ringing from the sitting room. I heard Marvalette's voice. It seemed like it was Aunty Cora.

"Aaron. Come. Fix yourself. Aunty Cora is going to take you by her place to play., just so me 'n' Daddy can get a rest. What a late night we had!"

I got up to go to make some tea in the kitchen. Marvalette was in there with Aaron, giving him some Weetabix.

"So, were you alright then?" he asked his Mum. "You and Daddy weren't back by bedtime and I was worried. Aunty Jen said you may have gone to the pub to talk with friends after."

"Aaron. You need to listen. This is serious. We are all ok, but you will hear about it on TV or from others, so we will tell you the truth. The police and some marchers had a fight. Daddy and I were not at that part, but we got arrested. Aunty Jemma came with a solicitor and got me out, but they charged Daddy. Don't worry though. Everything will be fine."

"Will Daddy go to prison?" asked Aaron, starting to get tears in his eyes.

"No, no. The Pumas will make sure of that. Don't worry. We are standing up for ourselves against injustice and we will win. Daddy will be fine."

Just then, the doorbell rang. I made a move to go and answer it, but Marvalette beckoned me back.

"I will answer my door." There was an edge to her tone. I felt uncomfortable. I noted how Marvalette had barely even said good morning, but I had put this down to her talking to Aaron.

Aunty Cora and Denison came in and Marvalette led them into the sitting room where they waited for Aaron.

"Would you like me to make some tea for everyone?" I asked.

"No, they are leaving right away, but you can make some for you and me. Norman is still sleeping."

Maybe I am just being sensitive, I thought. After all we had all been through a terrible time, especially those two. Aunty Cora put her head round the kitchen door.

"You alright this morning Jen? I'm going to take Aaron over by me til later so you all can have some rest. I will cook food and bring for you all later."

I remembered I had seasoned the lamb for Marvalette the day before and put peas to soak. Let it wait, I thought. Then the three of them left.

Marvalette came back into the kitchen and I handed her the tea, offering to put some toast on.

"Stop, stop, stop." I didn't know what she meant and my confusion was plain to read on my face.

"I mean stop trying to run my house – answer the door, make the tea, making me toast. Like you are my Mum or something. I'm not incapable. Or is that what you think? That you have to rescue me? Cho!" She sucked her teeth and put some toast under the grill.

"I'm just trying to help as much as I can. You and Norman have been through an ordeal and I am just trying to be thoughtful. Of course I don't see you as incapable. That's not fair."

"Not fair? Not Fair? Dis is wha' not fair." She rolled up her sleeve and there was a massive bruise; she pulled back her hair from her face and there was another just coming out. She lifted her nightgown and there was another on her leg.

"I know that's not fair," I replied, feeling that somehow Marvalette wanted to take out her anger on me. "I know you have suffered and you are probably in shock. I know I am and I didn't even go through what you did. But it was pandemonium in the police station last night. What happened to you two was terrible. I just wanted to be there for you, to help you. It IS your struggle, but I wanted you to know I was behind you, supporting you."

Marvalette sucked her teeth again.

"You want to know what is your problem, Missie?" (I couldn't believe she called me that and I was now feeling really uncomfortable.) "is like you just want to sit on the side and hobserve wha' go on. Like is some kinda drama game fe yu. Go live in de ghetto an' dish out you 'support' fe we struggle, like yu is Florence Nightingyale or some bloody damn thing."

I was shocked to hear Marvalette talk to me in that way. Only two days before we had been sitting together as friends and I had shared my confidences with her. I knew she was angry and hurt, that it was the reality of the extent of the racism she and Norman and the others had gone through that was behind the bitterness in her words. But the words stung and I started to cry. I did not know what to say. A racial divide was carving into our friendship and I did not know how to handle it.

"Is that how you see me? After all the weeks I have lived here and we have got on so well and I thought we were friends? Is that how you see me?"

I wasn't making sense.

"What happened to you and Norman and everyone was awful. It was not my fault, so don't take your anger out on me, please. I have done my best to be a friend, to show you gratitude for your kindness, to go the full nine yards for you both when you were in trouble. I am so sorry this happened to you both. I never knew about racial prejudice and discrimination til I moved down these sides. I am not just peering in on your lives. I am living here too, experiencing this reality and I want it to change too. This is what I am learning. This is what I want to do – to make the world a better place – for all of us. Not just me, but through doing my bit."

My tears rolled down my face and my nose was snotty. I reached for some kitchen roll to dry my face but the tears kept rolling. Marvalette just sat there.

"Can we talk about this calmly?" I sniffed, wondering what was coming next and feeling like my world was about to crash – again.

"I am calm. Look like is you who is hysterical."

"I just don't know what to say. You and Norman have been so kind to me. I would do anything for you. It's just about living in a kind way. Not about thinking I have to rescue you."

Marvalette turned to look out of the window.

"Norman thinks you should move out."

"What do you think? Do you think I should move out?"

"I go with what makes Norman happy. And right now he is very unhappy. In dat room is a broken man. Broken. My man. My 'usban'. Him come first and last before any friend. If 'im wan yu fe move out, is move yu movin'."

"Oh my God. How is he? He looked awful last night. But I heard Barbara say she would get him off?"

"Like I tol' you. He is broken. I never see Norman so. Never. So whatever 'im say, is dat me a do."

"When do you want me to go?"

"Now."

The shock of this echoed through me. The insecurity of my position with totally no-where to go on a Sunday morning, just like that.

"What? Move out all my stuff and everything today? Where can I go? I have nowhere to go? It's Sunday and I can't even go to a flat agency? Who do I know to take me in? And why does Norman want me to go? I just stood bail for him. When Jemma called to say what happened, I called Cora and came straight away. Why does he want me to go?"

"Do you know what the fucking Babylon policeman said to him? Do you?"

"No I don't."

"After dem beat 'im pon de street, after de white people, what's left of them and who dared put their head out dey windows, callin out 'go on, get the niggers, run them out of our streets back to where they belong' and all that shit – I hear it too. Ol' white 'oman come push me - 'fuck off back to your jungle then' she said before sneakin' back into she doorway. Babylon push me and pull me, I fall, dem drag me, "As she got a wig on?' I hear one o' dem say and they pull my hair to see. One grab my breas' as they lift me and haul my arse into de van. I don't even know where is Norman. I'm callin' for him, but in dat mess I can't see who is who. It was like slavery days as one sista seh to me. Like when de white man separate us woman from man on de slave ships. We coulda see dat same wickidness in de white man eye."

Marvalette paused for a moment. She was fighting back the tears. I said nothing and waited for her to continue.

"It was like the same wickidness of my white stepfather when him do nastiness to me. Yu neva know dat bout me is it? When my father die, my mom marry a white man. She have me and my two younger brothers. At firs' it was fine, all lovie dovie and she t'ink she land pon two feet, car 'im 'ave a good job an' a nice 'ouse. She get pregnant and from den it change. 'Im seh 'ow 'im cyan feed so many pickney mout' and 'im pressure she to sen' my brudders back 'ome. She say she nah go do dat, so 'im beat she and 'im beat dem and den tell social workers 'ow my muddah beat dem. So, dis and dat 'appen and boof they get taken away; put inna home and me neva see dem for time. Now 'im free to start 'pon me wid 'im nastiness. Me run away and dey ketch me and put me inna 'ome too. All de while me neva know where my brudda dem stay. So is all dis a flash back on me. I was 16 when I lef' de care 'ome. Ran away. It was Norman who foun' me. Me tell 'im I was eighteen, but two two's I was pregnant with Aaron and then de whole story haffe come out. It break Norman 'eart, but 'im did love me and I did love him. Norman married me and from dat day me know no-one coulda harm me again, nor take him from me. But they nearly did last night."

I was shocked, stunned and I didn't know what to say. There was just so much hurt here. Slowly, I began:

"I never knew that was your background.... what you went through. So, when they took you into the police van, it was like when they took you into care and then you got a flashback of what it must have been like in slavery when they separated the women from their loved ones. That must have torn you apart. When did you hear what happened to Norman?"

"Not til dat Barbara Sington-Smith turn up."

"Yeah, Jemma brought her and another solicitor called Michael something – they are supposed to be very good. She said it was important to get them rather than you have any old duty brief that the police came up with."

"Whatever. It's she tell me they arrest Norman and wanted to charge him with assault as well as riot and affray. To be fair, she manage to cut that down, but me neva see my man til dey let we bot' out. Him ask de police fe me and me ask fe 'im, but dem nah let we know. Not til we did come out did I know what happen and las' night 'im tell me wha' happen to 'im too."

"Did you want to tell me – what happened to him? First, I would like more tea, but would you like some too?"

Marvalette shook her head, then said that she would. So I made two cups of tea and then she finished telling me what happened. She took one of Aaron's pencils and tore a piece out of his school book so that she could draw a map of where stuff happened.

"Right. Dis is de 'arrow Road, Dis de carna o' Bravington Road. Half of us – say that's about where I am, right, sort of about three in from the side. Babylon let about half of us turn and den dey moosh their way into de crowd to slow it down and den, before we knew it, 'alf of us was in Bravington and the other 'alf still on the "arrow Road. Me was 'ere. Norman was a bit behind so 'im was dere. Big set of Babylon now in between. And fracas start. The people on de back end of the march was not happy and the police start jostling about and next ting is fight. I ran back to try to find Norman, but dem tek' im first, thru' 'im a marshal, dem pick off de marshal fus', so discipline gone an all hell bruk loose.

"In de van deh trow 'im and a few of them got han'cuff and beaten as deh get trow in de van. Dat van lef de scene, Dem 'tink dem have de leaders so dem wan break dem first. But Norman is no leader, but dem suspec' same way. Deh fin' some o' we leaflet. Two coppers start question Norman inna de station, but 'im know 'im nah haffe seh nuttin' til him get a brief. So, deh shut 'im two box, but 'im still seh nutting an 'im ask fe mek a call. As for me, when dem hol' me, me did ask fe call Jemma, but is still me wait two hours or more and from dat, she call you. But dem nah let Norman mek no call at all.

"Dey lef 'im and two, t'ree brothers in de cell as by now all hell bruk loose in de station as they bringin' in van loads of people dey arrest – about 30-40 in all, so Barbara say. Cho, it was only 150 or so on de march!! Firs', Barbara deal wid me and get me out – me neva done nutting, so she manage to show dem up good and so dem let me go, no charge. But Norman now, she haffe argue an' argue to see 'im. Dem jus' keep seh 'inna minute, inna minute.' But meanwhile, Babylon go inna de cell and tell Norman is no-one dere fe 'im. But dem cyan' keep dat up long long, but before dey let her see 'im, dem taunt 'im. How 'im fight fe black power, fe de right fe self determination – and is what? A white 'oman come fe bail 'im and a white 'oman come fe respresent 'im as a brief. Dem tell 'im 'ow 'im pathetic and 'ow 'im cyan stan pon 'im own feet as a black man and 'ow im only can crawl widdout a white 'oman fe 'elp 'im, an' all dis shit. But den Barbara get in and do she bits and pieces and gets 'im out."

"It's a terrible story, Marvalette. Sounds like they wanted to undermine him, break him down, like you say, with that taunting. It must have made him feel terrible. Is that why he wants me to go?"

"Norman's grandfather was a Garveyite. You hear 'bout Marcus Garvey? Well Garvey used to say how de black man must stan' 'pon him own two feet, have race pride and stuff. But Norman always used to say how we is all made equal by de Almighty, an' how no white person is born a racist and how no black man or woman is born inferior and so if you live like how you believe – that we are all equal, that way you will create the world you want, by believing in it and doing it, sort of thing. Dat is 'ow Norman see t'ings and me too. Well, up 'til yesterday. What happened shatter dat for us. We feelin' like we jus' can't believe dat dream again. Maybe Garvey was right after all."

"And so you want me to go? Is our friendship over because of what happened?"

"Yes, and possibly. We just need to be in our little family, to get over this, Jen. Maybe in time, things can be different."

"And the house in Kensal Rise, with me being a tenant? Forget that too?"

"Jen, if Norman gets convicted, that's job gone and house out the window, so I think you can say we have other priorities right now."

"Ok. I understand that what has happened has made you see things differently than before and only you can sort that out. I can't make the world better for you, but I can try to make myself a better person. I can and will always stand up against this kind of oppression and try to change that way of thinking in white people. But I have to say that what has happened here this morning has broken my heart. That you have such little faith in me as a person. It feels like you want to make me pay for what happened. Not just our friendship but now I have nowhere to go. I don't speak with my family and I can't go back there and I have lost contact with all my old friends and the only people I know here are you, Bev, Jemma and Gabriella."

Marvalette thought for a few minutes. I was praying that she would say it was ok and that I could stay after all. But it was not to be. "I will talk to Aunty Cora. She has a room spare and not too far from your work – she is in Shepherd's Bush. You can't stay here. Sorry Jen. Me neva wan' dis fe 'appen. Maybe inna few weeks, when we feel more better in weselves. You is not a bad person. An' we is bot' grateful fe all yu do, but right now Norman is a broken man and we jus' need we own space. Try fe unnerstan?"

"Yes. Aaron will miss me. You know Marvalette, yesterday, Aaron told me about stuff he is gong through at school, about being called names and about the teacher not believing him. He said he was worried about telling you as you all have enough to worry about – but he felt at least he could tell me. I told him he should tell you, that nothing is too much for you when it comes to him, so I'm telling you, so you know he has stuff to talk to you about."

"So, now yu feel fe yu is some big someone fe tell me 'bout me own chile?"

By now I had had enough. "If that's what you want to think. I am going to pack up my stuff. Please let me know what Cora says. Meanwhile I need to catch some sleep."

I walked out of the kitchen and back to Aaron's room. I shoved my clothes into a black plastic bag and went back to bed.

I wanted my Mum. But how could I tell her any of this? I could never go back there, not ever. Since separating from Liz, all my friends were black. I had no intention of ever making up with her though. I thought of some of my white friends at college. Like Sarah, who moved up to Hertfordshire and Suzie who had got married. Neil and Jake who I never saw out of college anyway. I didn't even have their numbers any more. At work, I was friendly with Gabriella, but as for white colleagues, I knew Jacqui's number, but she was not someone I wanted as a friend. What a complicated muddle my life had become.

92

All this swam round in my head. But surprisingly, I managed to fall asleep, like my brain just had to switch off from all the various traumas of the past 24 hours.

13.   The respite.

When I awoke it was well into the afternoon. Norman and Marvalette were up and I could smell food cooking and the sound of music playing quietly in the sitting room. It then all came flooding back into my head about what Marvalette had said and about how Norman had wanted me to leave that day. Tears began to flow again. I had only tried to do what was right and kind for them as my friends and I felt as if it was being thrown in my face and despite what Marvalette was trying to explain, I didn't really understand it. Perhaps I did need to get some distance so that I could work it out a bit in my head. Marvalette had said I should stay with Cora for a while, but I was not so sure and would have preferred to stay by Gabriella so that I could get some distance from the whole crowd. I decided to phone her as soon as I had sorted my stuff out.

I went to the bathroom, had a quick bath and cleaned my teeth. Then I realised I needed to take my flannel and toothbrush and my bits and pieces from the bathroom to pack. This brought tears to my eyes again. I felt so sad, lost even. I had been so happy here for the past two months. I went back to Aaron's room and got dressed. I made the bed and then thought Marvalette would want me to wash my sheets and towels so, I stripped the bed and left it in a pile by the door while I continued to pack stuff I needed for a while until I got a flat. That done I went into the kitchen and put the bedding and towels in the washing tub and made a cup of tea. I didn't feel like eating; I felt so sick inside. However, I decided to put on a brave face. I had to go into the sitting room to get my records together and even though I didn't know what on earth to say to Norman, I couldn't avoid him.

I knocked on the door. Marvalette called out "Come," so I walked in and said I had just come to sort my records out, did they mind and that I hope I was not interrupting anything. Marvalette said it was fine, so I started sorting my stuff, with the odd tear escaping down my face. How embarrassing. Then Norman spoke.

"Jen. Sit down 'ere so a minute. Some t'ings yu does need to 'ear from me straight." He beckoned me to the sofa and I sat down. Marvalette went out of the room, coming straight back with a box of Kleenex.

"Here," she said giving me the box. I could see from her eyes that she had been at the box too, and Norman was looking none too happy either. I guess it was a very difficult emotional time for each of us in our own way. Inside me I was hoping and praying that they would change their minds and say sorry it was all said in haste and that they wanted me to stay. We sat silently for a few minutes. Norman broke the silence.

"Marvalette spoke to Cora and you can go by her for a few weeks. No pressure. Til you get a place fe yu'self. It'll be a'right dere fe yu. Dem is nice people."

I didn't know whether to say I would rather go by Gabriella, but as they had fixed it for me I thought it impolite to refuse. Anyway, Gabriella might not have wanted to take me in, so at least this way I was not homeless.

"Thank you. I just wish I could stay here with you. I have been so happy here, happier than I have been for years. You are so kind and such good people and I didn't mean to upset you and, and..."

"I's a'right Jen. We know. We did enjoy yu bein' 'ere wid us too, don't get me wrong. Is just dat, well, what happen yesterday, well, it did leave me shook up an' t'ing, an' Mavalette, an' we just need to get weself sort out from de shock."

"It's more that that though isn't it? It's to do with me being white ......and you don't want white people in your house .... Not after what you all went through, the racist behavior of the police and all that." I was trying to make sense through the sobbing.

"That's not what I said. Cho!" said Marvalette, sounding a bit defensive. I wanted to reply, 'yes you bloody well did', but thought better of it. Everyone was raw and I knew I had to be careful not to make a row. I would just make everyone feel worse.

"Can you explain to me, Norman, so I can understand from your point of view?"

Marvalette began to jump to Norman's defense but he quieted her and looked at me.

"Jen. I's hard to hexplain 'ow me feel. I's like me as a black man took one set of humiliation an' t'ing. I was glad o' yu 'elp an' glad of Barb'ra too, but Marvalette did tell yu wha' de police did seh to me, is it? Dem seh if me is a black man an' want black power, why is me depen'in' on white women to 'elp me? Can yu imagine 'ow me did feel? Car in a kinda way, dem is right. An' I haffe change dat."

"Do you want me not to stand bail for you then?"

"I t'ink dat woulda be bes', Jen, no tru?"

"If you say so. Who will do for you then?"

"Denison."

"So why didn't he say that when we went there?"

"Cos, Jen, yu 'ad it all sew up. Yu was stan'in' bail and dat was dat. No-one gets a word in about it."

"It wasn't like that. Jemma called, in a right state, telling me about what happened, that you both had been arrested. She asked me if I could stand bail. I didn't think twice about saying yes as it was an urgent situation and at that moment if she said would you cut off your hand for Norman and Marvalette I would have done. Why? Because you are my friends – we have been living like family and I would do anything for you to help you in difficulty. Just like you helped me. None of that has anything to do with white or black. I didn't say to Jemma, no, go find a black person in case Norman gets a hard time because a white woman is helping him. No. As far as I see the struggle against racism is about everybody, not just black people. We all have to be on the same side."

I stopped to let out a few more sobs. Norman was about to reply but Marvalette chimed in.

"So why you never ask Cora an' Denison? Dem's family – family – who should come to de our aid, but no, you call Cora to babysit and ask Denison to chauffeur you as Miss White Lady come to rescue the poor niggers dem so you can get in on de action at the police station. Yu shoulda stay 'ere with Aaron and let Cora and Denison help we."

"Marvalette. Das enuff o' dat talk. Yu cyan see 'ow dat 'urt she? It was a difficult t'ing. Jemma call and she did answer sey she gwine 'elp we. Like she sey. She nevva t'ink twice. Dat is a good fren'. We appreciate dat Jen. But we mus' now support we own. Y'unnerstan? Marvalette? Yu does unnerstan? Don' let dem damn nasty police spwoil yu fren'ship."

"Yes. Sorry Jen. Me's still in shock. Me don' know what to think, in trut".

I burst in to tears again; Marvalette was sobbing too. To my surprise Norman took my hand and then Marvalette's. He kissed her hand and said,

"Me know. Me know you's in shock. Right now yu don' know wha fe t'ink, fe tru'. Yu min' is all over de place and yu need some space. But in all o' dis we mus' keep we dignity. Me nah go let dem Babylon fill me 'eart wid 'atrage. So neider yu. Jen is yu good good fren."

Marvalette folded herself up next to him; he let go of my hand and he comforted her for a few moments til she pulled away to get a tissue. Then he took my hand back.

"Jen. We will always be yu fren'. Jus' try to unnerstan dat we jus' need we own space. Yu' done nuttin' wrong. Yu is not a racis'. Yu does try to live good wid everybody. Yu been learnin' about how life tough inna de ghetto. Yu done your bes' and we grateful fe all yu' do."

"Thank you Norman. Despite what has happened today, I have loved living here. Marvalette, you have taught me so much and even though things have been said today that have hurt deeply, I can see how this is a painful situation for both of you and I respect the fact that you need your space."

Norman took my hand and Marvalette's hand and held them together.

"You two. Yu fren'ship is a good t'ing. Hol' on to it. Get t'rough dis pressure time and come out de odder side. We mus' hol' on to we principles. We mus' not let our terrible hexperiences mek we 'ate anyone fe dem colour nor dem creed. If we do, we become like Babylon. An' we betta dan dat. Yes maan. Better mus' come! No tru?"

Marvalette looked at him, looked at me and then hugged me really hard. "I'm sorry for what I said. Jen, yu is de bes' fren' me eva had. But Norman is right. We need we own space a while. I feel so angry I wanna explode so I's bes' you ain't aroun' me girl, case I bite yer 'ead off again innit!"

I smiled and hugged her. Despite the hurt I felt, Norman had helped me understand and he had helped Marvalette calm down. He had actually stopped our friendship from falling apart.

"Yu bes' not!" I answered lightening up with a little joke. "I could do with a cuppa tea after all this."

Norman laughed. "Well, I coulda offer, but neider yu like 'ow me mek tea."

"Yu ain't gettin' off that easy mate," joked Marvalette; "Bung the kettle on and I will fix de res. At leas' me can make you a cuppa. An' Cora bring we some cake. So we can do de 'ole t'ing Hinglish style."

I laughed. Norman went to the kitchen to put the kettle on. He came back and put some music on, selecting some of my favourite tunes by the Techniques. I loved that Treasure Isle sound. Marvalette went to the kitchen and minutes later I heard her yell.

"Eh! Come rinse out yu laundry. Nah me fe do – den 'ang dem up."

Things felt a bit more back to normal now and I went to the kitchen to rinse the washing in the twin tub and then put it in the spinner then I hung it up in Aaron's room on the airer. When I came back to the sitting room, Marvalette appeared with a tea tray, teapot, jug of milk and sugar bowl, with cups and saucers. Cora's fruit cake sat on a plate waiting to be cut into three slices.

"I'll be mother then. One lump or two" said Marvalette in a posh accent. We laughed. Norman did not like the cup and saucer tea, but he held his little finger up as we all parodied the English upper classes having tea.

The doorbell rang. It must be Cora, Denison and Aaron. I was glad we were all sorted out before Aaron came back so he did not have to face an atmosphere like earlier. I took the tray back to the kitchen and washed up while they chatted with Cora. Aaron came into the kitchen.

96

"Why are you going, Aunty Jen?"

"Oh, it's just so Mummy and Daddy can sort out what has happened together. You all need to be a family again now and I need to find my own flat so you can all come to have dinner with me. Would you like that?"

"Yep!," relied Aaron. "I will miss you Aunty Jen. 'Specially when you read me stories. Can you read me one now before you go?"

I agreed and he brought a book back to the kitchen for me to read to him. Marvalette came into the kitchen to tell me it was time to go.

"Mummy, you will have to read to me now Aunty Jen's not here. Will you?"

"Course I will. Now let Aunty Jen get her stuff. Can you help carry a bag for her?"

Bless him. Aaron tried to struggle with the biggest bag, but Norman took it from him. I was only taking three bags, leaving my household stuff for the day when I would have a household to put it in. Perhaps this was a good thing in the end as I could get my own place now. It was time.

I hugged Aaron then Marvalette, then Norman. I stifled my tears as I got into the back of Denison's car. They said their good byes too and we drove off.

"Alright, luv?" asked Denison, cheerily.

"I'm fine now. It's been hard to understand but we have all learned. I think we will always be friends."

"That's good," said Cora.

"Yeah. That's good then, innit," added Denison.

That's all that was mentioned about it that night and I was glad of that. I didn't know Shepherd's Bush very well – apart from going round the market a couple of times with Marvalette to get boiling fowl to cook for Norman. They used to wring the live fowl's neck there and then, plunge the bird and take the feathers off. They would cut off the head and gut it, keeping the neck, giblets and the egg from the chicken's belly. It was delicious cooked, but Marvalette hated all that cleaning of the bird. She just did it for Norman, I could tell.

"I hear you can cook good," said Cora, lightening up the atmosphere. "I hope you can give me some lessons!"

"I doubt it. Your cake was delicious and I have heard you make wicked steam fish."

"Haha. We gonna get on jus' fine."

We soon got to Wormholt Road, where they had a sizeable Edwardian house. They had the downstairs like a flat, with a bedroom, sitting room, diner, kitchen and small bathroom at the very back. They rented out upstairs in two flats. They also had a bedsit room that shared the bathroom with the first floor flat. I was to have the bedsit room, but they assured me I was welcome to come to the lounge or their kitchen any time. I wondered if I should have brought the rest of my stuff after all, but Cora said it was all sorted out for me. It was three pounds fifty a week rent plus two pounds for food. I thought that was very reasonable.

"You know, Jen, you can stay 'ere as long as you like as a tenant. You don't 'ave to move out unless you want to." Denison took my bags and showed me upstairs. "The tenant only left last week and we ain't even 'ad a chance to let it, so you're doin' us a favour, innit. Saved us advertising and references an' all that lot. You will be comfy enough and anything you need, let us know. You're more like family than a tenant."

"Oh Denison. That's so kind of you and Cora. I do appreciate what you are doing for me. I had thought it was only temporary til I find a flat. But we will see how it goes."

"Fair enough, girl. Mind you, if you wanna flat, I will keep a look out as I am doin' up places all the time, like, for landlords and that. Some of 'em's bastards, but a lot's ok. I know a few who have places come up from time to time down 'Olland Park like. I'll give you a shout if I hear anything going."

"Wow! Holland Park. Sounds expensive."

"Some is, some ain't. There's a lot of them 'ouses owned by old boys and they dies and the 'ouses go for auction. I been lookin' meself, but no luck yet. Some of them need a lotta work, some been better kept. But I also work for landlords in Notting Hill Gate and Bayswater, so if I hear I will let you know. Right, I will leave you to get settled like and then come down for yer dinner. We've got a bit o' chatting' to do about that bail. OK?"

"Yeah, yeah, that's fine. Thank you so much. I will be down in about half an hour."

'Ok. No rush. Take your time. Anything you need, gis a shout. It's all electric in here and it's included in your rent. No separate meter like. You do have to slot the gas for the bath though. About a shilling, sorry five pence, will do it. Oh and you can wash clothes downstairs in our washin' machine, but you have to hang 'em in 'ere or take 'em to the laundryette to dry. It's just over the road and down a bit. Ok. I'll let you get on then."

"Ok thanks. See you in a while."

Denison shut the door and I looked around the room. It had seen better days. The bed was Ok and it was well made up with a nice cover and pink woolen blankets and pink and white striped sheets. There was a little sink and a small Baby Belling electric cooker that sat on the worktop. There was a fridge – thankfully – but it was a bit noisy in the room. Something to get used to then. I hung my clothes up in the old musty Victorian wardrobe. I opened the drawers in the chest of drawers and they looked old and stained, smelling of mothballs. I left them open to air and thought I needed to paper line them before I put my stuff in there and maybe get some lavender bags to improve the smell a bit. There was a little table and a dining chair as well as a small easy chair. It was clean, but dingy and I wondered whether to get my stuff to cheer it up a bit or leave it for a while. Anyway, can't think of that now. Food was seriously on my mind. Denison had left some keys on the table and I worked out which opened the door. I locked it to go down stairs.

There was music playing:

> 'Ooh yeah...Sunday's coming, uh.
>
> Better get some rice and peas
> Better get some fresh fresh beans, uh
> When you bring some Sunday sweets
> When you hear the church bells ring, ding ding.
>
> Ooh yeah..Sunday's coming'[vii]

Cora's kitchen had that lovely smell of West Indian Sunday dinner coming from it. I loved that smell and wondered what she had made. Stew beef, red beans and rice, boiled dasheen and chocho, with sliced beef tomatoes in black pepper and oil. Cora said she always made squeezed orange juice on Sundays and that would now be my job – to squeeze 20 or so oranges. I said I didn't mind and sat down to eat. Her food was really good and I stuffed myself full.

"We don't eat your English puddings here, so I hope that's ok for you."

I laughed. "Aunty Cora, that is just fine. I will wash up for you – don't worry, Marvalette taught me to wash up properly, rinsing dishes and scrubbing the pots to shine!"

"Oh good," joked Denison, "that get's me off the 'ook then!'

After I washed up, Cora made hot drinks and we went to sit in the lounge. Denison poured himself a whisky and we discussed the arrangements to transfer the bail for Norman from me to him. He would call 'the Nick' in the morning and find out what we had to do.

I went to bed about ten o'clock that, exhausted, physically and emotionally. I set my alarm for six in the morning as I was on earlies and was not sure how long the journey would take me – bus down the Uxbridge Road to Shepherds Bush Sation, then train to Ladbroke Grove.

14   The Welfare

The next morning I was woken up by a hulabaloo upstairs. The TriniDadian couple in the top flat were arguing. It sounded like she was yelling because he did not come home last night and had not given her money for the house since Friday and where was it. She accused him of gambling it away and sleeping with another woman. Doors banged, something was thrown across the floor, kids screamed, more banging about and yelling on both sides. I got up fast and rushed out of my room, forgetting my key, shutting it before I remembered the Yale was on. No doubt Cora had a spare key – I would need to get used to this.

"Cora, Cora. Denison. Where are you?"

"In here, love." Cora's voice sang out from the kitchen.

"The people upstairs. They are having a hell of a row. Things are smashing and the kids are screaming."

"Cho. That bloody lot. They will have to go soon. I will call Denison. DENISON! Come quick. That lot upstairs, Veda and Winston. They fightin' again and the place getting smashed up."

"What you want me to do? Get involved and get smashed up meself?"

"Their kids are up there, screaming. They could get hurt." I said, urging Denison to go up and do something.

"Cora. Jen. Never come between a man and wife arguing. Last time I did that – it was this couple in the street, on Goldhawk Road one night. He's layin' into 'er something rotten and I goes up and tells him to ease off and they both turns on me. Never again."

Anyway. The situation sorted itself and Winston came crashing down the stairs with a suitcase in his hand.

"I fuckin' gone from dat woman. I leavin' miserable she and she miserable chil'ren. I ent has to do nuttin' to she and she keepin' up noise. I gone brudda."

100

With that, he opened the front door, flung it wide open and left, leaving the door wide open and the three of us just standing there.

"Blasted small islanders. Nothin' but trouble. I told you Denison. Now we got her and no man and the rent's not been paid for weeks. She'll have to go, that's what. I'm not running a home for blasted small islanders that keep having pickney dey can't min'.

Cora was mad. Denison still did not want to get involved.

"'Ere, Cora. What about we 'ave breakfast and a nice cuppa and sort it out. Jen, sorry about this. What time you goin' to work then?"

"Oh Christ. I'm meant to be on earlies and its half seven already. I'll be late. I better get ready fast and run."

"You'll be runnin' for yer life love. Get ready and I'll drive you in. Cora go up and see Veda. Sort out what she needs – like National Assistance or Supplementary Benefit, whatever it's called these days – and we will talk later."

"Oh. I forgot. I locked my key in the room. Do you have a spare? Sorry. I just need to get used to putting the Yale up when I come out of the room."

Cora dug about in a drawer and gave me a spare key, which I promised to return on my way out and no, I would not leave it in the room again. I ran up, got my stuff, forgot all about needing to slot the meter for gas, washed in cold water, ran back to my room, got dressed, and, both keys in hand, ran downstairs, gave Cora back her key, grabbed a banana, all in time for Denison to say "Ready Jen?"

I nodded and we sped out of the house, almost as fast as Winston, although we closed the door behind, leaving Cora to pick up the pieces with Veda. I got into Denison's van that was parked next to his car and off we sped, nipping round the back streets of White City and Latimer Road to end up on the corner of Lancaster Road right near to the nursery. He dropped me there and I ran, making it just in time.

Matron was on leave and her deputy poked her head out of the door. The deputy, Alice, was new and it was clear she and Matron had different ideas. She was in a difficult position, but you could tell she wanted to bring in changes. She started organizing staff meetings, but Matron blocked her by saying they would have to be after the nursery closed at six. We had two, but Matron blocked her agenda and no-one would say anything unless it was to moan about the parents. I said if this was what we were going to do I was not going to anymore. Oops. That was me in trouble, but Alice came up to me afterwards and said well done for speaking up and she agreed with me. However, she thought we would not be having any more staff meetings, but as Matron was retiring in a few months she was prepared to sit tight and hope things would change.

I could see she was not impressed with Matron. That morning, I asked after Matron's health and mentioned how she needed to have her Tonic Wine. Alice said nothing. I said that Matron kept it in the cupboard where she also kept the carrier bags of spare supplies that did not fit in the main store. Alice's eyebrows raised for a moment. I ignored that and sped off to my room. Later that day, we had a visit from the Service Manager from the Town Hall. Matron's door was shut for some time. No-one knew what was going on. We didn't take much notice, but I wondered if Alice had discovered Matron's secret stash.

Two days later we were informed that Matron was retiring. Yipee! It was thought that Alice was still too new to act up as Manager, so one of the other deputies came down to act up while the post was advertised. Matron's office was cleared from top to bottom and some people called auditors came down from the Town Hall and an inventory was made of every single thing in the nursery. They went in and out with papers and files. Every member of staff was spoken to about resources from toilet roll to Lego. We began to get the impression that Matron went out on a bad note. We were all told that she was not well enough for a leaving do and there was a small collection, but it was just from our nursery. We got her a book token and a potted plant – some reward for 30 years service.

Gabriella and I had a brief gossip about her, but the most important thing was that I wanted to talk to her about what happened over the weekend after the March. One of the staff mentioned a 'riot' off the Harrow Road during breakfast break. I said it was not a riot but a legal protest march against police brutality. I didn't hang about for her reply but hurried back to my room. Gabriella said I should go round that evening, but I had forgotten to take Cora's phone number with me to let her know if I would be late and said Wednesday would be better for me. Gabriella agreed to that and I looked forward to it.

When I got back to Cora's that Monday evening, she was muttering about the woman upstairs, saying I should go up with her as Veda had not let her in. Cora said she had been yelling at the kids all day to shut up and be quiet and how she never wanted to come to this kiss me arse country. How back In TriniDad they had servants and look what he had subjected her to. Cora said she was worried about the kids, what with all that shouting going on.

"What do you think I can do that can make a difference?" I asked Cora. I was tired and wanted to put my feet up. It was 5pm and Denison was not due back til half past six, so Cora had not started to cook yet.

"I dunno. Maybe if there is two of us she might talk? Anyway, help me get this meat season – I hear you do it good! And peel off this yam and dasheen. Then let's go up."

"Ok." I agreed to help, and we prepared dinner in no time. While we were doig that Cora explained how she and Denison had taken them on as tenants less than three months ago. They had advertised the flat in the local newsagents. It had only been in the wndow for a couple of days when a nice-looking young man came to see about it for him and his wife who was expecting a baby any moment. He said they were homeless as their previous landlord's place was not fit to live in as it was only one room, with shared kitchen on a landing and this sounded better for them.

"I felt sort of sorry for him, what with his wife due to give birth any time. He said he was working and showed me wage packets – good job too, with the Council. So I said yes. As usual, feeling sorry for people. Anyway, he took a quick look round and said he woulp pay a deposit and a week's rent and could they move in the next day. Well, I could hardly say no. Next day he came with a friend with their bits of furniture, took it all upstairs, came back down and said, 'Soon come.' And off he went. Half hour later, he's back with a very pregnant Veda and two babies that he says he told me about, but I didn't recall. I was so taken aback I couldn't say anything. Next day, midwife arrives and there was little JoJo. Poor little scrap. Denison said I was mad – 'too blimmin' soft by 'alf', he said!"

"So you hardly knew her then?"

"No," Cora continued, "I'd hear him leave for work every day in the morning, but he's come home all hours and sometimes not at all at weekends. I was beginning to see that her life must be hell, Jen, but Denison said to keep my nose out. One day, Mrs Adekunle popped down and said how the baby crying kept her and Mr. Adekunle awake at night. I'm thinking what does she think I can do about it? Shut them all up with a magic wand? I said I would go up and talk to her, but when I went up it was all quiet and she didn't answer, so I left it. Didn't go back up again until now. We had better get to it, Jen!"

We braced ourselves to go upstairs. Cora knocked at the door quietly.

 "Veda, Veda, love, can me an' Jen come in a minute to have a little chat?"

"Is what all'ya want to talk to me about? I ent in no mood for guests, at all, at all."

"I was just cooking me dinner and thought you might like some for you and the kids. You eat for the day?"

"Nah. Me ent eat nuttin' for t'ree days. Winston take his whole damn wages and gamble. No food for me at all. I jus' have two/ t'ree Farleys and milk for the kids dem."

"Veda, I'm so sorry to hear this. Let us in and we can talk."

Slowly Veda opened the door. She had a big bruise over her eye. The room was a mess and it stunk of piss. In this room was a red leatherette sofa and two red and black chairs. The dining table was stacked in pieces behind the door, broken, as were the two chairs. There was a cooker in the corner, an 'easy work' kitchen cupboard with broken doors and glass missing. In the bucket was a pile of broken crockery.

103

"Dat was my good good set, my mudder send for me. Winston just smash it so. I can make all all'ya tea if you want."

We both said yes just to not make her feel bad, but did not really want to have anything made in that room. She had done her best to tidy up and we sat on the sofa and waited for her to make the tea.

"Where's the kids?" asked Cora. "I heard them crying earlier. This must have been frightening for them to hear all that fussing."

Veda burst into tears at that point.

"Dat man. Winston. He sen' for me, come Inglan to married he. I had was to leave my Mudda's nice house. Big, comfortable house, wid garden an' flowers and servant to wash we cloze, an' help min' pickney. An' dat man bring me to DIS! Married me when I was jus' 16 and fill me up wid one pickney after another and now dat damn blasted Winston leave me with t'ree pickney - de baby, de one year ol' and de two year ol'. How I is meant to cope wid dem? If my Mudda only knew. She would kill him, yes! Me doh had no money. Nuttin'. Dey is in de crib, out o' de way. I gi' dem Farley tea an' put dem in de crib. All dem do all day is make noise and I ent able right now wid dey carry on."

Veda took off her gold wedding ring and threw it on the table.

"Veda, is the bedroom mash up too, like this? Can I see please?"

I figured Cora actually wanted to see the condition the kids were in rather than her property. Veda agreed reluctantly and told her to be quiet then. Cora went off to see the bedroom. She called me "Jen, come, come quick."

I looked at Veda.

"Oh gaawd!" she exclaimed. "Wha' she go do to me?"

I went to the bedroom. Cora had put the light on. I'd never seen anything like it, or smelled anything like it, in my life. All three babies were sleeping in the one cot, with a towel over them. The floor was sodden with wee. There were some nappies in a bucket, just thrown there. A second cot stood broken in the corner. There was a double bed with a stained candlewick bedspread as a sheet and one thrown on the floor.

"Veda. This is terrible. You can't keep pickney like this. It stinks in here. Why are they not in nappies?"

"Yu t'ink I has money to soak an' wash nappy? I look like I have laundry money to you?"

"You could wash them in the house. Throw the shit in the toilet, rinse them and boil them in a big pot like my mother used to."

"Me? Wash dem stinking 'tings? In TriniDad we have servant to do that. Winston supposed to take care of dem t'ings."

"No love, you are supposed to. These kids could catch cold, catch pneumonia and die, just left like this and I hear you cuss and blast them this morning. They never go out, do they? Lovvie, sorry to say, but it seems to me like you don't have a clue. Now where are those baby nappies and clothes?"

Veda looked sheepish and pointed to a cupboard. Cora opened it and inside was a box of brand-new nappies and clothes, never worn. Cora said nothing other than to give Veda a very bad look.

"Do you want the government to take your pickney dem and put dem in a home? Because that is the way you are going. Now get those pickney outta dat bed and get dem downstairs, first to my bathroom."

We each carried on of the children, all boys, downstairs to Cora's bathroom. Cora slotted the gas and ran them baths. They weren't keen but I soon took charge of that part bathing each one in turn, Jojo, Matthew and Steven. The one and two-year old had bruises and flinched. I thought we should call welfare or the police. We had kids like this in the nursery sometimes, but that didn't help me know what to do. Cora went upstairs and pulled all the dirty bedding off the beds and brought them down to her own washing machine, except the dirty nappies that went straight in the bin. I bathed the kids, dressed them in some new nappies, sleepsuits and a babygrow and took them to the kitchen. I sat Matthew and Steven in the armchair that Cora had in the kitchen and held the baby.

"Veda, have you got a bottle please?" I found some cornflakes and fed the older boys and boiled the bottle that Veda brought down before making the baby a fresh bottle of cooled boiled milk. The kids looked like they had not eaten for days. I stayed on kid duty while Cora and Veda set to on the bedroom. I got some cushions and made Jojo a bed on the floor, putting him down so I could start the dinner. Denison was due home and at least the food should be cooking.

Cora, fired by rage, ordered Veda to help her get the damn stinkin' mattress out of her house, followed by the carpet and both cots.

'Those things are not staying in this house another night." I looked at her thinking she meant the kids, but then I realised she meant the stinking stuff from Veda's room. Then she filled a pail with hot water tipped half a pack of Flash and a bottle of Dettol into it, gave Veda some rubber gloves and a scrubbing brush, saying

"Scrub. The whole of that room. Until there is no more piss smell. And open the blasted window while you are about it."

Veda looked at her, but before she could protest, Cora added:

"If you want somewhere for you and your pickney to sleep tonight you will do as you are told. When you done, you can come eat."

Cora came into the kitchen, clearly distressed about what she had seen. And shocked that this had happened in her house. We talked as she started to cook.

"Jen, you know about these things, what do we do?"

"I don't know that much, but I think we have to talk to Veda about what she wants to do and make it clear she can't go on treating her kids like this. She's on her own now with them and she has got to get organized or they will take them away from her and who can blame them."

"I don't know why I didn't call the welfare from this morning when I heard her cuss and beat them, but I never knew things were that bad. No wonder the man left her."

Just then Denison walked in wanting to know what the bloody 'ell was goin' on. Denison was angry and upset, thinking Cora and I were fools for getting involved and not just calling the welfare on her.

"The poor girl is miserable because of how that man treat her, starving' her and the kids while he's gamblin'," said Cora. "She needssome help and a chance to come good."

The boys were still sitting on the chair and had not moved. Cora dished them up some food and I fed them. Meanwhile she and Denison went to find a spare cot and a mattress from the cellar, calling out the Veda that her dinner was ready. No answer.

Cora went upstairs only to find the bucket in the bedroom, the gloves and scrubbing brush on the floor and no Veda. The wardrobe was empty and there was a note saying 'Mind my pickney. I soon come. Veda'

"Blasted damn selfish woman," cussed Cora. "How can I mind these poor little ones?"

"Cora. You can't mind them," reasoned Denison. "You have to call the welfare or the police and get them taken into care. Don't argue with me. You are in no state to take 'em on. Who knows if she'll ever be back. It's up to the police to find 'er. Fer Crissake. You know she was only nine'een, don't ya? Just a kid 'erself."

Cora looked at me. I was holding little Jojo, so small and scrawny from underfeeding.

"Denison is right. It's awful but it has to be done. She can't cope and at the moment she doesn't even seem to want them. Poor little things. The welfare might find her and help her to have them back. We have had kids a bit like this in nursery, but I've never seen anything like this."

Denison went to the front room to make a call and within the hour a social worker and a police officer came. They said they would find a foster family to take them, the baby going to one family and the two older boys possibly somewhere else. I thought that was sad, but they said it was near impossible to find a foster family that could take three children under three and that they may even have to go into a home, although they wanted to avoid that. It took a long time getting through the paperwork, taking our statements and filling out forms. Cora showd them all the rooms and the stuff we had thrown out. Even though the kids were now washed and dressed it was clear they were in a very poor state and looking very confused. About nine pm they had finished what they had to do and took the remains of the kids never worn clothes that were in the cupboard, bundled up the poor babies who made no sign of protest and off they went.

Cora cried and Denison comforted her. We went and sat in the front room and Cora rang Marvalette to tell her all what happened. I left them discussing the ins and outs of black children going into care and went off to my room. Denison went up to scrub the floor so that the smell of piss did not permeate the house as now the door was open, you cold smell it on my floor, if not on the ground floor. The Nigerian man, Mr Adekunle, and his wife, came out to see what was happening. Denison said he did not have time for no chat right now and where were they when Cora or even Veda needed help?

Mr Adekunle took Denison into his bedroom that was under where Veda's bedroom was and showed him the ceiling. It was stained where presumably the nappy bucket had accidentally overturned and had soaked through. There was a urine smell to it. Denison shook his head and I heard him ask why the bloody 'ell he hadn't told him before. Mrs Adekunle said she had told Cora about the poor babies, but she had done nothing. Mr Adekunle just shook his head.

"We did not know what to do. It is not our business, but you West Indians don't live like us."

"Don't we? In that case, 'ave a week's notice."

"Ah! But we have paid our rent to the end of the month. You cannot do this to us. We will report you."

"End of the month then, but you are out. I am selling the house. Take me to court if you want or just find somewhere else to live – your decision."

I heard this conversation from my room. Why was it that trouble seemed to follow me like a lost lamb? I started thinking I was a jinx – everywhere I went to live ended up in a drama.

As I thought about it I fell asleep.

15   The connections

I managed to get through the next day somehow, and the next few Uneventful weeks, settling in at Coras and getting over the event that had happened – well all the events – Leroy, Norman and Marvalette and Veda. I had had the all clear from the Clinic and had come off the Pill, vowing no more men until I was more settled and surer of myself. I went in to work on a late shift one Wednesday andthe whole nursery was buzzing with questions about what on earth was going on with Matron. Our Acting Matron, Sue, was very good; she and Alice called staff meeting at 5- 6 pm, after having asked the parents to pick up early if they could that day. In the meeting they told us that the Council Managers and the Auditors had finished their investigation and there had been a few things that the auditors had picked up that they were not happy about. Apparently, they said Matron had not been following Council procedures over the finances. She said the Head of Service said Matron was not very well, that it was quite serious, and so they had offered her retirement, at last, I thought. And with immediate effect.

There were going to be changes. Sue said that the Council were no longer going to call the matrons 'Matron' anymore, that they were to be known as Officers in Charge and that from now on us Nursery Nurses would be called Nursery Officers. The new Officer in Charge post would be advertised and in the meantime, Sue would be Officer in charge and Alice her Deputy. She said they had been asked to do a review of what worked well and what needed improving in the nursery. They were keen to improve the nursery's image, as well as modernize our practice. They were going to interview all the parents as well as all us staff and the Head of Service was going to come in and observe our practice.

I was glad, but I had so many other things on my mind I felt my mind drifting. I was on lates anyway, like Gabriella, and neither of us wasted any time in getting out of there. Gabriella had invited me back to hers, but I didn't feel like it.

"Gabriella, I am so tired and it's late. Can I come one day when we are on earlies?"

"Sure. Actually that's better for me. In fact I am off next Monday, come then when you have finished about half five."

I agreed to do this and said my goodbyes and walked off towards the train station to go home.

I had been living at Coras for about six months and had settled well with her. She was more like an Auntie to me, furthering my cooking education and teaching me to crochet. She was caring without taking away my independence, which I liked. Denison would make us laugh and it was his Sunday thing to make his Guiness Punch and play the music. Sometimes he would play my records too, otherwise I didn't venture to the lounge to use the record player without permission. I stayed home a lot, saving money, but sometimes went out with the girls from work. I missed Marvalette but Cora said it wasn't the right time to try to repair the friendship and to wait until Norman's court case was over – whenever that might be. She always said Norman or Marvalette had asked after me, or had sent their love, so this helped me still feel connected to them.

One evening after work, one of those chilly October evenings when the clocks have gone back and it is dark, I was making my way to the station when I heard a man's voice call my name.

"Jen, Jen. Wait up."

It was Leroy. I wasn't in the mood for him at all, but as he was Marvalette's cousin I didn't feel I could just run off and ignore him. I stopped and turned back, waiting for him to catch up.

"What do you want, Leroy?"

"Dat's no way to talk to an ol' fren, Jen. Wha' gwan?"

"If you call giving me crab lice and gonorrhea being my friend, I hate to think what you would do if we were enemies."

Leroy stopped and I could see his little brain ticking over those months back and what he did to me. Clearly, he had conveniently forgotten. He looked sheepish.

"Well? Cat got your tongue?"

"Jen, come on man. You know me neva mean to do dat to you? Don' get on so."

I was furious.

"What do you mean you never meant to do it to me? You know damn well they call you Crab-I because you deliberately gave it to other girls to get your own back, 'cos one of your girlfriends gave it to you. I've got no time for you Mister Leroy. Plus you went and told that slag Liz where I was living. She said you were going out with her – is that true?"

"Nah man. She did seh 'ow she wan' talk to yu an' t'ing; bout 'ow you was in trouble an' she need to contac' yu. I never know she was troubling yu. An' I never went out wid 'er."

"Lying cow."

"Jen. Me sarry bout de crabs and de gonorrhea. No hexcuse. Me was goin' t'ru' a 'ard time and me never knew wha' me was doin'. You is a nice girl and me did like you, but me 'ead was fucked up at dat time. Please - forgive me nah?."

"Twat. Ok. I accept your apology. But I have to get a train. It's late and I have to get back to Shepherd's Bush as Cora will wonder where I am."

"So, you's by Cora? What 'appen to Marvalette? You an' she fall out?"

"Sort of. Not exactly. We are still friends. They had a hard time at the March. Both got arrested. They charged Norman but let Marvalette go. You must know that much Leroy. They were both in shock and felt they needed space. So I moved out and that's about it. I am staying at Cora's, but we had more dramas there with one of her tenants a while ago and Denison is saying he is going to sell the house. I am supposed to be looking for my own place. Know anywhere?"

"Cho, man! Denison a hidyat! 'Im always t'reaten fe sell de 'ouse, but 'im cyan do it. Co' it belong to Cora. Her mudder leave it fe she and she nah sell dat! Jen, me workin' pon some big nice 'ouse in Westbourne Grove. T'ree big 'ouse. All let off. But de ol' man what hown dem did die and leave dem fe 'im son. De 'ouse dem in a mess. Not a bit o' work since before de War, so yu can imagine. De son hire builders fe fix dem up and me and me team decoratin' dem right now. Yu hintrested?"

"Leroy, don't be giving me a set of old talk because I am not in the mood."

"Jen is fe real. Tru an' real. Yu wan see dem? Me go tek yu dere fe show yu."

"If I go there to look, I want to see the landlord or his agent, I don't trust you as far as I can throw you."

"Okay, okay okay. If yu don' believe, come Sat'day at half t'ree. 'Im due fe come an' pay we, so if you's dere yu can see 'im, but I will call and hask 'im firs' to mek sure all is ok. Allright?"

"Give me the address then and I will think about it."

I gave Leroy some paper and he wrote the address down for me. I said I had to go now as I was tired and had a train and bus to catch. He offered me a lift and I was so tired I decided to accept. It was his work van and he was very fussy about making sure the passenger seat was clean for me to sit on.

"So, you been any Duke Tam dance lately?"

"No Leroy and I'm too tired to talk right now."

"Ok, tired one. Me jus' drop yu 'ome and see you Sat'day."

"Yeah, that would be good."

We remained silent until we got to Wormholt Road. He pulled up outside Cora's and we said good-bye. I went in, and found Cora and Denison having an argument. They stopped as soon as I went in the kitchen. I had my dinner and then went upstairs, had a bath and went to bed. I figured they were arguing about selling the house. I wondered if Leroy was serious. I hoped he was. A redecorated place in Westbourne Grove would be ideal for me.

110

Saturday soon came. I was exhausted from the happenings at Marvalette's, then at work and then at Cora's, where there was still an atmosphere. No for sale sign had gone up, so I figure Denison had not got his way. However the Adekunles did move out. No new tenants moved in as Denison said the house needed fixing up after all the mess from those damn small islanders. So that weekend, he started work replastering the ceiling in the back-bedroom underneath Veda's old room. More old smelly furniture and carpet was slung out. Cora got to work cleaning the curtains as she said she could not afford to chuck out everything.

I left them working and went off to meet Leroy at the address on the paper. I got there at five minutes to three. No-one was there. Leroy's van nowhere to be seen. It must be the right place, I thought, as you could see there were skips in the street and work was definitely taking place. I waited til half past three and I was nearly in tears, thinking he'd duped me, when a blue Jag pulled up. A well-dressed man got out and went up the steps.

"Excuse me, hello, excuse me." The man turned round. "Are you the landlord?"

"Ye,s I am," he replied, "Who are you? Did the agency send you?"

I told him my name and how Leroy said to come here and see him about a room or small flat.

"Ah Leroy, Leroy. Where indeed is he? I have brought the men's wages. I bet they are in the pub."

Just then Leroy pulled up in the van and said Hi to the man.

"Where's your men, Leroy? You are late and I have their wages. This young lady says you told her to ask me about a room."

"Yes She de one I tell you 'bout. Yu could fix her up? Soon come."

He disappeared into the pub over the road and the man shook his head.

"Leroy didn't tell me your name, Mr...?"

"Feltz. Rueben Feltz. I suppose Leroy told you my father owned these houses. He bought them when he came here after the War in 1946. He let them go a bit, but they are lovely houses. A lot of the old tenants left - got rehoused by the council, and I am looking for a better class of tenant. Where do you work Jenifer?"

I told him and he seemed mildly amused at my job. I told him what I earned and how long I had worked there. He seemed ok with that. He took me into the house, right to the top floor and said he had a room for me. However, my heart dropped. It was the size of a matchbox and was five pounds a week. That was twenty pounds a month. I could afford it, but it was too small and I said so. I said I could pay up to seven pounds fifty a week and did he have anything for that. He took me downstairs to the ground floor and showed me a huge double room which was at

111

the back of the house, overlooking a large garden. It had a small kitchen area and its own little bathroom. He said it was eight pounds a week, payable monthly with a month's rent in advance. I said I'd take it.

I reached into my bag and took out my cheque book.

"Ah Jenifer, Jenifer. You are in a hurry. First we have paperwork to do. I need references from your work and your current landlord as well as a bank reference. I give all my tenants a rent book."

"Oh. I can get you a work reference and one from the bank, but I haven't really had a landlord before. I have been living with friends since I left home. I moved down here to be near to work and one of the people I know through work let me stay there. She will give me a reference if that's ok?"

Bit of a lie there but how could I risk a possible bad reference from Mrs. Cameron - Old Nosey Parker?

"Not to worry, not to worry. Work and bank will do. Many young women your age can't even provide that. Jenifer you have the pick out of the eight pounds a week rooms. Do you want to see any more?"

"Oh. Ok. Sure. Thank you"

Mr Feltz showed me six rooms at eight pounds a week. Then he said he had a final room to show me, but it was more expensive. I looked at it and fell in love with it immediately. It ran from front to back of the house and had really high ceilings. Separating the back from the front parts of the room were some double doors that were almost to the ceiling. All had been painted white. There was a larger kitchen area with room for a cooker, fridge and washing machine, a small hallway and a compact bathroom with a tiny bath - although I wasn't worried about that. It was perfect.

"How much?" I asked.

He knew I was hooked.

"Ten pounds fifty a week. It won't leave you much money for the electricity or food."

"I will get a pay rise in April, I can eat at work and I can get a Saturday job and I'll manage. Maybe I will try to get a better paid job. I've got savings and I can furnish it nicely and I will be a good tenant."

"Go on, go on Jenifer. You can have it for ten pounds a week. I am in a generous mood today, but when you earn more and get that better job, I may have to put the rent up. Is that OK? It's fifty pounds for the deposit. And if you have your boyfriend here make sure you are on the pill as I'm having no babies here."

"I don't have a boyfriend and I'm not thinking about having any babies. No, Leroy is definitely not my boyfriend."

"He's a hard-working boy, Leroy with a future ahead of him. You could do worse Jenifer. But then if you set your sights higher, who knows who could be your boyfriend. The world is your oyster."

Just then Leroy came in.

"Mr Feltz, 'ere de men dem fe get dem wages. Ah Jen. Is dis de room yu like?"

"Yeah well. I like it and yes I am going to take it. I just have to pay the deposit and fill out papers, get my references and then – move in!! I expect Denison can help me bring my stuff from Marvalette's, but I will need to get some furniture too. Gosh, it's exciting."

"Cho, man! Me gwine 'elp yu move. Any t'ing yo wan'. Me have t'ings to do fe mek up fe being a hidyat."

I laughed and told Leroy to wait for me. I signed up the papers for Mr Feltz and gave him a cheque for the deposit of fity pounds. He gave a receipt and the rent book and said I could move in Saturday week, giving enough time for the references to come back. He said there was a few things he had to do, like put down the carpet and asked me what colour I would like, and I said brown or cream as long as it was plain – no patterns. He also said the Gas Board had to come to fix in a new gas cooker and a gas fire. Wow, so much new stuff and a lovely room all freshly painted white. He asked me if I wanted him to leave the shutters on the front windows and I nodded my head madly. It was so all amazingly lucky.

Leroy dropped me back at Cora's. As he pulled up, he asked me if I would like to go to a dance later. I wasn't interested and stopped him mid sentence about who was playing and where it was.

"Leroy, I just want to stay home. I have things to plan and think about and I think Cora could do with company tonight as it's Denison's Domino Night – some tournament somewhere or other. Cora's not bothered about going, so I said I would keep her company."

I think Leroy half expected a refusal anyway – he could hardly think that he could worm his way into my good books that easily – but then again, Leroy got by on being bold, but that didn't mean I could not keep him at distance. To be honest, I did feel attracted to him and he had personality, but after what happened I would need a lot more than a sorry face to sway me. I said good-bye and thanked him for the contact and the lift and said he also could call me at Cora's.

Cora was in the kitchen when I got in; I called out "Hi, it's me" and went upstairs to take my things off and get my slippers.

"How did you get on?" called Cora from the foot of the stairs. I knew she was pleased for me as she hugged me when I told her about the flat. We sat and discussed the whole thing over tea and then I told the whole story again when Denison came in an hour later.

"Wha's 'is name? That landlord?"

"Feltz," I replied "His old man died a while ago and the son has taken on the houses and he's been doing them up. He has made them quite smart. Leroy's team has been decorating there."

'I knew the old boy. Miserable and tight as a dog's arse. The 'ouses could 'ave fallen down – well the roof did cave in in one of 'is 'ouses - and 'e would just shrug and say, 'What can I do?' until the Council got be'ind 'im. The son's worth a bob or two, so for 'im to spend a bit on the 'ouses it's like a tax dodge for 'im, plus it improves the properties, so 'e's laughin'. But that Leroy – that boy could 'ave got us a work there, and he never. Cheeky little so and so. Wait til I see 'im!"

Cora stepped in. "How could you say that? You've had work til you nearly fall off the ladder with tiredness, so how could you have taken on anymore?"

"I'm just sayin', just sayin', that's all. Leroy could have asked us."

"Well maybe Feltz already had it sewn up. Otherwise, Leroy would have put the work your way. You know that."

When they had finished the discussion of Leroy's loyalty, I carried on telling them about the flat. Denison felt it was expensive and that I could have got a cheaper place around Westbourne Park Road, but I told him I wasn't interested in being too near to where half the nursery's parents lived.

"The thing is," I began, "it's unfurnished. I will need to look around some secondhand shops. I will want a new bed, but I hope to find a wardrobe, chest of drawers and maybe a little dining table and a couple of chairs secondhand. I will want to paint them, so if you can give me some tips, Denison, I would be grateful."

"Sure. You can get good stuff down Uxbridge Road, but what about the 'bello? Lots of second 'and shops there, and up the Gol'borne. You could nip out on your lunch break to 'ave a gander?"

"Jen, I have a couple of bits in the cellar. Have a look and see if they are any good for you to paint. Mind you. I never heard of painting furniture. Spoils the look of the wood if you ask me."

"Thanks Cora. I'd love to have a look. Painting old stuff just gives it a new lease of life – freshens it up and you can fit it into modern colour schemes. I was reading about it in a magazine."

114

I'm not sure Cora was convinced, neither Denison, but they let me get on with my planning and colour scheming, chuckling at my excitedness. Later, when Denison had gone to his Domino Tournament, Cora took me down to the cellar. She showed me the bits she had in store there. She had a small table with sides that could come up to make it bigger, 'drop-leaf' she said it was called, and four kitchen style bentwood chairs. They didn't match but were perfect for painting. White, I thought. But maybe red – or orange! She said she would give me as a starter present. She also had a large pine chest of drawers. I asked her if she would sell me that. She thought for a moment. It was her mother's she explained, maybe she would want a quid for it. No. Second thoughts, anything I wanted I could have for free and was I interested in the wardrobe? It was a large pine wardrobe with a mirror, a shelf and a large drawer underneath that would be perfect for sheets and towels. I loved it. It had carved features on the doors and even though it was quite big, the bedroom area was big enough to take it. Cora also pointed out an old wall mirror – the sort you put over a fireplace and said I could have that as well as a little glass fronted cabinet, a carved coffee table and an old wooden box. I wondered why she was so keen to give me all this stuff and I asked her.

"You know Jen. Maybe Denison is right. This old house. You know it was my mother's. When she died, she left it to me. I grew up here, with my sister. My Mum and Dad bought this house when they came here in 1955. They got it in an auction for £750. Yes. Can you believe? They rented out, just like we do now and that paid for it. Then my Dad died. It was 1961. He was only 49, Mummy was 42 and I was 21, my sister just 19. The room you are in – that was my sister's old bedroom. Mummy never really got over his death; he was the only man for her. She got on with life, but never found anyone else. My sister married a worthless guy – Mummy told her not to. There was a big argument and we never saw her again. Mummy died three years ago, leaving everything to me, so Denison and I moved back in and I took over running the house just like she did. It was how I coped with her death, keeping it all like she had it. Not letting go of her furniture – nothing."

Cora stopped and tears came to her eyes. Now I knew why Denison was so keen for them to move – he wanted her to let go of the past and move on. The house was far too big, and all the responsibility of the tenants was a huge burden. We went back up to the kitchen.

"What happened with Veda and those poor little kiddies of hers. That's shocked me. I keep seeing that sight of them in that room. The smell....my God. Awful. Denison was saying we should move. He's been saying that ever since we got married. But I wanted to stay here. To be close to my Mum. Perhaps, I always hoped that one day my sister might come back, and I was too scared to move away in case that meant I missed her coming here ....to find me again. Daddy too. The house was his pride and joy. He, well both of them, worked so hard to get it. It was to pay for them to go back home, but they ended up in a grave before that could happen."

Cora got up to put the kettle on. I said I would make the tea and Cora sat back in the chair. Then she went to the cabinet and got a box of old photos. Over tea we looked at pictures of her and Flora – her sister, her Mum, Aveline, and Dad, Bernard.

"So, Denison wants you to sell the house and you don't want to because of the memories it has for you. But now you say he is right, and you are giving me lots of your stuff. Does that mean you have changed your mind?"

"I think so. Maybe he is right. We could buy a smaller place. I could go back into nursing, maybe just part time. He has money put by so we could buy between us, a nice area, not like here. Kingsbury, maybe. Or Chiswick. Or Ealing. With enough in the bank for a place in the Caribbean and we can go for holidays. I'd love to go. There's so much we could do, he always says. He is right. Ah Jen. I've made up my mind. I will tell him later. He will be so pleased."

"That's fantastic! And your Mum. She would want you to move on in life. It must be hard being a landlady, having tenants in the same house as where you live. You hardly have any privacy."

"None at all," agreed Cora. "Jen, this is the right thing to do. I see it now."

I was glad she had made this huge decision – glad too that it meant I could have all this furniture. I went off to bed that night with my head swimming with ideas for organizing my place. With all this furniture being given to me, all I now needed was a bed and a sofa. Perhaps I could afford a new sofa? I also needed to get a cooker and a fridge – maybe even a record player and a TV. Oh and a sewing machine. I would definitely need one of those to make curtains and cover cushions. Plus I would need to make my own clothes from now on as I couldn't afford to buy them, now the rent was taking up most of my money. Gosh, I thought, I would soon be in my own flat. A one bedroomed, self-contained flat in Westbourne Grove. Perfect.

As I lay in my bed that night, I thought of Cora as a child in that house, maybe even in the same bed, and it being the way, the only way, she felt she could stay connected with her beloved parents. And there was me, couldn't even be bothered with mine. I felt guilty. No matter all the horrid things they said, they were still my folks and they had sacrificed so much for me. I resolved to call my Mum as soon as I was settled in and invite her over.

16   Another new life begins for me

Through that week I spent all my spare time – lunch breaks and the odd hour after work - shopping and ordering. I had made a list of priorities already and was trying to budget. I had three hundred and fifty pounds in my savings account, less the fifty pounds for the deposit, leaving me with three hundred. I felt rich! The new things I needed were the bed, sewing machine and the record player. I went off to John Lewis to get the sewing machine and came back with a nice little Frister and Rossman portable one for seventeen pounds. I bought a little sewing box, scissors, needles, pins and some reels of cotton. I looked at fabrics for ideas, but thought they were expensive. One lunchtime I went down the Portobello Road to the decorating shop and bought some brushes, white spirit, and some undercoat. I had not decided on the colours yet, but at least I could make a start. I popped into the Electricity Board showroom and made note of a fridge that I thought would fit.

I took another look in the daylight at the furniture that Cora was giving me; the chest of drawers and the wardrobe were old pine; Denison had brought them up and left them in the kitchen waiting for my moving day. I thought they could be stripped back and then waxed. Denison didn't really appreciate my idea about the waxing, but suggested I rub them down and then apply a coat of varnish. That would give them a shiny look, which I did not want, but he said I could use a matt varnish. However, I was definitely going to paint the table and chairs using rather bright colours, mismatching, and using printed colourful fabric for cushions for the chairs to bring the look together. Cora and Denison just looked at each other and then looked at me as if I had a screw loose, but I showed them a picture in a magazine and they saw it was effective, although, we agreed, not to their taste.

I asked Sue, our new Acting Matron for 2 weeks leave; this was no problem as no-one else was off in early November. This meant I could have a week before moving in, doing all this painting and a week when I was in, doing all the sewing side and getting it all nice. In all of this excitement, I had almost forgotten about going to Gabriella's that evening as Kenneth would be there with some news about the aftermath of the March and what was happening to the people who had been charged. It just seemed to be taking so long.

When I got to Gabriella's I could see she had made a real effort. The table was set for dinner for three and I thought that this included Sharlette, but Gabriella said she had eaten earlier, and the third place was for Kenneth. I hoped there would still be time for me to just chat with Gabriella, without Kenneth.

"I invited Kenneth to stay for dinner as it would seem mean not to. He will be good for you to talk to as he knows what is going on more than I do and anyway, he said he would like to talk to you about what happened with Norman."

"It's fine. I just hope there can be time for you and me to chat, that's all, but I am grateful Kenneth has shown an interest and is happy to share some of what he knows."

"Well you can come and help me finish preparing and fill me in on what's happened since you left Marvalette's."

I sat in the kitchen and told Gabriella everything that happened on the Saturday night of the March as well as what happened with Marvalette and Norman the next day and why I had been at Cora's for the past six months.

117

"God. You are like a little waif and stray, you are. Always finding yourself in trouble and needing to be helped out. You always manage to land on your feet and how you always manage to get black people jumping up to help you, I don't know. Most times, they wouldn't even bother to help their own, so you must be lucky somehow!"

I wasn't sure how to answer this, so I moved the conversation on a bit and told Gabriella about the flat.

"So you see, I will be independent at last. I will have my own flat and be independent of everyone. But I will invite you for dinner too, and Sharlette."

"I'm only joking with you. Don't take me seriously. To be honest, I don't know how you took all that from Marvalette. She was a bit below the belt I think, but then again, she was hurt and angry and it seems like she wanted to take it out on you. You know, since you moved down this way and fell out with that Liz, I notice its pure black people you deal with. Have you ditched white people or something?"

"Well, this is the point I wanted to get to Gabriella, so you've hit the nail on the head. I have seen that myself. Don't get me wrong. I don't have any objection to anyone, and I am so grateful for Marvalette and Norman's help. I was happy with them and they were planning on buying a house and were going to rent me a room. It was just all too ideal really. Cora and Denison have been really kind to me too, but it also gave me the kick up the backside I needed to get myself independent. Yes it's true, these days I seem to only know black people. I feel like I ought to have white friends as well, but I don't meet any and I need to think about the kind of white people I want to have in my life. Not like that Liz, that's for sure."

"No rednecks like your family then – or like Carol Clarke and Big Mary!" joked Gabriella.

"Definitely not. But I don't know where to meet other white people that are on the same thinking track as me."

"Kenneth can help you there. He has seen how you are with the politics and that – I think you even have more interest than me – and he knows a few white women that you might like to meet and some organisations you might like to join."

The doorbell went and Gabriella went to let Kenneth in. When she came back we took the food into the living room and set it on the table.

"Good to meet you again, young Jenifer," said Kenneth, sounding like an old man addressing a child. I don't think he meant to sound patronizing as I think he genuinely liked me.

"And you too. How's Jemma and the Campaign going?"

"We are all very, very busy, as you can imagine. After the demo, the police arrested 35 people at the final count and then charged just 10. Two have since had charges against them dropped at the CPS said there was not enough evidence – Norman was one of these. We just heard today, and I have just come from his place earlier this afternoon. I heard they asked you to leave. I think they feel very bad about that, especially Norman, but Marvalette has been badly affected by it all and she is still not herself. I said I was seeing you later and they sent their love. Norman said it doesn't mean you shouldn't call round – Aaron is missing his story-teller!!"

I tried to reply, but I got choked up and a few tears came out, although I tried to hold them down.

"I thought they were the loveliest people I have ever known. They were so good to me; I learned a lot from both of them and Aaron is such a sweet clever boy. I was so happy there. I would have done anything for them, but they felt me standing bail for Norman added to the humiliation and that I should have gone to family. Denison is the surety now and I can understand but ... oh it was awful at the time. All this race business is so complicated."

"Yes it is Jen. Very complicated and it's not everyday we find a young white woman who has so genuinely worked so hard to understand the issues, become aware of her own attitudes and where they came from in order to move on from that. It must have been very painful for you. And what impresses me Jen, is that you did not use that pain as an excuse to indulge in crude prejudices, like your friend Liz, but used it as an experience to learn from and still keep your principles and your kind heart intact."

"Thank you Kenneth. That means a lot to me. But I was saying to Gabriella, it seems like my whole life since I lived down here has only involved black people, but I don't know where to meet white people that are on my wavelength. Surely I should have both black and white friends?"

"Well I hope to help you there. The struggle is a wider class struggle and we all have our part to play. Oppression affects us in different ways, but the black struggle is only one strand of the wider movement for freedom from all oppression. It is unusual that the black struggle has been the key to have opened your consciousness as a young white woman, but that's how life has played itself for you. I would like to introduce you to some Socialist Worker friends of mine and a woman called Beth Hastings who is very involved with Women's Liberation and runs a group in Westbourne Grove. I am sure you will get along with her and learn a lot from them."

"Oh! I am moving there in two weeks. I will be really close by, so I would love to meet her."

"Does that mean you will be burning your bra and growing the hair on your legs?" joked Gabriella.

"Is that what they do then?"

"No, don't mind Gabriella. I think you will like Beth. And Women's Lib is not all about hairy legs and bra burning. There are some serious campaigns that they are involved in – and Gabriella you know that. Look. Here is Beth's number – she is expecting your call. She will also tell you about the SWP, but in the meantime I have brought you a few of their papers, so you can get an idea."

The conversation now turned to what was going on in the nursery and how Matron had left so suddenly a while back. It seemed that Kenneth was in the know about what happened; must be from those friends he had in the Town Hall. He was a bit cagey, but Gabriella pushed him.

"I think she was fiddling. Jen saw her packing stuff into shopping bags – and she caught her on the Tonic Wine. Plus we never had money for equipment and all the other nurseries seemed to have more than us."

"Gabriella, you know I can't reveal what I know. Just think if it got round what might happen."

"Yeah," I put in, "it might even get into the papers and then the whole world would know what she was really like. Cunning old mare."

Kenneth laughed. "Jen, sometimes retribution seems like a good idea, but you have to look at the long-term result. What is it we really want to achieve here? Surely, that the nursery is properly managed from now on. If you all put your energies into that, you could really 'Seize the Time' as Bobby Seale says, and make the changes you want to see."

I looked at Gabriella and she looked at me. "Could this be our moment then to start to implement the practice we want to see? I have got lots of stuff I have been reading and taking notes, lots of books for children, ideas for activities and stuff, from babies right up to five. I have been doing lots of stuff here with Sharlette and I was also thinking of opening a Saturday Club for black children and their parents to learn about their history, develop pride in themselves and for parents to come together to support each other. But that is for the black community – what we have to do is make the nursery a place fit for black children, to meet their needs as well as be a place where white children don't grow up with the same old conditioning. Like I said to you before, it starts with us in the nursery."

"Gabriella has been developing some very fine ideas. Now, you two, this is the bit that is hush. I know the powers that be have their eye on Alice and they want her to apply for the new Officer in Charge post. By all accounts, Alice is very good; she worked in Brent before and was a Deputy at a nursery very similar to yours. The Officer in Charge there was a good friend of mine's wife, Maureen Skeet. They are both part of the education group I have mentioned before. What I am suggesting is that Gabriella, you should apply for the Deputy job and you, Jen, should apply for the room supervisor job. The three of you can then act as real change agents. The old guard will leave, and you will be able to bring in people that chime with your way of seeing things. It could be a very exciting time for the Nursery."

"Wow," said Gabriella, " as usual you have it all worked out for me don't you? What about my dream to do teacher training next year? Do you want me to drop that? And, don't forget that the Council put Sue in as Acting Officer in Charge and she's so got her feet under the table it could be that they will give her the job and not Alice. "

I kind of felt that I was watching the tensions in their relationship unfold here a bit. Gabriella had said how Kenneth looked at her like she needed His Guidance as if she was not capable of directing her own life. Probably that was because when she was younger she was very quiet, and Kenneth felt he could mould her into shape. This was why they split up. But more and more, Gabriella was coming into her own and her thinking was not based on what she was told by Kenneth, but from her own studies. I think he was proud of her and wanted to encourage her, but he still had this annoying habit of planning her life for her. He realised his mistake, and I could see he felt a bit embarrassed that some of their issues had been exposed to me. None the less, he was quick to make amends.

"Gabriella, more than anything I want you to realise your dreams of teacher training. I just thought that as a strategy for implementing change, this could put you in a more powerful position and would also go well for you if you were to apply to be a teacher."

"Just as long as you know," replied Gabriella standing firm to her ground. "Does anyone want a coffee or tea?"

Kenneth looked at his watch and said it was time for him to go. He asked if I needed a lift. I really wanted to talk to Gabriella on my own, so I asked her if I could stay on a while, or did she want to go to bed. She said it was fine to stay and we could clear up and then talk more about Kenneth's ideas.

As it turned out, we talked and talked, not realizing the time.

"Oh my gosh. It's nearly eleven. I have to go. I hope I am ok for the train and buses at this time of night."

"I think you will be fine to about half eleven, but it's late. Why don't you stay here the night and call Cora and let her know?"

I agreed. Cora was none too pleased about my late call, but she accepted my apology and said she appreciated me letting her know so she would not worry. Gabriella and I sat up til gone twelve and we agreed that Kenneth's ideas would be really good.

"I just wish he would stop knowing what's best for me. It's so annoying. He thinks I am still the naïve sixteen-year-old he met all those years ago. I am not – I am a big woman now and can do my own thinking!!"

We laughed as she took him off calling me 'young Jenifer' like he was an old man or something. Nonetheless, we agreed he was sound, he knew a lot and was quite influential. He was also fair minded and, in his own way, supportive of women, so like Gabriella said, having him around was more pluses than minuses at the end of the day.

Gabriella went to fetch me a spare nightdress and gave me a new toothbrush, which I offered to pay for. She refused, saying it could stay at hers in case I stayed again. She got me some blankets and made a bed up on the sofa for me, then she bid me goodnight.

As I lay there, I felt good again, thinking it was about time I called Marvalette or went to see them, even. What with the new flat looming and all the plans for changes at work, and the new circles of potential friends that would balance my social circle out a bit more, I felt excited about life once more.

Sharlette woke me in the morning, telling me Mummy had breakfast ready. It was six thirty in the morning and I recalled we were both on early shift. Gabriella left Sharlette at her Mum's who then took her on to school, but it still meant we had to get our skates on to get washed and dressed, fed and ready to go. But we made it anyway and with Sharlette duly dropped off, we made out way to the bus stop.

'The number seven buses are a nightmare after half seven in the morning. Either full or late or both," observed Gabriella wryly. "That's why I prefer doing earlies any day."

A man at the bus stop joined our conversation to agree with Gabriella. It was a particularly cold morning, and it was still dark, leaving you with the feeling that you really ought to be still tucked up in a warm, cozy bed rather than out here with the world's early shift, shivering and stamping your feet, wishing the bus would hurry up and come. Ten minutes, and ten frozen toes and ten numb fingers later, the bus arrived – late and almost full. We made our way upstairs to the upper deck which was misty with cigarette smoke and coughing smokers. We found a seat each though, and I began thinking about my Christmas plans.

Imagine. It would be my first Christmas in my new flat. A little tree in the window, some lights and some tinsel hung around. I was lost in my own festive daydream, when Gabriella called out "Come on! Wake up! It's us next stop." Christmas plans were discussed as we walked briskly the rest of the way to work, arriving at ten minutes to eight, giving us a few minutes to down a quick cup of tea before we set up breakfast for the children who arrived early. I used to feel sorry for the babies who were in at eight in the morning until six in the evening. It was a long day for them to be away from their Mums and some were really miserable. The words of a Delroy Wilson song came to mind as I thought of how hard our parents worked, especially the single mothers with full time jobs.

> "I've been trying a long long time
> Still I can't make it
> Everything I try to do seems to go wrong
> It seems I have done something wrong
> But they're trying to keep me down

122

Who God bless, no one curse
Thank God I'm past the worst

Better must come one day.."[ix]

Janine's Mum never had time to give her breakfast and she was one of the first in, often with last night's nappy still on, reeking of urine, so changing Janine and then feeding her was first job of the morning. Ryan was also an early bird; his Mum, Faith, was up at five thirty in the morning to get him and his two older sisters ready before dropping the girls at seven thirty to the childminder in Latimer Road who took them on to school, then making her way over to the nursery for eight. Ryan was ready for more breakfast, but sometimes the poor little one was half asleep in his bowl. Being a working Mum was not easy. The toddlers fared worse; invariably they would be half asleep and grumpy in the morning and not happy for Mum to go and then grumpy again in the evenings when it was time to go home. Ryan had started biting and Mum was less than patient with him, telling us we should bite him back, like she did at home. Gabriella would tell her that we did not do that as it would only teach him that biting was ok. Ryan had started settling into the next group and he was finding it tough without Gabriella, who had cared for him since he was three months old. Mum said he would just have to get used to it, but we used to feel that this was a tough life for a little one and I vowed I would not be in a rush to get back to work if and when I became a Mum. In fac.t, all of us nursery nurses said we would never put our babies in a nursery. No matter how much you cared, you could not replace their Mums and love them in the same way. Babies needed that, we used to say, not us and our shifts.

Faith worked in one of the big stores in Oxford Street. She had been able to work Monday to Friday for the past two years, apart from when she was off for 6 weeks having Ryan. She didn't get sick pay when her kids were sick and nearly lost her job when she had to take time off when Ryan was unwell. They got every bug going, those babies, on the first year in nursery and employers were less than sympathetic. That morning Faith was in tears when she told us that the store was introducing a late-night opening and that she would have to take her turn for a late shift every alternate Thursday and they were thinking of stopping the Monday to Friday privilege. Her husband was a student, both of them being Nigerian, and she supported him though one failed exam after another. She seemed close to breaking point, as life was such hard going for her. In this job you could really see just how hard women worked, being both a Mum and having a job outside the home. There was no weekend off for these Mums either, as that time was taken up with cleaning, washing, shopping and generally running round after kids and husbands.

Gabriella was the only member of staff who was a working Mum in our nursery at the moment and she would say she could not do it if it was not for her Mum helping her with Sharlette, what with the shifts and the long hours. It was really annoying when you heard staff criticising the working mothers, as Carol Clarke and Big Mary used to. It wasn't up to any of us to judge what these parents took on and felt was important for them, whether that was having babies and having jobs and husbands. Many of our parents did not work and they had shorter day places. Their children came to us because of various reasons. Some had disabilities and needed the stimulation that our facilities could offer them; some could barely talk by the age of three or had behavioural problems. Occasionally, some were with us because their parents could not cope and some even were thought to be at risk or had been known to have been treated badly. I wasn't sure that coming to the nursery was always the best place as they hardly got one to one attention, which some of them needed. Sometimes the nursery place prevented the child from going into care as it helped the Mum, but I used to think that if we really wanted to help the Mum, or Dad for that matter, take better care of their children, then they ought to spend time with us too. I had heard they did this at the local family center, and I wanted to get into that kind of work eventually, but for now, I had a senior's job to get until such time when that opportunity arose.

And arise it did. Later that day, Alice spoke to us all individually, telling us that Sue had been appointed at the new Officer in Charge, leaving the deputy post open. She would still be with us for a further month to make sure Sue settled into the new job well. Alice had not applied for the job after all as she found the travelling too hard, so the space was there for Gabriella to apply. Kenneth's plan would not be overly railroaded, as long as Sue was amenable to changes. We were sad Alice was not going to be our new boss and hoped Sue would prove as forward thinking as she was. However, the Under-Fives Research Project was underway and they were doing interviews with staff and children. They told us the report would be out in June 1972. Why did these things take so long? We had recently got two new staff members, Marion and Clare, to replace Carol Clarke and Big Mary; they seemed ok, but I did not know them well as they both worked with older children. Marion lived in Shepherd's Bush and I had seen her on the way to work a couple of times when she had told me that she had been out with a 'black bloke' a couple of times and said she had found out he was married and finished it. She never mentioned his name and I thought not to ask. It seemed that she was seeing him again, but did not talk much about it – who would want to openly declare they were seeing a married man?

Anyway, we hoped that the next Deputy would not be appointed quickly to make sure people had a chance to apply. Apparently, Gabriella told me, Alice had encouraged her to go for it. This had meant a lot to Gabriella. Under old Matron it was as if she did not exist, but I was pleased for her that Alice, and Sue for that matter, had seen her for the conscientious person she was and for her real gift for working with young children. I knew she would apply, and I wished her all the luck in the world.

Marion suggested we should all go out on the following Friday after work, suggesting a pub in Kensington. I wasn't keen at first, but Vicky was going and Clare, so Gabriella and I decided to go along, at least for a while. Elizabeth, Denise and Val said they would go as well, and shouldn't we ask Sue and Alice too? This was unlike anything we had known under Matron, so Marion asked Sue who agreed, for this once, as it was like celebrating a new lease of life for our team. Gabriella reminded me not to mention that she was applying for the Deputy job, just in case Val was. Val had also worked in the nursery longer than Gabriella and was also a room senior, but she seemed less interested in her job than the house she and her husband had just bought in Wembley that she never stopped going on about.

The Deputy job was advertised internally to start with, and the closing date was imminent. Gabriella got her application in, with a little help from Kenneth, dropping it into the Town Hall before starting her shift. I was on leave, sorting out my flat and getting ready to move in, but I managed to take time out from my painting and sewing to meet up at the pub as planned.

17   The big move

"So when are you moving in to your flat?" enquired Marion.

"Tomorrow morning. I picked up the keys this afternoon. All week I have been getting stuff ready, making curtains and cushions, painting furniture and looking for bits and pieces to make it nice. Luckily I was given loads of stuff and I found a secondhand sofa which is lovely and comfortable."

"Secondhand sofa?" interjected Val. " Aren't you worried it could have fleas so something? I would never buy second hand. Alf wouldn't let me for one and my mother would have a fit, but I suppose you can't afford much on our wages, especially as you are not much beyond being a trainee."

"Actually, it's practically new. It's a white leather Chesterfield and I was lucky to get it for twenty pounds. It was one of those that get taken back when people have not paid the HP and then sold in the secondhand shops. As for my wages…I can manage well enough."

"So when can we come round and see you?" Marion re-joined the conversation. "I would love to see your flat and how you have done it. We should do that more – meet up at each other's places and all bring something to share for a meal – as long as work talk and wages are not discussed!"

"That's a great idea," agreed Clare. "What do you think, Vicky? Jaqui? Bet?"

"Well I live miles out," said Val "and Alf would definitely not like a hoard of Nursery Nurses descending on our cream carpet."

We ignored her and agreed that those of us who lived near could organize a monthly get together taking turns at each other's places. Marion suggested we all go on to a club. I declined as I had to get up early next day, but I was keen to go another time. Dreams in Kensington was quite popular; more of a soul and pop music club, with expensive drinks, but it was nice enough. Then I remembered that I would have to plan my clubbing carefully, with not much money left over from my wages now I had so much rent to pay.

We all left the pub, Gabriella and I went our ways home as did Val, Sue and Alice leaving the rest of them to go on to Dreams. I took the bus down to Hammersmith with Sue who was going to get the tube back to Acton, while I got the bus to the Bush and then another bus up to Wormholt Road to where I would be sleeping for the last night. I got in about nine pm and went into the kitchen where Cora was sitting. I could see she had been crying.

"What's up?" I asked her. "Why are you crying? Is everything OK?"

"Don't mind me, darlin'. Denison put the house with the agent today and they will be putting up the 'For Sale' board tomorrow. So what with you leaving, and all the tenants being gone, the house is empty and lonely and I am missing the sounds of my Mum and Dad's voices, - my sister's too. It's like the memories flooding in like old ghosts. I miss them all so much."

I hugged Cora and made her some tea. On the table were details of houses in Ealing, Greenford and Wembley, as well as some smaller flats.

"I'm finding it hard even to look at these. But I know Denison is right. If only I could find my sister. Once I have gone from here there will then be no way for her to get in touch."

"But you can be in the phone book – especially if you put the phone in your name. She can always look you up. But I am sure there a people you can contact to help you find 'missing persons'. Maybe if you look in the Business phone book you could find some sort of missing person agency or private detective."

"You can do that? They have people who can look for missing relatives? Maybe you are right. I can still try to find her. If I do and she does not want to know us still, then at least I have tried. But it's about the house too. She never forgave Mummy for leaving the house all to me and nothing to her. I feel I am taking something of hers by leaving the house. I always felt the house belonged to both of us. Oh, I don't know. I suppose selling the house is bringing it all up for me again."

"Are you having second thoughts about selling then?"

"No, no. My mind is made up and Denison is right, but I will do as you say Jen, and see if I can find an agency to look for her. Then it will clear my conscience. Anyway, it's your big day tomorrow, isn't it? Have you told Marvalette yet?"

"No, not yet. I was waiting to actually move and then invite them all round. Would they come do you think? You too, and Denison – you are both welcome if you would like to come and see me anytime."

"Well, I have to admit, Jen, I let it slip when I spoke to Marvalette. Sorry about that. I told her you have been busy-busy getting stuff ready and that you would call soon. She sad she hoped you would."

126

"I will call from here in the morning then, if that's ok, before Leroy comes for me. But for now I need a good sleep – and you too. Everything will seem better in the morning. It's a new day for you and Denison as well. And things are looking up at work, too. Anyway, did Marvalette mention what is happening with Norman, and how is he anyway?" I didn't mention the conversation with Kenneth.

"Norman's fine. The police have dropped the charges for riot and affray, but they have charged him with obstruction. It's not so bad, but it's still an offence and will go against him. That's how they do it, see? Try to do him for something less so they have more chance of getting a conviction through and making sure he gets a criminal record. So they are not out of the woods yet, by any means. However, they now have a West Indian lawyer, a Chinee, they say. Mr Fook. He's from TriniDad. He works for the same firm as the one before – the woman, what was her name? Oh , Barbara, wasn't it? So they are on the same side, and he's feeling pretty good about that. But Marvalette will fill you in."

I said good night to Cora and went to bed for the last night in Wormholt Road, thinking how Kenneth never said anything about the obstruction charge. I would have to wait until I spoke to Marvalette to get the latest. Denison had been working hard on the house for the past couple of months and his team had been in, re-plastering, laying new floorboards and thoroughly airing the smelly back rooms. Leroy was due to come in with his team to redecorate where it was needed – which was actually everywhere, but Cora would not spend the money to do the whole house as they were moving. It was actually a very attractive house and would make lovely flats, but at that time Cora would not hear of it.

As I lay there, my thoughts turned to my flat. Mr Feltz had been true to his word and had laid brown carpet in the living room and bedroom. It wasn't best quality but it was fine. There was some tile effect lino round the kitchenette area and in the bathroom, so that was flooring all ok, and he had had curtain poles put up at all the windows, keeping the shutters at the front. I had noticed that there seemed to be a connection for a phone and asked Mr Feltz if I could have a phone put in, to which he agreed. I phoned the GPO and they said the line was still live and it would only be a reconnection charge, although I would get a new number. Perfect.

The bed and the fridge were coming on Monday – I would just sleep on the sofa til then. I began to plan where everything would go, including my little Dansette table-top stereo, when I fell into a deep sleep. I was awoken at what seemed like minutes later, but was actually a whole night past, and Cora was banging on the door telling me it was nine am. Gosh, Leroy was due at ten, although he would more than likely be late. I grabbed my stuff and got ready quickly as I still had a little bit of packing to do. Phoning Marvalette would now have to wait.

I went into the back storeroom, where I had been working on my furniture. It was freezing in there, but Denison had rigged up a little heater, warning me to keep chemicals away from it if I did not want to end up as roast turkey!! He had introduced me to the wonders of Nitromoors and I had used that first to strip the varnish off the pine wardrobe and chest of drawers and then I spent a day sanding it before applying wax. Oh My arms! How they ached! Denison had advised me not to strip the table and chairs but just sand them and give them a couple of coats of undercoat. Leroy had given me some half-used tins of eggshell paint in various bright colours and I had mixed them up a bit til I got a coffee brown for the table, with orange and red chairs. He had been round in the evenings helping me with that as well. I had painted a small coffee table and the little bookcase (now record cabinet) white to blend with the sofa. I had also found a small carved square table for the bedroom which I had also painted a bright turquoise blue.

I had found some long beige velvet curtains in a junk shop – more than I needed, but I bought the lot – about six in all. I couldn't afford to dry clean them so I washed them and Cora pressed them out for me. That was the bedroom window taken care of. I would do the others for the main window next week as Cora pointed out, shutters may look good but they did not keep the draught out. I also found some orange nets – Cora nearly puked – but I made them up to hang café style along the main window and some left over was just right for the bathroom. I had also made a couple of cushion covers in some bright material I had found in the market and had more to do next week. School sewing lessons had served me well as I remembered at least the main things to get me going on the home furnishings. So, I had achieved all of that – and I still had a fair bit in the bank left over for a rainy day.

The doorbell rang as I was having a cup of tea. It was Leroy – bang on time for a change with his little van.

"Yu ready fe Freddy? I's your big day an' me only have a small van!! Serious! Like me haffe mek two, t'ree trips, so yu bes' get goin'."

"Leroy, have some tea first and rest yourself. Don't rush us on our last breakfast with our Jen. You want an egg and toast?"

"Yes please, Aunty. Yu comin' fe 'elp Jen fix de place?"

"I don't think Jen needs me, she's so independent, but I am happy to if you want me Jen."

"That would be great, thanks," I said, then adding "but I'm not sure how we will all get in Leroy's van. It will be like the Tardis from Doctor Who."

Leroy then went into his impersonation of a Dalek and we all laughed, with Denison saying Cora was not going in no Tardis and offered to help bring her down and some of my stuff in his van – which was a bit bigger than Leroy's.

I rounded up all my boxes and bags leaving them in the hall, with the guys putting all my furniture into their respective vans, with Leroy yelling to Denison to min' the paint or he dead! After an hour we were all set, when the estate agent turned up with the 'For Sale' board. Bad timing! Denison asked him to come back Monday – thereby avoiding any more emotional stress for Cora that day. He moaned but agreed to anyway. That done, we set off for Westbourne Grove.

I will never forget that morning. Crisp and cold, but sunny, with a real 'new beginning' feel to it. We sped down Uxbridge Road, then down Holland Park Avenue to Notting Hill Gate, from there into Chepstow Road and then left into Westbourne Grove and to number 164 – my new abode. Tada!! Leroy parked outside and Denison, close behind. I went up to the door and propped it open along with my flat door and the guys carried all the stuff in, while Cora stood guard, she reckoned, to stop anyone nicking our gear. The two guys started pretending they were removal guys for real.

"Where d'y want this ma'm?"

"Oh. Over there, my good man. Ta so much." It was silly banter and we all giggled til Denison said:

"Anyone seen the kettle? Could well do wiv a brew."

"Yeah," said Leroy, "where de kitchen t'ings dem?"

"Oh no." I joked. "Maybe I left them behind. Leroy, can you take me back to Cora's please?"

"Yu joke man!"

"No. Serious." I reached for my coat.

Leroy looked flabberghasted. Then I said I was joking and said I knew where the kettle was and he was lucky because the gas man had been to fix the cooker that week. However, he seemed not to have appreciated the joke and didn't really laugh. Denison caught on and joked him out of it while I got on and made the tea. Cora took some sandwiches and cake from her bag and we all had some lunch before the men said they had to go. Cora said she would stay and help me sort out and unpack. Leroy, who had dropped his mood and was chirpy again, asked if there were any more man jobs that needed doing. I said no, but he said he would come back later to see if I was OK.

The first thing I put together was the little Dansette stereo. I put it on top of the glass cabinet that held my records, even the LPs and that sat in the alcove. On went my tunes that I had not played for ages and that kept us going while we unpacked my stuff and put it all away. We were done by 2pm and sat back and had another cup of tea. The flat looked amazing. Even Cora conceded that the bright colours looked cheery and fun. Then I remembered I had not called Marvalette and looked at Cora in dismay.

"Look, you've got all this stuff to do. Just get on with that and call her when you have time."

I agreed this was probably best. I was now just five minutes from the Portobello Road market and I was dying to nip down to see if I could find a few little bits and pieces to add some decoration and I wanted to get some old-fashioned cups and saucers. Cora said she had to get home too. I didn't want her to go. It would then make it final. I hugged her and we both shed a tear. Then she reached for her bag and opened it.

"Jen. Look. While you have been by me, I have put aside the money you paid me for food and I would like to give it you back, plus a little extra from Denison to help you with your fridge or your phone. I would like you to have it please."

I thanked her from my heart. She was just so kind. I didn't want to look in the envelope, but she made me. There was fifty pounds in it. It was a lot of money and I was so grateful.

"It's so kind of you – perhaps I might use it to get a TV!!"

"You get whatever you want, whatever makes you happy. This is a lovely little place. You are going to be twenty in a while so call it a little early birthday present for your first home."

Just then there was a tap on the door. It was Mr. Feltz coming, as agreed for his first month's rent which I had ready for him. He looked around approvingly and laughed at my ideas for my bright dining chairs.

"Don't worry, My Feltz. You won't come next time and find green and purple walls!!"

"I am glad to hear it Jenifer. White is best, or something a little less loud perhaps, but make sure you ask me first and get it done properly. Anyway, you have made a lovely job. Muzeltof. That is what we say to wish you good luck. Now this is your rent book. I am here every Saturday morning at eleven o'clock or Monday evening. You will pay me monthly on the Saturday or Monday after your payday on the 15th of the month. Always call me if there are any problems. Enjoy your afternoon ladies. Goodbye, Goodbye."

We wished him goodbye and then got ready to go up the road, with Cora going towards Notting Hill Gate to get the bus, leaving me to explore the wonders of Portobello antiques market before going down to the fruit and veg end to get some grapes and bananas.

I knew Leroy would be back, and as I did not yet have the fridge I had not got meat to cook but intended to make some corned beef and rice for him with some tomato salad and fruit after. I got back to the flat about half past four, set the table, put on more music and had a bath, changing into my jeans and a white shirt before starting on my first supper in my new place. Leroy arrived at six o'clock with a beer and some orange juice. He knew I hated beer.

"Leroy. You know this is just a thank you supper and nothing more, don't you?"

"Yes, yes, man, Jen. Me nah rush t'ings again wid yu. Yu know me like yu and me know me do wrong, so me ok to wait a while til you mek up yu min'. Me know yu

130

like me too, but me wan' show yu' wha' me is really like, so yu know me as a man and not a damn fool bwoy, seen?"

I smiled. I did like him but was not going to rush like before. I wanted to make sure he was for real and not messing me about. Just to impress me, he even cleared the plates and washed them up. Then we sat and played some music.

"Jen, who else live in de 'ouse so far?"

"Only me, I think."

"Yu nah 'fraid? Cho! An' is only a Yale lock on yu door. Me gwine get yu a Chubb lock, mek sure no-one cyan get in and tief yu!"

"I'm fine, but an extra lock would be good." I did not want him to see I was a bit nervous in that big house by myself. To be honest, I was not sure if I trusted Feltz or not. I knew he had keys – of course he would as he was the landlord. Maybe that's why Leroy suggested I should have an extra lock."

"Is Feltz OK? You know, like can he be trusted? He wouldn't try to use his key to get in?"

"Nah, man. Me nah t'ink 'im a do dat. Yu can put up de catch pon de Yale to mek yu feel safe if you want."

I was thinking I was looking a bit worried to be there on my own and I hoped he would not take that as an oblique invite to stay.

"Leroy. I know tomorrow is Sunday, but if you are round this way in the morning could you just look in on me for 5 minutes. Just to make sure."

"Course, man, course. No problem."

"Thanks. Well, I had better be getting to bed – though I'm sleeping on the sofa til Monday when the actual bed comes."

"Sure. Unno mus' be tired. Me gone, seen?."

"Good night Leroy. Thank you so much for all your help today."

"Is cool, man. Is cool. Me go see yu tomorrow marnin'."

With that, Leroy left and I did as he suggested and put the snib down on the Yale. I put my old blankets out on the Chesterfield, curled up and went to sleep.

18   The letter

Leroy kept his word and popped in to see me at ten o'clock the next day. It was just a flying visit and he was glad to find me still alive and in one piece after a night alone in that large house. Just after he left, I heard a bang and a thud downstairs in the basement and nearly had a heart attack. I looked out of the window and saw that I might have a neighbour. There was a moving van and a guy in bell bottom jeans and a fur jacket giving the orders to two removal men.

"In here, sweeties. Yes, mind the steps. In we go. Welcome to Francis' new Paradise Pad."

He sounded very effeminate and constantly flicked his longish blonde hair away from his face, gesturing what the men should take out of the van next and directing them into the flat with it. Francis, as I assumed he was named, did not seem to do much himself, but took great pleasure in admonishing the men.

"Mind how you go with that, duckie. That cost Francis a FORTUNE! Oh. Careful now. Christ! Bulls in china shops springs to mind."

It was rather funny, and I was pleased that I would have such an entertaining neighbour. Queer definitely, but none the less rather funny and I could not wait to meet him. I waited until all the moving had been done and the men gone, made a mug of tea, took the biccies and the sugar and made my way downstairs to his flat.

I rang the bell. No answer. I rang again.

"OK OK. I'm coming I'm coming. Said the actor to the bishop, haha! Who is it?"

"I'm Jenifer, your neighbour. I've brought you some tea."

"Oh my days! That's so sweet of you. Come in. All sixes and sevens here, but I suppose you are too. When did you move in Jenifer? I'm Francis by the way. Pleased to meet you."

"Hi Francis. I moved in yesterday, so yes, I am still in a muddle – unpacking and finding places for stuff I had forgotten I had. I am in the flat above you."

"Ooooh! I hope I won't disturb you. I am a bit of a late bird."

"Oh. I'm afraid I have to be an early bird in my job, so I am an early to bedder. I hope that does not mean our lifestyles will clash. I work in the nursery down in Lancaster Road, so I'm out just after seven in the morning when I am on earlies!"

"Hmm. Feltz mentioned that you were probably a morning lady. I'm not that bad really. My last neighbours just loved me!! I am a hairdresser by the way. Coiffeur to the stars and my neighbours, just to keep me in their good books."

"Don't worry. I could sleep through an earthquake, so I am sure all will be fine. I just hope my music does not disturb you."

"I'm not sure how often an earthquake might happen down here. I don't often feel the earth move these days. But there's always hope. What music do you like?

132

Beatles? Slade? Chopin. Oh I do hope not Country and Western!"

"I am a soul and reggae fan." I waited for the bombshell effect.

"Oh darling. I just love all that Caribbean razzamatazz."

Francis started to do a Carmen Miranda impersonation, which was a bit crass, but I just laughed. At least he was not hostile.

"Well. Thank you so much for the tea. Reached the spot as they say. I am sure we will get on famously."

"I hope so. I must go now as I have so much to do as well."

"Well, TTFN. Let's have a proper get together when we are both settled in."

"Sure," I said, as Francis opened the door for me. I bid him goodbye.

When I got back upstairs, my mind was on one thing. Mum.

I considered going out to the phone box, but I did not feel too good about phoning her and the pips going half way though, running out of money or, worse, Dad answering and giving me short shrift. I decided to write.

And say what?

Exactly?

I sat and thought for a while and made a few notes about what I wanted to tell her about. I began.

2nd December 1971

Dear Mum and Dad

Start again – just to Mum, giving love to Dad at the end.

2ⁿᵈ December 1971

Dear Mum

I am sorry I have not been in touch before now. I spoke to Liz a while ago, who told me she had been in touch with you. Heaven knows what she said. She seems to make it all up these days. I have not seen her in months, not since we parted at the flat in South Kilburn. Lots has been happening and, I am pleased to say, all good since Liz and I parted company.

My job at the nursery is going really well; I have been there over 18 months now and I have had a pay rise, plus a cost of living increase and I am on fairly good money. I was staying with friends and have been able to save up, which came in handy as I have just moved into a new flat. I am living on my own - a bit daunting, but all going well so far. It is a one bedroomed place with little living room/kitchenette and a small bathroom, all self-contained and unfurnished.

It has been really exciting getting it altogether. I was given some stuff and have painted it all up and found some good secondhand bargains just leaving me to buy a good bed and a little fridge brand new. I bought a sewing machine so that I could make cushion covers and things for the home - I will probably need to make my own clothes too now to save money as the flat is quite dear for me by myself, but it is lovely and I am really pleased with it.

You remember I told you about the dozey old Matron at the nursery - well she's retired now and some of the miserable staff have left too, so we have a new manager and there may be opportunities for me to apply for a promotion to room senior soon. I love the job, Mum, I really do and I am learning so much all the time. Some of the children have very hard lives and I am getting more interested in going on to do work supporting families who find it hard to cope. But all in good time as I need more experience first.

I would love to see you and Dad and it would really please me if you both came over to see my little place. Then you would see for yourself that I am fine and you would not worry about me.

I hope you and Dad are both well. Don't mind anything Liz says. She got in with a bad crowd and had a terrible experience. I want you to be reassured I am not keeping bad company and even though I know you don't approve of black people, or coloured as you put it, but I have been helped a lot and been taken good care of by my friends who are all good people.

Jenifer. Xxxx

PS I don't have a phone yet - but hope to get one connected soon, then I will let you have my number. Miss you both. xxxxx

I wasn't sure if I should have said all that about Liz, but I figured if she had been on the phone, maybe even Liz's Mum, then my poor Mum would have had her ears well and truly bent. I bought a nice card, wrote it out and put the letter inside and posted it that afternoon, hoping it would reach them by Tuesday at least. I realised I felt quite excited. Writing the letter made me feel like I missed them and I just wanted my Mum, in particular, to accept me and be pleased to hear from me and write back to me soon. I pictured them coming over and seeing how well I was doing and being really proud of me. But maybe that was too much to ask.

I came back from the post box and thought I needed to get the curtains up before it got dark. I did the nets in the front room. Yep! The orange nets in a modern woven design – no flowers or birds. I had the wires and the hooks already in place. They looked good, allowing a golden glow in the room when the afternoon sun shone through. The bright tables and chairs went in the window alcove perfectly, looking bright and cheery. I would need a help in fixing the main curtains at the front, but the back curtains were ready to go up. They were really heavy and I balanced them on my shoulders to keep them from being too weighty as I was putting the curtain hooks into the rings. I took my time and at the end, they were up and looked good, coincidentally co-ordinating with the carpets perfectly. I now thought of where the bed would go and repositioned the wardrobe and chest of drawers before putting all my stuff away. I couldn't wait to get my bed and to set it all up with my nice bedding with the turquoise and cream satin bedspread. Ah, Monday night would be pure bliss.

It started to get dark and I pulled the shutters across in the living room. Cora was right. It was draughty, and curtains would be better than the shutters in keeping the warmth in. My little gas fire seemed to eat up the small change, so I put a 50p in and hoped it would last longer. There was a little electric Dimplex in the bedroom, and I had not yet used that. It was cold though, but the heavy curtains helped a lot. The bathroom was freezing as the window rattled away and the draught came in with a gale force against which the orange nets were no good, but what could I do? I would ask Denison if he had any good ideas. There was an extractor fan so maybe I could block the window or cover it up with plastic or something. I switched on the fan and realised there was no hope in that direction as it did not work.

I finished washing all the kitchen stuff and got rid of all the newspaper packaging and broke up the boxes, ready for shoving in the bin on my way out the next day. When everything had been dried and put away I found a tin of soup and some bread and ate that, followed by some grapes. Tomorrow, when the fridge arrived I would be able to think about shopping.

That evening I got on writing out the rest of my Christmas cards and budgeting, thinking how it would be nice to have a little black and white TV – couldn't afford colour. My home was perfect. Almost.

After another uncomfortable night on the sofa, I was glad when the shop delivered the bed at 9.30 the next morning. It was a divan, so simple to put together, and I took out my bedding and made the bed up. Perfect! I just needed to finish painting an old wooden headboard I had found on a skip. Turquoise, the same as the table, and then the bedroom was done. I had found a turquoise vase in a junk shop that I put on the chest of drawers. I was thrilled to bits with the whole thing and could not wait for to get in the bath that evening and get to bed.

Just as I had done that, the fridge was delivered. It said you had to let it stand for a few hours before switching on, so that would mean no shopping today. I decided to go out for lunch and found a little café to have egg and chips and a mug of strong tea. I posted my cards on the way back and as I got to the flat I saw Leroy coming down the steps.

"Eh! Where yu been? Me was just passin' fe hail yu up and see 'ow's tings?"

I invited him in and showed him what I had done, saying I needed help with the curtains for the front window. He seemed to approve of my flat's style and admired my hard work. He went to get a step ladder from his van, coming back to fix up the curtains at the front window. I want sure if they went in front or behind the shutters, but he said that I needed to close them first and then the curtains should go over from the inside – so that was how he fixed them, allowing for them to clear the windows completely when pulled back.

"So, yu done, or is more to do?"

"Just to finish the headboard and a few sewing jobs and yes, I'm done. I want to get a little TV and an Xmas tree, a few lights and stuff and then I am all set. I wrote to my Mum by the way."

"Good, good. I hope you an' she can get along now. I miss my mudder bad bad. Yu know how Winny sen' fe me, an' 'ow 'im look after me? Set me on de right road fe tru' or me woulda hend up gwan jail or sometin'!"

"Yes, I hope we can get along better now, too. I have told her how my job is going well and that I have this nice little place and I hope they can come and see me here. But if my Dad objects, she won't and it's him who is more of a problem."

"'im nah like yu coloured frien' dem, is it? Or rather, 'im nah like 'im dahter wid a black man, is it Jen?"

"Something like that, yes, Leroy. But they just have to accept this is a different time and their old ideas just don't fit today's world. It's my sister and her husband too, and I bet Liz has told them all kinds of rubbish about me."

"Don' pay Liz no min'. I see she de other day, yu' know. At the Buccaneer in Kensal Rise. An' yu' know dat is a black man pub, pure reggae and t'ing. She look a bit drunk to me, all over some poor guy. Me did feel sarry fe har, but me neva went to talk to she. Me stay far, yes."

"Strange. Last time we spoke she couldn't hate black people more. After what Gregory did, she said she never wanted to have anything to do with them, especially as she seemed to have fallen right back in with her parents and they are like the National Front, I'm telling you. She is someone I don't want to know again."

"For real. Anyway Jen, me doin' a job right now, but me soon come again. Me haffe do a likkle more wuk fe Feltz in de 'ouse down de road so. I 'spec' T'ursday me will pop in an' check yu. Anyway. Me gone."

"Ok. Bye then."

After Leroy had gone, I set up the sewing machine and started on the rest of the cushion covers. I had found some odd bits of velvet in all colours as well as some bright prints. The doorbell went just after I got settled. I thought it was Leroy – maybe he had left something behind, but I couldn't see anything, so looked out of the window. It was Francis, waving at me from the steps. I went to let him in.

"Sweetie, are you running a motorbike up here? Or setting up a dental surgery – what's that noise I'm hearing?"

"Come in Francis, how are you today? The only noise here is my sewing machine and it's hardly a Harley Davidson."

"Darling – it was just an excuse for me to come and see you in your pad. Just nosey that's all. I thought you might be sewing and just wondered if you could run up a little something for me – I would pay you – or give you a new hair do. When last did you let a hairdresser near you? Months? Years?"

"Guilty as charged. Not in at least two years. It has got a bit long and straggly; I admit. Swapping is great, but I am not sure my sewing is a match for your hairdressing skills. I am only doing a few cushions. See?"

I showed him the orange and red velvet ones I had made and was just about to embellish them with some frills made from the patterned material – I was experimenting with being creative and, so far, it was coming along. Francis was impressed. I showed him round the flat. He raved and raved in his exaggerated way saying he could get me more fabric if I wanted – all designer stuff from his interior designer friends who he wanted to show my flat to.

"It's superb. Fabulous. How old are you Jen? You are in the wrong business, darling. You could make a fortune designing for the stars!"

"Come on Francis, you are pulling my leg."

"I never touched you dear. Your legs are not my thing – but your décor style is truly after my heart."

"Would you like some tea?"

"Nothing stronger?"

"Certainly not. Just tea or instant coffee."

"Tea then please, two sugars and let me hear some of your reggae."

"Ok then."

I made Francis some tea and played a selection of music to him. He danced like a loony and knew it. We both laughed.

"You know Francis is as queer as a coot?" he asked.

"That much I have sussed, I think!" I answered.

"Oh," he groaned, "is it that obvious?" Francis sat down, crossed his legs and flicked his hair at me. "Surely no??"

I was falling about laughing. I had never actually met a homosexual man before – not to talk to like this anyway, and I really liked him.

"I think we are going to get on really well."

"Was that your beau I saw earlier? Rather handsome, tall and dark with those little plaits?" He fluttered his eyelashes as if to say how attractive he thought Leroy was.

"Not exactly, but he'd like to be, I think. He paints the houses for Feltz. I like him. His cousin and aunty are good friends of mine."

"Aah. A Caribbean culture fan. Me too, darling! Yes I think we will certainly get on well together, but I have to go now. Thanks for the tea. Mwah."

He gestured me a kiss and left. He was right. He was as queer as a coot, as he put it, but he was amiable and good fun. I wondered what Leroy would make of him, though. But by now I was tired so I ran that bath I had promised myself and got into my lovely bed early and was soon fast asleep, not stirring until after ten the next morning. Goodness, I must have needed that.

I finished all my sewing that day leaving me the rest of the week to paint the headboard and finish off my shopping. I got the fridge set up and nipped out to get some milk, butter, eggs and cheese, some vegetables, seasonings and a couple of lamb chops, which I cooked later with some rice with sweet corn. I was just about to dish up when the door went. It was Leroy.

"Just in time for dinner," I joked.

"Nice. Car me 'ungry no blouse 'n' skirts. Is who dat man downstairs? 'im is a batty man?"

"Yes. He moved in Sunday. His name is Francis and he is a right queen, but he is ok. We introduced each other and so far he seems fine"

"Yu and 'im is frien'?" Leroy looked unsure.

"You know Leroy, he is fine. At least he is not going to chase me round the bedroom and, so far, he seems to be a nice enough neighbour. I popped down to him with a cuppa on Sunday and he popped up here yesterday – very impressed with my flat too. Said he is going to get me some designer fabrics."

I mimicked Francis' exaggerated responses and Leroy lost his scowl and laughed.

"Well, if yu say 'im is Ok, den me go tek yu word. Mmm – food taste nice. Marvalette did teach you good."

"What about you? Did Winny teach you to cook?"

"Not Winny as such, but my mudder did learn me fe cook. One time I couldna' even touch a pot car it remin' me o' she. But is a'right now, so one day, is cook me a cook fe yu too. Ah. By de way, me bring yu dis."

Leroy handed me a carrier bag. I took it and looked inside. It was an LP. Jackie Mittoo. I was thrilled.

"Yu like 'im?"

"Oh yes and thank you so much." I switched on my stereo and put it on to play.

"Come, dance wid me?" Leroy beckoned me to his arms. We danced a whole tune, nothing too amorous, but it reminded me of the night at the party when we were both stoned and got too carried away. I kept myself in check and Leroy could sense it.

"Jen, me nah try nuttin', so don' fret. Me jus' wan' dance wid yu – mek sure yu nah forget!! Long time yu nah tek in a dance, is it?"

 "Yes, it's been a good while. When I am settled here I can work out my budget and maybe start going out again. The girls at work went some place in Kensington last week, but I wasn't in the mood that night, but I might go with them another time."

"Well, dat is up to yu, but me was t'inkin' yu might like to come a dance wid me some time before de Chris'mas as plenty party a gwan. Me can carry yu a Tam dance if yu wan'. 'Im get better and better – pure Studio One."

"Ok – that is a temptation I can't resist. A Christmas dance with Duke Tam playing a Studio One selection – you are on!!"

139

Leroy laughed. We had one more dance together, then danced separately with him showing me a new step or two. He put on Queen of the Minstrels by the Techniques and started to sing along.

Queen majesty, may I speak to thee?
So much I've long (I've long)
To speak to you alone
Truly I agree, I'm not of your society
I'm not a king, just a ministrel
But my song to you I sing.

Tho' just a ministrel
Our worlds are far apart
Royal Queen, I see love in your eyes
Your eyes, I love you too.

Is it really true
These things I ask of you
Oh, your majesty, could you really care for me?

Tho just a ministrel
Our worlds are far apart
Royal queen, I see love in your eyes
Your eyes, I love you too. [x]

"Oh, pack it in Leroy. Trying your luck with your ballading! It will take more that a sweet serenade to get around me."

"Ah. Jen, Don' pay me no min'. I's just a nice song with pretty harmonies."

"That's true. And you sing it rather nicely as well. Maybe you should make a record!!"

"Nah man. Is paint me like to paint. Hey. Gimme dat 'eadboard and de paint. Me go paint it up nice fe yu, OK? Itta be bes' fe spray it. Me can do dat."

"I think that would be very nice of you – and save the flat stinking of paint as well."

I gave Leroy the headboard and the paint. He looked at me twice when I handed him the turquoise, but when I showed him the room, he agreed it would look nice.

" Ok. Me gone. See you Sat'day. Yu wan' tek in de market?

"Ok. That would be nice. Thanks. About eleven?"

Leroy nodded and off he went with my stuff, skipping lightly down the steps, waving as he got in the car.

I turned away from the window and replayed Queen Majesty, singing along myself. Leroy was right, the harmonies were pretty and I loved how the singer pronounced minstrel as 'ministrel'. It made it sound so, well, Jamaican.

Chapter 19 The telephone call

Right, today is Tuesday. Mum would have got the letter. If she replied today I would get a letter next day – but maybe she would wait days, talk to Dad, or my sister first, maybe she wouldn't even write back at all.

Wednesday I did not get a letter, nor Thursday. I couldn't bear it. Now all my jobs were done and my shopping completed I was left with nothing to do but worry. I couldn't stand it anymore. I figured Dad would be at work and that she might be home. So I got dressed and went out to the phone box, took a few coins with me and plucked up the courage to dial her number. Mum answered.

"2947 Hello."

"Hello Mum. It's me, Jen. Did you get my letter? How are you and Dad?"

Silence. Then,

"Hello Jenifer, dear. Yes, I did get your letter and I am glad to hear from you. I had been worried as I had no number or any way of calling you. We have had some bad news. Six weeks ago your Dad went into hospital. He was having trouble breathing. You know how he gets. Well, I'm afraid it's, well, it's cancer. He's dying Jen and I think you should come and see him."

"Mum, I am so sorry. Sorry to hear he has been so ill and I am so sorry I have not been in touch sooner. It must seem so selfish, but it wasn't meant to be. I just wanted to get my self settled before I called you. Have you seen Veronica? Has she been a help to you?"

"Jen, I have missed you. Veronica and that pig of a husband of hers, Ron, have moved up to Newcastle. She came a week ago for the weekend but had to get back. I would love to see you."

"Mum,
I am on leave from work and I will be over tomorrow morning as early as I can."

"Thank you dear. That would be a great comfort to me. Where are you calling from?"

"A phone box outside my house."

"Love, you must be freezing! Hang up now and go and get yourself back in the warm."

"Actually Mum, I could come this afternoon, and if you like I could stay over and come back tomorrow."

"Are you sure dear? You must be very busy with your new flat. I'm so pleased everything is alright. That Lizzie has been round, and her Mum. What a right pair they are. I will tell you all about that when I see you. What time can you get here?"

"Well I need to get in, pack a few things and get down to Euston. I will get a fast train up to Wealdstone and then pick up the little line from there. I will call you from the station – I reckon I will be with you in about three hours from now."

"Ok dear. I will be here for you. Bye for now"

"Bye Mum."

I put the phone down, still reeling from the shock. I used my last ten pence to call Leroy but he was not home. I got back inside and wrote a little note to him and left it with Francis, asking him to keep an eye out and let him know I had gone to my Mum's.

"Oh poor you," sympathised Francis. "I will hold the fort for you and keep an eye out for Mr Handsome."

I laughed, slung my duffel bag over my shoulder and went off to the bus stop to make my way to Euston.

It was indeed about three hours later when I got to my Mum's. I rang the door bell a couple of times and there was no answer. I called though the letter box, but there was no answer. I even looked under the mat for a note, buy there was none.

"Cooeee. Jen. Cooee." It was Mrs Coggins from next door.

"Your Mum's been called to the hospital urgently. It's your Dad. He's taken a turn for the worst. She only left about half an hour ago – she said for you to get down to the hospital as soon as possible. I can give you a lift if you like."

"Oh, thank you Mrs Coggins. I would appreciate that."

I sat in the car, hardly knowing what to say. At least Mrs Coggins seemed to get the idea I was worried and in no mood for polite chat. She just filled me in a bit about when Dad had been taken ill and what had happened with my sister. I couldn't help wondering what she knew, or thought she knew, about me. Thankfully, we got to the hospital within ten minutes. I thanked her and got out of the car.

"He's in Camelot Ward. Third floor," called Mrs Coggins. I yelled out a thank you without turning round and made my way to the entrance. I asked someone at reception how to get to the ward and he showed me where the lift was.

"Third floor. Turn left Camelot is signposted."

I got to the ward and took a deep breath and walked in slowly, looking for Mum and Dad. There they were, he in a bed in the corner and she sitting with him holding his hand. I went up to the bed and Mum got up and hugged me.

"I'm so glad you are here, Jen. He's very poorly. He hardly knows I am here. He might not recognize you."

I hardly recognized him. My Dad was a strapping handsome man, always the strong one who fixed things and lifted heavy stuff, got rid of spiders and kept everyone safe. For that moment, I forgot all about why he and I had grown apart and about his racist views. They seemed almost insignificant as I looked at him. My Mum's tower of strength, her rock, lying on the bed in that hospital. Weak. Frail. Grey and drawn, his eyes sunken into the hollows of their sockets, his cheeks non-existent. An oxygen tank was by the bed and various other contraptions, but they hardly registered in my mind. I just saw this shadow of a man who was my Dad. He breathing was noisy, wheezing and gasping. He had been a heavy smoker all his life and was now paying the price. I was glad I had given up when I went to live at Marvalette's and thought how the weed needed to go as well.

"Dad? It's me Jen. I'm here with Mum." I took his hand and his head nodded a weak recognition of my presence.

"Sit here," said Mum, walking round to the other side of the bed where she took a chair and took his hand while I stayed holding the other one. A nurse came by.

"This is my daughter, Jenifer."

"Nice to meet you. I am Nurse Jones. I am here to make sure your Dad is as comfortable as we can make him. He is on Morphine now."

I looked at Mum, who nodded and mouthed at me 'He's dying," so that Dad would not hear her saying the words. I felt tears welling in my eyes as various memories flooded into my mind. Him horse-playing with me when I was little, reading to me, teaching me to swim, coming to my school events and being so proud of me when I did well.

No doubt Mum was thinking similar thoughts as she looked at him, stroking his hand so lovingly. I knew we would be here until he passed.

Nurse Jones checked the contraptions, wrote up notes on his chart and adjusted the drip that I hardly noticed was in the hand I was holding.

"Be careful of the drip. That's his Morphine. We are relieving his pain with that."

"Can he come home?" I asked, naively.

"I'm sorry Jenifer. Dad is too ill to be moved now. He is quite peaceful. He has you both to sit with him. Mum has asked for the Priest to come."

Mum and Dad were both Catholics, not staunch, but my Mum took a lot from her faith to help her through life. She wanted the Priest to give him the last rights before he passed. It brought it home to me even more that Dad was dying and was not long for this world.

Mum said very little and I did not feel like saying anything either. We hardly noticed an hour had passed before the priest came.

"Good afternoon Father. I am so glad you could come. He's fading fast."

Father O'Malley said the requisite prayers for Dad, asking God to accept him and forgive him his sins. Then he went. I thought it was a bit rapid, but like Mum said, he probably had more people to visit that day. My version of the reason for his speed was more cynical than that, but, of course, I said nothing.

The nurse came round and asked if we wanted a sandwich and some tea. We both said yes, but Mum hardly touched hers, although I was starving and ate mine, and the rest of hers, too. We just sat and sat.

Nurse Jones went off Duty at four o'clock that afternoon and Nurse Hammond, a male nurse came on. He was very kind too. They were clearly well trained to support dying patients and their families. Mum spoke after being quiet for what seemed like hours.

"It's like when you were being born, Jen. This time it was Dad sitting just holding my hand. You started, then the labour stopped. Everyone flapped a bit, but Dad said 'Baby's just taking its time. It just wants to be in the cosywarm of your tum a bit longer. It'll be out by and by. She or he knows we are waiting.' And with that I had one massive contraction and within the half hour you were here. It's like that now. He will be on his way by and by. GranDad and Grandma are waiting for him and Uncle Eric – his favourite brother. Say your goodbyes to him Jen. He's fading fast."

I started to talk to him. Slowly and quietly.

"Dad. It's me Jen. ….…..I love you Dad. .……..Sorry for being so aggravating. I hope I have not hurt you. I love you………. You were a brilliant Dad….. I'm doing really well at work and I have a lovely flat now. Watch over me Dad, won't you."

Just then, amazingly, Dad rallied for a moment. "I'll always………. watch……
over………. my girls…… Love…….. you all…….. too." The words struggled out on his rasping breath, but they were clear enough.

Then he made a sound as if the last of the air was expelling from his lungs and that was his last breath.

"Nightnight, Ernest. Sleep well my love. God bless you and keep you safe." She closed his eyes and we both sat there. I called Nurse Hammond over. He saw immediately what had happened and went to talk to Mum.

"When you are ready Mrs McKay, let me know and I will call you a taxi to take you home. Will your daughter be staying with you? Oh Good."

"I think we want to go now," said Mum. So the Nurse called down to the reception to call us a taxi. We made our way down and waited five minutes for the cab. Mum said nothing. I just held her hand. The cab came and were home at Mum's very soon. I paid the cab and Mum went in the house, bursting into tears as soon as she got in, as if she had been bottling that up all day.

I went to Dad's drink cabinet and got her a Brandy, then I made us a pot of tea.

'Jen, in the morning we will talk about all that has to be done, but right now I just need to go to bed. There's a bed made up in the spare room. You can have that."

"Mum, can I sleep with you tonight please?"

My Mum smiled and put her arm round me. "Of course you can dear."

So I slept next to my grieving mother as we both felt the loss of Ernest McKay and found comfort in the nearness of each other. It was a restless night as we both slept in fits and starts and my Mum cried and I cried and we hugged each other. Eventually my Mum fell deeply asleep and I lay there beside her until I too went to sleep.

Chapter 20   The grief

I woke however at half past seven in the morning; she was still asleep, so I got up and went downstairs to get the heater on and to make some tea. There was the porridge, still in the same old tin, so I made some for both of us.

As it was early I took the opportunity to call Leroy, hoping to catch him before he went to work. A very sleepy Leroy answered the phone.

"Leroy. It's me Jen. I'm at my Mum's. Dad was taken very ill and he died last night so I won't be home for a couple of days. I just wanted to let you know as I won't make it back before Sunday evening as I need to be here with Mum."

"Oh Jen. Me so sarry fe 'ear dat. Tek time wid yu Mom. She will need yu right now. I meet yu neighbour by de way, las' night as me pop roun'. Him did seh yu 'ad gone by your Mom and I did get your note."

145

"Oh good. Glad you got that. I will call you later. I have to go now. Mum is getting up. Bye for now"

"Yeah man. Later. Me right 'ere if yu need me. Ok?"

"Thanks Leroy. I will call later. Bye"

I hung up and turned to see my Mum standing at the kitchen door looking so vulnerable and sad. I went over to her and held her while she sobbed in my arms. I cried too and we both stood there in the middle of the sitting room, held together by our grief for what seemed like ages. Then Mum pulled away gently.

"I'll get us a tissue," she said, reaching into her handbag and handing me one from a small pack. She always carried tissues in her bag, those little small packs – just in case – as she always said. There was no greater moment that a tissue was needed than this one.

"I've made us some porridge and the kettle has boiled. I will make us a pot of tea. Shall we have it in the sitting room in front of the fire, like we used to when I was little and it was cold outside."

Mum nodded and sat down on the sofa. Her and Dad now had an electric fire, but when I was little Dad used to be up early cleaning the grate and making up a fire for when we came down. I missed looking into the flames of a coal fire and hearing it crackle. Mum used to make sure the fire gurad was always in place and told me and my sister off if we got close, telling us stories of girls whose nighties caught fire, getting badly burned. She used to buy flameproof wincyette to make our nighties, just to make us safe. It felt strange to be back in the old house with all the memories flooding back.

I went to bring a tray with the teapot, cups and saucers, milk jug and sugar bowl, just the way she liked it served, as well as two bowls of steaming hot porridge. We sat and ate in silence, Mum smiling at me and patting my knee, as if to say, 'thank you'.

"I can't eat all of this," she said after a while, doing her best to get the porridge down her. "I'm hungry, but I just can't eat. Funny that." Her voice sounded vague and faint, distracted by the thoughts in her mind and the grief in her heart.

"I need to sit and talk with you Jen. Pour us another cup, will you dear? Ah, thank you.

"Your Dad had been ill for some time, as you know, and we had sat and talked about what he wanted. He wasn't one for beating around the bush and as soon as we knew it was terminal, he said it was just something we both had to face together. I am well provided for and the house is mine. He has left you both a little sum, £500 each for now, and £1000 in five years time. That is to help you with whatever you need, but you know he would like you to be sensible with it.

146

"Dad and I discussed what he wanted for the funeral – it's all written down somewhere. I will find it later and go through it with you. After the funeral, I will put the house on the market. I have already been looking for something else. I was showing Dad a couple of days ago. Seems funny doesn't it, me and him talking like that. But it was like he wanted to be a part of setting up my life as a widow. It made him feel sort of useful, I suppose, and it was also a comfort to him to know I would get on with life. Not that I feel like it at the moment. Right now, I would give my right arm to have him back here, but it's not to be."

Mum stopped a while, to drink her tea, but she was really stopping because she was choked up with tears again. After a while, she went on.

"I don't want to stay in this house, Jen. Too many memories now, plus it's too big for me. I don't want to spend the rest of my life cleaning and polishing!! I am looking to get a little two bedroom flat somewhere near Harrow-on-the-Hill. It's nice there. Livelier than here and near to the shops, plus I need to be near transport as I don't drive and don't suppose I ever will. Then, when I am settled, I may go back to work – just for the company and to keep me busy. And I am going to have holidays, at least two a year and go to all the places Dad and I were going to see when he retired. This is what I am doing Jen. It's what I want and it's what your Dad and I discussed."

"Mum, whatever you want is fine with me. It's a great idea about moving to a flat, but wait a while, as all the upheaval so soon after he has died will be very hard."

"Bless you dear, thank you for that. I was worried about telling you and your sister what I was going to do. Veronica will now doubt go mad and as for that interfering controlling husband of hers, he will probably put his oar in. Which reminds me I need to give her a call. Can you pass me the phone, please love – and could you wash these things up, there's a dear?"

I passed her the phone, cleared our breakfast things and went into the kitchen so that she could talk to my sister in private. Soon after, I heard Mum raise her voice, sounding very distressed.

"I told you how bad he was the day before yesterday and I remember saying to you that you should come down.....I did Veronica......No, she just phoned out of the blue..........No, I don't know.....No.......That's not fair......Veronica, he died last night late I came home and was too exhausted to call you straight away, that's why I am calling you now.....I hardly think this is the time and place...Look, I'm not staying on the phone to argue with you. It's been a bit of a shock to all of us. You and Ron are both welcome to come down for the funeral of course, but there's no need now to jump on a train. Veronica, stop going on so. Look, Father O'Malley is coming up the path, I'd better go and let him in. Bye dear."

I looked out of the window of our front door but could not see Father O'Malley anywhere. I went back onto the sitting room. Mum was on her knees on the floor sobbing.

"What happened? Why did you say Father O'Malley was here? I heard your voice raise, you sounded upset. What did she say?"

"That was just so as I could get off the blimmin' phone. Your sister said I should have called her before, like when he was dying and when he had just died. She accused me of not wanting her to come down on account that I don't like Ron. Well, he is a controlling bully as far as I can see, and she will wake up to the fact one day. I had asked her, a couple of days ago if she would like to come down, but I don't think it registered with her that Dad was actually dying and she didn't see the need to rush. I said it was up to her. The she went on about you and what were you doing here and would Ron be welcome if they came for the funeral. Always got to turn anything round to her, your sister. She didn't even say she was sorry to hear he had died or asked if I was OK. All about her. Selfish little cat."

I thought that all was fine with her and Veronica; they had had their ups and downs a few years ago, when Veronica was in her teens, and I knew Mum had liked Ron at first, but it was as she got to know him that she saw him differently. I thought it was awful of her to fuss like that as Mum was grieving. But it was as if Mum read my mind.

"It's OK Jen. She's in shock too. And she's right. I should have called earlier but I knew there would be a drama about something, so I left it 'til now. Anyway. Put that to one side. I need to do one or two things today. Phone the Hospital to find out what I do about getting the death certificate, phone the Undertaker and then Father O'Malley. We may have some running around to do later. Mrs Coggins will probably help. Get yourself washed and dressed while I make a couple of phone calls and then can you pop into Mrs Coggins and ask her to come over?"

I nodded yes and left her to make her calls while I got washed and dressed, then I popped next door to get Mrs Coggins. I told her the news and she seemed very upset. Well they had been neighbours for over ten years and my Dad used to go fishing with Mr Coggins. They did not have any children, but were always so lovely to us, although we never called them Aunty and Uncle. My Mum hung on to these old formalities.

Mum was still on the phone when I brought Mrs Coggins in and we sat in the kitchen. I made another pot of tea for everyone.

Mum popped her head round the kitchen door.

"One moment Rita dear. I just need to get myself decent."

Mum ran upstairs to get herself decent as she put it. Another one of her little formalities – never let your neighbours see you in your night clothes!

A few minutes later, she joined us. Mum had composed herself a little now, although you see she had been crying. Mrs Coggins offered her condolences on behalf of Mr. Coggins and herself and asked if there was anything she could do.

Mum said yes there was and would she mind taking us to the hospital to pick up his things and to get the death certificate. She had made an appointment for the undertaker but had not got hold of the Priest. Just then the doorbell rang and, talk of the devil, it was Father O'Malley.

"I've just popped by to see how you are bearing up, Mrs. McKay."

"Thank you Father. Would you like to come in and have a cup of tea? I won't keep you long, but I would like a little chat."

Father O'Malley came into the kitchen and was surprised to see us all sitting there around Mum's large teapot. I poured him out a cup.

"Jen is staying for a couple of days and Mrs Coggins has just called round. She has offered to take me to get the death certificate."

"There's no hurry to do these things. God likes us to take our time so as to spare our hearts too much agony all at once."

When my Mum's mind was made up and she had her plans made, agony or no agony, there was no telling her to slow down.

"Thank you Father. We all deal with things in our own ways. I want to get these jobs done. No point in waiting around. Plus I want to do them while I have my daughter here for a couple of days to help me. Taking my time just makes it more agonising for me, not less. I was calling you to make an appointment for the funeral arrangements. Next week would be fine, if that's Ok with you? Monday, perhaps?"

"Yes, shall we say half past two, at the Church?"

"Yes that would be fine. Ernest knew what he wanted for the funeral. It's all written down somewhere. We spoke about it and I want to follow his wishes."

"That's no problem at all, Mrs McKay. Just call me when you have found your papers and we can take it from there. I look forward to seeing you on Monday. I will leave you all to get on now and bid you a good day. May the grace of Our Lord be with you and bring you comfort."

"Good bye Father and thank you," said Mum as she led him to the front door.

"I will pop and get my coat and the car keys," said Mrs Coggins.

"Right you are," said Mum, " best get cracking and get the worst of it out of the way. Jen, thanks for washing this lot up. I will get our coats."

We were out of the house and on our way to the hospital. Mum sitting in the back with me, holding my hand, and looking out of the window, not wanting me to see the tears welling in her eyes. I knew anyway and reached into her bag for a tissue to give to her. When we got to the hospital, Mum could not move.

"You can always do this another day you know, Mavis," said Mrs Coggins. Mum steeled herself, got out of the car, muttering to herself as much as anyone else.

"Let's just get the bloody job done."

It was rare to hear my Mum use any kind of bad language at all and as she spoke, she braced herself for the ordeal. It was by far the worst thing anyone could ever do, I thought. The cold formality of getting a piece of paper that signified the end of my Dad's life - that certified his final status as being dead. Nothing more, nothing less. Just dead. Now I was upset and I found it hard to hold off the tears. Mrs Coggins took my hand and found me a tissue. I struggled to compose myself, just for Mum's sake, but excused myself to go to the loo, where I sobbed a while without feeling guilty or weak, before going back to join Mrs. Coggins. It seemed as if we were there ages, hours and hours, but in fact it was only fortyfive minutes until Mum came out, carrying an envelope and a grey plastic bag.

"Let's get out of here. How about a nice cup of tea in the Cottage Tea Rooms, with one of their lovely scones, or a cake. I just need to cheer myself up. Ernest and I often went in there to cheer ourselves up if we were fed up and it would cheer me up today. Plus, I haven't had anything other than half a bowl of porridge since morning, and if we are lucky they might still be serving food. I fancy a poached egg on toast. What about you two?"

We all agreed it would be a nice thing to do, so we set off for the tea rooms and this time Mum sat in the front. But before we left, she got out of the car, went over to one of those great big bins and chucked in the grey plastic bag. We said nothing, but we just looked at each other, me and Mrs Coggins. It was just what Mum had to do. Then we set off. It was funny sitting there having poached eggs on toast and a cake, but when I looked at Mum, it was as if she was sitting there with Dad, all calm and serene. It really came home to me how much they loved each other, despite their bickering, how deep their connection was and how he was there, holding her together, through this time.

We got back later that afternoon, it was already dark and frosty, being surprisingly cold for early December. Mum thanked Mrs Coggins and they hugged, then we both said goodbye and went back indoors. We put the fire on in the sitting room and sat on the sofa together in the dark for a while. It was Friday – we always had fish and chips on Friday, but Mum was in no mood to cook and neither of us were very hungry, but I offered to go round to the fish and chip shop anyway and get something for both of us.

When I got back Mum was on the phone to Veronica, who had my now calmed down and was sorry for earlier. She was coming down on her own on the train on Monday. Mum was trying to put her off, but to no avail, so she gave in.

"She's not just coming down to see me, there's something up that she's not telling me. Ah well, I suppose I will find out sooner or later. I just hope she has not got a bun in the oven for that husband of hers. Not that I don't want her to have kids – just not for him. She'll never get rid of him if she does. Now, let me have a little bit of that fish and chips and then I think I want to go to bed. Do you want to sleep the little room tonight Jen? I'll make you up a hot water bottle and put the fire on in there for you if you do. You know how it gets perishing cold in there."

I nodded and went to put her supper on a plate, which she ate quietly.

"Mum, is there anything you want me to do tomorrow – you know like washing or cleaning or shopping, especially as Veronica is coming?"

"No, leave all that for Veronica –it will keep her occupied. Tomorrow, I would like to go through the funeral plans with you. Can you get the time off work? I would appreciate of you were here the day before and went back the day after. Would that be all right?"

I said that would all be fine and that I had booked leave to the end of the week. "Can we look at old photos tomorrow?"

"That's exactly what I had in mind. And another little trip to the Cottage. I feel like your Dad is there with me."

I smiled. "Mum, may I make a phone call when you have gone to bed?"

'Of course – to your young man is it? Is he a coloured boy? To be honest Jen I don't care what colour he is. Life's too short. I've learned that."

"Well, he's not exactly my young man, but I think he would like to be. I will tell you about him in the morning."

After Mum went to Bed, I tried to call Leroy, but he was not in, so I rang Marvalette to tell her what had happened. She was genuinely sorry to hear my news and asked if she could do anything for me. I said just to be my friend again, like before, to which she answered we would always be friends. We talked a while about how Aaron was and about how Norman's case was getting on, but I was not taking it all in. I told her about the flat, about Francis and about the very keen Mr Leroy. I said I wanted to invite her and the family over for dinner one Sunday, but probably after the funeral. She said she'd hold me to that and then went on to tell me about Bev being pregnant again, and more fool her, and about Jemma having seen Marcia, who was looking better than the last time she saw her. I hoped this would not go into a conversation about Gregory, so to avoid it, I said I heard my Mum calling me and that I had to go. I tried Leroy one more time, and this time he was home. We talked for a while and I said he could come round Monday after work and we could have dinner. Then I thought I ought to call Cora, but it was getting late, so I put it back for the next day.

151

Then I too crawled upstairs, tired and drained, and went to bed in my old bed that was now in the little room – or guest room. It was warm and cosy and before long I was fast asleep.

Chapter 21   Leaving Mum

I woke up early the next day and Mum was already downstairs so I told her I needed to go home tomorow as I had some jobs to do and prepare for work again for the following week. Veronica was coming in a couple of days so she would not be on her own. I had slept better the previous night but Mum looked awful. I could tell she had not slept well.

"Mum, why don't you go back to bed. I'll bring you up some tea and porridge. We don't have to be at the Undertakers til two this afternoon."

"That's nice of you, dear; I had a terrible night. I just can't sleep. I seems so strange to be in the bed without him. Everytime I hear the floorboards creak when you walk about, I think it's him and that he's going to open the bedroom door and hop into bed. He was so warm to hold. I felt so secure, safe, you know, when I was in his arms. Any troubles I ever had just dissolved when I lay in the warmth of his arms. Oh Jen. I miss your Dad so much. Oh, why did you have to up and die, you silly old bugger." Mum looked up to the heavens and shook her fist, not angrily, but just to get it out of her system.

"I expect he feels bad about going too. He probably misses being cuddled up to you, as well! Come on, get yourself back upstairs. I will come up in a mo with breakfast and we will both have it in your room."

Mum pulled herself out of the chair and slowly dragged herself upstairs. I went to make us both breakfast and took it up to her. She was holding his pyjama shirt, smelling it and sobbing. I put the tray down and held her while she let it all out. She seemed to be coping ok yesterday but today was another matter. Perhaps Father O'Malley was right after all.

"Shall I cancel the Undertaker appointment and remake it for next week?"

"No love. I'll be all right in a bit. I'd rather go there with you than Veronica. It will be all her histrionics next week, I'll bet. I'd be better going with you. You're so calm. You take after your Dad."

"Why don't I get the old photos out then and I can hop in next to you and we can look at them together."

"Yes. Let's do that. Now, where's that tea?"

We had breakfast and spent the rest of the morning in bed looking at old photos. They were all in bags – my Mum liked to have them all organized. I picked up each bag and held it up.

152

"Which ones shall we look at first then? Take your pick. Ernest growing up. The McKays. Vi Growing up. The Corbetts. The girls. Holidays 1962, 1964, 1966, 1968. Misc."

We started with Dad, then Mum when they were young, before they got married, then us as a family. And there before us, on the eiderdown, was spread out their entire lives. And us as a family too, with Veronica and I as babies and little girls. Then we looked at the extended family. Mum told me old family stories – there was even a picture of the old house in Dollis Hill, in Chapter Road. I wondered who lived there now. "Coloureds or Irish, I expect," said Mum, but I said nothing in reply. This reminded Mum of who we needed to invite to the funeral. I went to get paper and pen and she called out names and I made a list. Then it occurred to me that the phone had been very quiet; neither had Mum made many calls.

"Isn't it about time we started telling people, like Auntie Ada and Uncle Bert, and your cousins, as well as Dad's workmates and friends from his club?"

"Yes love. That will be a job for Veronica."

"Fair enough. But isn't it leaving it a bit late? It will be almost a week by then. Why don't you let me make a few phone calls? Dad's side of the family at least will be upset if they are told a week late. Plus his work, so they can send you on any wages outstanding."

"No love, I'll do it. You are right. I need to make all these calls. I just can't face people saying how sorry they are and having to tell the whole story over and over, but I suppose it's got to be done. If you do a bit of tidying up, I'll do the nearest and dearest, his workplace and his club. I'll only have to call them all again when I get the funeral date sorted out. What I would like you to help me with is the wake after the funeral. But we will sort that out next week. Basically, your Dad wanted to be cremated and the ashes scattered in the crematorium, where mine will go too. I am sure Dad's club will let us use their hall and they will put on a nice spread for us, take all the strain off me. I tell you one thing. I'm not having the bloody coffin in here; it can stay at the undertakers. Makes me shiver that does, but some of the older ones, they like all that. Curtains drawn for days, all the drama, feathered horses and carts, but we will have the cars and none of that Victorian malarky."

"Mum, you are funny. You seem to have cheered up a bit, so let's get cracking. I will help with whatever you need. And Mum, why don't you try sleeping in the back room? I can make one of the beds up in there and maybe it might help you sleep?"

"I don't know if that will help. I get a bit of comfort being in our bed that we shared for almost thirty years, but it also has too many of the memories. Tell you what. Make a bed up for me and I will see how I feel."

I started to tidy and do the chores for Mum while she got dressed and started on her calls while I got myself ready. Mrs Coggins popped in and asked if we needed a lift into the town center. As it was a twenty-minute walk, Mum accepted the offer, but told her not to hang around for us and that we would find our own way back. Mrs Coggins came back at half past one and dropped us at the Undertakers. Mum did all the paperwork with them and they discussed the funeral arrangements, hymns, readings and all that sort of stuff, although we still had to discuss all that with Father O'Malley. We came out at half past three and Mum said that while there was a bit of time left why not go into Mallory's (the dress shop) and look for something for the funeral and would she like me to buy something. I told her I had a black cat suit, but she said that was not suitable and I needed a black skirt, not one that was 'half-way up my backside' either as my Dad would have said, and a black top.

"That's kind of you to offer, but please nothing from Mallory's. There's a Chelsea Girl and a Dorothy Perkins in Harrow and I could pop down there tomorrow. Their stuff is more my style."

Mum laughed and said she would come with me. As it was, there was nothing Mum liked in Mallory's – it was all a bit old fashioned, even by her standards.

"Actually, Harrow does have more choice. There's a Marks and a Debenhams and that other store – what's its name? Anyway. It's the whole outfit we need. Shoes, hat, bag, coat, so we will be bound to get kitted out there and we can pop down to Wembley if we can't find anything in Harrow."

"Or there's Watford, if you really want to spree." I said laughing.

"Well, it will cheer us up a bit. And I want us to look really nice – all of us, Veronica too, I'll be treating her as well. He's only going to have one send off and I want to do him proud. Dad often took me to Debenhams to treat me to something nice. We'll go shopping early and come back to do more blimmin' phone calls before you go off – when was it Saturday or Sunday? Why not go Sunday morning?"

When Mum spoke in this more upbeat way it was when she was remembering things they used to do together that made them happy and it was as if she sensed being with her, encouraging her, holding her together. I agreed to stay til Sunday.

'That's good. I will call us a taxi to take us to the station; we can get the train to Wealdstone and hop on a bus from there. I tell you, the sooner I move from that house back to civilization and a decent bus service the better. Ooh. Look, there's the Estate Agent."

Before you could say "house for sale" Mum was through the door and sitting on the chair talking to the agent. It seemed that he knew her as she and Dad had been in a few weeks back to get details of flats.

"My husband's passed now, Mr. Patel. Just the other day. And I want to put the house up for sale. This is my daughter, Jenifer, by the way."

154

I shook Mr. Patel's hand and sort of stared vacantly about while he and Mum discussed the details of the sale of our house. Mum told him when to call, nice and early, just to get him in and out before Veronica arrived. I chuckled to myself. Certainly the sight of Mr. Patel measuring up our house would send Veronica into what Mum called histrionics, so this was the best thing to do. Mum said she wanted no viewings until after the funeral, but she wanted to get the ball rolling. Mr Patel assured her that he understood; then he went to a drawer in a tall filing cabinet and came out with some sheets of paper with details of some two bedroomed properties that had just come on the market.

"Thank you Mr Patel. We must rush now as our bus is due in fifteen minutes. I will see you next week, as arranged. Bye for now."

Mr Patel said goodbye as Mum and I turned to leave to get our bus back to the roundabout – we still had a five-minute walk from there, but that was nothing. It took us past the corner shop and Mum went in to get a frozen chicken pie, some frozen peas and a few potatoes.

"It will do for tonight," she said almost excusing the fact that it was not a home-made pie, like she used to make. I said it didn't matter and we could pick up a couple of chops and some veg on our way back from Harrow on Saturday.

So that night, after getting through part two of the phone list, we had our chicken pie, then Mum went to bed in the back room, I called Cora for a brief chat and then read the details for the properties, imagining what they would be like before I went to bed myself.

Mum slept much better and we were both up and out by half past eight in the morning to make our way to Harrow, getting there an hour later before it got busy. It was one of those days when shopping went perfectly. Debenhams had everything we needed. We both found a black dress each, black shoes, a black coat and a new handbag. Mum didn't fuss over my choices and I found myself not complaining that her choices were old fashioned although we did disagree over hats – I hate them, but in the end I settled for a beret, that Mum accepted as being 'nifty.'

We picked up our chops from the butcher and did a small bit of grocery shopping, then laden to the hilt, we headed back home, arriving exhausted, but satisfied at least. Mum set to on stage three of the list while I cooked our chops. I did them like she liked them, resisting the temptation to do them any differently. Shh! Don't mention garlic to my Mum!!

That evening we curled up on the sofa together and discussed the funeral plan and the properties. We also went through part four of the list – that was the insurance company, companies that Dad had subscriptions or memberships with plus the pension people. Mum said she would do all that next week after Mr. Patel had gone and before Veronica got there. Then that just left sorting out the date with Father O'Malley and the Undertakers and then Mum said she could relax and let Veronica get on with letting people know the funeral date and tying stuff up in that department.

That night, Mum went back into her room and I could hear her sobbing while I was on the phone to Cora.

"Don't worry yourself too much about her crying. It's natural and she needs to do it. She has lost a dear husband and she will feel grief for a while to come. What about you Jen?"

It was at that moment that I realised that I had been bottling things up so as to be strong for Mum, but to Cora I let out my feelings, how much I missed Dad, how I forgave him his silly attitudes and remembered him for the lovely times. Cora asked me what time I would be home the next day and said she would get Denison to drop her over to me for an hour or so that afternoon. Bless her; she knew my grief was buried in me and wanted to help me cope with it, allowing me to lean on her and I was so grateful. Before I finally went to bed I called Leroy. He was at home – surprisingly for him at the we ekend– but he said he wanted to wait in for my call and would see me Sunday evening if that was Ok.

Before I went to my bed in the little room, I checked on Mum – she was not in her bed. I panicked a bit, then checked the back room. She was there, fast asleep.

Chapter 22   Friendship

I said my goodbyes to Mum in the morning and left with all that I came with, and more. Mum seemed Ok today, so I was not too worried and I said I would call her when I got home – if the phone box was working! As I walked away to begin the twenty-minute walk to Oxey Station I thought about the last few days. I had certainly bonded deeper with Mum than in a very long time. Perhaps it was because at this moment in time she needed me, so let her guard down and I wondered would it have been the same between us if Dad had not died, or for that matter, what she might be like with me in a few months time when things had settled. Perhaps, I should stop worrying and just be as positive and supportive as I could. But there was something about the rift between us in the past that made me doubt her and not trust her. Maybe she felt the same about me? Anyway, only time would tell if this would be a true re-bonding of mother and daughter. I would try my best anyway.

The other thing that was coming through to me was that through being so involved with Mum over the past few days, attending to her, supporting her grief, I had not really allowed mine to surface. I was beginning to feel that I might be cold, that I had no grief or sorrow that was more than skin deep. But now I was approaching home, on my own, feelings were beginning to flood into me. On more than one occasion I felt tears coming to my eyes – I just wanted to get home as quickly as possible so that I could let it out and feel my grief.

I got back to Westbourne Park Station about two o'clock and decided to walk from there. I was a sharply cold afternoon, dull grey sky and maybe cold enough to snow. I hoped not! As I was walking down Ledbury Road, I heard a voice behind me.

"So Jenifer, you still walkin' de streets? Hah! Where yu fren' now?"

My blood chilled. It was Gregory. Ok. Jenifer. This is the moment you have been dreading. You have to face him out. Go! I did not slow down my pace, but kept walking, trying to give him the brush off.

"Hi Gregory. Look. Just leave me alone. My Dad died the other day and I just want to be left alone. OK?"

"Oh. So sorry, I am so sorry. Oh poor Jenifer's Daddy died."

Sarcastic bastard. I just carried on walking. Not to be put off, he followed me. I began to think about what happened to Marcia and Liz and was worried he would follow me home and push his way in and worse.

I thought of going up to Jemma's in Powis Square but thought against that in case that opened cans of worms and, anyway, it just was not a good idea. Who could I call? I dived into the nearest phone box, praying that it was working and that I had the right change in my bag. Luck was on my side for once so next was to call Leroy – I knew his number by heart – and hope he would be in. He was. I told him what was happening and he said he would drive over and meet me outside the house in twenty minutes. I was relieved yet petrified of what might happen in the next twenty minutes. My heart was beating like crazy. Gregory was on the other side of the road. I came out of the phone box and he started following me, calling out from the other side of the road.

"So. You a call out de cavalry? Call fe back up? Yu 'fraid o' somet'ing? Nah me?"

I stopped walking.

"Gregory, I am not afraid of you. I just had to make a call to let my friend know when I will be home. What do you want with me, anyway?"

He came over the road to me. I was afraid but assumed he could do little in the middle of the street.

"What me wan' wid yu? What me wan' wid yu? Like yu ent know?"

"This is what I know, Gregory. I came home to the flat and found my friend battered and raped and the place in a state. She tells me you raped and beat her. I took her to hospital. She said she did not want the police involved but the hospital called them. I came home and cleaned up her room so that we could swap rooms around so she did not have to go into the same room when she came home. But her Mum came and took her home. They know about you because her Dad knows

157

Big Dave and they are all mates with big wigs in West End Police, so they want to get you for what you did. I have not been called as a witness because they think I am a liability. Don't ask me why. Liz's Mum thought I was getting rid of the evidence to protect you. As if! I just didn't think. I thought I was helping Liz. Other than that, I don't see Liz anymore and I don't care what happens to either of you. It's not my business."

"Ok, Ok, Ok. De t'ing is. It was never me rape nar beat Liz. I drop she home and some man musta follow she in. The whole o' dem frame I and through yu and' yu debil works, me lose support from my community. Dat is my beef wid yu. Seen? And yu haffe pay!"

As he said this he gave a me one of his leering grins.

"No-one can say if 'is me rape an' beat Liz and if some foolish gyal a clean up de evidence, me gaan clear. Dem fit me up, dem beat me up and you, you wid you big mout' did pull back all my support and even me good good solicitor did a drop me case. So, you howes me, Miss Jenifer."

With that he made as if he was pulling a knife across his throat as if to say I had better look out. I was minutes away from home and wanted to get there soon where Leroy would be waiting and I could feel safe. But Gregory had more to say.

'Me know where yu stay. 164 Westbourne Grove. De 'ol whore 'ouse. Me know it well. Me used to look after old man Feltz, collec' 'im rents and look after de gyal dem. But since he die, de young bwoy, de son, 'im a clean up and in walks you, right into my web, said the spider to the fly. But me have every key to dat house, and me know 'ow to get into any window, especially the one pon' de firs' floor. Yes. Yu' fraid now. You wants to be."

"Thank you for telling me that. I'll be getting along now. Goodbye."

I walked off, wondering if he was following me. I heard him suck his teeth and laugh, but I did not turn back. I turned into Artesian Road and then into Needham Road, which was where Leroy usually parked his van and hoped I would see him. No van was in sight. Maybe he was on the main road, but no. Oh, Leroy, where are you when I need you, I was thinking. Anyway I might as well dive into the phone box and call Mum, which I did, telling her I was safely home and that I would call on Monday when she had the date set for the funeral. When I came out of the phone box, Gregory was nowhere to be seen, and still no Leroy. Oh well.

I ran up the front steps and got into my place as soon as I could. What Gregory said about that house and Mr Feltz was now sinking in. Maybe that's what he meant by being an accountant! Collecting rents – with menace no doubt - and controlling prostitutes in that very house - the very apartment, no less, that I am in.

I was terrified. I locked the door and double checked that I had locked every singe window, working out how anyone could get in. I would have to talk to Denison to get better security. I was not leaving that flat after all the work I had put into it, so Gregory and his threats to get lost. I made myself some tea, trembling as I did so, trying to compose myself by putting on some music – oh how I had missed my sounds – and putting my stuff away.

I checked the time. It was two thirty. The door rang. I looked through the window, hoping to see Leroy, but it was Cora and Denison. Even better! I let them in and, at that point, burst into tears. Cora had brought me some dinner and a few groceries as I had not been home for a few days. In fact, I had meant to pick up some stuff from the Everopen store but forgot in my haste to get home.

I blurted out all the stuff about being followed by Gregory, forgetting that Cora and Denison did not know the whole story. I just said that I was afraid he could get in, so Denison took a look around and said he could put in better window locks and some limit catches to help make me more secure.

"I 'ave to say, though, Jen, if a man's got a mind to break in, there ain't much you can do to stop him breakin' a winda but you can try to make things a bit difficult along the way. What a shame, eh love, and you got this place so nice and trendy like. I'll pop round tomorrow after work and fix a few locks for you, but I will leave you an' Cora for a bit. What time do ya want me to pick you up, love? "

"About five, dear, if that's ok. If that's all right with you too, Jen?"

I said it was fine. I also said it was freezing cold and I hadn't yet put the fire on and how we were all standing there in our jackets, freezing cold.

"An' tha's another thing. Them winda's are rattly and draughty. I'll get you a bit o' draught excluder. It don't make much diff'rence, mind, but it'll 'elp tone it down."

"It's perishing, as my Dad would say."

"'An 'e weren't wrong and tha's a fact!!" laughed Denison

We all laughed with him as I put on the heaters in both rooms and even put the oven and burners on for a few minutes to get the heat going, suddenly remembering I needed to check the gas meter and make sure I had enough coins and thankfully I had a couple of fifty pence pieces that would keep me going for a couple of days, at least.

Denison said goodbye and left Cora and I to put away the things she had brought me and we heated up the food she had cooked. I laid the table and even had a candle for the center.

"I should be cooking for you," I said as we sat down to eat.

"Plenty of time for that. Now start from the front. Tell me all about what happened with your Dad. I am so sorry to hear that he died. How old was he – too young to go, too young to go. I am very sorry Jen."

159

I told her a bit about what happened, but I was still holding back tears. I wanted to eat my dinner. It seems a daft thing to say, like I was planning when it would be convenient for me to cry. After dinner, over a cup of tea! But tears got the better of me and at long last it all came flooding out and I was so glad Cora was there. I told her how things were better with me and Mum, but how I was worried that it would not last.

"Jen, it sounds to me like your Mum was glad of you. You are calm and kind. And that's what your Mum needs right now and she won't forget that. You were there for her, not the other way round, like it is with your sister."

"And her histrionics, as my Mum calls it. I never realised how much she got on Mum's nerves. I thought she was Mum's favourite as she was older than me and they used to gang up on me together. I hope that does not start again at the funeral. Families eh?"

"Well, all families have ups and downs but that's part of life. We have to learn how to cope and do the best we can, not letting petty things get to us. If we always face things with the best mind, usually people respond the same way. If you are miserable, you will make people miserable with you back. So keep being positive, calm and kind and I am sure everything will be fine with you and your Mum."

Cora led me to the sofa and told me to sit there with a blanket round me while she washed up. It was as if she was giving me the mothering that my Mum could not in her grieving time. I was ever grateful to Cora for her kindness. I was just dozing when the bell rang. Cora looked out of the window.

"Oh, It's Marvalette and Norman, with Aaron. I told them about your Dad and that I would be here, so they said they would pass by." Deep down, I was sad it was not Leroy, but I was glad to see them, nonetheless.

"Jen, Jen, how are you lovie? Me sarry fe 'ear 'bout yu Daddy. We brought you some t'ings. You know it's kinda traditional when somebody dies to bring food an' ting."

"Well," said Norman, "is Marvalette bring de food and me bring de t'ing! Sorry to hear bout your loss Jen. Is a 'ard t'ing to lose a fadder."

We all hugged, the biggest hug of all came from Aaron though, who had made me a card with a picture of a black angel on it and a heavenly sky.

"Dear Jen I am sorry that your Dad died. I hope he goes to heven and has a nice time there. Xxx From Aaron. I love you."

I was touched and said I hoped he was happy in heaven too. Then I shed a few more tears and sat down again letting Cora and Marvalette organize the kitchen. Cora said we had just eaten, so Marvalette said the food she had brought would

160

stay for a few days in the fridge, but she had also brought some cake and fruit. At this rate I would not need to shop for a week!

"Look like y'ave some post too," said Marvalette handing me a wodge of letters, most of which seemed like junk, but there was a letter from the GPO saying the engineer called and could come again on Monday. Yippee, I would be on the phone!

"Dis a nice likkle set yu 'ave 'ere, Jen" said Norman looking at the my record player.

"Yes, there's some new music there too. Leroy brought me a couple of new tunes, and an album, but I have not had time – or money lately. But feel free to play some sounds."

"Yeah, an' don't bother putting de music louder dan we talkin'" said Marvalette, joking with Norman, knowing he had a fondness for volume.

"No, No, is jus' so me go play – ok?"

"That's great." I added, "So what do you think of my pad then – go look in the bedroom."

'Oh it's nice. You did all this? How you get the whole place furnish so fas'?"

"Well Cora gave me some stuff and I got other bits from second-hand shops, except the bed, I painted stuff and Leroy helped as well as Denison, who showed me how to do it, and I bought a sewing machine and made stuff too."

"Whoah, girl, you have ideas galore hee? Yu mus' come fe do we interior design when we move!"

"So, Marvalette, have you found somewhere or do you just mean, like, later on when you find somewhere."

"No, love, we are on the move!" Marvalette wiggled in her chair as she said it. "We decided not to let Babylon interfere wid our plans. We have found a place in Kensal Rise, like we said. It's a little two-bedroom house with a sittin' room an' a dinin' kitchen – kitchen diner as you say."

"Wow. That's' great news. When do you move?"

"Well. Is early days yet. We get a margage agree and we jus' now doin' de legal side," added Norman, also pleased with what was happening. I noted they had found a smaller property, I assumed cheaper, which would make it more manageable for them.

"I bet you are wondering how we can afford to do that innit, what with Norm's case coming up. Yes, they are doing him for obstruction as it would be easier, so they think, to get a conviction, but we are not that easy!! But back to the house. I had a turn up for the book as you English say!! My stepdad (the bastard) died, leaving everything to my Mum. She got a lawyer to find me and has given me half the money for the house. She gave me five grand!! I reckon it was to ease her guilt about putting me in care, but she's ill, too, and quite alone. My brudders will have nuttin' to do wid her and I don't know how things really stay wid my younger 'alf brudder. But me nah jus' tek she dunzie and run – me keepin' in touch, so me go fin' out. So it looks like bot' o'we find we mudders again."

"And both of us lost our fathers. I can imagine now how it must have felt when your Dad died when you were a kid. At least I am older and he was there for me through my childhood. He was a good Dad really. I just wish he did not have those shitty attitudes. Let's try to make the best, then, of our relationship with our Mothers."

"That's right," joined in Cora. "I lost my Mother and Father and I miss my Mother every day, so if you can pull it together with your Mum, it can only be a good thing."

We carried on like this talking about our mothers while Norman and Aaron were playing music – quietly – then they went over the road to get some cold drinks from the Everopen store.

While Aaron was out of the way, I asked about the case and if there was any news. Marvalette said there was a date set for June next year and that the solicitor was good and she was sure they would all get off. It was very clear that the whole thing was provoked by the police. They had photos of police attacking them with truncheons, and of white residents waving their fists and shouting at the marchers. It was clear the police caused the trouble, but they would back each other up and try to set up the marchers. The Guardian newspaper had run a few articles and publicity for the cause was gaining.

"Well, I just hope Norman gets off. It makes you sick to think he could get a conviction while that bastard Gregory gets off scott free."

I then told them what happened and Marvalette said I should leave that flat if anything dodgy was going on. I said that I didn't think that the young Mr Feltz would want to employ Gregory nor let the house turn into a 'whore house', but I was afraid that Gregory was out to get me.

Cora told Marvalette that Denison was going to help me make the locks more secure.

"And help get rid of that perishing draught," I added.

Norman and Aaron arrived back with some Top Pops and some orange juice – he knew how I hated those fizzy things – and we poured drinks and Norman rolled a spliff. They didn't mind about smoking in front of Aaron – but I opened the window a tad to clear the air – it was only me and he smoking – as Marvalette declined. Strange, I thought.

The door went again – surely not Francis – I had given up hope of Leroy, but to my surprise, Leroy was indeed at the door, carrying a big bunch of flowers. To soften me up – I could have been murdered in the time it had taken him to get here!

I asked Norman to let him in – he was surprised to see a full room! Cora took him to one side and explained that they had all come round to see me to see how I was after Dad dying and that I had told them about being followed by Gregory and what he had said – and where was he?

Leroy came over to me and handed me the flowers. He was clearly agitated and very sorry. The van had broken down and he had to fix it before he could get here. I accepted the flowers and the apology and asked if he wanted some food. Cora, got up and fixed him a plateful while we sat there talking. And the doorbell went again – Denison coming back for Cora, making it a full house of all my friends. I wanted Mum to meet them soon.

Cora and Denison left, as did Norman, Marvalette and Aaron, leaving Leroy and me together, talking about the Gregory incident. It was getting late and I half wanted Leroy to stay, but I was not ready yet to sleep with him. It also made me aware of the fact that I was not on the pill, nor did I have a GP yet round here, so that would have to be sorted out. I knew Leroy was wondering whether he should make a move, so I just came out with my answer before he asked the question.

"Leroy, don't think that this gets you into my bed. But I appreciate deeply what you have done for me. We do have a date to keep and a dance to go to, but that's it. OK?"

"Awhoah. Yu can be on de nail – eeeh? Yes, man, but we mus' talk. For now me jus' a seh dat me like yu big time, Jen. Yu is all I t'ink 'bout. But is up to you, so if is time yu wan' tek, den lewwe tek time."

"I like you too Leroy. You have shown me your character, your kindness and helpfulness and I know you are a hard worker and you have ambition. I like that about you, but right now I am not interested in a relationship with you. Right now I need some time – I need to get over my Dad's death and get my life settled.

Leroy laughed and got his coat, ready to go. We hugged, but I refused a snog as I did not want to be tempted – and I was, believe me!

But when he had gone, and I had finished tidying up, I began to wish he had stayed as I was afraid in the flat after Gregory's threats. I also did not feel I was ready to go back to work and as the GPO man was coming the next day I thought I would call in work and ask for another day's leave. I started to sing along to a John Holt song:

Take my hands
I'm a stranger, but I love you
Hold me, don't be scared
I need you right now.

I'm glad that I met you
This is the start of something new
Come to me, oh please
'Cause I need you right now.[xi]

I wondered, indeed if this was to be the start of something new – and did I really know what I was doing. Was Leroy on the level, or just charming me and possibly leaving me high and dry like last time? I would have to see and take things SLOWLY, Jenifer. Got that? SLOWLY, I said to myself again.

23   The Surprise

I hardly slept at all that night, panicking at the slightest sound and so wishing I was not alone. I got to sleep eventually and woke in one piece, thankfully! I rushed about getting myself ready and nipped out to call work. Francis put his head out of the window and called out to me.

'I am broken hearted, Jenifer! You got back yesterday and did not call into see me. How's things with you?"

"Sorry Francis. A lot was going on yesterday. The GPO are coming today to fix the phone and I hardly slept last night. Can I pop down later this evening and I will fill you in on what's been going on."

"Sure, sure, my little poppet, just make sure you don't leave Francis out of the details!!"

I laughed and waved him goodbye. Later on that morning I saw GPO van pull up outside. I nearly died when I saw who got out of it. It was Benjamin. Please not coming here. I felt my stomach churn, then butterflies and he sprang lightly up the front steps. Oh well, at least I was getting a phone and it was not Gregory!!

I opened the door and saw a look of surprise on his face to equal that of mine!

"The lady of the house, I presume?"

"Indeed. The man from the GPO, I presume!" I replied. "Come in."

"Wow. Nice place. Renting furnished?"

"No, unfurnished, and I put it all together myself. Only been here a couple of weeks, but I love it. I can walk to work and get to the market. So I am happy. Would you like some tea? Toast?"

Benjamin was clearly taken aback by how nicely I was set up here and he looked a bit uncomfortable. Good. I asked after his girlfriend. I had forgotten her name, only that she was Maggie's sister, the one with the miserable face, although I didn't tell him I thought that.

"Valerie," he said. "Yeah, she's Ok. And you? Any man in tow? Not that creep Crab-I?" he laughed – seemingly at me.

'No, I am not taken by anyone at the moment. And a good job too. I have a lot on my plate at the moment, Benjamin. The first call I will be making on this phone is to my Mum to find out the date of my Dad's funeral."

"Oh – I didn't realise. I am so sorry to hear that he died. But I thought you two did not get on, on account of you going out with me?"

"Yes but that's water under the bridge now."

"So how are you coping? You OK with your mum these days? I seem to remember you fell out with your family big time when they found out you were going out with me."

"Like I said, Benjamin, water under the bridge. I've just come from her place and we are fine, more than I expected even."

"Do you see anything of Liz?"

"No. Not these days. Not after what happened. Have you seen her at all?"

"No – but what happened?"

"Oh Liz got herself in big trouble and I am implicated, but I don't want to talk about that now. It's a long story and I would just rather cope with my Dad's funeral right now. Do you want me to put on some music?"

"What and slip into something more comfortable?"

"No – but if that's how you are going to be I won't put any music on."

"Oh Miss uppity customer. If that's how you are going to be I won't fix your phone."

"You have to. It's your job."

'So what's your job then?"

"Same as before. Working in the nursery. I just have got today off."

"Oh. Well you know what used to go on in these houses years ago, don't you? I thought my luck was in when I got the ticket to come here."

'What? You thought you'd struck it lucky to land a two-bit prozzie, is that what you mean? God Benjamin, give me a break. My Dad has just died and I am not in the mood for your flirty dirty jokes."

"Sorry. I'm just being flippant. Don't take me seriously. I am really sorry that your Dad died.

'Don't worry Benjamin. I will never take you seriously again. I got into trouble with that before."

I put some music on and Benjamin got on with pulling out bits of wire, clipping bits off and leaving little bits of brightly coloured wires on the floor. I left him to carry on for a bit while I did a few chores.

"You know Jen, there's a bit of a problem here. I'm afraid it's not a straightforward reconnection. What I am supposed to do is go back and get them to book it out as a re-wire, but that will cost you more, so I am just going to put in a new wire for you. Some of these cables are buggered and need replacing, that's why I can't get a connection."

'Thanks Benjamin, I appreciate that. Would you like some lunch? I have a load of food here. Cora and Marvalette brought me food over yesterday when I got back from Mum's. There's loads. Would you like some?"

"Erm..well, what do you have? You know I'm not a roast beef and cabbage person."

"No, it's West Indian food – fried fish, fried dumplings, plantain, chicken and rice and peas – oh and some banana bread."

"You eat all that stuff? Yes please. Chicken and rice and peas then please."

'I not only eat it but Marvalette and Cora have taught me to cook it as well, but this is their hand today. It was nice of them to think of me." I heated the food up for Benjamin and had a small bit for myself.

"Oh, maybe I should taste your hand one day then." He took my hand and made out as if he was eating it. Then he kissed it.

He was, I knew, only gently flirting, but a feeling like 1000 volts of electricity went through me and I flushed hot, surely going red in the face. I walked away to hide my face and got him some juice.

"So when did you give up being a postman and change to this job?"

"About six months ago. The postman hours are ridiculous for a man who likes his bed in the morning and this is more money. Plus they send you on lots of training and you can work your way up."

"I bet you like that. Working your way up?"

Benjamin laughed. He was always up for a silly joke and love messing about with double entendres.

"Oho! Trying to beat me at my own game? But yes, and plenty of opportunity to get the ladies all wired up for a ding a ling!"

"Idiot man! Just eat your dinner. What do you think of this record?"

It was the latest Jackie Mittoo. I loved it but it was instrumental and Benjamin said he preferred vocals so I changed it to a Pat Kelly, which was one we used to dance to. Stupid me, I thought as it started to play. Why did I have to choose this one?

"Madam, may I have this dance?" He held his hand out to a cushion. Then took the cushion in his arms and danced with it. Making the cushion say inane female things while he chatted it up.

I laughed but was not prepared for him to then put the cushion back and hold out his hand to me. I was barely aware of walking over to him and accepting his invitation, folding myself into his arms as he began to rock me to the music. As Pat Kelly sang something just came over me. When he held me, I felt transported back months to the night we went to a dance in Brixton and we stayed at his sisters and made love for the first time.

'Kiss me each morning for a million years
Hold me each evening at your side
Tell me you love me for a million years
and if it don't work out
then if it don't work out
then you can tell me goodbye.

Sweeten my coffee with a morning kiss
soften my dreams with your sigh
Tell you love me for a million years
And if it don't work out,
then if it don't work out
Then you can tell me goodbye.

Oh but if you must leave without saying goodbye
then it's the right time to say it now.

But of you must go I won't tell you no
So we can say that we tried
Tell you love me for a million years

167

Then if it don't work out
Then if it don't work out
then you can tell me goodbye.[xii]

It was an old song that we both knew the words of and sang them to each other often, as we did today.

"Was it the right time to leave without saying goodbye?" Benjamin asked me.

"No, you should have stayed to sweeten my coffee with a morning kiss and kissed me each morning for a million years."

"Do you want me to kiss you now?"

"Yes," I muttered weakly and feebly. And he did, long and slow like always before and for a million years that I wanted to feel this kiss for. And before I knew it I was leading him to the bedroom and we lay down still kissing and wanting more. Every feeling I had ever had for Benjamin, my first love who had left me with my first broken heart, was here again, kissing me, moving me, and I began to pull his shirt from his trousers, slipping my hands up his back to feel the velvet smoothness of his skin. Here was I, in a passion impossible to stop, after things were cautiously blossoming with Leroy. And I wasn't even on the pill for God's sake, and here I was about to make love with Benjamin. And as he began to remove my clothes and fondle me in every which place til all I could feel was this need for him, to love him, and please would he come back to me, forget about old miserable face Valerie, and be with me, just me. As he entered me, that emotion poured from me, although the words stayed within and I imagined I heard him say he loved me and he wanted me back and that he would leave old misery face, that I was his love and oh please would he just love me again, just love me again just like in this paradise place of pleasure, for a million years, or would he just tell me goodbye?

Benjamin reached his climax soon, while I was still in deep passion, but I stopped for him, thinking that, like before, he would kiss me again and soon he would be ready for really giving me a long, long loving. But he was up and nipping to the bathroom, back in a trice and getting dressed before you could say old misery face. I said nothing and went to the bathroom, washed quickly, straightened my hair, came back, and dressed myself while he was fiddling with my telephone wires.

I went to straighten the bed, deeply regretting what just took place; what a fool I had been. There he was – like nothing had happened, saying

"Well it looks like you wires are in working order Madam and your bell is well and truly rung."

"I think I just made a big mistake there Benjamin. I got carried away with my feelings for you. They all came flooding back and I let you do that to me and I'm not even on the pill. I have been really stupid."

168

"Oh come on Jen. It was just a nice likkle piece of something for old times sake. Nothing to get emotional about. Cos if it don't work out, if it don't work out, then you can tell me goodbye."

"Have you finished with that phone, as I think I would like to tell you goodbye. I was weak and you took advantage of that. My Dad has just died, I've got stuff going on in my life because of that damned Liz, all my emotions for you came up and I lost control. I should not have done that." I didn't know if I wanted to cry or hit him.

Benjamin could see I was serious and even he could see this was now no time for messing about. He came over to me and sat me on the sofa, sitting next to me.

"You know, there was a time when I had feelings for you and I was afraid. I was too young to be getting serious and I didn't know what to do. Then I saw you leave the Night Angel with that other guy and I just thought that was it. It was over. That's why I left you, why you didn't hear from me."

"I was only leaving with him, he put me in a cab - alone. I told you this already - what happened and that and I don't want to go over it now. But I did love you. You were my first real love and when you did that to me I was broken up. Today, I got carried away with memories and I felt that old love surging through me and I thought, stupidly thought, for one foolish moment that you wanted more than just for a quick fumble and I feel so stupid now. And I am angry that you did that to me. Insulted even."

"Look. Your phone's working. This is your number. Don't get on so. I am going now. Don't be upset. Please. It is making me feel bad and I didn't mean to hurt you. I thought you were just up for a frolic. Please don't get emotional over me. I am with Valerie now and we are getting married. She's pregnant."

"Oh, Benjamin. That is rock bottom. Well, Good luck to her. Thanks for fixing the phone. I think you had better go now."

A sheepish looking Benjamin left the flat. And a very worried Jennifer ran a hot bath. I wanted to flush every last drop of his semen out of me and looked around for a plastic bottle that I could squirt inside me with. I found some Dettol and an unused lacquer bottle that I had had for ages. I experimented with the spray, but that did not get inside me, so I took the lid off and filled the bottle with a Dettol solution, lay in the bath and contorted myself into a position to insert the bottle head and give it a powerful enough squeeze to get as much of the fluid inside me as high as possible. I repeated this about six times. Surely that would kill any little sperms floating about. I lay there in the bath sobbing and feeling at my lowest ebb for a long time. I did not want to see Benjamin ever again.

Jeepers. I leapt from the bath. I had not called Mum to find out what was happening. It was still early evening, so I called Mum's number and she answered. Phew, glad it was not Veronica. Mum sounded a bit short with me. Was she stressed, or had she reverted to the old Mum, now that Veronica was there?

"Hi Mum. How are you?" Mum said she was fine, thank you.

"I am calling you from my home phone. It was installed today. Do you have a pen to take the number?" Mum went to get a pen and she took down the number.

"Have you been able to fix a date for the funeral?" Mum said yes and I took the details down. All Saints Church then on to Vicarage Road Cemetery to scatter the ashes and on to the Working Men's Club for the Wake.

"Is everything ok, Mum? You sound a bit short." Mum said she'd had a busy day and was tired. I asked if there was anything I could do and she said no not that she could think of and if she did she would call me.

'Is Veronica with you." Mum said yes she was.

"Everything ok?" Mum said yes, sounding impatient at my questions.

"Ok, well if you need anything, give me a call, otherwise I will see you on the day."

'Right you are, dear. Good-bye then."

I put the phone down and just burst into tears. It felt like two rejections in one day. Just when I was feeling so vulnerable. Benjamin was a dick head, I decided, and I was foolish to have got carried away, but Mum. That was another matter? It was like she really had no time for me.

I remembered I had promised I would pop in on Francis, but I was not in the mood. I went to bed instead – it was only about half past six, but I was exhausted in everyway. Then I remembered that Denison said he was coming round to fix the locks for me, so I quickly straightened the place up and got dressed again. I wasn't in the mood, but I figured it was necessary. I called Cora and left her my new number so that Denison could call me back when he came in. When he did call back it was a quarter to nine and was a bit late to come round, so he rearranged it for the next evening. That was a relief and I just went to bed, to sleep away my guilt and embarrassment.

I woke up the next day with that back to work feeling and itching terribly down below. Not all that palava again, please, I thought, but there was no getting away from it. I dug out the leaflet I had been given from the clinic the last time I went there. Itching…..ah yes, possibly thrush. Not sexually transmitted, so that was a relief but I could not ignore it. I had yet to register at a GP locally, as Dr Samuels did not cover this area, and anyway I would like to find another one a little less old fashioned. I checked the times at the clinic and saw that I could go the next evening as they were open late and as I was on earlies that would fit in and then I could have a bit more time finding a doctor to register with. That meant I would also have to rearrange with Denison. I rang Cora before I left and sorted that out.

I also wanted to talk to Mr Feltz about Gregory and what contact he may still have with him. There were lots of questions here. Plus my Mum was on my list as well as popping in to see Francis.

Chapter 24   The Case Conference

As soon as I entered the Nursery to start my shift, Sue called me into the office to brief me as to what had happened in baby room while I was away. We had a new baby settling in – Jasper who was 8 months old. His Mum, Bernadette, was only 17 and she was a single mum. Jasper was mixed race – his Dad was from St Lucia and she was Irish – and her parents had disowned her. Jasper's Dad was not on the scene, or so the social worker said, but Sue was not so sure. Bernadette had been living in a Catholic mother and baby home since she was pregnant and had refused to give the baby up for adoption. Social services came in and told the nuns they could not force her in this day and age so she had been given a one bedroomed flat. She got some money from charities through her social worker to get some essential stuff for it, like a bed, table and chairs and stuff, but it was still pretty bleak, apparently. Sue had done a home visit with her social worker and had seen her place. She had noticed a bottle of men's cologne in the bathroom which made her think there was a man around somewhere, but whether he was Jasper's Dad or not was another matter. But these things had a habit of coming to the surface in time. Bernadette was due to start a college course in January, just basic skills like literacy and numeracy; she wanted to train as a cook, so she needed to get to a basic standard first. I wondered what hope there was for Bernadette and Jasper with such a poor start to life for both of them – she being thrown into adult responsibilities from so early on and he being so vulnerable because of that. Sue wanted me to settle Jasper in and be a support to Bernadette.

Another thing was that there had been an incident involving Janine last week when I was on leave. She usually came into nursery with last night's nappy on and not having had breakfast. Sue was not happy about that and she had spoken to Linda, her Mum, about it. Linda had not responded very well and had not brought Janine into the nursery the next day – or for a few days after that. Bella, another parent, had come into the office and said she had seen Janine being taken to a babyminder who was well known in the area for looking after many children and not being registered with the council. Sue rang social services who went to visit the illegal babyminder, finding Janine sitting on the floor, crying, in a filthy nappy, left with the woman's older children while the childminder was out. The other children did not even know if Janine had eaten or had a bottle. The social worker called Mum at work and she was not there, saying she had left 6 weeks ago, and as they could not find her at home either, they took Janine into emergency care.

Apparently, Linda was found later on, trying to find money for drugs – well, begging, actually. They visited her at home – the place was a mess with nothing in it – not even a cooker, as Linda had been selling everything to pay for heroin. It was a dire situation. Now that I knew what was wrong with Linda, it fell into place why she looked so awful in the mornings when she rushed in to drop Janine and rushed out again. Anyway, there was going to be a case conference and I was to prepare a report for Sue to take along with her; Sue handed me a sheet of paper with what I needed to cover in the report, like how Janine came in every day and what she was like developmentally as well as any observations or comments on Linda. Just when I was meat to write that was anybody's guess. My breaktime, I supposed, as I would be tied down with Jasper and Bernadette for most of the morning.

But, yes, there was more, as Sue said when she saw my eyebrows raise. Ryan's Mum, Faith, was going through a hard time. She had split up with Wilfred and he was making her life difficult, following her and yelling out to her in the street and threatening to kill himself. All of this was in front of the children. Ryan was very anxious, crying a lot, not eating and generally quite stressed. The older girls, Bola and Abi had been behaving badly at school and were wetting the bed. Faith was still trying to keep everything together, going to work every day and now also trying to manage the late night on a Thursday without a childminder. Bola, who was ten, was picking up Ryan and looking after both children until Faith got back at 8.30pm.

Sue said Faith had been in tears, feeling like she was unable to cope, and Faith had to tell her, as gently as she could, that she could not turn a blind eye to Bola collecting Ryan and looking after him and Abi. It was not acceptable, and she explained all the dangers, which Faith acknowledged, but asked what choice did she have? Sue had suggested that she cut her hours and claimed some benefits, or even stopped work altogether for a while until things were straightened out at home and the kids more settled. It was then that Faith told her that she wasn't legal in the country and was not entitled to claim any benefits. Apparently Wilfred had sent her a ticket to come here and told her that she was entitled to stay over her visa as she was married to him. But what he didn't say was that he too was on an extended visa and had overstayed himself. Sue had made a call to various organisations to get immigration advice for Faith who was terrified she would be made to return to Nigeria and her kids taken into care here. She would also try to find a childminder to help her with the kids and was hoping she could get it paid for by social services.

And I thought I had problems! When I told people that I worked in a nursery, they would say "Aw, how cute. That is such a nice job – playing all day with little kids." If only they knew what it was really about. We had hardly been trained for that sort of thing – bit of child development, stuff about recognizing measles and mumps or how to make a book of nursery rhymes. Nothing about all the difficult family stuff we had to deal with. Some of our parents had it so hard. This was just in baby room and there were more families having real difficulties in the other group rooms too, as well as children with emotional and behavioural problems health conditions or disabilities. Within half an hour, the fact that my Dad had died, as well as what had happened with Benjamin and with Gregory, seemed to be a million miles away.

"What's happening about the vacancy for your job, then?"

"Well, it has been advertised internally and Alice has applied as well as another Deputy, but I can't tell you who. The interviews are next week Thursday. "

"Oh, that's the day of my Dad's funeral, and Mum wants me with her the night before and the day after. I can work on the morning before and just have the afternoon as TOIL, but can I have the other two days as leave, please?"

"It's actually Compassionate Leave. You can have 5 days, so if we take off yesterday, last Thursday and Friday, then you can have those two days, but you need to put it in writing for me. How are you coping anyway? How's things with your Mum?"

I told Sue how things were on that front, but I kept it to the minimum, mainly because I was aware of the time and did not want to keep her any longer – we both had work to do, but I was grateful for her concern.

Gabriella was doing breakfast in the baby room; she had been waiting for me and was pleased that I was back after everything that had gone on in the last two weeks. Bernadette had been told to come in at ten, and as Janine was not in we were low on numbers that day. That meant that Jacqui might have to cover in the Tweenie group as Vicky was off. I could see it was going to be a busy week.

The day went fast enough and I left on the dot at 4pm to get to the Clinic to sort out my itching nether regions. As I sat in the waiting room, I reflected on my conversation with Bernadette earlier. She was doing her best, but she was not the brightest in the class, as my Dad would say. She told me what her Mum had said to her when she eventually could hide her pregnancy no longer.

"An' me Mam says to me 'What a disgrace you are, an' all. What do you think the Doctor will think of you when you open your legs and that black thing crawls out? We won't have anything to do with it, me and your Da. You will have to have it adopted, sure you will, for it's not coming into this house.' That's what she said, and they put me into the Catholic mother and baby home. The Nuns, they were ok, but they said I would go to hell for what I had done and that if I wanted my baby to grow up without the taint of my sin I would have to have him adopted. I phoned my Social Worker and she told them they weren't to talk to me like that and that things were different these days. I was determined to keep the baby , so I was. I will be a good Mum, I will."

She was very loving to Jasper, but she said she was dreading when his hair grew 'hard' as she put it, as she didn't know how to manage it. She said he would just have to have a crew cut and freeze in the winter like her brothers did on account of the nits. Gabriella told her not to worry, and that one of us would show her how to comb and plait Jasper's hair. "All in good time," was my response. She fed him well and played with him, enjoying the time with nothing else to do than sit on the floor and amuse him. She talked about her course and her plans for the future. I asked about Jasper's Dad, and she cut the conversation, quickly changing the subject. I wondered how she was managing with getting her flat comfortable and

173

thought I would talk about that the next day. Anyway, my thoughts were interrupted by the Doctor calling my number.

It was the same Doctor as before; he checked my notes and then seemed to recognize me. I wasn't sure if that was a good or bad thing. I told him what had happened and what I had done with the Dettol and now what an itch I had.

"When is your period due?"
"Erm…Friday actually."

"Are you on the pill?"

"No, I came off as I was not in a relationship, but I want to go back on it now. I wanted to wait until I could be with someone that I really like, but I made such a silly mistake with my ex-boyfriend."

"Not the first silly mistake you have made is it? You can't make a habit of silly mistakes, Jenifer. What if you are pregnant? Dettol douching is not a method of birth control, you know, and it's no wonder you have an irritation. However, I will do all the tests anyway as we should rule out other nasties."

I waited for the Nurse to call me into the examination room and from there I went through the same uncomfortable process as before, but I gritted my teeth and just put up with it. I got dressed and waited again to be called in for my results. Thrush was the verdict, nothing else, but I would have to go back for the results of the cultures to make sure. I was given Nystan pessaries and cream.

"What are you going to do about birth control?"

"Well I wanted to find a new GP as I have only just moved, but I am worried a bit as they don't all seem to want to give you the pill if you are not married."

"Have you heard of Family Planning clinics?" asked the doctor. I said that I had not.

"I can give you this leaflet, but make sure you go there and get yourself sorted out. It is quite possible that having sex so late in your cycle will prevent you from being pregnant, but it's not a given and you don't want a recurrence of this. I would also like to say to you that you should not use Dettol in your bath or anywhere near your vagina. It is a very powerful disinfectant, more suited to cleaning floors. Your skin, and your vagina for that matter, is made by nature to ensure there is plenty of good bacteria to do the job of keeping bad bacteria down. Dettol kills the good bacteria, so here you are with thrush. No more disinfectant please Jenifer"

I was not even sure what he meant about 'my cycle' or having sex so late in it, but I did not to want to look an idiot, so I did not ask. I just nodded and took the leaflet, promising not to use Dettol anymore. I didn't dare say my friends all used it – I had got into the habit as Marvalette had recommended it to me. I realised though that I did not know enough about my body and needed to find out more

With my little bag of pessaries and cream in my hand, I left to get the bus back home. I had been waiting ages for the 23 before it occurred to me that I only lived a 15-minute walk away, so I gave up waiting and walked the way home, stopping off to get some food for the week in the Everopen store.

Before I went home, I knocked on Francis door. What a welcome! Hugs and kisses, like I had been gone for a year! He invited me in, told me to put my feet up and made me a cup of tea. I filled him in on my news – well, the shareable bits anyway – and then asked him what he knew about the old Mr Feltz.

"Oh, Jenifer, my sweet innocent, you do not want to know about the old Mr Feltz. The very name makes me shudder. You know what this house was don't you? I got chatting to Mrs ...er, Mrs erm, oh, Mrs Something –or –other, next door. What a carry on. Apparently he had this black guy as his henchman, or so she said."

"Oh Francis, I am not that innocent. I know what this house was before and I do know about the henchman too. The thing is, what is Feltz Jnr's game? Does he follow in his father's footsteps or is he a new broom in truth?"

"No idea, Jenifer. He seems OK and well, you and I are not showing red lights in our windows and we have respectable jobs, so I imagine Feltz Jnr. is more of a new broom than a chip off the old. By the way, you have a new neighbour. Another girl to keep you company. Her name is Anthea. She is a journalist for an alternative magazine. You two will get along just fine."

"Have you given her the once over then?" I asked laughing.

"Well, I just want to know who lives upstairs and I need to make sure you will be OK."

"Francis, I need to tell you that I know the henchman and that he has been threatening me. He is bad news, believe me – his name is Gregory. I can't go in to all the story tonight, but me and Gregory's paths have crossed via a friend and I am afraid, as he said he has keys and can get in any window in the house."

"Ooh. So scary Jenifer. I think that you are safe as far as keys go as Feltz Jnr did say he had all the locks changed. You could put up a bolt, or get a new Chubb lock put in, rather than just your Yale."

"My friend's husband looked at the windows and put a temporary lock, well it was a nail, but he said he would fit some secure window locks for me. He is coming the day after tomorrow."

"Oh you are making me all nervous now, Jenifer. Would he put some in for me?"

"I am sure he will, but he will charge you. But I am also going to have a talk with Feltz about what's going on. Perhaps he will pay for locks on all the windows? I do know that Gregory is dangerous."

'Oh my God. I'll not sleep a wink now. I will have to call my bodyguard friend – big, tall and muscly Italian – quite a show-stopper!"

"Oh Francis, you are incorrigible! Anyway, I've got to go home now and get my dinner. By the way, I have a phone now – here's my number. You can give me a call if you are worried and vice versa. I must go now though as I don't want to miss Denison"

"Well, that's something at least. But don't run up bills for the phone, where a visit would be much more civilized."

I reassured Francis I would not and bid him goodnight.

What a relief it was indeed to get into my flat, get the heater on and find myself something to heat up from all the food that was still left over from Sunday. I called Cora to see if Denison could come that evening and she said she was not sure as he was still stuck on this same job and they needed to finish. She said she would let me know anyway. I then called Mum, who was fine with me, but a bit cagey as Veronica was sitting there. Then I called Marvalette just to give her my number and have a brief chat, then Leroy. I didn't stay on long as I felt so guilty about what I had done. What was wrong with me? Had I no self-control? After the Leroy fiasco the first time, had I not learned? Why did I not just tell Benjamin to stop? And, finally, what would I do if I was pregnant?

Too much to worry about – make a plan instead. I looked at the times on the leaflet for the Family Planning and I thought about when I could call them for an appointment –probably after my period due date had passed as a period or otherwise would shape the direction that was going in. Now for a bath and to try out the pessaries.

I was just running the bath when there was a tap at my flat door.

"Who is it?"

"It's Anthea. I'm your neighbour. I live upstairs. I only moved in today and I just wanted to say Hi and introduce myself. I could come back another time if you are busy."

I opened the door and let Anthea in. I did want to meet her – at least it would not freak me out to hear footsteps upstairs if I knew who she was.

"Hi. Come in. Please go and sit down. I won't be a mo. I was just running a bath, but I will turn it off for now. It's great to meet you. Welcome."

I ran to turn the bath off and came back and offered Anthea a drink.

"Oh it's ok thanks. I don't want to disturb you."

It's fine. I had only just turned the water on, so it's no bother and I would like a cuppa anyway."

"Oh. Ok. In that case I will have tea, weak, black and no sugar. Just dip the bag in."

I made the tea using the same bag for both of us. Anthea was a bit older than me – I imagined in her mid Twenties. She had auburn hair cut in a bob, not very fashionable, but it suited her. She was dressed as one is when just having shifted boxes all day.

"Have you eaten yet? I have some food here left to heat up and we could share if you want. You are probably still wondering where you packed the knives and forks."

"That would be great. Thanks. What do you have? I am vegetarian."

"Oh. Right. Well I have some West Indian food here that my friend made. I can heat you up the rice and peas, the plantain and slice you some tomatoes. That should be ok. Better with gravy, but I could give you some pepper sauce or ketchup. What flat are you in by the way?"

"Oh. the large bedsit directly above you. Food sounds great. I am grateful as it saves me running down the road. Gosh, it's turned cold."

I heated the food and she sat at the table, commenting on the flat.

"I like how you have done your place. You really have an eye for colour. Are you a designer at all?"

"No," I replied laughing. "Actually I work in a nursery not far from here. And you?"

"I am a journalist. At the moment I work for an alternative magazine called Underground News. Nothing to do with the Tube!! It is alternative political satire. Are you interested in that at all?"

"Well, I would be happy to read a copy. I am not very up on politics, but I am getting clued in fast, living and working in the community down here."

We got to chatting about our backgrounds which were rather different. Anthea came from a quite well-off family from Kensington and she had been to University and had studied History and Political Philosophy. It all seemed like another world to me, as I suppose my humble background did to her. But she seemed very interested in me and we hit it off, chatting for about an hour. She told me she had met Francis and thought he was cool. I told her about the local women's group that I wanted to check out and she said she would love to come with me; she seemed less keen on the Socialist Worker Party.

177

"I used to hang out with them at Uni. They can talk a good talk, but not many of them walk the walk. Most are a bunch of privileged hippies and have very little contact with your real cloth cap working class. But maybe round here it is different. I like the idea of the women's groups as they seem more turned on to what all women are going through, the things we all share, regardless of our background."

"Round here there is the Black political scene too. I know some people involved with that and that is very much a real issue movement, I can assure you"

Anthea sat agog. At first I thought she was shocked but then I realised she was full of some kind of weird admiration which was equally uncomfortable. I thought it best to let this novelty effect die down before I shared anything further with her. I was also nervously aware of her being a journalist and maybe on the look out for hot stories. I did not want to expose any of the people I knew, such as the Pumas and the case coming up from the march, as what she might think was sympathetic publicity might backfire.

"You know Anthea, Just one thing. I know we have only just met and stuff, but I hope that what we share and talk about within these four walls does not go further – like into your paper or anything."

"Oh no. Of course not," said Anthea looking genuinely shocked. I apologized for being so bold, but I did have this habit of saying what I wanted to say upfront.

'Well, you never know. There may be a time when publicising what's going on round here might be a good thing, but you have to take the cue. Stuff goes deep here and you never know whose toes you are treading on. There is something I need to tell you about this house as you will hear eventually."

Anthea was all ears and I hoped I was doing the right thing in telling her about old Mr Feltz and what happened in the house before. I also wanted to make sure she knew about Gregory as I needed to be sure she would never let him in without realising who he was. I didn't tell her the whole story, just that he used to work for Old Feltz and still thought he had connections here. I did say that he had threatened me and that we had to be careful as he was known to be bad news and to make sure he never came in the house, always to keep the front door shut etc etc. It sounded a bit like a bad trip, but she could see I was serious and said she would be very careful. Living in an ex house of ill repute seemed to excite her a bit as being rather daring!

Anyway, I said I would find out about the Women's Group and maybe we could go along together. She seemed happy with that, and saying she was tired and that she too needed a bath she said she would let me get back to mine.

As she left, I thought that I liked her, but I felt she was a bit naïve and I worried about Gregory using that as a means to gain entry into the house. I was still very scared on that front but tried not to let it get to me too much.

Anyway, I had my bath and got to grips with the pessary and then went to bed. What a messy business they turned out to be as I woke the next morning, feeling less itchy, a bit, but my knickers were stained yellow from the pessary and cream. I would use an S.T. in future.

I thought I ought to call Mr Feltz, but I was a bit hesitant as I wasn't sure how to approach the subject – mainly about Gregory. When I got in the next day, I got on the phone to him.

"Mr Feltz? Good evening. This is Jenifer, from 164 Westbourne Grove"

"Ah, yes Jenifer. How do you like your new neighbour? Have you met her yet? Very nice girl, very nice indeed. Good family."

"Yes she came down to see me yesterday. I like her. Have you got any more tenants lined up yet?"

"I'm looking and looking. I want to make sure I get nice girls like you two, or nice young men like Francis – a colourful character, but I hope he is a good neighbour."

"He's great, Mr Feltz. I hope you find the kind of tenants you are looking for. Can I ask you something, please? I hope you won't be offended."

"Go on, my dear, ask away! Not much offends me."

"Thanks. I wanted to ask, well, about the house as it was before. It's just that there's a lot of rumours."

"I see. Jenifer, I will be as honest with you as I can. First of all to reassure you, nothing like that will ever happen again. My father was very old and he was going a bit, well, demented, you know – kept forgetting things – and he got taken advantage of. He had a rent collector.."

"Gregory?"

"Oh, I see you have heard a lot! No, actually before Gregory, he came later on. This man, Billie, well, he was very deceiving. He told my father he would help him look after the properties, find tenants, make sure the rent was paid and get them out if they didn't pay or were any trouble. Bit by bit, he made a couple of the houses filled up with 'ladies of the night' and would take money from them – so yes it was a brothel I suppose. My father did not really cotton on, he wasn't involved, not to my knowledge anyway. He was just an old fool being taken advantage of. Billie took on Gregory as one of his gang he used to frighten people out of the houses.

"But Billie,…. well, it got out of hand and Billie got cold feet and he moved on. No-one really knows where he went as my father never heard from him again, but this Gregory chap just took control. At that time, my father never discussed this with us, but I began to get concerned and some tenants pulled together and went to the police. So my father began to get a bit concerned and, to cut a long story short, he wanted to get rid of Gregory, but he had such a hold that my father could do nothing. So he started to sell off the houses and he just kept these two, the ones that were the brothels and two properties over the road where Gregory had a flat. He used to stay there to watch the girls' activities – spy on them really…"

"Does he still have that flat?"

"Not that I know of. It's the one above the Everopen shop which I sold on. When my father died, about a year ago, I had a hell of a job getting all the girls out of the house, it seemed that they did not all live there, but lots of them had keys and would use it for their activities. Gregory was put out that I was not interested in his services and because he knew I was on to him, he moved out of the flat and I am not sure where he went. So, no, he's nothing to do with me. Like I say, I sold the flat and then I sold the house over the road to someone who wanted to make it back into a family house and now I only have these two. As you can see, I am most particular who comes in as tenants, so please rest assured, you are safe and I am sorry you have had to hear all of this gossip."

"That does put my mind at rest and I am so sorry your father was used in that way. What I need to tell you is that I sort of know Gregory. He is not a friend of mine, first of all – I need to make that clear – I know someone who went out with him and she came unstuck and he knows that I know that. He has been harassing me. I am not scared of him as such, but he tried to frighten me, saying he had keys for all the rooms and that he knew everyway to get in the house. My friend's husband looked at the window locks and said he would fit me some better ones - would you mind about that?"

'Dear me Jenifer, I would have never thought a nice girl like you would know someone like Gregory, but as you say, it was not by choice. By all means improve the window locks. Ask your friend – is it Leroy, by any chance? – to call me."

"Well, actually, it's not Leroy, but my friend's husband, Denison – Leroy knows him. He's a nice man. Helpful."

"Right. Get Denison to call me and I will get him to put better locks on all the windows. I was thinking of getting a caretaker in, but that's how the whole problem with Billie started in the first place. What do you think?"

"I think that Gregory will get fed up and move on eventually. Getting the security up to scratch would be good and then we feel safer, I know you did change all the locks, but Denison said how easy those Yale's were."

'Well, it's an Ingersoll that you have on the front door. That's pretty safe and the back door is a Mortice lock – you all have a key for that – and there are bolts. Just be careful to lock up and keep an eye out. Call me if you are worried. I hope this is not preventing you from enjoying your little flat. I will be around on Saturday, about 11am, so I will see you then. Can you ask your friend Denison to get in touch?"

"Thanks Mr Feltz. I will do. I am very happy here and intend to stay that way."

"That's good. That's good. Good night."

I bid Mr Feltz good night and felt a lot happier. What a story! Now who else did I have to call? Oh – Beth Hastings from the Women's Group and Family Planning. It was their late evening, so I gave them a call to make an appointment. There were so nice and we arranged for the week after the funeral. At this rate I would be fixed up for Christmas! But that led me to thinking about Leroy and that made me recall how guilty and unworthy I felt and that I was not sure what to do – tell him or keep it to myself, like my guilty secret. Perhaps in time I would forget about it. However, I was not really a dishonest person and what I really felt I wanted to do was confess it all to Leroy. Then he would know what I had done and either accept it or walk away, but at least he would know I had been honest. I didn't know what to do really. Certainly wait for my period and decide then.

Now for Beth – hopefully I could then get some dinner and relax.

"Hi, can I speak to Beth, please?"

"Speaking. Who's calling?"

"Oh. My name is Jenifer McKay. Kenneth gave me your number and said to call you about the women's group. I would like to come along, and there is someone else in the house who would like to as well. I only live up the road from you."

"Hello Jenifer. I had been expecting your call. Kenneth told me you were interested in coming to the group. Shame he doesn't suggest it to Gabriella, but there you go! Who is your friend?"

"Her name is Anthea. She lives in the same house here. She works as a journalist for Underground News."

"Oh? Interesting. I'm not sure if that's a good or a bad thing. I mean I like the paper, but I wouldn't want our meetings, you know, what we talk about, being publicized in her paper. What's she like?"

"Well, I only met her yesterday, but she seems fine. I suppose you would just need to get her to agree to keeping things confidential."

"Yes, well, we meet on the second Friday of the month, but we won't be meeting til after Christmas now but I can come and see you for a coffee, or you can come over here. I am very close to you. Opposite in fact."

"Oh, do you live in the big house that used to be old Mr Feltz's?"

"Yes, my husband bought it, but we split up and I live in it with our three children."

"Three? How old are they?"

"Five, seven and nine. Two girls and a boy. So in age order, Tammy, (Tamsin), Ollie (Olivia) and Benji (Benjamin). All at school now, so I have time in the day, otherwise am in for evening visitors."

"OK I will pop over tomorrow if that's ok – shall I bring Anthea, if she is free?"

"Lovely. About half seven, when the mob are in bed. Fine to bring Anthea, so see you both tomorrow. Must rush. It's bathtime"

"Ok, see you tomorrow."

What a small world! I popped up to deliver the news to Anthea, who said she would love to come with me and would come down at 7.20 tomorrow. Should we bring anything? Wine? Cake? I thought cake would be best, so we agreed on that, said good nights and I came back downstairs to call Cora and leave Feltz's number for Denison to call.

I finished off the last of the left-over food and then wondered what on earth I would eat for the rest of the week. I would need to be better organized with shopping, and would get on that soon, but for now, I would settle down on my sofa with some back copies of Underground News, potter about a bit, have a bath and get down with the messy pessary again. Oh bummer. I forgot to buy STs so used some loo roll instead. It really was messy stuff. No-one told me you had to go through all these palavas as a woman!

25   The deep end

I had a heavy day at work. Bernadette was not in, so I told Sue and she said she would give the social worker a call. Ryan cried all day and just wanted to be held. Another parent, Maria, who was using the nursery for child-care to go to work was settling in her baby, Dean, and you could tell she did not want to be there and was making comments on some of the other children. She was a bit hesitant about the fact that so many black babies were in the group. Well, we only had 4 white children including Dean out of the nine we were allowed. She commented about Ryan and said he looked old enough to be in the next group and why was he miserable and how she didn't want Dean picking up on that. Dean was just over a year and a lovely little chap, keen to explore, but he made the mistake of coming to talk to Ryan who was sitting on my lap and Ryan bit him. Maria grabbed him up and said "Naughty boy" to Ryan who cried all the more, after only just calming down.

Well, Maria was angry. Gabriella saw and took her to one side, saying that Ryan was very upset at the moment and needed to be with me. She said it was not nice for Dean, but that many children went through this phase and we just had to be patient. Maria said we should punish Ryan and Gabriella took a firm stand and said it was neither our job, nor our belief, to punish babies and that the way we worked by being kind and understanding was the best way to get the results we were looking for. Maria left the issue there but took Dean home – which she was due to anyway, but we felt she did it more to withdraw him. We knew she was not happy. Jacqui said that the next day she would take more time with Maria and Dean while I focused on Ryan. Him, on top of settling Jasper and getting to know Bernadette. It was going to be a busy week. Gabriella, as the room leader, had been asked to take a little boy, Ade, under her charge. He was 9 months and was blind and the parents were worried about him not crawling yet. The medical team was not sure if he was totally blind or if he had some sight. We thought he could detect light, as he would turn to the window when the sun shone through or look up when the light went on.

So we had our work cut out and we all felt rather dismayed when Sue came round to our room after tea and said that Maria had made a complaint about a child biting her child and about the way Gabriella spoke to her. Gabriella was very upset. We had heard how quietly and politely she had spoken to Maria, but at the same time explaining the way we worked. Sue said she would need to speak to us all one by one and report back to her manager at the Town Hall. In the meantime, Maria had said she was not coming back to this nursery and wanted a transfer. So, miraculously, they found her a place at another nursery. So that was the end of Dean. Gabriella felt that Maria had been racist and could not accept her authority nor the fact that more than half the babies in our room were not white.

"Then we don't want her here. The other white parents are fine and we have a lovely group here, so it's her loss," I ventured.

"It's not the point though,' replied Gabriella. "The issue is that the powers that be in the Town Hall have pandered to her, like they are ashamed of how mixed our nursery is. I bet they put her over the other side of the area, in Golden Lane, as there are hardy any black children going there. Also, it's the same old story. They eventually gave me the senior job, but anytime there's something like this, they take the side of the white person."

It was true, I could see that, but Jacqui said Gabriella was too sensitive, which did not go down well at all. Gabriella was quiet for the rest of the day. Gabriella went on her break leaving me to talk to Jacqui.

"You know, Jacqui, Gabriella has been here a long time, and she has a good idea of how things work. Old Matron was miserable to her and she had to put up with untold crap from Carole Clarke and Big Mary. She spent years before just feeling like she was walking on eggshells. Give her a chance. She is an amazing worker and she is really overlooked and not given the credit she is due. It upset her when you said she was being sensitive."

"Well, she goes on a bit too much. Like she's got a chip on her shoulder or something. She should just brush it aside."

"You know Jacqui, that's not fair. We don't know what it is like to be black and face what Gabriella faces. I've seen what she's had to put up with and neither of us would like it, so why should she take all that? Either one of us would be upset if Maria had reported us for saying what Gabriella said, so give her some support. That's the best way to deal with it. Give her the support we would expect from each other if it was us."

Jacqui shrugged her shoulders. "Would she support us though?"

"Of course. How could you say that? Come on now Jacqui, she's our colleague and room leader, and we are a team, so let's act like one."

Gabriella came back into the room and Jacqui swanned off to go on her break. I would like to be a fly on the wall in the staff room.

"Don't mind her, Gabriella. I just told her straight and she's offended."

Gabriella said nothing but went off to the bathroom to do the nappy bucket. Meanwhile, I took Ryan and Ade to the book corner and Daisy came along too. Bonnie, Earl and Donnal were sleeping in their cots, so this was a nice time. Ryan was fine. He was protective of Ade, and he liked Daisy, so was happy to sit as we all looked at books while Ade chewed one.

When Jacqui came back she went over to Gabriella.

"I'm sorry I upset you. I don't know how you put up with it all. You ain't sensitive. You're strong."

Gabriella smiled, and unusually for her, she let Jacqui hug her and hugged her back.

"Thanks." She said. "Right are these babies ready to wake up yet. It will be home time for Donnal soon. And how's my Ade baby?"

At the sound of her voice, Ade turned towards Gabriella and held up his arms. She scooped him up and sang to him. She really was quite something and Jacqui had recognized that today.

I was still thinking about this on my way home. I thought of calling Gabriella to talk to her about it, but then reflected on the fact that she was quite a private person and maybe its would be best to leave her be.

I nipped into Everopen and bought some groceries, some fruit and cake to take over to Beth's, then went home and made some egg and toast for myself. The phone rang and I went to answer it.

It was Benjamin. Hmm. My first reaction was to out the phone down.

"Hello Benjamin."

"Don't sound so cold Jen. Look, I won't keep you long. I just wanted to call you to see if you were Ok."

"No, Benjamin, actually I'm not. Because I was so afraid of being pregnant, I tipped half a bottle of Dettol inside me and that has given me a dreadful irritation called thrush so I had to go to the clinic and get checked out and get that sorted and I'm still waiting to have my period which is due next week. Plus I feel ashamed and guilty and me and Leroy had been getting close as friends and now I feel I can't look him in the face."

Silence. Then,

"I'm sorry. I am so sorry. I was selfish and behaved badly. I don't know what I was thinking and I feel guilty too. Both for doing that too you, as well as for cheating on Valerie."

"Maybe you should think before you get your trousers down. But I also learned a lesson. I just got transported back to those feelings all that time ago and just wanted to feel all of that again. But it wasn't like it was before and I misread you. We both made a mistake. I don't know what I was thinking as I know you have been with Valerie for some time, I just imagined that I could get you back, restake a claim on you, regardless of your relationship with Valerie, so I am sorry for that."

I was choking back the tears by now and I could hear that Benjamin was sorry and guilty.

"I know. I know. You know, Valerie fell pregnant so fast and everyone expects that I will marry her, but I am not sure and yet I feel I can't get out of it. It seems like I am making mistakes too, but at least you are not about to make the biggest mistake of your life."

"You don't have to get married. Why not wait until you are sure. When the baby comes you may feel differently. You must have feelings for her, else it wouldn't have got this far."

"She tried to get rid of it, as I asked her to, you know, but it didn't work. So she is as trapped as me, but she wants it and she wants to get married. She is a nice girl and she wants the whole family thing."

"How old is she?"

"Same age as you. She's not like you. Independent and confident. She's shy and just wants to be a wife. She says it's easier for her to accept than me."

"So, if I hadn't bothered to get on the pill and just got pregnant, would you have married me? If I find out I am pregnant now, would you marry me?"

"Don't ask those questions Jen. I don't know. How could I answer that?"

"Well, maybe if I hadn't been sensible, I would be in her position and getting married to you. Maybe that's all I wanted. At the time."

"Well, Jen, we can't re-write history can we? We are both where we are at and we can't go back. Look, I hope you are not pregnant. It would be a disaster for both of us and I don't want to ruin three lives plus two pickney. I hope you get it together with Leroy, if that's what you want. He doesn't have to know what happened, does he?"

"But this is just it, Benjamin. I feel I ought to tell him what happened. Otherwise it will be on my mind and I will feel like I am hiding something from him. Oh. I don't know what to do."

"You're good you are! Fancy risking your relationship by telling him. How do you think he will react to that? You know Leroy has had that happen to him before and look how he went off. Jen, keep the whole thing to yourself. Sit on it."

"So, will you be sitting on it, as you put it? Or will you confess to Valerie? How can you build a relationship on lies from the start?"

"Jen, they say what the heart don't know, it can't grieve over it. Just let it go."

"Seems to me like you don't want me to tell Leroy in case he comes after you, or even tells Valerie himself."

Benjamin, let out a sort of chuckle. "Well there is that as well, but to be honest, I was more thinking of you. But you do need to be aware that once you let things out of the bag, they could go far."

I couldn't help momentarily thinking how that could go my way. If Leroy told Valerie, that would be the end of them and then I could have him back. I brought myself back to planet earth rapidly as that really would be the last thing I wanted.

"Well, I will think about it. But thanks for calling and for your apology. I hope all goes well for you in your marriage and with the baby. Bye then"

"Ok. Thanks for being understanding and for accepting my apology. Take care of yourself and I hope you come on. Call me if you don't, won't you? Bye Jen."

As I put the phone down, I thought to myself what on earth did he think he could do if I did call him to say I was pregnant – take me up some backstreet abortionist or something? Period – please come.

Crikey, I checked the time. Nearly seven and I hadn't eaten yet, so I quickly made an egg and toast and got ready to go over to meet Beth. Anthea came down at 7.20, and picking up the cake, we left to go over to meet Beth and chat about women's liberation. Boy, did I feel I needed liberating.

186

Chapter 26 The Liberation of Women

Anthea and I got to Beth's house on time and rang the doorbell. It was answered by a blonde child in a long nightie, whom I presumed was Tammy.

"Who is it Tams?" called a voice which sounded like Beth, only shriller than the voice on the phone.

"Who are you?" asked Tammy.

"I'm Jenifer and this is Anthea. Mum is expecting us."

"Beth. It's Jenifer and Anthea. Shall I let them in?"

"Yes, do. And bring them to the lounge. The kitchen's in a frightful state."

"Come in then," said Tammy. "This way."

She led us to a magnificently huge room with high ceilings and ornate plaster work, but that was where the magnificence ended. Two huge sofas that had seen better days faced each other in the center with a large carved coffee table in between. Plates and glasses festooned the table and kids stuff littered the floor. Anthea and I looked at each other and removing some kids clothes from the sofa we sat down. I felt as if I ought to make myself useful.

"Shall I take these plates to the kitchen for you?"

"If you want" answered Tammy, shrugging. "We used to have a cleaner, Marina, but she left and Mummy said we ought to do our own clearing up, but I hate it."

"I know what you mean," answered Anthea, "at the end of the day, it depends on what you hate most – clearing up or being surrounded by mess. I gave in to cleaning up, but it was a hard choice."

Tammy laughed. "I will never give in to cleaning. But you can bring the stuff this way."

She led us to the kitchen which was equally in disarray. Anthea and I looked at each other and rolled our sleeves up and began to tackle the mountain of plates and pots that were, well, everywhere.

In no time – well about fifteen minutes - we had the washing up done and had even managed to recruit Tammy to helping by putting stuff back in cupboards and drawers.

"Goodness me!" It was Beth, sounding astonished. "You didn't have to go to the trouble, honestly, but thanks anyway. Being a single Mum with three kids and a big house is not easy I can tell you. At least let me get the kettle on and make us some tea."

"We brought cake – and I'm Anthea."

"And I'm Jen."

"Well, I am Beth and this is my eldest daughter Tamsin, or Tammy for short. Now, Tammy, off you go. You can read in bed until 8, then it's light out. OK?"

Beth collapsed into a dining chair and swept her hair away from her face. She looked as if she was in her early thirties and wore jeans and an old jumper which looked as if it had some of supper's spag bol on it. She had the look of one exhausted, so Anthea and I finished making the tea and found some plates for the cake.

"What must you think of me? You have come here to discuss Women's Lib and meet me who is a disheveled heap and so oppressed it's not true." Tears came into her eyes. "I cannot remember the last time someone made me tea. Or brought me cake."

"Don't worry, we are just pleased to be here and meeting you. This is a massive house. It must take some elbow grease keeping it organized and with three kids as well – that's enough for anyone to contend with."

"It's all too much sometimes. I mean it's a lovely house. My husband bought this a couple of years ago, before the divorce. He left me for his secretary – would you believe? Younger, slimmer, has time to get her hair done, no kids to worry about. Makes me sick. Anyway, while the divorce was going through he let me live here plus he paid me maintenance. The divorce settlement was that he made half the house over to me and would allow me rent free on the rest, so that counts as maintenance. So I have a great big bleeding house, but I can't sell it – that's in the contract- and no money. I get my Family Allowance every week which just about feeds us and I am trying to get Supplementary Benefit. But they count the waivered rent as maintenance and say I am not entitled. I am fighting this but it is just so hard. I do a little freelance work to pay the bills and the cleaner. I am a designer, fashion designer, by trade, but work is hard to come by and who wants a fashion designer looking like me? My last contract was for a 'fashion for the over fifties' firm, so that's what I have been reduced to. To be honest, I didn't really want to do fashion anymore anyway. It's not exactly Women's Lib is it? But what can a Mum with three kids and a degree in Fine Arts actually do?"

"Tammy said you used to have a cleaner, - Marina."

"Yes, I had to let her go. On one hand it was great to have her, but the kids took advantage and now they are spoiled. Also how can I be said to be representing the revolution when I employ a domestic to do my scrubbing for me?"

"We all have our own oppressions in our own way, according to our circumstances, including social class, race etc." Anthea responded. "Middle class women are oppressed too, you know. Behind the veneer of privilege, there are layers of oppression just like you describe. Being controlled, financially, mentally, sexually by the patriarchy – in this case in the form of your husband and how he is constraining your life, making out like he's so generous, but really just controlling you and making life bloody hard, not seeing that his kids are suffering as a result. And it's no biggie to employ help – it's about how you value the work that person does and treat them as an employee that matters. Stop being guilty!!"

"I was going to rent out a room. An interesting West Indian chap applied – the only one so far. Tall, quite handsome although he had a scar on his face. Said he used to live in a flat next door and how this would be handy for his work. He is an accountant. I was actually renting the back room but he said he would pay more for a front room, but I am not so sure"

"Not Gregory, by any chance?" The shivers were going through me and I looked at Anthea. She looked at me.

"Yes – actually that's right. I thought it might be nice for the kids to have a man about the house."

"But please, not that man. He's no good. He has a terrible reputation, I can't go into the details, but I can only beg you not to let him through your door. You haven't agreed with him yet have you?"

Beth looked shocked as I was so emphatic about Gregory's undesirability. He clearly saw renting the room as an opportunity to spy on me.

"Thank you for telling me. One is just so vulnerable. Not I had not agreed, I said I would let him know. He left me his card to call him back."

"Please call him and say you are not renting the room again and take the ad down from where you had it. Keep it quiet for a while until you get a plan B together."

"Sure – but meanwhile are we supposed to starve?"

"Of course not. I have an idea," continued Anthea. We have been looking for a designer for our paper for ages. It's part time and does not pay well as we are just a small alternative paper, but you should clear about £10 a week and with your family allowance would that be better?"

"That sounds great, but I am not sure I have the right skills."

""Bit of bluff, bit of pazazz and you will pick it up as you go along. Plus you will be doing something you like. Do you type?" Beth nodded. "That's a start – and you design – that sounds like a winning combination to me!"

How easy, I thought, for the privileged to fall on their feet as I compared this with the lot of Faith at the nursery, but I said nothing. I was just glad that Gregory would not be moving in.

"More tea? I'll make it this time."

A rather cheerier Beth got up to make some more tea.

"What I had really wanted to talk to you two about was setting up a consciousness raising group. I am getting fed up with being in the SWP and all they talk about is the working-class revolution and how we have to take control of the means of production. Then we can be liberated. Marx says that our social relations are determined by our relationship to the means of production. This means the hierarchies of the workplace are echoed in the world outside the factory and woman is of course at the bottom of that. Some of us have been raising the question though that if we take control of the means of production how does that change life for us as women? The men are either not interested or just fleetingly so and they cannot understand what we are saying about the narrowness of our lives as wives and mothers and are not prepared to look at patriarchy and their own role in furthering oppression of women. They just shrug it off and say after the revolution we will have child-care and birth control and big communal laundries and kitchens, so we won't have to worry. But I say, who is going to work in those places? Will it be the men – or just the women? So for me the revolution seems to be about business as usual for us women. The whole point of consciousness raising is to start from where we are at as women. Many of us have not even been given the chance to voice our dissatisfaction, our unhappiness and loneliness of being at the bottom of a patriarchal heap."

I thought of the women, the mothers, at the nursery and how oppression affected their lives – of Bernadette and her baby, of Faith with the fear of deportation hanging over her head, of Lynda and Janine and how the cycle could come round full swing if they were not given the chance to improve their lives. I voiced these thoughts.

"But revolution, Jen, is not so much about making little changes to the system so that people can get better chances but creating a whole new system where our human rights as women, as mothers, is at the heart of a new society." Beth was in earnest, but I was not sure. Surely a revolution was about bloodshed and suffering and look at who pays the price most.

Beth anticipated what was on my mind.

"Look revolution does not have to happen as a result of an armed struggle but when people's consciousness has been raised and moved so that it is the collective will of the people that drives a social revolution. I am not defending armed struggle. I am a pacifist. But I am suggesting we need to revolutionise our thinking, specifically as women and that comes from sharing our experiences, challenging the things that oppress us –especially those things which we have internalized about ourselves – so yes, those mums from your nursery, they need to be a part of this, as do we all."

"Well, I'm in," said Anthea, "what about you Jen?"

"Sure. I am not sure where it will lead, but that is part of the attraction of it. Do we tell our men friends or keep it as a women's secret?"

"Oh yes - like the Greek women's mystery schools of Eleusis. Or like a coven!"

Beth laughed and rubbed her hands in a witchy kind of way. "So, when will we three meet again?"

I knew that was from Macbeth, but I did not have a clue about this Eleusis, but I did not want to show my ignorance. I was beginning to feel a difference, a gap, based on class and all that brought with it, but I was determined to bridge it and not allow myself to feel left out or inferior to them. I just put it down to them having more education than me – with their degrees and stuff.

"So. With this consciousness raising thing – how does it work? How many do we need for a group? Does it have a leader or an agenda? Do we have a clear objective to achieve?"

"No, no, nothing like that? Am I right in that Beth? We just get a few women together and start meeting, say, on a monthly basis and we just start to unravel our stories. We begin where we begin and end when we feel it has ended. No leader or agenda and our only objective is a purely personal one to gain an insight into our personal oppression and link that to the experiences of other women and then we may decide to work on issues that arise from that in a collective way."

"Well, I'm in too. Do you have any other women interested?"

"So far, at least four from the SWP group – the others think this is a middle-class reactionary diversion. So that's seven of us in all. What about some of the women from your nursery Beth?"

"Childcare" I answered.

"Well, said Beth. They could bring their kids here. Tammy is really good with kids and we have loads of playthings."

"And it would be bedlam! Seriously Beth – can you imagine and anyway, kids are meant to be in bed. They would need baby-sitters. Would any of the women in your SWP group be prepared to babysit to liberate a sister for a few hours once a month?"

"I'll ask. But first Jen, do you think that any of the women you work with would be interested?"

"I will ask – also among my colleagues. Look, if we each get another two women to come along we would have eleven – ish. I'd think though that the group needs to be as mixed as possible so we can learn from a wide range of experiences and perspectives."

"Ok," said Beth, "so that's all agreed. No point in arranging a first meet before Christmas, so what about 2nd Friday January and then we do second Friday in the month after. Let's run for a year and see where we go. If you don't mind us meeting here – I have the space, plus that means I don't have to worry about childcare."

We all greed to the plan and said goodnight to Beth. It was nearly ten o'clock and we wondered where the evening had gone. As we walked back over the road Anthea asked me what was happening about the locks and I relayed to her that Mr Feltz had agreed to get Denison in to do for the whole house and I would check with him and find out.

I said good night to Anthea. I was too tired for coffee and chat, but I said I would come up Saturday morning for breakfast. "Great plan," she replied. "Goodnight Jen"

When I got indoors my flat was cold as I had turned the heating off when I came out. I went into the bedroom and found the window wide open. I froze in horror. I knew I had not left it open. I knew it was Gregory. But how? Was he still in the flat – the bathroom being the only place left? My heart was beating and pounding inside my chest as I threw open the bathroom door. There, slumped over the bath, with his head pouring with blood, was Leroy.

Immediately, I went to the phone and called an ambulance. I could hear him groaning as I tried to make sense to the emergency services. They said I needed the police as well and they said they would send someone over. Leroy groaned in pain as I dashed back into the bathroom to sit with him until the ambulance arrived. They said not to move him just hold a cloth to stem the bleeding, but as he came round, he shifted himself onto the floor and I found a towel and held it to where his head was cut. It looked worse than what it was and as he came round he started to tell me what had happened.

"Dat damn Gregory, Jen. Me was jus' passin' to see if you was back yet from yu fren' dem as me 'ad some keys a me yard dat belongs to Feltz dat 'im len' me when me was workin' 'ere. Den me see de light in yu sittin' room tu'n on and den off, so me t'inkin' yu mus' be back so me come up de steps and ring yu bell, but dere was no answer. Me worried now, so me use de key fe open de front door, jus as 'im was coming out of your door. Me push 'im back in an me seh is wha' gwaan? Nex' t'ing, is 'im turn fe start wrestle wid me and him was getting de better o' me, an' him drag me inya so and bus' me 'ead pon de bath. Fock me, man. Me wasn't prepare fe dat. No sah."

"Leroy can you remember if the window was open in my bedroom?'

"Yes, maan. Me notice dat co' de place feel col'".

"The question is how did he get in here if he went in by next door?'

"Me no know, sah, but de police gwine haffe wuk dat one out. All me know is dat me 'ead feel bus' up bad and pain me no raas!"

Just then the door went. It was the ambulance. They came in and I showed them to the bathroom.

"That's a nasty old crack to your head, mate. Don't worry we'll get it fixed for you. What your name?"

Leroy told them what happened and I could see they looked like they did not believe him, but they got on with cleaning up the wound."

"It's quite a nasty cut there and will need a stitch. Do you have any other injuries? Are you Ok to walk?"

Leroy shook his head and nodded at the same time as he dragged himself to his feet. He said he felt dizzy, so they went to get the stretcher chair for him and carried him out to the ambulance. I wanted to go with him but I was afraid to leave the flat. Just then Anthea came down looking like she had seen a ghost.

"My God. What is going on? I went into my flat and everything looked ok, but when I went into my bedroom just now and I found it was ransacked. What has happened here? Is that Leroy?

I burst into tears. I didn't know what to do. The ambulance man was great though as he could see I was frantic.

"Look, love; we'll take care of Leroy. We will take him in to casualty and they will stitch up that cut and give him a check over to make sure he is ok. He'll give you a ring later. Meanwhile you need to be here with your friend and wait for the police."

"Well, they haven't got here yet, and they don't know about Anthea's flat. Oh Gosh! I hope they hurry up. I am scared for us to stay here."

"Is there anyone else you can call? Your landlord?"

"Yes," chimed in Anthea, we must call Mr Feltz."

The ambulance men left and they drove off, leaving us to wait for the police. Thankfully Francis appeared, having been oblivious to all what went on – so he said. Frankly, if he could hear my music or my sewing machine, then I wondered how he could say he had not heard the ruckus between Gregory and Leroy. But he came in and offered to make us some tea while we waited for the police and called Mr Feltz.

Chapter 27   The Interrogation.

Mr. Feltz was shocked. He believed us – well, Leroy's story anyway – which was a relief. He started to tell a tale about the 'old houses' where there was access between the two houses, but he said the builders had not found it, so he assumed it was a myth. The stories were that punters would get taken to a room, parted with their money and then the girl would disappear. The pimps – or Gregory - would then lead the guys out and tell them not to come back. Of course the guys would never report it as they would not want it known that they were visiting prostitutes. But the so-called secret door – was that still accessible and was that how Gregory got in?

We said we were scared to stay there and Feltz said he would send out his emergency man to secure the windows and doors after the police had looked over. He asked if we wanted to stay in a hotel for the night, but we didn't want to leave our stuff. Francis said we could sleep in his place. We felt that was best and agreed to do that and Mr Feltz was happy with that.

Francis suggested that the window must have been opened from the inside – I was supposed to come in and find it and get spooked by it – however, I was even more spooked by my boyfriend-to-be being injured and by Anthea's flat being trashed.

Just then the door rang – it was the police. Francis let them in – two policemen, looking none too pleased to have been called out!

"Which one of you reported an intruder found injured in their flat?"

"Me," I said, "but it was not the intruder who was injured. That was my friend who had seen him and was trying to get him out, but the intruder smashed his head. I know who the intruder is. He also got into Anthea's flat and trashed her bedroom. The landlord says there is a secret door to the next house and that's how he got in."

"Whoah there. This isn't making any sense to me" said the tall policeman, whose face was vaguely familiar. Let's start with your names."

We each told him our names and the tale began to unravel in a more organised way. They went upstairs with Anthea. I went with her, mainly to make sure they didn't start meddling with her brain. Her bedroom was indeed a mess with stuff thrown around the room, but she said nothing was missing. But then she looked again and said she thought her building society passbook was missing. She was very anxious and the police sensed that and said to leave it for now. We were both told to leave everything as it was until the fingerprint team had been round.

We came back downstairs to find Francis had made tea for all of us. What they could not get their head around was Gregory's role in it all. They were trying to say that Leroy had made that up and that it was him who has broken in and was going to try to get out of the bathroom window when he slipped and hit his head.

All of us were shocked at the suggestion and so the police asked why I was so sure about Gregory's involvement and why the others seemed to support that story. Gradually it came out who Gregory was and the history of the house. One went outside and spoke on the walkie-talkie to get a background check on Gregory. That was when they believed us – or rather me. But then came the question of why. So then the whole story of Liz had to come out. They must have been interested but they kept it cagey. They then began to get interested in the story of the secret door.

"That's a bit unlikely, though, isn't it? Wouldn't you say that could be your imagination running away with you?"

"It was the landlord that told us," I answered. "I know it sounds far fetched and like a Famous Five story, but that's what he said."

They took Feltz's number and said they would speak to him the next day. Francis indicated he had something to say.

"I have lived round here for years and what I know about some of these old houses is that it's not a secret door – like a fake bookcase that opens from a hidden switch. No. It's quite simple really. Some of the attics connect, so you go up into the attic and somehow get through to the house next door. It came to light in a house I used to live in as there was a fire in the chimney and it spread through to the attic next door because there was no proper separation right the way through. I never saw it, but the firemen said that was the case."

"Oh. Please can you check?" implored Anthea. "It is just so scary."

You could tell they weren't that keen, but Anthea kept on. Partly to keep her quiet and partly to satisfy their own curiosity they went up to the top of the house. The flats up there had not been let yet and the doors were locked. The entrance to the roof space must have been through the top attic flat, which I only just realised was there.

"We can't break in, but we will call your landlord to come down in the morning and we will have a proper look. In the meantime, you ladies should take up your neighbour's advice and get some sleep. Someone will come and take a formal statement from you tomorrow."

Just then the phone rang. It was Leroy. He said the hospital was going to keep him in for the night and that he would call me in the morning. I briefly told him what else had happened and that the police would want to see him. Unbeknown to us, the police had also sent someone to the hospital to speak with Leroy, so they had his story too. They were trying to say that he was the intruder as well, but they eventually listened to his story and seemed interested when he mentioned Gregory. They told him to go into the station the next day to make a statement. He reminded me that his van was parked round the corner and asked me to keep an eye on it, which I said I would.

He hung up and I got some stuff and left the flat to go downstairs. The short policeman said it was ok the shut the window and lock it, but not to do any cleaning up. He looked at me in a patronizing way but I looked the other way. As we left and went downstairs, the tall policeman sidled up behind me, out of earshot of the others and said:

"Some people never learn – do they, nigger lover?"

Then I realised who he was. He was the copper who stopped Norman that night when we were all in the car. I pretended I had not heard and quickly caught up with Anthea and Francis. The two police drove off in their Panda car and we all went into the safe haven that was Francis's flat.

We sat up chatting with Francis about the night's events, then listened to Francis's entertaining stories from his 'Hairdresser to the Stars' repertoire. Some famous names were dropped in rather compromising ways and I was sure they would not have liked to have heard some of the tales that Francis told. But he had us rolling around the floor with laughter. Eventually we all nodded off, laying on opulent velvet and satin cushions on Francis' deep pile carpet.

It was Thursday the next day and I should have gone to work, but I called in to say that I had been burgled and that I was waiting for the Police. Sue said I would have to take the time as annual leave and asked if I could come in later as we were short staffed. I said I would let her know. We all looked like we had gone through hedges backwards when we woke up the next day and all I wanted to do was to get in the bath and change my clothes. I wasn't sure what to do. After the last fiasco of interfering with the scene of the crime I was reluctant to go upstairs and get some clean clothes. Francis had the number of the Police Officer dealing with the case and said we should phone and find out as Anthea was feeling equally grungy and wanted to access clean clothes too. Francis said we could 'avail ourselves of his bathing facilities' and came out with a pile of towels, soap, bubble bath and anything you could think of to make our bathing experience one to remember – so he said!

I told Francis I would rather he called the police as I did not want to have to speak to the one that insulted me, calling me a nigger lover. Anthea said she would call for both of us before we got a bath, so Francis handed her the phone saying that had better be now then.

To cut a long story short, it was a policewoman who said she did not want us to go in the flats until they got there, so we just bathed and put back on our same clothes that Francis had ironed for us so we didn't look like 'a couple of slags after a night on the town'. We chased him round the room chucking cushions at him for his cheek – but it was all meant in good fun.

I could faintly hear the sound of my phone ringing upstairs and I wondered if it was Leroy, but Francis phone soon rang straight after, so I guessed it was him and

Francis handed me the phone, pulling a face at me. I supposed that meant Leroys was not too pleased.

"Is wha' yu a do in Francis' place, man? Yu nah been to yu bed at all?"

I explained why me and Anthea were still in Francis' place and that we were waiting for the police to come to look at the attics and take statements.

"Yu know dem hol' up Gregory innit? Backside! Dat save my life, co' dem wan hol' 'im up long time and is t'rough me and 'im did 'ave dat fight, dem a ketch 'im. I hope dey locks 'im up long time. An' pelt 'way de key. The police did come last night an' took statement from me so me nah haffe visit Babylon yard after all. Anyhow, darlin', me comin' over your side right now. Me haffe get outta dis damn hospital, so as soon as de doc a sign me out, me right dere. Me van ok? Good. Me gwine pick it up an' lef outta your sides co' me have a work fe do down Shepherds Bush. Yeah – fe Denison and Cora. If me see police dere, me nah comin' in co' me nah stickin' aroun' fe dem chat shit in me ears and' me have work fe do."

"OK Leroy,' I said ' I'm going to be busy with everything here, so phone me later. Oh, by the way. One of the police last night was the same one who called me 'nigger lover' that time when they stopped us all in Norman's car that night. He recognized me and came with his same racist crap – why do they have to be like that? Can't they just spend their time on real criminals and leave regular folks alone? They make me sick – but I have to say I am worried – well more uncomfortable really, like it's not the last I will hear from him or something."

"Jen, nah worry yu 'ead 'bout tings dat nah 'appen yet! Yu jus' mek stress pon yuself. Worry 'bout what you 'ave pon yu plate a'ready. Cho! Blasted police dem! Me check yu later, ok? Gimme a buzz at Cora's if anyt'ing."

I said goodbye to him and, as Anthea was now out of the bathroom, I dived in and got ready to face the police.

Chapter 28   The Plot Unravels

While I was in the bathroom, Anthea rang the police again to find out when they would be back to take statements and to look over the rooms and check the attic. They said as soon as they got in touch with Feltz they would be over as they needed keys from him. They said they had been trying to call but he was not there. So Anthea rang Feltz who said the police had not phoned him and he had been in all morning waiting for their call. Liars I thought. Look how they waste peoples' time as well as insulting them! Feltz said he would call them but also that he would be right over to see us.

He arrived half an hour later bringing Chollah bread, eggs, cream cheese, smoked salmon and real coffee, thinking we might need some nourishment after our ordeal. Francis was delighted and made off to the kitchen to prepare a platter of scrambled eggs, with the cream cheese and smoked salmon to which he added sliced tomatoes and some crisps to go with the Chollah bread which he sliced and buttered. This was followed by a jug of orange juice and a big pot of percolated coffee. We all dived in chatting about what had happened when the police arrived. Thankfully, without PC Racist.

Feltz left and went upstairs with the two officers to look at the attic. Anthea had wanted to go with them, to see for herself and was told no, wait there and finish eating. When they came back, Feltz said it was as Francis described and that from the room at the top there was an attic access and yes it led right over the house next door. As Feltz owned that one too, he said he would call the builders right away to get that bricked up, not just to prevent access but, as Francis also pointed out, in case there was ever a fire and to stop it going through both houses.

The police asked how Leroy could have got in and asked me if Leroy had a key. I said I thought Leroy had mentioned somethind about still having a key on hm from when he was decorating. That he's seen a light going on and as we were out he was worried. The police said that was Leroy's story too but that Gregory said he was there already and let him in. I saw Feltz looking as if he was about to say something, then changing his mind, looked away. I hoped the police had not seen this and it seemed they had not as they then asked Anthea to go upstairs to look at her room to see if anything was missing and then they would come back for me.

When they had gone, I asked Feltz what it was he was going to say earlier. He looked at me as if he was not going to reveal and then said,

"Jennifer, Leroy did have a set of keys from when he was doing the painting and I am not sure if I got them back from him. There was a whole bunch from all the houses he was doing, so he may have still had that set and I didn't notice. I will have to ask him to give them back."

"I'm sure he means to – that's wht he told me anyway."

He looked annoyed.

"Jenifer, I do not want to get your Leroy in trouble. He's a good lad and I don't want the police on his back. That Gregory sounds a real undesirable and I have no hesitation in backing Leroy to ensure Gregory is apprehended. I am sure there's a lot more matters that the police want to discuss with him. Ah! Look. Here they come with Anthea, I expect it's your turn now."

"Mr Feltz. Please would you come up with me. I feel a bit intimidated by them. Oh and thanks for sticking by Leroy's story. I would certainly feel safer with that Gregory locked up .And Leroy was actually bringing the keys over for you."

"Yes, Yes. So he says. As far as Gregory goes, if only the law were that simple,' replied Feltz, 'and yes of course I will come. I will tell them that, as you are under 21, I feel a bit responsible for you – which actually I do," he added.

Just then, Anthea came back into Francis' living room.

"All OK.' She said. 'Nothing missing, just a bit messy, but my door was actually broken into. I only had a Yale lock and had not got round to getting a mortice lock like you said, so it was easy. Anyway, one police officer took fingerprints and the other took a statement. Nothing too arduous. So, when they match the prints to Gregory's we shall have our crook nailed."

"We will need to take some fingerprints from Leroy," said one of the policeman – he was one that was with PC Racist last night. The other one, the short one, spoke to me.

"So, do you know where he is then? His van's still here. Has he been back here this morning?"

"No. He called from the hospital to say he was coming to collect it but had to go straight off to a job."

"Any idea where?" asked the short guy, to which I replied that I did not.

"Can we go and check Jenifer's room now? I'm sure she would like to make sure everything in her little flat is ok and I can see if anything needs attending to. By the way Anthea, I will send a locksmith round later to change your Yale and fit you a Mortice lock."

Feltz edged past the policemen and I followed, with them behind us. We went upstairs and through the front door to where my door had closed in the usual way. It certainly had not been forced and I remembered only putting it on the Yale and not double locking. So either the person got in with a key or in fact had come through the window after all. I had left the window open as I had found it and the flat was freezing because of it. The police dusted for prints as well as over the bathroom where I had found Leroy slumped over the bath. The bedroom table had been knocked to the floor and an ornament broken. Now the picture started to make sense. Leroy might have seen someone in my place through the window, used the key that he still had to get in, found Gregory coming out of my flat and they had a fight. Gregory pushed Leroy back inside my flat, left him over the bath and gone out leaving my door shut after him. There was blood on the side of the bath which fitted with Leroy saying Gregory had hit his head on the side of it, which was when he passed out. What I couldn't understand was the window. Why, if Gregory had got in through next door and over the attics, down into this house, had he appeared to have broken into Anthea's room and got into mine via the window?

Then the police officer said to us to come outside to the hallway as if to demonstrate something.

"Look at this' and he shut my door, took a knife and ran it down between the door and the frame and 'click' my door opened. 'This is how Gregory got in," he said

"The open window is just a smoke screen to get you worried that he came in that way. You have locks on your window don't you?"

"Yes, and I am sure it was locked and Feltz said he is going to fix a Mortice lock for me because I remember he said how that Yale was not safe. I hadn't locked it as I was only over the road for a couple of hours."

"Well it seems pretty clear your boyfriend was telling the truth, so we won't be needing to talk to him anymore. As nothing appears to have been taken we won't be fingerprinting or investigating any further,"

"What's happening with Gregory?" I asked, wanting to hear he had been locked up and they'd thrown away the key.

"Oh. He will be helping us with our enquiries a bit more Miss, but we can't say further than that. Your landlord here could apply for an injunction to keep him away from the premises. That means if he ever does turn up, you just call us and we will come out and arrest him straight away."

'Thank you," I said looking at Mr Feltz, who did not seem so keen.

"I don't think it will come to that yet," he said "I don't think we will be seeing Gregory for quite a while". He said this with such an air of paternal assuredness that I did not dare say anything. It was like when Dad would say something – the Final Word he called it – and that would be the end of the matter.

The police then left and Feltz took a look round the rest of the house making sure everything was ok before he left, making some notes about what work he would need to have done and chatting to me and Anthea. Then he asked to have a word with me in private and taking me into my flat, he closed the door and looked furious.

"Jenifer. I have to say to you that I am not pleased about the events that have taken place here over the past 24 hours. I have said to you in the past that I am determined to change the bad reputation these houses had during my father's later years. All the comings and goings with prostitutes and pimps including that one Gregory who seems to have followed you right here. I cannot doubt that if you were not here he would not have come anywhere near the house. He would have had no need. I do not want to say that West Indians bring trouble and I told you, I like Leroy, he's a good lad. But I have to ask why he still seems to have a set of my keys and co-incidentally, he just happened to be returning them tonight? Very convenient. Uh? I do not want my other tenants to feel unsafe and both of them have asked me for my assurance that this will not happen again. So, you see, I feel bound to say this. I do not mind West Indians coming here to see you if they behave themselves and act decently as I am sure many of them do. But I am not allowing the reputation of this house to fall again because of the people who come here to visit any of my tenants. In other words, and I wish to make myself perfectly clear, if there is any further episode like this involving you I shall have to ask you to leave. Understand?"

"Mr Feltz," I began, fighting back the tears as I felt he had just delivered a below the belt full on punch, "I am sorry for what happened. But it was not my fault. I didn't ask Gregory to come here and indeed I am the victim of his behavior as is Leroy. It may seem like an odd co-incidence to you that he was bringing the keys back but I have no reason to doubt his story. Leroy is trying to build his business, not destroy it. As for Gregory, he has never been a friend of mine and never will be."

"Jenifer. You do not know what you are getting into in dipping your toes in with having coloured friends. The criminal element goes deep in their midst, I'm afraid, and once you are in deep you will be tainted by association. The police asked me to speak with you in a fatherly way, as it were. None of them would be happy if their daughter was going out with a coloured chap and I can't say I would be too pleased if it were my daughter. You are headstrong, we know, but you are sensible and I can't tell you what to do or who to associate with but I am saying to you to be careful. Don't waste your life. Leroy is a good lad, but where's he going to get you? Hmmm? Just think about it Jen and remember, absolutely no more trouble, do you understand? By the way, do you know where he left the keys, or does he still have them with him?"

"Yes." I said, and "I will ask him about the keys and make sure they are returned to you as soon as possible," adding nothing further to prolong the conversation. I felt as if another racist had wormed their way out of the woodwork. Two faced or what? Gregory had nothing to do with me – he has been Liz's boyfriend and look at the trouble he had made. None of my West Indian friends were like that and they were being tarred with the same brush. Damn that Liz and damn Gregory. As for Francis and Anthea – had they really complained to Feltz about me and my friends? I would have to find out. Plus I needed to phone Mum. The funeral was almost upon us and I needed to plan.

After Feltz had gone I tidied up. I didn't want to tackle Anthea or Francis straight away while I was still reeling in shock, so I sorted a few things out, did some washing, changed clothes and made a shopping list as I wanted to cook for Leroy later. I had some tea and toast and then went down out down the Portobello market to shop for some chicken and some sweet potato and plantain. I got one of those lovely big beef tomatoes too and some fruit. I got home, seasoned my chicken and then decided to see Anthea and Francis. But who first?
Anthea. I popped upstairs and knocked on her door.

"Who is it?" she asked sounding nervous.

"Only me." I replied, "just popping up to see how you are."

"I'm fine thanks, but I'm resting right now.' I'll come down later."

"OK," I replied, not sure if this was a brush off or if she really was resting and needed to be alone. I just felt as if I could not trust the ground I walked on. What I had thought was sure and steady was turning out to be the opposite and again, race was at the heart of it. I could not understand how people could allow prejudice to shape their whole outlook on life and how they saw and interacted with other people. I tried Francis next.

"Hello trouble", he said jovially as he opened the door with a big smile. "Have you survived the ordeal."

"Yes," I replied, "but blimey the ordeal was nowhere near a shock as the telling off I just had from old Feltz."

"Go on," said Francis like someone making out they don't know what you are going to say, but they do really. I told him what Feltz had said. Then I asked him to tell me truthfully if he had spoken to Feltz and if he felt uncomfortable because of my friends. Well, not so much my friends, maybe, as my nemesis, Gregory.

"Well I did ask him just to make sure you were safe and that none of us wanted a repeat of that Gregory business. He is a criminal and a nasty piece of work – nothing to do with race. My gosh darling, I am the last person to be racist – I just adore those hunky dark-skinned men!! But then again, I also have some tales to tell about my escapades – not known to Feltz, you understand – and yes I have to agree there is a darker ('scuse the pun) side of West Indian life and you need to make sure you don't get drawn into that –which I know you won't because you've told me all about your friends and I've met them and they are just lovely. But your friend Liz, now, she wasn't too careful and like how she got caught and then it's spilled on to you. Maybe that's all Feltz was saying eh? Darling there's good and bad in all. Even among us homos, there's some very nasty characters I can assure you and, by the sound of Liz's family, crooks come in a whiter shade of pale – and in uniform - too. I think Anthea has taken it all quite badly. I overheard her saying to Feltz that she was beginning to think twice about living in this house. She's never been exposed to people of different backgrounds, let alone Black Men." He pulled a scary face, "Maybe she feels threatened."

"I tried to talk with her but she almost told me to go away."

"Don't mind her. Let her calm down and talk when she's ready. And if Feltz did ever try to chuck you out of our *belle maison*, he will have to deal with me!"

Francis gave me a reassuring hug. He had a way of just brushing aside things that stood in the way of being happy. I decided he was right.

After a few minutes I came back upstairs and went into my place to phone Mum. But first I found my calendar and marked off the days when I would be off work. We did not automatically close during the Xmas week in case social services needed a place and for the 'at risk' children to be able to come in if their parents could not cope. Some parents had to work as well, but most of them tried to get the week off too. I would be off Xmas eve, Xmas day and Boxing day and with a few days annual leave I would not be going back until after New Year. Lovely!

I wondered if I should go to Mum's or invite her here – after all we could both sleep in my bed and, if need be, or I could kip quite comfortably on the sofa. If she came here it would at least allow her to get away from past memories in the house and she could meet some of my friends. However, the thought that we still had not had the funeral – which was next week - sobered my thoughts as Mum might well not want to think about Christmas til that was out of the way. I decided to take the lead from her, so I picked up the phone and rang my old home number. Surprisingly Mum answered straight away – she must have been sitting by the phone.

"Hello Mum. How are you?"

"Hello Jenifer. I'm as well as can be expected thank you, dear – and what about yourself?"

"Oh! I am fine, Mum. Thanks. I was ringing to find out about the funeral – Thursday isn't it?"

"Yes that's right, dear. I'll be glad when it's over. Your sister's been here trying to organize me and tell me what and what I should do and who to invite and, to be quite honest, she's driven me mad. She went home yesterday. Thank God. I don't understand why she can't see this is MY day, to say Goodbye to MY husband, the man I loved and was married to. Anyway, I have still got it mostly my way – you know, things like wreaths and readings. I like traditional things, but she says it's all old fashioned but we ARE old fashioned. It's just who me and your Dad were."

"I see what you are saying Mum and I agree, you should decide how the funeral should be, but maybe all she meant was that he is our Dad and maybe she thinks she ought to have room to say a goodbye as she wants to. As for me – I'm happy with anything you want."

"Well, I know that really, and I'm happy for her to have her reading included – but do you want to read something? I would prefer it was religious though – this is where we disagreed as she wanted to write a poem. Anyway, we agreed that she could choose one from a book of Wordsworth's poems – Dad liked those."

"I'd like to read the 'In my house there are many mansions' bit from the Bible – can't remember where it is but I'm sure Father O'Malley will remind me! Would that be OK?"

"Lovely!" Mum answered with a sigh of relief as if she was glad that was sorted out so easily.

"Do you want me to come up the night before to help out? How's the wake planning going?"

"All under control. I have booked the Club where Dad used to go and they will cater for 50 people. All the invites have gone out –oh and by the way, it will be a cremation don't forget, so none of that weeping round the graveside. Jen, I can't

203

tell you how I want to get it over with – I wish funerals were private things I really do. But – that's the way it is and I suppose it will be nice to see some of the old family and our friends from way back."

"So, when do you want me to come up?"

"Well, nightmare and co are coming the night before but they are driving back up – providing he's not half cut – that night. I would prefer you come here on the day, about 10 in the morning; you can leave your stuff here and we can go in the family car. I would like it if you could stay over that night and maybe another night. I've got a surprise for you. I've seen a flat and I'd like you to see it. Not a word to Veronica, mind, I don't want her and her husband poking their noses in. I told you Veronica is pregnant, didn't I? Oh well, she's made her bed, as the saying goes."

"Wow, Mum, that's a lot of info!! Yes I will be there at ten in the morning and yes I can stay overnight, and the next night too. Yes, you did tell me about Veronica and Mum, yes, it is her life and I think you've got more important things on your mind."

"I agree – and thank you dear. I'm looking forward to spending some time with you."

"Me too. I wondered if it was also a good time to ask you about Christmas – or if you would rather wait til after the funeral."

"Actually Jen, I'm glad you asked as the last thing I want to do is spend it here – I will go mad. My sister has asked me to go up to her, but I'm not sure and I'm definitely not going to Veronica's. I'd love to come to you, though, if there's room for me in your little flat. I'd like to meet some of your friends and have you cook for me for a change – none of your garlic though!"

Well that took me back – she took the words out of my mouth! "I'd love that Mum and I wanted to invite you. Perhaps if you come Christmas Eve and stay over Christmas Day and Boxing day, going home on the Saturday when the trains are running again."

"That sound fine Jen – but let's leave the details til after the funeral."

"Ok. That sounds fine and hey – I'd love to see the flat!! I hope you are sure about all this"

"Very sure, dear – now I'd better be off. See you Thursday."

"Bye Mum. See you Thursday"

Just as I put the phone down it rang! This time it was Leroy.

"Is who yu a talk to? Me been trying long time and just beep beep engage all de while?"

"Hi Leroy. How are you? I'm well thanks. Actually, I was just talking to my Mum, making arrangements for the funeral."

"Jen, please come get from de 'ospital. Murderation in ya, fe true. Me cyan stan' it. De food taste like shit. De doctor done fix me arready an' me good to go now. Yu could reach me in a hour?"

Leroy sounded really down, so rather than tell him all what had been going on, I said I would come for him and bring him back here.

"T'anks Jen. T'anks. You could call Denison and mek 'im come drop we off at yours?"

"Sure. If I can't get him, I will just come for you and get you back in a taxi. Anyway, I thought you had to go over to theirs and do a job for them?'"

"Nah, Jen. Dat nah good. Me coat mash up wi'blood. Taxi man nah go like dat. Jus' wait fe Denison and ask 'im fe bring me a coat. You can do dat please? De doc say me should res'up a couple two days til de swellin' gone down a bit, so Denison will haffe wait. Eh – yu plannin' on cooking up a likkle somethin' later? Me 'ungry no raas!"

"Ok. I will call Denison and see what I can do. As I can't call you can you ring me back in half an hour and I can tell you what's happening? You know you have to see a Doctor to discharge yourself, don't you?"

"Cho. Me nah ha' time fe dat. Me jus' gonna walk out so."

"Leroy, it is important to see the Doctor, just in case he needs to tell you any advice about medications or dressings and just to give you a last check over. It may take a while, but it's best and anyway we don't know how long we will have to wait for Denison, so you might as well. I will come straight over anyway. And bring you a pattie on the way if you like. Oh, and yes, I am cooking later"

"Arright, arright den. If it so, it so. If yu cyan get hol' o' Denison, call Norman. OK. I will call back nex 'alf 'our and I will tell de nurse dat me wan go 'ome."

Just then the pips went cutting us off. But I called Cora immediately. She answered straight away and I told her the long story of what had happened.

"Lord Jenifer. Trouble like you, eeh? That blasted Gregory. I wish he would just voom off the face of the earth! Denison is right here. You just caught him love. Here he is."

I waited a couple of seconds while I heard Cora give Denison a brief run down of what had happened. I heard him mutter something about Leroy being a lot of trouble.

"All right Jen? That Leroy in trouble again? Wha's 'e dun this time? I dunno."

"Denison – Hi. I'm alright thanks but Leroy was attacked. Yes, by Gregory, and he's in hospital. He asked if you could pick him up and bring him back to me and bring him a jacket as the one he has is covered in blood. He daren't go outside in it and no taxi would take him in that state, so he asked me to call you – and Norman - in case you can't help."

"No love, it's fine. I can do it, but not til after four. You want me to pick you up or you gonna make your way down there from now?"

"That would be good, thanks. Yes, I'm going down to Paddington Hospital now and four o'clock will be good as he has to wait to get the doctor to discharge him."

"Oh, if you have to wait to see the doc I might as well take me time. They don't rush you know."

"To be honest Denison, even though I am trying to get him to wait to see the doctor to discharge him, I think as soon as he sees you, he will be out like a shot – he's that fed up!"

"Alright Jen – I'll 'and you back to Cora. See ya later.'

"Hi Jen – I take it that's all sorted with Dennision. I will find one of his jackets he can lend Leroy – I'll come too if that's OK and we can all go back to you to cook, if you've got enough. I can bring cake and a little drop of rum."

"Thanks Cora – I've got a whole chicken seasoned and enough to go with. Rum and cake sounds good and I've got some orange juice so we are all ok."

"Good girl – see you later then, bye."

I said bye to Cora and got myself ready to go to the hospital. Just then, Anthea knocked on the door, apologizing for earlier. I explained that I had to go and get Leroy and that we would all be back later and I would be cooking. I extended an invite to her, for politeness, but to my surprise she said ok and that she'd love to come down. That settled, I sped off to get two patties and a tin of Nutrament from the Everopen shop and hopped on the bus to the hospital.

It was just after two o'clock when I got there. Gosh I was glad of the rest and the quiet when I took the bus – the morning had been one thing after another and my head needed to settle. I was still pondering about what Feltz had said. It was nothing but racial stereotyping really disguised as a fatherly chat 'for my own good'. I resented it and it made me think about whether I really wanted to stay in that house. But I couldn't just up and go. Then I wondered whether to tell Leroy. He would be mad for sure and bound to go back to Feltz and say something, probably a hot something, and then lose any futher work. Say nothing was best, I decided. My head was spinning.

The bus turned into Praed Street and I got off at the stop, finding my way through the maze that I was now getting used to in the hospital. Leroy had been taken to Casualty yesterday but was now on a ward and I forgot to ask where. Luckily the man at reception helped me find the right place and directed me where to go. Leroy was tucked down the end of the ward and was sleeping. I stood by the bed and touched him lightly to wake him.

"Hi hon," I said quietly.

Leroy opened his eyes and looked at me. He looked relieved and took my hand and kissed it. I kissed his head and then felt stupid as if I was like a Mum kissing his poorly better, but he didn't seem to mind.

"Me feel better already fe seein' you. Where Denison?"

"The cavalry is on the way. Him and Cora will be here about four, then we will go back to mine and cook some food and you can rest up at my place. He says not to worry about the work. It can wait til you feel better."

"De doc say me mus' res'up fe a week or two but is 'ow me can do dat when me have wuk fe do. T'ree people a wait on me fe some decoratin' and me need money, man. Me 'ave rent fe pay and is Chris'mas soon. Cho! Damn dat blasted Gregory."

"Leroy, just rest for a few days and see how you feel. You can call your customers from mine and let them know what's happened. Perhaps Denison can help out."

"Well me no know about dat – is my wages me worried about. Oh. Me jus' 'member. Did yu gi' Feltz de key bunch? Me lef it pon your table?"

"I didn't see any keys," I replied immediately panicking that Gregory might have taken them, imagining that he now had keys to all the rooms. Leroy saw the look on my face.

"Nah fret, sis!" he laughed. De room keys is all de old ones from when me do de work fe Feltz. Is since dat 'im change de locks".

"So why did you keep the keys?"

" 'Cos what dese lan'lords do, Jen, when dem do a locks change, is swap about. Locks cos' plenty monies. So dem take locks from one 'ouse and swap wid anodder. Dat way, dem save. Seen?"

I nodded. Skinflint, I thought, but said no more. "Do you want a hot chocolate from the machine and some biscuits?"

"Maan – me no like dem sweet t'ing dere sah but dese Pattie an' Nutrament yu bring me will do me fe now. Lord – me 'ungry!"

I laughed and went off to see what I could find. It was only an hour or so before Denison and Cora would be there, so I got a hot chocolate which would suffice for me along with a packet of crisps and a Mars bar.

"No wonder all yu English teet' dem a rot an' fall out." He joked as I ate my sweet food.

We sat and chatted quietly until the doctor came around half past three – good timing. It was all good news. The X ray showed no fractures, and the cuts were superficial, so no need for stitches. There was swelling due to bruising and Leroy would have some pain for a few days. He told Leroy to take it easy and not to work if he was having pain, for which he prescribed pain killers. He said there was some concussion as Leroy had passed out and so to be wary of feeling sick or dizzy. As he hadn't shown any signs of that in hospital they would agree for him to go home, but that if he did become sick or dizzy or unusually sleepy, then to get him back down straight away. We nodded our heads in agreement and thanked the doctor. Leroy took the prescription and put it in his pocket. I knew he would not take the medication – he had his own kind of pain killer, which Denison would no doubt bring along.

So, after thanking the doctor we bid him and the nurses goodbye. Getting Leroy's stuff together we went to wait for Denison. I found a payphone and called to say where we were waiting. Denison said no problem he would be there within the hour, but it was more like two and Leroy was not amused.

"Is wha'appen? Like yu jus leave man fe freeze in disya col' place?"

It was cold indeed in the lobby where people waited to be picked up as the door kept opening to let in cold air every time someone went in or out. Denison looked taken aback and Cora pulled a face.

"Nice way to greet a friend, innit?" Said Denison, clearly put out. "I'm doing you a favour mate. I 'ad to finish a job for Cora – couldn't just leave it, could I? Then we got stuck in Sheherds Bush and all the way down 'olland Park Avenue was chokka with traffic. I dunno. Christmas shopping I thought, but nah. Accident by Nottin' 'ill Gate. Soon as we was past that and into Bayswater we was alright, but then it took us a bit to find a place to park. Circled round outside a bit and then we got lucky and got right outside. So you better 'urry up , mate, before I get nicked."

"Sarry man, sarry! Me jus' wan fe get back a Jen's and eat some food."

" No worry about that, Leroy. I spent this afternoon cooking so all we have to do is heat up and eat up!"

"'T'anks Cora. T'ank you. Me appreciate dat. An' me require some 'healin o' de nation' fe dis raas of a 'eadache."

Leroy looked at Denison who looked back as if to say he'd got it covered. He helped Leroy to his feet and led us out to his car. Gadly, not the van, I mused to myself.

Chaper 29   The Resting and the Revelation

It was good to be back at mine. I had left the gas fire on low so the flat was warm. I settled Leroy down and went out to his van where he said he had a bag with clothes and stuff and brought it back for him. I ran him a bath and Cora got on with heating up the food. We ate and they stayed for a while playing music and having a smoke. Cora and I were chatting about her house hunting and how she may have found a buyer for her place. Denison had tried to persuade her to convert the house into flats like others had done in that road, but she said she couldn't bear all that work going on and wanted to sell it as a family house. Denison had pointed out how she would make more money that way or kept one to rent out and sell the others. Who, these days, he had explained, had families so big that they would need such a huge house? He bet that a buyer would want to buy it but only to develop it and then pocket all the money. "Laughing all the way to the bank", as he said and why shouldn't that be her? Leroy and I saw Denison's point, but I could also see that for Cora that would be like chopping up part of her life. Denison said she was something else and we all left it at that, sensing Cora was feeling unhappy.

"Lovely cake" I said, changing the subject and, as everyone was agreeing, and looking around for more, the phone went. It was Francis asking if he could visit the patient. I agreed and minutes later he was at the door with flowers for me and a stripey knitted hat for Leroy.

Leroy looked taken aback, but was pleased, nonetheless. Later he confided that was the first time a white man had ever given him a present just so. Not a gift after doing a job, but just from being thoughtful.

"Well, we want to keep the injured head warm – it's frightful out there, darling, frightful!" cooed Francis.

"Yeah and you wanna cover it up mate 'cos your customers will think you look a frightful sight and won't want you if they fink you've been fightin' an' that!" added Denison, unnecessarily. But seeing that Leroy looked worried he added 'Nah mate, only joshin ya!"

"Francis it's nice to see you again. Have you eaten already? Or would you like some food?" Cora got up to get the self-confessed hungry Francis a plate of stew beef, rice and peas and dasheen that she had brought. He succumbed to the flavours, savouring his plate quietly, as if devoutly enjoying every morsel.

"Thank you, thank you, Caribbean Queen of Cuisine," he charmed to Cora. "That was delicious and I feel like a new man!"

Cora laughed and gave him cake and a tot of rum. Clearly this was heaven , round two, and Francis was speechless again. I finished arranging the flowers and by now that atmosphere of my flat had changed from one of violation back to one of friendly warmth and comfort.

"Have you seen anything of Anthea?" I asked Francis.

"Well. Actually. Yes. Quite a revelation. May I reveal all now, or would you rather wait until your company has retired to their quarters?"

God. He had such an exaggerated turn of phrase, sometimes it felt awkward. Nonetheless, I thought, everyone knew the whole story so far as it had been the topic of conversation all eveining, so in for a penny, as they say.

"Spill all, Francis," I said encouraging him to take the floor. Which he did, literally rising to standing and gesturing for us to hush as he did not want the sound to echo into the hallway.

We sat with baited breather while Francis geared us up for the moment.

"Get on with it then," teased Denison.

"Francis, do you think you could sit down and tell us as this feels a bit dramatic – and we've had enough drama for one day" I added, beckoning him back to the chair.

"Well.." he began slowly. "Promise me no killing of the messenger?"

"Fer cryin' out loud," muttered Denison.

"Talk nah man," encouraged Leroy.

I think Francis enjoyed the build up to the story and this was how he really engaged attention – which he loved!

"Okaay. In that case. I spoke to Anthea earlier. We had a long chat. She came down to see me while you were out. God she looked a sight. Ok, she had had a bath and changed her clothes, but had been crying. Eyes all red and puffy. I don't know. This crying business - it may be good for the soul but it plays havoc with the visage."

We all sighed out loud as if to say get to the point mate, but we could also all see that Francis was about to drop a bombshell. He took a deep breath.

"Well.." he continued, "in brevitas. It was Anthea who let Gregory in."

We gasped. Leroy sucked his teeth.

"But how? She was with me all evening and we both left the house and came back together and she did not leave Beth's house. Plus, I had told her about him on the day she moved in and expressly said not to ever let him in. What did she think she was playing at?"

"Apparently, she let him in before you came home from work. He told her his name was Leroy and that he worked here for Feltz and just had to finish a job upstairs. She didn't think anything of it and knew you had mentioned Leroy was your friend. She let him in and he went up to the top floor. After a while he knocked on her door to say he was done and left. So she thought. She heard the front door slam and had no reason to think he was still here. But it seems as if he scooted back upstairs and hid til you all had gone out."

"But why? I said, struggling to make sense of this.

"Jen – has Anthea ever seen Leroy before last night? Has she ever seen Gregory?" Francis went on. " She didn't realise until she saw Leroy there and realized her mistake."

"So why didn't she just say? Did she tell the police?" I had so many questions. It just did not add up.

"'An 'ow comes har place a get mash up too? 'Im do dat, innit?"

"Well – the story gets messier, I'm afraid," continued Francis. "She could hear when you went in that you kind of gasped in shock and when you saw Leroy you were distressed and she could hear you. So she came back downstairs, but you were on the phone calling the ambulance. She took a peep in the bathroom and saw Leroy lying there and realized it was not Leroy who she had let in earlier."

"Me t'ought me did see someone but me was still confuse' and me t'ought it was Jen. So why she neva say nutin' to Jen, den? She a run back up or what?"

"Not only that" I said, now feeling really angry, "why did she SNEAK back down and not call out to see if I needed help? My God. What was she thinking?"

"Look. I know this is all wrong. What she did next. But she panicked. When she heard what was going on, she was frightened that something was amiss and it crossed her mind that she may have been taken in by none other than our dear sweet Mr Gregory. When she saw proof of that she ran back upstairs to her flat, made the bedroom all messy and came back down and the rest you know."

"Why the fuck, scuse me, did she do that, the silly bloody bitch?" Denison seemed as if he was about to pop a fuse.

"Yes, why?" I added not knowing whether to shout or cry.

211

Francis went on. "Look Jen – and Leroy – people do the stupidest things when they are afraid. And she was. She wanted to make it look as if the intruder had been in her room too. That she too was a victim and thereby deflect the blame."

"Put us off the scent like. Devious cow." Denison was fuming and Francis' exposition on the psychology of fear was not impressing him. I kind of understood, but it did not make me feel forgiving or any the less angry. Fancy wanting to make herself look like a fellow victim when Leroy had clearly been so badly assaulted.

Denison sucked his teeth loudly. Followed by Leroy.

"Wait til marnin'. Me gwine talk to she and tell har wha' me t'ink. All o' dat nearly get me de blame wid Feltz too."

"That's a point." Cora, who had been quietly listening, with no other comment other than facial expressions, asked whether Feltz had been told this and if so what was he going to do about it.

"Cora, this is the part I am just coming to. I did, indeed, say that she must tell Feltz. She was, as I am sure you can imagine, worried about that. But no, I said. You must tell him. And the police too. I said she had a responsibility to tell the truth and that this would give further ammo to the police to help them deal with Gregory."

"Dat fuckin' man. Me gwine deal wid him meself when me ready."

"Leroy," scolded Cora gently, "now is not the time to play big man. You would only get yourself in serious trouble and that could ruin everything for you."

"Yes. No time for all that hot 'ead talk, Leroy. Don't go lookin' for trouble, mate" added Denison. I just looked at Leroy and he knew I agreed with both of them. He sucked his teeth again. "Cho, blood claart," was his considered reply.

Sweat was beginning to appear on Francis' brow, a clear indication that this was hard work for him. I admired him for that as he could have just told Anthea to get on with it and sort her own mess out. I offered him a cold drink and Cora said he looked as if he needed something stronger and gave him another tot of rum with orange juice and ice. We all looked on jealously. Cora took the hint and made three more, but just orange juice for Leroy as she said he should not have alcohol, what with that head going on.

"Please carry on." I was exhausted by this story but needed to know what was the outcome. Francis, somewhat refreshed, continued.

"Eventually she agreed with me and we rang Feltz who came down about half past three this afternoon. We told him everything and you could tell he was not amused at all. Understatement. Hmmm! He was most displeased but holding it in as he thought that was needed. Of course, he had to call the police, which he did from my place and spoke immediately to whoever. The police said if she had made a signed statement that could have got her in a lot of trouble, but as that was not the case she could make a correct one when they came on Monday to take statements from everyone."

"Dem tek a statement from me arready. In de 'ospital" Leroy informed us.

"Well yes. They were going to do that today, but I said you were not back yet so they said they would leave talking to Jen til Monday. And it's a good job too, as did you know, you can smell your weed from the hallway? I'm just telling you this as if you get snitchy neighbours moving in, it may be trouble. For future reference, if you see what I mean."

Francis could see that no one was in a mood to be reminded about weed smoking, but I did make a mental note that this needed to be thought about seriously. I opened the window, despite protestations from all present and aired the room for a couple of minutes. We let Francis continue, uninterrupted.

"Feltz said that one thing was certain. Leroy was telling the truth and that was clear with the police too."

"So..dem nah gwine 'ang me. Cho!" interrupted Leroy momentarily, clearly and understandably put out that he would even be suspected of lying or anything else untoward. Francis nodded sympathetically.

"Quite, Leroy. Feltz then went on to tell Anthea that he was very concerned about her lies. The fact that she made a mistake and let Gregory in was forgivable, and I can see you are all nodding in agreement. But the subterfuge was unnecessary and potentially damaging to Leroy and obscuring the fact that Gregory has one victim in mind. Jenifer."

In all the fuss over Leroy, which he deserved as he had been injured and all to defend me, I had let the fact of Gregory's real intended victim slide to the back of my mind. Leroy squeezed my hand.

"Jen. Feltz likes you and wants an end to all these problems with Gregory and also for any future tenants. Even though Anthea did the wrong thing, please also see she is scared of Gregory herself now. And I can't say I'm too comfortable either. He is also of the view that, even if none of you were here, Gregory would still somehow be haunting this place as he also wants to get back at Feltz for not giving him a job, or even renting him a flat. So, he too, is worried about Gregory's continued presence in our midst. The police also seemed convinced he is big trouble and are keen to see him behind bars. But all they said was 'leave it with us'. Then Feltz said he would think on things over the weekend and then decide what he would do. He will be round Monday to talk to all of us."

"Well that's me set for getting chucked out. He must think I've been nothing but trouble"

213

"Don't say that Jen" Cora tried to reassure me. "Surely he can't just chuck you out of your lovely place when you've made it so nice and cosy. You haven't done anything wrong."

"Jen – there's nothing to worry about on that score. Feltz is aware of that. He had a chat with me after and said after the way Anthea also lied to him and tried to cast a shadow on you two, that it was her who is in the bad books. But he said he wasn't making up his mind til Monday. Phew. What a load that was to deliver. Can I leave you all now to talk it over as I need to get ready to go out? A date. Very charming, but no money. Oh well."

Francis got up to leave. He hugged me and told me not to worry. He shook everyone's hand and kissed Cora on the cheek, thanking her for the dinner and then made his way to go. I saw him to the door, thanking him and apologizing for all the trouble I had put him through. Then, quietly, he mentioned that earlier this evening, after Feltz had gone, he went over to the Everopen and saw Anthea going into Beth's house, no doubt to tell all over a cuppa 'n' cake – as he put it.
As I shut the door, my heart sank again. What was Anthea talking to Beth about and how would she be playing the story to her? But that would be for another day to reveal. For now, I had washing up to do and Leroy to see to. When I got back in the room, Leroy had his feet up on the sofa and looked all in. Cora was washing up and Denison was drying.

"Dunno where they all go Jen, love. I'll 'ave to leave the putting away to you."

"That's no problem, Denison. Thank you both for helping and Cora you should not be doing that when it's you who cooked."

"It's fine love. I reckon you two have been through enough over the last 24 hours so we will just tidy up and leave you to it. You should get another dinner out of what I brought and I've put it in the fridge for you both for tomorrow – unless you want to scoff it off tonight. There's some cake too."

"But you ain't having me best Appleton rum!"

"Denison!" scolded Cora.

"It's fine. Thank you both for all you've done. I reckon you deserve to polish that off yourself!"

Cora gathered her stuff, and Denison his best Appleton rum, and I saw them to the door. Leroy yelled "Later, bredrin" from the sofa and the door was closed to warm goodbyes, shutting out the cold night air. I went back in and sat with Leroy.

"Budge up, invalid."

"Is who yu callin' hinvalid'!"

I put on the TV and we snuggled up to watch some family game show or other and then a Peter Cushing movie. No more was said about the events of the past 24 hours. What we did talk about, at my insistence though was about the weed smoking and how you could smell it in the hallway. It was such a give away. My feeling was that for me, my dabbling in weed smoking was over and I had already been thinking that giving up in the new year was the way to go. I suggested to Leroy that saving the money instead could lead to brighter things. He was not convinced.

The other thing we discussed was who was sleeping where. We ended up with him in my bed and me on the sofa just to give him the space to rest. It was my insistence that he had the bed. He would have preferred company but I said not in his state. Back to reality, which I chewed over in my mind while curled up on the sofa. I was still on the thrush treatment, due to finish in a couple of days and I was waiting for my period also due soon. My appointment with Family Planning was on Monday, after work, so with Feltz's visit it was all happening. Feltz would just have to wait for me to come home after my appointment. It was becoming increasingly pressing for me to be on the pill. Note to self. Get an extra blanket. And a hot water bottle.

Chapter 30   Longing for a Quiet Life

Leroy left early with me Monday morning. He wanted to go home and felt OK enough to look in on the team of guys he had working for another property developer who was doing up flats for a Housing Association. He had a couple of private jobs to do but called to say he had had an accident and put the start dates back so he could take it easy for a couple of days. Leroy managed all this in his head and on scraps of paper. I suggested he needed a diary and got him one for the coming year ahead. Good start to the new year I thought. It seemed as if Leroy and me becoming an 'us' was on the cards. It felt as if we were coming together and building a relationship in a way that was effortless. We just seemed to fit like pieces of a jigsaw. So far it was becoming a comfortable friendship and I liked that. Leroy dropped me off at work at 7.45 – time for me to have a cup of tea, get changed and get the breakfast room set up. I was glad to be back at work at least for a couple of days before the funeral. And then I could spend a couple of days with Mum and have a bit of a break, although that too was going to be emotionally stressful especially if Veronica and Ron were going to be around. And now that she was pregnant, I bet the two of them would be sniffing around for any spare cash my Mum might have at her disposal. I carried on musing while setting up, as babies started to arrive.

As usual, Granny Simmit brought in Anthony. Mabel did not bring him ever since that to-do with Big Mary and, even though she had left, it was as if Mabel did not feel welcome in the nursery. That was a bridge that would take ages to rebuild. Sue had spoken to Granny about it and said how she would love to meet Mable and that she promised nothing like that would ever happen again, Mable still did not respond. She called though and had a chat with Sue telling her that everthing was fine and that it was just her work hours that made it difficult (she worked in a hospital)and that she preferred her Mum to bring Anthony in as it made it less difficult for her. Sue had managed to persuade her to come to the kids' Christmas party next week and she said would love to and would try to get the time off. Faith came in and dropped Ryan, in a mad rush as usual with a taxi outside. Was it worth it to work if all her money was spent on just facilitating getting there? She was still waiting to hear from the Home Office about her stay and was still so worried about being deported. How could she go back to Nigeria with three children and a failed marriage? Her parents said this was not a problem, but she was so worried that she would be a burden on them, although they said it was fine. She was worried the kids would not settle as they were happy here; she worried about not being able to find a job and the stigma of being a single parent; she was worried about Wilfred's parents, who lived close by, and if they would pressure her and, of course, she was worried that if she went back to Nigeria he would be there too, as it was highly likely that he was to be deported. What if the Home Office accused her of leaving him just to better her chances of staying here and what if Wilf's parents blamed her for his failures and his state of mind? She was so stressed, poor woman, and as much as I was happy to listen to her and give her time I had the kids to look after and I couldn't leave it all to Jacqui and Marion, so I redirected her to Sue who was in her office and was free to talk, although none of us could give her the legal advice that she badly needed.

At 8.30 Clare and Val came on duty and Anthony and the older children left our room and went to 'help' set up Biggies. Jacqui went to set up Tweenies leaving me and Marion to finish breakfast. She said how Janine's social worker said that she would be going home in the New Year if Linda continued to make progress and that Janine would be coming back to nursery. Maria, who was still with us after all and had calmed down after the biting incident, came in with Dean – it was his first day for being left all day while she went to work. She was worried and cried more than Dean did. Gabriella was due in at 9.30 and Maria wanted to leave Dean with her, but, in the end, was ok to leave him in my arms as he settled easily with me. Alice, our deputy, came round and saw we were a bit short handed and helped Marion set the room up while I comforted Ryan, who was a bit sad – always was - and sat Dean in his chair for breakfast. Donal arrived and his Mum settled him and fed him until it was time for her to leave as well.

One by one all our babies arrived and Gabriella came in carrying the presents for us to give to our babies from Father Christmas. We noticed that Bernadette had not brought Jasper in and, as he was still settling, any disruption to that, especially on a Monday, could set him back. Sometimes the mothers found settling-in awkward. Just to be there in the nursery while they had things to do at home seemed like a waste of time. Sometimes, too, they felt like we were watching them and with a few mothers it was hard to make conversation. On occasions, there were the odd few that thought that if they slipped the settling-in they could bring their child in on the start date and be allowed to leave them. Old Matron would sometimes allow this, leaving us coping with a distressed toddler or baby, but Sue was more insistent. If Bernadette thought she could do this, she would find out that it was not so. Just then, the door of the baby room opened and I heard Gabriella say 'Hello Jasper'. I turned round and saw it was not Bernadette bringing him in but a man. You guessed it. It was bloody Gregory. Sue had said she knew from the home visit that there seemed to be a man around in Bernadette's life, but she was cagey about it and we had no idea if this was Jasper's father or not. So, when Gregory walked through the door it mattered not whether he was the 'putative father', but the very fact of his existence in the lives of Bernadette and Jasper meant they were in danger. This then explained the fear in Bernadette when she was asked about Jasper's Dad.

Oh shit. These were the exact words that went through my head. Should I go hide in the sluice room or be bold. I adopted the latter decision and went up and took Jasper from Gregory's arms.

"How's Bernadette? Is she not well?" I asked, careful not to appear to be giving the game away that I knew him. Gregory immediately turned this around and blowing this cover, said

"Hi Jen. So this is where you work. Long time no see."

I gave Jasper over to Gabriella and asked Gregory to come this way please, straight to Sue's office.

"Good morning Emmett," she said to my shock horror, "how can I be of help?"

"I am not sure, Sue," replied Gregory in his best voice, " It seems that this person here has some sort of problem with me, but I don't know why." Gregory glared at me in a kind of way as if to dare me to speak out because he would have a way of letting it roll off. I had other ideas.

"Matron, sorry, Sue. This gentleman brought Jasper in this morning, and, as we have not met him before, nor know anything about him from Bernadette, I thought we ought to have a little chat so I brought him in to meet you."

"Thank you Jenifer. This is Emmett. I know him from my last nursery. Emmett, how is Junior?"

"Oh, he's fine, thank you Sue. I think his Mum have him in school now. He was five a while back. August, I think."

"I wish him well. He's a bright boy. Charming like his Dad."

Gregory smiled, hiding both his embarrassment and his gloating over me. I was not to be put off by a man who seemed not to know his son's birthday. This had not seemed to register with Sue who was smiling sweetly at him.

"Please can you tell us who you are in relation to Jasper?" I asked boldly. " we do need to know for our records."

"Well, not his father for sure." Gregory leered at me.

"So are you a friend of Bernadette, or neighbour? And can you tell us where Bernadette is today. She is supposed to be staying with him as she's still settling him in."

"I am sure everything is fine, but it would help us to know how Bernadette is." Obviously, we did have to know this, but I could see Sue was glossing over just who Gregory was in relation to Bernadette.

"I'm just a neighbor. I have a flat in the same house as Bernadette and she wasn't too well today, so I said I would bring him in. I'm just doing a favour, that's all. Nothing to worry about."

"Yes, well, thank you for bringing him in. He should only be in for half a day today but we will keep him til 3pm to help Bernadette out while she is not well. Who will be collecting him?"

Gregory looked at Sue, somewhat what flummoxed as if he had not thought through the fact that children brought in have to also be collected. Clearly that might mess up his day, but I had a feeling there was another reason why Bernadette was not in.

"Bernadette. It will be Bernadette. She just has to see the doctor this morning, so she will collect him."

"Thank you Emmettt. I expect you will need to be getting along and Jenifer, I think your colleagues and Jasper will be missing you and you need to get back to the room. See Emmettt out please. And perhaps a little less drama in future?"

Gregory smirked at me when we were out of Sue's sight. "Yu cyan touch me at all" he leered, "an' me got yu cornered anywhere you go in dis place. Yu hear? Yu and' yu damn fool bwoyfren' gonna fin' out who yu a deal wid."

Gregory left the building and I shut the door after him, taking a deep breath to calm the shaky feeling I had in my boots. Sue just HAD to know the truth about him and recognize the fact that Bernadette and Jasper were probably in danger. I walked determinedly back into her office.

"Sue. I need to speak to you urgently about that man. He's not what or who he seems. I am sorry to interrupt you, and I know I am needed back in the room, but I really need you to hear me out."

I was near to tears by now and Sue saw this. I could see she was not sure how to deal with my request but it must have been the look on my face that made her resist her initial instinct to send me back to the room.

"Ok. But first go back to the room and swap your break so there is cover. Jaqui will have to have second break and you can have this time as yours."

I did as she said and was back in minutes, despite the miserable look on Jaqui's face when I told her. I didn't have time to discuss it and made my way straight back to Sue's office where she had pulled up a chair for me. She made me a cup of tea and gave me a council digestive biscuit – to make up for me missing my break. That gave me 15 minutes. My head was spinning. Where to begin? From the beginning? The middle? Or the latest episode and work back?

"That man is dangerous and I am concerned about Bernadette." I kind of stumbled into it and I could see Sue thought I was being hysterical.

"Jenifer, I don't know what you know – or think you know- about Emmett, but I know him from when I worked in the nursery in Brent. His son went to the nursery for two years and I have never had any cause for concern. In fact we were supporting a case he was involved in – there had been a false accusation of rape made against him and we helped him and Gloria, his wife, find a solicitor."

"I can see you have been taken in…….."I began, but Sue interrupted.

"That is a very insulting accusation Jennifer. I am not sure that I want to continue this conversation and unless you can actually give me evidence, and not your very perjorative assumptions, then I will call this matter closed. We can't just go round hurling accusation like that at our families and people involved with them. Do you understand?"

I was shaking and knew if I didn't calm down, Sue was going to think of me as some kind of raging neurotic or something.

"I'm sorry Sue, I will give you the facts and everything I know about this man. I know him as Gregory, but I am aware he also goes by the name, his real name I believe, as Emmett Jonson. First of all, how I came to know him……."

I had decided to start at the beginning. I told Sue about Liz and Gregory at the club and what she saw that night. I told her about the state I found her in and that I was 100% sure that Gregory had raped her and beaten her up. I told her about Marcia as well and that led into my association with the Pumas and how I knew about the campaign to support him and how I also knew that they had dropped it. I didn't go into details of Liz's Dad, Frankie and what I knew about the police's part in the story.

"Jenifer, I don't know how you can expect me to believe this. This is not the picture I have had of this story at all and although I am inclined to believe you are not making it up, I am inclined to think you are mistaken."

"There's more," I went on, ignoring her. I told her about the flat and about old Mr Feltz and the fact that my landlord could back this up. And then I told her about what happened at the weekend and abou how he was virtually stalking me and how afraid I was.

I could see Sue was shaking her head. She said he was an exemplary Dad and how Junior was a well adjusted, bright boy with a lovely Mum who was a law student. As far as Sue knew, Emmett was an accountant and provided for the family well, although it was the case that their relationship seemed a bit 'on/off' as she put it.

"Sue, my first concern is that Bernadette is vulnerable and he is very manipulative and violent. She denies she has a relationship and we know that Jasper's Dad does not seem to be on the scene, yet we have seen on the home visit that there were some men's things in the bathroom. She could be in danger if she is with him. Secondly, he has used this as an opportunity to gain access to the nursery just to scare me. This is what he does." I told her about how he had tried to rent a room in Beth's house and emphasised again how he had fooled Anthea into letting him in the house and how he had threatened me on the street a few weeks back."

"Well, we can't just go barging round there because of this story of yours. What would we say? For heaven's sake. Bernadette's friends or boyfriends are not our business. Now I suggest that you need to stop your imagination running away with you. Perhaps it's all to do with the death of your father. I am not taking this further at all. Go back to your room now."

My heart sunk. I cried with despair and anger. My stress had come from being hounded by this man. I wanted to call the police but could not bring myself to as the thought of facing their negativity, nay, hostility towards me was too much. Feltz seemed to get on ok with them, and it was in his interest to get as much on Gregory as possible, so I resolved I would call him. I wanted to do it there and then, but I doubted Sue would let me use the phone. I would have to wait til lunchtime. Sue just had to find out the truth – especially after I had now revealed all the murky aspects of my life to her. If she didn't find out, then my job could be on the line.

"Jenifer. Go and take ten minutes in the staff room to compose yourself and I will cover for you in the room so Jacqui can have her break."

Now I knew exactly what the expression 'leaving with your tail between your legs' meant as that was how I felt when I left her office. I thanked her and apologised for taking her time. But, to have the last word, foolishly, I added that she would learn the truth and that I would make sure of that. Sue looked at me disapprovingly and just said "Enough. This conversation is over."

I didn't go directly to the staff room but stopped in the loo as I felt overwhelmed with my distress and needed to let out a good old cry. I must have been in there ages as the next thing I was aware of was Jacqui knocking at the door asking if I was ok.

I calmed myself and came out of the loo. Jacqui led me kindly to the staff room where I sat as she made me tea and plied me with more council digestives.

"Are you Ok? Matron said you were upset and over-reacting about that bloke who brought Jasper in. She said you were upset because of your Dad dying and we should look out for you."

"Thanks." It was all I said. Taking a deep breath, and realising how I had to get some self control going on so as not to look like a total idiot who was imagining things. I went back to the room. There was a small corridor inside the room as you came in the door where the babies' coats and bags were kept. Vision into the room was blocked but you could hear everything. And I overheard Sue speaking to Gabriella. I must have caught the tail end of their conversation. But I got the gist.

"Well. What did happen to Kenneth's involvement with Emmett? It did all seem to go quiet. Do you know if the case is coming to court soon?"

"Sorry, Sue. Kenneth doesn't tell me anything. I'm not really interested in all that Puma stuff so I don't know anything about it. To be honest I have never even heard of any Emmett."

"Look, I know you are friendly with Jen. Has she said anything to you about it?"

Gabriella laughed. "She doesn't tell me as much as you think, Sue, and I don't know if she has anything to do with the Pumas. Why would they want to involve her in anything anyway? Sounds like cock 'n' bull to me, Sue."

I felt a cold chill go through me as I wasn't sure what to make of Gabriella's reply. On one hand it sounded like she was covering up for Kenneth by not being prepared to give anything away. On the other hand it sounded as if she was discrediting me, as clearly Sue must have disclosed some, if not all, of our conversation. Sue knew Gabriella and Kenneth was a friend of Sue's husband. I would have to wait unil Sue dug for more information in her own circles. In the meantime, I opened the door quietly and shut it loudly so that they would hear and I walked back into the room.

"How's Jasper?" I asked as Sue was holding him. She passed him to me. " Good timing," she said, pulling a face. His nappy obviously needed changing so I took him from her and went to change him. Poor baby. He always looked kind of scrawny as if he was not fed well, but we knew that Bernadette was very particular about his well-being and appeared to feed him well. As I removed his nappy I was shocked as I saw bruises on each side of his inner thighs as if he had been held down while being changed. It was awful and for a moment I froze in panic. I called to Sue, who was still in the room. I showed her the marks.

"Oh. I suppose you are going to accuse Emmett of doing something to the baby now. Really Jen. This is going too far."

"I haven't said anything. But I do know you have to look into this as it's a non-accidental injury. Even I know not to accuse, but it has to be investigated by the social worker. Please call Bernadette's social worker. You know who it is. Cathy Mulhoun."

" I will indeed do that, but I will be speaking to her, not you. Do you understand? You will need to come round to the office later and fill out a statement. Do it in your lunch break. You've had enough time out of the room for one day."

I nodded, deciding to say as little as possible and carried on attending to Jasper.I had other babies to look after too and I wanted to get back into the room to do my job.

When Sue had left. I looked over at Gabriella. She was avoiding my look. I told her what I had heard her say to Sue and asked her why she had denied knowing anything and to me it was sounding like she was discrediting me.

"You and that mouth of yours. Always blabbing blah blah blah. What did you have to tell Matron all about that business for?"

"So what do you want me to do? Just keep quiet and let Gregory walk all over me. Do you know how scared I am? And what about Bernadette? She may be in danger – just look at Jasper's bruises."

"You? Scared of what? A big black man coming to get you in the night? Give it a rest, Jen. I thought you were alright, but the way you are hounding that man leaves me wondering."

"Do you know what he did to Leroy? Just Friday night gone? He could have killed him. You know, you don't know anything about what has been happening. You can't sit on the truth forever you know just to save your precious place at teacher training college."

" Just leave it Jenifer. We've got work to do. Just put your mind back on your job will you and leave me be. Jacqui will be back in a minute and I don't want her thinking something is wrong"

That suited me well enough and we got on with the rest of the morning, what was left of it, making baby feeds, taking the nappy pail down to the laundry, clearing away the toys and getting tables ready for the older babies lunch.

Meanwhile, Sue did call Cathy Mulhoun who said she was in the area around twelve and would call in to see Jasper on her way and that she would drop in on Bernadette to check that everything was Ok and to talk to her about Jasper's bruising. Sue dealt with Cathy and didn't ask me to say anything and she didn't even bother to pop in the room to see Jasper. She did ring from her office later to say Bernadette wasn't in, but that a man who said his name was Emmett answered the door and said Bernadette was not there and that he would be picking Jasper up. Cathy asked him if he knew anything about the bruising and he denied all knowledge, saying Jasper was fine when he left the house. Thereby casting suspicion on me and, of course, Sue fell for it. I was called into the office

222

and suspended immediately. I was so distraught I asked Sue if I could make a call and rang my house hoping that Leroy was there. He was, still resting after his ordeal but he heard how upset I was and said he would be there 'jus' now'. Which he was – for once he was bang on time! Granny Simmit answered the door and let him in.

"Wha'appen to Jen?" he asked her.

Granny shrugged he told me after and said "Yu know dem people an' dem business. Me keep well out. But, Jen is in trouble an' as far as I can see, it nah right. Nah right at all. Jen is a nice girl. One o' de best 'ere anyway."

Grany Simmit led him into the office where I was sitting, crying liberally.

"What 'appen Jen? Is wha' go on?" He looked at Sue for some kind of explanation but she was bound by confidentiality and could not say. She also reminded me of my confidentiality statement I had made when I started work which effectively meant I couldn't tell Leroy anything. However, I asked him to show Liz the head injury and tell her how he got it.

"Dat damn Gregory bus' me 'ead. I found 'im a break into Jen's flat after 'im tell de woman upstairs dat 'im was me so she let 'im in de house where 'im lie in wait, bus' into Jen's flat and dat's when me see de light from de road, so me 'ad Feltz key an' let meself in to see wha'go on and bap, de man lick me inna me 'ead an me en' up inna de 'ospital. Police go 'ol 'im up soon, man. Hope so anyway. De man is a debil an only do de debil wuk."

Sue looked taken aback. I'm not sure how much of the Jamaican dialect she had managed to catch, especially as Leroy had rattled his piece off at top speed.

"Hmm." She replied. "Leroy it was very good of you to come for Jenifer but would you mind waiting outside while I just finish off some paperwork with her. Leroy went reluctantly, not daring to question her authority. Sue handed me a handwritten letter telling me I was suspended on full pay and would have this confirmed by the Head of Service in a letter that would be sent to my house in a day or so. Meanwhile, Cathy Mulhoun would be back later to take Jasper to the hospital. There was to be something called a Case Conference, but in the meantime they would need to talk to Bernadette. I would be called to go to see the Head of Service after the doctor had submitted his report to the social worker. I listened to all of this and asked what were they doing to find Bernadette. Sue told me that I was now suspended so that was not my business.

"Call the hospital," I said fearing for Bernadette and also fearing that again, Sue would not listen.- which of course she didn't. I picked up my bags and walkd out fo the office.

"Jen yu aright? Come darlin'. Le's go 'ome. Me call Norman and 'im gonna bring a t'ing up to you an' Marvalette say she go pass wid 'im." I squeezed his hand.

"When we get 'ome, yu gonna put yu foot up an' relax. Me go mek a food fe yu an' den yu can tell me wha' go on 'ere, car me nah like 'ow it stay. Gregory again, innit?"

I nodded. "Thank you Leroy. First thing, I have a call to make – or two."

"Ok. Jus' don't stress yu brain."

"What? Anymore than it is already? That would be a tall order!"

We laughed and I felt a bit cheered up as we drove the few blocks back to my place.

Chapter 31   Justice at Last

There was something I had to do when I got home. It could get me into more trouble, but I had to prove a point. I knew I was right; I just knew it.

I picked up the phone and dialed the main switchboard for A and E at Paddington Hospital.

"Good evening. My name is Cathy Mulhoun and I am a social worker from the Ladbroke Grove Team. Do you have a young woman there by the name of Bernadette McMahon? 26D, Ledbury Road? "

"One moment please while I check."

A few minutes passed and my heart was thumping. A voice was returned to the end of the phone.

"Yes we do. She came in last night. Had an accident. Two broken ribs and a fractured jaw, I'm afraid. She is on Carraway Ward."

I knew it, I thought and thanked the woman and put the phone down. Who should I tell? Police? No – nightmare. Feltz – he could get straight to the top with the police, but it would mean dragging him in too and he would not like more Gregory sagas. So no. Sue? Did I want to be in more trouble – impersonating a social worker? No. That only left one person. Cathy Mulhoun. Yes, I would have to admit I said I was her, but I didn't have a choice. I looked up the number for the office and rang her. Yes, she was there, just walked back into the office and could I hang on? Whoever it was forgot to ask who was calling and in a few seconds Cathy came to the phone.

"Hello, sorry, they didn't get your name, who am I speaking to? "

"Jenifer McKay. I've located Bernadette McMahon. She is in Carraway Ward in Paddington Hospital. Admitted yesterday with broken ribs and fractured jaw. Now do you believe me about Gregory?"

"Jenifer, you had no right to do that. You are suspended from your job pending a child abuse investigation. I appreciate you want to clear your name but you have to let professionals do their job. Now I will follow this through, and on this occasion I will not mention it to Sue, but you really need to let the process take its course. Furthermore, you cannot simply assume that her injuries had anything to do with Mr Jonson. Now I have to go, so goodbye."

Ok, now that was out of the way I had one more call to make. Leroy said he was popping down the market to get something to cook so I had a few minutes to spare. I rummaged round in the drawer and found Jemma's phone number. I dialed the number and got through.

"Hi Jemma, this is Jen. How are you?" I thought I would do a polite warm up before launching. Again I didn't know where to begin or how much detail to go into.

"Hey! Stranger in town! Wha' gwan? Me alright, y'know. Still fightin' de good fight. What can I do for you?"

"That's good. Well, I wondered if you could get a message to Kwame as I need to talk to him quite urgently."

"Sounds serious, by your voice. Look , you can talk to him now as he's right here." She called out to Kenneth who must have been in another room. "Kwame. Phone. It's Jen. I dunno wha' she wan' but is yu she wan' talk to, nah me."

"Young Jenifer" he said sounding pleasantly surprised, but from the sound of his voice I knew he knew this was not a social call. "How can I help you? Has Gregory been causing problems again? I don't know if there is much I can do but tell me your side of things."

I guessed from this response Gabriella had already filled him in on her side. I wasn't going to discuss any of that, though. All I wanted was for him to try to talk to Sue, as he knew her quite well – or so I had understood.

Well, I'm afraid to say I lost all composure and started to cry. I felt an idiot but he was understanding and said to take my time from the beginning. I began from the time when Gregory followed me in Artesian Road and threatened me, when he tried to get a flat over the road, how he had conned his way into the house and how he had beaten up Leroy, right up to the part where he brough one of our babies into nursery and when I was concerned and told Sue, how she dismissed my story outright. I said how awful I felt when she appeared to know him as Emmett from another nursery, where he had given the impression of being perfect Dad and how she thought I was being ridiculous when I said he was dangerous. I then said how I had found bruises on the baby's legs and how he accused me, how I was suspended, but how I had also found out that the baby's Mum was in hospital with all these injuries.

225

"So what exactly do you think I can do, Jenifer? I can give you some advice, but not much more, I'm afraid."

"Well, I just wondered if somehow you could tell Sue that I'm not making any of this up and that Gregory really is a shady character. I thought you knew her husband. I really believe Bernadette is in danger. She is young and vulnerable with no-one to turn to and I am afraid for what is going on there."

"Sue? I don't actually know her. I know about Alice as she used to work with Maureen Skeet and I am friends with her husband, but I don't know this Sue or her husband either. As you know Alice did not get the officer-in-charge job at your nursery. I think the powers that be in the Town Hall are rather afraid of 'radical' people in influential jobs, so they employed this Sue from Brent, who is very efficient, by all accounts, but also very status quo, if you get my meaning. It also means that they may try keep on Alice as deputy, so they can use her skills, but also block Gabriella from a promotion opportunity. This is how they work. But, to get back to your request, I can talk to Paul Skeet and see what can be done, if anything. Now as you can probably imagine, Gabriella told me about what happened. As you know she doesn't want anthing to upset her future career plans. We talked it through and I have asked her to talk to Sue and be a bit more open with her and support you more. She is very worried about you, you know."

"Thank you, thank you," I replied. "But what else can I do to help Bernadette?"

"Nothing. Absolutely nothing at this time. Your main concern is how you can help you, Jenifer. I suggest you tell Feltz. If you go to the police you will not be taken seriously, but he has status and position and they will listen to him. After all you are his tenant. I would also advise you to move. Right out of the area and maybe change your job too. For now, can you stay with your Mum?"

I didn't like any of this advice, but I also thought he might be right. But I didn't want to leave my flat – why should I? It wasn't me who had done anything wrong. But Kenneth said that I just needed to be safe (as if I didn't know that). It seemed as if the police were on to Gregory and with a nudge from Feltz they might move in on him faster. He also told me to tell Leroy and see if he could stay with me while I was in the flat.

This had helped me to sort out my thinking a bit. There was nothing I could do now except let the whole process run its course. And he was right about Bernadette. The truth would soon come out and in its own time. He said goodbye and put Jemma back on the phone.

" Sounds like you're in a right old mess. Tell you what – you like Duke Tam innit? Well, Boxing Day night he's playing up in Hampstead Town Hall. Why you don't ask Leroy to bring you. Marvalette will be coming and the old posse so it will cheer you up. Yu can wine up on yu man all night!" She laughed.

I didn't yet know what was happening with Mum or where I would be but I badly wanted to go so I accepted her invitation and thanked her.

"OK. An' yu' stay far from dat bandulu man, y'hear. Me wan' see yu' in a rave not a grave! OK?"

I laughed and bid her goodbye. Perfect timing as Leroy walked back in the door. Oh Shit! I thought. I almost forgot. I had an appointment at Family Planning at six o'clock that evening and it was after four already. I could call them and rearrange it, but then I thought it was getting a bit urgent that I was protected. Plus, I was due on my period in a few days so even more reason to get sorted with the pill. I saw the look on Leroy's face. He looked very worried and he hugged me as I started to cry again. He sat down with me, holding me and kissing me of the forehead gently. He said he had guessed that Gregory had troubled me at work, that he was at the bottom of this mess somewhere. To which I nodded, and began to tell him what happened, first saying that I needed to go to this FP appointment at six.

" Yu wan' me drive yu roun' in de van? Me nah wan' yu' out dere by yuself right now. So tell me wha'appen and likkle more we go round de fambly plannin'. Me wan' yu fe get sort out becar long time me want yu fe true, and me cyan 'ol' out much longer!"

We laughed a bit and I held his hand, drawing it up to my face to kiss it. I could feel a warm tingling through me, which was, fortunately, dampened by the story that I then let out.

Leroy's advice surprised me. But I thought it was spot on. He said not to bother telling Feltz anything because if this was another story to take to him, I could end up worse off, like getting told to leave the house. He said no, I had to work my brain harder than that. After all, Feltz had no vested interest in seeing Gregory locked up, but one person out there did – and in a big-time way.

"Who?" I asked – cluelessly.

"Dat Liz Dad, man. Wha' 'e name again?"

"Oh. Frankie." The penny dropped. Leroy could be right.

"Yes, man! But lewwe t'ink on dat, car yu nah wan' jus' jump in. We go fix we brain pon' it later, sleep 'pon it an' den mek we move. Seen?"

I was beginning to relax now, and Leroy let me doze on the sofa while he got some food ready. He made some corned beef and rice as something quick and simple, but we left it to have when we came back. Leroy was fixed on coming with me, but I didn't want him in the actual doctors with me in case any awkward questions were asked. More than ever now I didn't not want anything about the Benjamin mistake coming out. So I put him off from that part but said he could wait outside for me. Later on at home, after we had eaten, we looked at the leaflets together and explored the packs of magic pills – I had three months supply. I could see Leroy had thought that I would be starting them that night and that they would be effective immediately. His faced dropped when I showed him the condoms that I would need to use in the first month – that was if he became a lucky man!

We spent a warm and cosy evening together, with him attentive and kind. I had calmed down a lot, but I just didn't want him to go. I was afraid still. So he said he would stay and take care of me like how I took care of him and I remembered he had to change the dressing on his head which had paint splattered on it. He just couldn't stop working and let 'de bwoy dem' get on with the job in hand.

"Jen. Me go stay a couple two night 'ere wid yu, but me go sleep pon de couch, car me cyan trus' meself fe lie down wid yu, so no' feel no way."

I laughed and said "Men!" and went to get him some covers. As I went to the bathroom before I went to bed I found I had come on. Phew! I was relieved and most pleased that I could start the pill in a few days from now.

Just before I went to bed, Leroy asked me if I had seen Anthea. I looked at him as if to say, 'that's all I need right now' and he took it no further. As I lay my head on the pillow, I thought more about what we had said about talking to Frankie and I decided that I would indeed do that the next day.

Chapter 32   Snared.

I had developed a taste for fresh coffee – percolated in one of those little pots that, if you don't turn down the gas as it boils, it will spill grouts all over your cooker. I was muttering away about cleaning up grouts at half past six the next morning after my attempt to make Leroy and I breakfast before he went to work. I managed well enough plus giving cause for some general hilarity which was an achievement in itself at that time of the morning. Leroy watched me as I slid back into a vacant frame of mind, thinking about what we had talked about the night before. It was as if he read my mind as he leaned over the table and stroked my hair. I looked up at him and took his hand.

"I was just thinking about what we talked about last night – you know about calling Frankie. I don't know if I've got the courage – I'm scared, I suppose, as I can't predict how he will react and if that will make things any better or worse for me."

Leroy sucked his teeth. " Cho man, Jen! Me know yu can do dis. I's gonna be 'ard yes, a gamble, but yu has to be strong. Me know yu can do dis. Me know. Seen?"

I felt reassured, if not convinced, but nevertheless, I promised Leroy that I would call Frankie. Leroy gathered his stuff and said he had to go to work and that he would pop in or call me around lunch time. I locked the door after him and went back to bed. I felt quite unwell, but I was not sure how to describe it. I had cramps and possibly my mood was to do with PMT, but I also felt overwhelmed with lethargy. I was exhausted in every bone and muscle of my body, so numb I could hardly catch my feelings to name them before they sank back into the depths of me. Was this how depression felt? A sense that you had lost whatever fight you were fighting, now resigning yourself to your fate, whatever that may be. Somewhere, a voice told me I could not let these feelings steam roller me into some forgotten flatness. I thought of what Leroy had said and tried to hang on to it as a drowning woman might grasp a branch from a tree, only to find it snapping off in her hands.

It was eight o'clock. I listened to the clock ticking. Should I make more coffee to keep me awake or go back to bed and sleep some more so I would not have to think about anything? But I had promised. And I held on to that. I told myself this was a strong branch and it would not snap, that I could make it to the otherside, despite the voice in me urging me to drown, drown, drown. It was too early to make any calls, so I could have been excused from wanting to go back to bed. I forced myself, instead, to get in the bath, and lay there until the water was too cold and I was shivering. Imagining, as I watched the water turn a translucent red, that I had just slashed my wrists and it could all end just like that.

Bloody hell Jen. I snapped out of my musing and pulled the plug, getting out of the bath as fast as I could as if I wanted to get away from the most dreadful thought I had ever had. How can your mind twist and turn and take you down thought paths that should be marked 'Prohibited' and 'No Entry'? I got dry and then dressed, summoning all the mental and physical energy I had. I made more coffee – no spills this time – with liberal spoonfuls of condensed milk for the luscious sweet creaminess. I could feel my mind steeling and concentrating as I was willing it to do. I decided I needed to write a brief account of what had happened with dates and names so that I could try to keep a track of what was going on. It was clear that Gregory was out to get me, that was for sure. And the only person who could stop it was me. ME. ME. ME! I caught a reflection of myself in the mirror.

"Gregory Emmett Jonson you will not get the better of me." I said it over and over, until I felt a surge of something I can't quite describe flood my whole body. A heat like energy. I decided to call it my Jen-force and took it as a sign that I was indeed empowering myself to move forward and not let this awful sequence of events make me ever feel that low again. I tidied the flat with a sense of purposefulness, deliberate as if to make sure that I could feel that it was really me doing the tasks. I put some music on, quietly and danced madly about the flat really enjoying the sense of this power surge in me that I had never known before. I then settled down to writing my 'statement', as I called it.

That took me til about midday. Right, now to call Frankie. I found Liz's parents' number in an old address book – lucky for me I still had it – and dialled the number. I had my fingers crossed that he would answer so that I did not have to explain anything to Jean and get lectured. Second stroke of luck! Frankie answered. I felt myself flush with fear as I heard his voice.

"Is that Frankie? I mean can I speak to Frankie please?"

"Frankie speaking. Who is this?"

"It's Jen. I used to be friends with Liz. I really need to speak with you?"

" Do what? Yes, I remember who you are alright. Liz's friend you say. Some definition of friend you have. What the bloody hell do you want?"

If I could just get over this hostility to get him to listen to me. I decided to go directly to the point and not ask about how Liz was or get into anything where I would feel I would be pressed into apologising or explaining anything that was not immediately relevant to ME. Remember ME.ME.ME!

"I need to talk to you about Gregory Emmett Jonson. It's urgent. He is stalking me and is very threatening. It's getting worse. It's all because I turned the Pumas against him."

"Well you could say you've turned me against you an' all, but I figure if you've got the guts to call me then it must be serious. Part of me wants to tell you it's got nothing to do with me and for you to get lost, but you might just shed light on a few things that would help my mates get him nailed. Tell you what. I don't wanna discuss this on the blower. Face to face. Where are you?"

I was a bit taken aback at his seemingly eager response, but I was still afraid. Anyway, I replied that I was at home and he said he would prefer to come and see me. I gave him my address and he said he would see me in the hour. I wondered if I should see him alone or get back up? I called Francis. He wasn't there. Mind you. Francis had not exactly been a direct witness, but he did know the history of the house – but then it occurred to me that so did someone else and that person was much more credible. Feltz. I dialled his number.

"Mr Feltz? It's Jen here. Are you free as I would like a quick word?"

"Go ahead. Although with you, my dear, it never seems to be a quick word. Please tell me it's got nothing to do with Gregory. I really can't stand hearing the name of that pestilence anymore."

"I'm afraid it is. There was a development at work. He turned up bringing one of the babies in. The baby had bruises and he is accusing me – which it could not possibly be - plus the Mum is in hospital all injured and I am sure it was him and I reported it to the Officer-in-Charge and she did not believe me as she knows him from a while back where he presented as some kind of model Dad, so now I'm suspended while there is an investigation." I stopped to catch my breath and before Feltz could fill the silence with even the shortest syllable, I went on. "It seems clear he's really got in in for me. I've phoned the Dad of that friend I used to know – the one that started this whole thing – you know, the one he raped. I've phoned her Dad -Frankie. He's an ex West End copper . He's coming here. I know they want to get him. Can you come in an hour? He will be here. If you tell him what you know and what you've seen I'm sure it would help getting him out of our lives. Please?"

"Jenifer. I am getting tired of this. But before we start I know I owe you an apology for not being sympathetic to Leroy as I now know that it was Anthea who let him in. Have you seen her by the way? I know she is desperate to see you and apologise to you."

"No. Not yet. I don't know. But can you come over? Frankie will be here around one or half past."

"Ok. But I need to warn you. This has to stop. Otherwise I will have to give you notice to leave. I know it's not your fault, but I can't have this going on. I am trying to run a business here and I have new tenants lined up for January – mainly medical students and hospital staff. I have to have a trouble-free house, Jen. I'm only coming over as it seems this may lead to something being done. I also want you to be safe. I am concerned about you too. It's not all about my business. I do have a heart too."

I was relieved that he was coming, although not that impressed with his heart-of-gold-inside line, but he meant well. As long as this meeting could lead to something positive happening, I would be happy. I wondered if Leroy would be turning up. Another witness, and perhaps Anthea? Ok, she wants to apologise. Now's the time. I ran upstairs, first locking my door securely, and knocked on her door. I was about to go back downstairs, thinking she was not in or not answering when I heard her asking who was there. I said it was me and she opened the door.

"Hi. I hear you had something you wanted to say to me?"

"Yes. Yes I do. I am most terribly sorry. I didn't realise and I was scared. Such an idiot. I am so sorry for your boyfriend being beaten up."

"Yeah, well he was after me. And Leroy stopped it. But it hasn't ended there. Look. I need to talk and there is an ex-copper coming over in a while and I wondered if you could come down and say what you know. I can understand if you don't want to get involved, but maybe it could be a way of making up to me for what happened? It would really help me."

Anthea thought for a moment. Then she said she would join us. I suggested she come down to my room as soon as she could. She said to give her 15 minutes and shut her door. As I went downstairs I began to feel suspicious. She had only opened her door a chink as if to want to hide something – or someone – in her room. Oh come on, I thought to myself. Maybe her place is a tip and she does not want me to see. I decided not to let my mind run on things that were not fact. I ran back downstairs and could hear the phone ringing. Luckily I got there in time. It was Social Services. Apparently, Jasper had been seen by the doctor who had made his report. In his view, the bruising could not have been made that day and were at least two days old, taking us to the weekend. I was silent, I thought I would just let her go on.

"What that means, Jenifer, if that you are exhonerated and we have told your Head of Service that you should be reinstated immediately and your personnel record

231

must show that. We have also seen Bernadette in hospital and are following up your concerns with the police. Clearly I cannot go into more details with you, but you will be invited to attend a case conference. We will confirm the date and time with you later."

I was gobsmacked, although relieved, and wondered what had happened to Jasper.

"He is with foster carers while Mum recovers and we will have to think about his long-term future and Mum's ability to look after him. If he goes home, then the nursery will have a big part to play in their lives. But we have to get together first to discuss what has been happening."

"I see. But what about Gregory, the one that Sue calls Emmett?"

"Again, I cannot go into details, but we have received a full police report on him. I can tell you he has been arrested and I think Sue is now a bit clearer about this individual. I am sure we will all learn more and be able to find a way forward after the meeting."

"Yes. I will expect you to tell me the time and date later and confirm I will be there. And thank you. Do you know if the Head of Service will call me or Sue?"

"I imagine both. See you on Friday. Oh. And I hope you are OK. This must have been a very difficult 24 hours for you."

"Yes it has. It has indeed. But I am relieved now. See you at the meeting."

We bid each other goodbye. I sat for a moment to let that sink in but then there was a knock at the door. I was Anthea. She held out her arms and have me a tearful hug. I thought that it should be me in tears – and then, of course, I started to cry too. We stayed like that for a moment, until I started to laugh and went to get us a tissue.

"Tea? Coffee?" I asked her.

"Oh! Tea please. I've got some biscuits although I think we could do with something stronger"

"So do I. But we can have that later as I think I have news to celebrate. Would you like some cheese on toast?"

Anthea nodded and I told her all what had happened and how my name had been cleared. She said it should have been obvious to that Sue about the bruise and talk about a knee jerker. Somehow though, I did not feel angry with Sue, I was just pleased it was all over. Then I told her about how Gregory had been arrested.

"Good! And double good. But now tell me about this Frankie and what's going on with Feltz."

"Well, they are gonna be here any minute, hopefully and maybe the less you know of the details the better, so it won't look as if you've been primed up. Here, take your cheese on toast. Do you want any Lee 'n' Perrins? Salt and pepper?"

"Yes to everything," she replied. "Have you heard from Beth? I saw her on the weekend. I have been able to find her a job in my office and she's over the moon. She said with that, and her Family Allowance, she can manage without having to beg from that ex of hers. Also, we thought she could possibly find a sort of semi-aupair who could live rent free and do a bit of housework and babysitting for her in exchange for the room and then the rest of the time would be free for studying. She thought a student would be good. Anyway, it's looking up for her and she also want to know when we can all meet again."

"Well that's all good, but I would rather get all this done with and out of the way. So maybe after Christmas?"

"I think she was more thinking socially. Maybe over the Christmas. A party or something. Invite your friends and Francis. It would be fun!"

To be honest, partying was not on my mind, but I did see it could be something to look forward to and lift all our spirits, but I was still too distracted to even think that far ahead. The phone rang. It was Leroy calling from a payphone. I briefly told him what had happened and that we were waiting for Feltz and Frankie to arrive any minute and did he want to come too?

"Jen. Me all de way down Stokie right now on a job, so me jus' givin' yu a quick ding.WE go talk 'bour Frankie later – but me proud o' you fe call 'im. Me glad 'bout de job, too, man. Me did pray fe dat. Dat dis cloud roun' yu woulda lif' offa yu. Yu gwine be safe. Trus' me."

I thanked him and said I would see him later. He said he would pick me up at half six that evening and we would go over to see Marvalette for dinner. He'd arranged it. I smiled. I was feeling more and more for this man. He just seemed so right for me. And just then, of course, the doorbell rang. I took a deep breath.

Chapter 33   The Tying of Loose Ends

I looked through the window before I ventured to the door and was very pleased to see Feltz standing there. I was glad that he had arrived before Frankie. He had brought a Jewish Honey Cake with him – to sweeten things along a bit as he put it. I checked I had enough milk for tea and put the kettle on, passing mugs and plates to Anthea to set on the table.

"Out to impress then, Jen?" Anthea smiled at me. It wasn't that I wanted to impress as such but just create the right impression and I thought that was different. I tried to explain, but Anthea thought I had taken her comment too

233

seriously. I was nervous and perhaps not in the mood for frivolity. My head was aching with tension and, frankly, I just wanted his over with – whatever 'this' was going to be.

"Do you want to brief us so we appear, at least, to know what it's all about and so we can make some positive contribution to help you here?" began Feltz. I guess we all have good reason to ensure Gregory is brought to book by the law, not least you, Jen."

I really felt as if my head was spinning with a million thoughts going round at once. I said I would prefer that we did not look as if we were rehearsed, especially as I had not told Frankie that there would be anyone else than me. Feltz disagreed, but he saw my point; moreso, he saw how unsettled I was and asked if I was feeling OK.

"No. I don't actually. My head is splitting and going round and round. Do you have any asprin?"

Anthea said she had Anadin in her bag and rummaged about frantically until she found a rather dog-eared pack, but I didn't care. I swallowed two with lots of water and then waited for it to take effect. Anthea put her arm round me sympathetically and tried to reassure me.

"My biggest fear is that Frankie just wants to focus on what happened with Liz and that whole mess and how he blames me for not being able to get Gregory behind bars for what he did."

"Well, you can't get yourself in a tiz over that. You have to remember that you have plenty of information about Gregory that can also be of help to Frankie, plus you have us behind you."

I was grateful for Feltz's support. I looked at my watch. It was nearly one thirty. Where was Frankie? Maybe he wasn't going to come after all. I sighed one of those sighs that you do when you feel all is lost.

"What does he look like, this Frankie? There's someone outside looking a bit burly, grey hair, beer gut over Farah slacks – could that be him?" I could not help laughing at Anthea's description and took a look out of the window. It certainly looked like Frankie, but his back was turned as he pulled a piece of paper out of his pocket and then turned as if to check he had the right address.

"It's him! Frankie!" I started to fumble about to get to the door, but Feltz stopped me and told me to sit down and for Anthea to finish making a pot of tea. He went to invite Frankie in.

"Excuse me. Am I right in thinking you are Frankie? My name is Mr Feltz. Jen's landlord. We thought it might be helpful for me to be here and another young lady, a tenant of mine in this house also. We all want this Gregory chap dealt with by the law. Please come in."

Feltz had this businessman's air of being in charge and of being someone to take seriously (unlike me, I thought). He and Frankie shook hands and he brought him inside, introducing me and Anthea and inviting him to take a seat at the table. He took his jacket and asked him if he wanted tea.

Frankie wasn't really prepared for this reception but he took his seat an accepted tea (two sugars, love) while Feltz cut us all a piece of cake. I began to relax, slighty.

"Alright Jenifer. I havn't come all this way to drink tea and eat cake so let's get to the point shall we? You called me, saying you wanted to talk – so talk. I'm listening."

I found my piece of paper that had all the events involving Gregory written down in date order. I said I wanted to start at the beginning – with that awful night with Liz being raped. Frankie's face hardened but I carried on with each part of the tale and how it all seemed as if Gregory really had it in for me and how afraid I was. I ended up with the latest that he had been arrested for beating up Bernadette and hurting her baby.

Frankie just said "Right." Then turned to Feltz and asked him how he came into the story, so Feltz told him about his father owning these houses and how Billie Boy and Gregory had turned them into houses of ill repute and embezzled his father out of £ 5,000 in rents not paid. I didn't even know that part, but I suppose it was no surprise as old Mr Feltz was not at all with it at that time and very vulnerable to being conned. Feltz said he was concerned that Gregory was 'relectant to let go' of his connections to these houses and that his harassment of me was bad for his business and that he did not want his tenants to leave- including and especially me. He went on to give me a bit of a glowing reference and said he felt protective towards me.

"More tea, Mr err... Frankie?" Anthea broke the rather tense atmosphere and Feltz said he would get the kettle on. Frankie just took a deep breath in, puffed himself up and then breathed out slowly, as if that said a thousand words. It certainly got us listening attentively to what he was about to reveal.

"All right, All right. I will have another cuppa, thanks - and that cake's a bit tasty if there's any more going?"

He seemed to be softening a bit and thinking things through, saying nothing while he slowly ate his second slice of honey cake. Then after another deep breath, he started to speak.

"I dunno what you think I can do. I'm not in the Police Force any more – been retired a while now. Arthritis. Painful. Got it in me 'ips and me legs, but that's not your concern. I'm gonna begin with you, Mr Feltz. I knew your old man. He used to be a canny bugger then he went soft in the head, poor sod. You know he had properties down the West End don't you? You shake your head - but he did, son, he did. Gambling house in Greek Street, strip joint in Peter Street, rooms he used

235

to rent above the shops too – not too many guesses what for! That's when he was married to your Mum and you were a little nipper. Your Mum and you came here from Germany when you were a baby in 1939. She set herself up in Belsize Park with a house and she rented rooms. She thought your Dad was fighting in the resistance – well he was for a while, but it's not hard to imagine where he ended up. When Auswitz was liberated in 1945, he was found alive and because of his contacts with British Intelligence he was able to come here and be reunited with his family. That was in 1946 – you would have been about…"

"Seven. I was seven. He never spoke of being in Auswitz, but we knew, Mum and I. We saw his camp number tattooed on his arm, although he always tried to hide it from us. He was never quite right mentally from all of that. Now, look, I only knew he had houses, but frankly I don't think you have it right about that seedy stuff in the West End. Dad just wasn't like that. He was well respected in the Synagogue and helped a lot of fellow Jews resettling here after the war. My mother was very proud of him. So, I'm not sure where you get all this story from, Frankie."

Frankie sniffed and continued.

"He bought his first proper house in Finchley, where you moved to as your family home. You went to a posh private school and he didn't want it coming out what lines of business he was in, and your Mum knew nothing of it. He sold those businesses in the mid fifties and bought some houses, these two and the one over the road, plus a couple more near Swiss Cottage. Houses like that went for a song in the auctions in them days, so he bought them up cheap; he set them up as rentals and got caretakers in to run them. His problem was that his circles were full of people from the shady side and he had a hard time keeping them at bay. The Swiss Cottage houses were OK, so were these until the mid 60s when he got old Billy Boy in, followed by Gregory. So, I can hear you asking how did the likes of Gregory get in on the act?

"I'll tell ya. Him and Billy Boy weren't just taking advantage of a demented old fool. It was blackmail, rather, retribution. They had two things on him. First. Your Dad liked young lads – smart 'n' smooth he liked them. Had a little dirty secret – yeah don't look at me like that – I'm telling you what was common knowledge. We never caught him and he was making a few of our boys, well, let's say, quite comfortable, being kind to them, if you see what I mean. Now, our Billy Boy knew all about that, he had material to prove it too, so he knew how to get his own way with the old boy to make sure he was comfortable too. Then he saw an opening to make things even more cosy and took up a job here as caretaker. Had the old man over a barrel.

Then a few years later, Gregory gets involved as a rent collector. Old Feltz never needed no rent collector. He had Billy Boy for that. It was Gregory who started the girls lark. But they kept it low key, no advertsing cards, just links with the night clubs in the West End. First, Gregory would procure punters and act as chauffeur. This is when the money started rolling in and Old Feltz was getting none of it. So what was the connection? Now, Mr. Feltz, what I am going to say will come as a shock, but it's true. Gregory's Mum used to work for Feltz in his strip club for quite a few years. He was born in 1949 and she had started to work for him as a receptionist in '48. She was quite a favourite with him until '52 when she died, but their affair had long finished. In that year she was pregnant again, not by him, but the bloke she lived with along with little Gregory. Feltz paid for her to have an abortion; he had told her it was safe, that the woman was a retired doctor. Of course she wasn't. Just some old back street crone that girls in the family way would go to. But, of course, he didn't know that. She died, anyway. Gregory's Mum. Audrey her name was. Bled to death in her own bed. Gregory found her. He was a nipper then –'bout three he must have been. His Dad, well, Audrey's man that she lived with, couldn't cope with the responsibility for a child who wasn't his, and put him in a children's home in Kent - terrible reputation it had too. Her boyfriend was none other than Billy. Old Billy Boy kept in touch with Gregory throughAudrey's sister, Mavis. One of the other girls knew Audrey had been to the old crone and told the police. She got put in prison and Feltz denied all knowledge of it. When Gregory left care, he went to live with Mavis and that's how he got in with Billy Boy, who told him about what happened to his Mum. So now Billy knows that both of them had grudges against your Dad and they had a field day with him and his money. It was never blackmail in the true sense of the word, but it was extortion and serious taking the piss. We knew about it but didn't do much – well you know how it goes; they was protected. Your old man was, by then, no longer interested in his young men so they couldn't nick him for it, but the boys just kept on fleecing him. Then of course he dies and as far as the properties go, you know what happened next. Gregory becomes a West End pimp. He liked to think he modelled himself on your father. He used his middle name, Emmett, and married a girl in Harlesden, bought a house and appeared to live a model life. His wife never knew what was going on, which was how he liked it. That's how your boss knows him and why she never believed you."

There was a silence. Clearly, Feltz was shocked, embarrassed and, I imagined, ashamed of his father. Anthea said nothing but looked uncomfortable. I was just wondering when he was going to come to the Liz part. It sounds awful to say this but I didn't feel a thing about the background story. I suppose he was building up to it.

"So as you can see, Gregory is, let's say, on the edge of criminally insane from all he's been through. He's dangerous but knows how to wheel and deal and manipulate to keep himself just about clear of the law. Then he starts on my daughter. I don't know for sure, but I reckon he knew just who Liz was, so he really wanted to reel her in like a trophy prize. She wouldn't listen to me. Oh no. Or her Mum. Then she was living with you in that basement and we just thought she'd made her bed, so let her lie on it. Then that bastard did what he did to her. That was bad enough. Then she was pregnant and lost the baby and that did her head in. Next thing she's back and forward down that pub in Kensal Rise and now she's with some other black idiot running around rolling punters. She won't take it no further about the rape and said you refused to stick up for her and wouldn't go to court and even Jean thinks you cleaned up to destroy the evidence."

"But Liz said you didn't want to call me as a witness. She said you said I was a liability. And I didn't realise what I was doing when I cleaned up and Liz knew

237

that. I would stand up in court for her happily to see him put away for what he did. And now he's coming after me 'cos I've blown his clean-cut image and I'm a real threat. Even though he's been arrested over Bernadette and the baby, she's vulnerable and scared, so two twos she will deny it was him. I'm very scared and that's why I called you. We've got all this – raping Liz, Marcia, beating up Leroy, Bernadette and the baby, stalking me, worrying Anthea – is there not enough to put him away yet?"

"Jenifer. He's a bit psycho for sure and, yes, you are in danger, but the police will say there's nothing they can do until he actually does something. Leroy is willing to go to court but it will be a minor charge of ABH. Six months suspended max. Bernadette, as you say, might wobble and withdraw her statement. Social services will pursue the child abuse but there's not enough evidence for the CPS to prosecute on. So, in short I don't know what can be done, but I will go and have a word with the old boss and see if they've got another angle. I'm sorry, but that's all I can say."

There was an uncomfortable silence. Then Anthea said she had to go. She told Feltz she would call him later. That's it, I thought, she's leaving. I didn't really blame her. I didn't know what to say and Feltz was still reeling about what he'd heard about his father, and we were all clearly very down hearted that Frankie reckoned the police could do nothing.

Frankie, sensing the atmosphere in the room, said he would see himself out and said to me to call him again if I was worried. He thanked us for the tea and cake and left. That left me and a very dejected looking Mr Feltz.

"I'm so sorry he said all that about your Dad. It must have been a shock. I just don't know where we go from here."

"Well, I'm going home and I'm going to think things through. When my head is cleared I will call you. Bye for now."

And he left. Just like that. Even though I felt sorry for him after hearing all those revelations it was still me who was in danger. I locked the door, cleared up the cups and sat on the sofa and cried until I went to sleep. When I woke up it was half past four. I went to the loo and splashed water in my face. A tap on my door startled me.

"Who is it?"

"Anthea"

I opened the door and invited her in. Then I noticed her cases packed.

"I'm leaving. I'm moving in with Beth until I find something more suitable. I'm not far, so I – well, and Beth – can keep an eye on you. I think you should move too. Get away from here, get a new job, just get away from here. I wouldn't want to be in your shoes right now but that's what I'd do anyway. Anyway. Just popped in to say goodbye."

I was gobsmacked. Not having anything to say in reply I just said something like thanks for telling me and shut the door. I felt more tears brimmimg in my eyes. Then I stopped in my tracks. I was NOT GOING TO LET GREGORY WIN. OH NO! I looked for an old single "Let the power fall on I' and put it on, singing as loud as I could til I could feel myself feeling strong. I decided to call work and speak to Sue.

"Hello Sue. This is Jen. I had a call from the social worker this morning and she says I've been exhonerated so that means I should no longer been suspended - am I right?"

"Yes. That was good news, although it's not up to me about what happens to your suspension. That will be down to Andy McCrae and personnel to call you in for an interview. That will be after the case conference. But until then I would just enjoy your time off and relax. I imagine this must be quite difficult for you. I will be at the case conference, so I will see you then."

We said goodbye and that was it. Short and sweet. Abrupt, I thought, wondering if Sue was miffed with me for proving her wrong about Gregory. Anyway, she said I was to enjoy the rest, and, in that, she was not wrong. I remembered that Kenneth said Gabriella was going to call me, but she had not done so yet. I wondered to myself what I really thought about her – was she a true friend? Could I trust her? Well, I would just have to wait and see as I was not about to call her. Leroy was coming to pick me up at half six to go over to Marvalette's for dinner. I might as well get ready then.

Chapter 34   The Future Takes Shape.

We spent a lovely evening at Marvalette's. Leroy had bought a new Heptones album and Norman, as always had some new pre-release singles - Gaylads, Cables and quite a few more, listening, as I was, from the kitchen where I was helping Marvalette and playing hangman with Aaron. When he had gone to bed, I told everyone what had happened.

"Do you think old Feltz is Gregory's father?" asked Marvalette.

"Who knows. But I bet the thought of him being Feltz's brother does not please. Feltz was not happy with the whole story. I really don't think he knew anything about it. But, the thing is what's he going to do next?"

"I think you should move from that place. You are not safe there. Maybe even change your job."

"Yes, man. Dat place jinx like is a duppy yard. Me know yu love dat place, but safety is a mus'" added Norman.

239

"I don't see why I should budge – that would be like handing Gregory the winner's rosette on a plate. However, I see your point. I admit the thought has crossed my mind but I will see how things go by the end of the week. I'm in no state to make decisions right now."

We sat around chatting and playing music until about half ten. I was starting to feel tired and Leroy noticed, so he asked me if I wanted to go. I said I did. We said our goodbyes and got in the not so smelly lift laughing about it having had its annual council clean. I was glad Leroy had the van with him and we were soon home.

I had left the fire on low (Leroy said it was dangerous, but it was freezing out) and I was glad to come home to a warm place. There was a letter pushed under the door. Part of me didn't want to look at it. It could only have been from Feltz as it was hand delivered for one and only he, hopefully, had a key.

"Looks like my notice to quit letter." I joked to Leroy.

" Nah man, Jen. Feltz nah go on so. Read it an' see. I'll make a hot chocolate for bot' o' we."

I looked at the letter again. Might as well get on with it then. It was typed.

> *Dear Jenifer*
>
> *After today's discussions I have given the matter of the future of my properties in Westbourne Grove a great deal of thought and discussed with my wife and my solicitor.*
>
> *I have decided, regrettably, to sell the houses. You may be able to stay on with a new landlord, but if I were you, I would think seriously about moving out of the area. I don't want to leave you with nowhere to go so I have some ideas that I would like to propose to you which you may find attractive.*
>
> *I shall call you tomorrow and arrange to come and see you. Please consider a time when Leroy can be there too.*
>
> *At this time, please do not say anything to Francis. I will let him know and make him a suitable offer when I have come to a satisfactory arrangement with you.*
>
> *Best wishes – and don't worry.*
> *J. R Feltz*

"So what do you think that's about? It's like he's kicking me out, but not? Jeez, I really can't take any more of my life being turned upside down."

Leroy came over to me and said to forget all about it til morning. He put his arms round me and kissed me, long and slow. It felt safe and warm and I liked that.

240

"Shall we drink our hot choc in bed then?" Leroy smiled.

"I'll jus' get a quick bathe and join you."

"I'll run you a bath" I said.

By the time we had both had a quick bath, the drinks were cold, so I warmed them up and took them into the bedroom. Leroy was sitting up in bed in his vest and pants complaining that cotton sheets were so cold. I got the hot water bottle and that seemed to make him feel better. My mind was spinning – sex, period, pill, rubber – I couldn't cope. Leroy sensed that I was distracted and guessed why.

"Let's just drink up and go to sleep. No pressure."

We slid down under the covers together and I sank into his arms. We kissed and stopped. Kissed some more and then Leroy said:

"Hush now. I'm here. Plenty time a'come for makin' love. Me love yu, yu know Jen. Dese las' few weeks me getting' to know yu good and me like yu style. From now on, I would like very much dat it's you 'n' me, like yu is my 'oman."

" I am starting to feel the same way about you too" I whispered. I admit I was taken aback by his admission of being in love with me – it was a bit early days for that, I thought, but I also felt we were getting very close and certainly there was a sexual spark that could ignite tonight if I did not determine to go to sleep right there and then. So far, Leroy was proving to be loyal – in my corner, as Marvalette put it- and I felt that I had a real friend in him. It was not long before I fell asleep, feeling safer than I had done in a long time. I must have slept deeply too, as it seemed like no time at all that I felt Leroy stirring and heard the bathroom light being turned on. When I looked at the clock it was half six, so he must be getting up for work. I got up to make him something to eat before he left, but, by the looks of the place, he had already made himself a fried egg sandwich and a cup of coffee. I put the kettle on to make myself some tea when he came into the living room, dressed and ready to leave.

He kissed me on the forehead – so sweet. "Mornin' darlin'. Me 'affe go work now, so me ketch yu later. Go back in yu bed and res'up. Tell Feltz me can be 'ere fe six o'clock tonight, if dat suit 'im. Den me go take yu up by me yard in 'arlesden to sort out a few bits an' pieces and come back a' you' yard. Me wan' stay wid you for a couple night until yu feel safe." Then he kissed me, picked up his work bag and left.

The flat seemed empty without him, but I refilled the hot water bottle and took my tea back to bed. I sat up making a note of the things I had to do and after I had drunk my tea I went back to sleep til after ten. I was surprised to have slept so long, but it felt good and I felt the benefit of it. I decided to get up and clear the kitchen area, but, catching sight of Feltz's letter, I wondered what he meant he had as a plan. I thought of going out for the paper to start looking for places, but today,

241

I thought, would be better spent relaxing after the storms of the previous days. I had not given Xmas any further thought and decided that would be the focus of today's efforts. I tidied up the rest of the flat had a quick bath, got dressed and made myself some toast. Finding a pen and paper, I started on the Xmas card and present list, checking off what I had or hadn't done. It felt like an effort, but I made myself do it. Then I rang the bank to see how much I had on my account. Good. Enough to do some shopping. I wanted to get out fast, but Feltz had not rung yet and so I hung around to wait on that call. I continued with Xmas ideas – decorations for the flat, after all I might as well as I would not be budging before that and it would be cool to do it up – get a tree and some garlands. I laughed to myself as I remembered the paper chains we had been making at nursery til everyone felt sick with the taste of the glue, before Marion had the idea to get a bowl of water and a sponge. I was trying to cost the list when the phone rang. I hoped it was Feltz, but it was Gabriella.

"Hi Jen. How are you?"

"Tired, but coping." I replied, wondering what she was going to say.

"Are you home today – I mean, can I come round? I'm off and I would like to see you."

"Well, I am home at the moment, but as soon as I have finished a call that I am waiting on I was going to go to Ken High Street to do some Christmas shopping."

"Ooh. I'd love to come if you can handle company. I haven't started on my list yet and there are a few things I would like to get there."

"Great. Ok then. If you can come here for me, then we can leave here together. I have to be back by six though."

" Right! You're on! See you in half an hour. I will walk round."

We said goodbye and I finished getting ready, hoping the phone would ring. It did and this time it was Feltz. We exchanged customary greetings and then agreed for him to come over later at six o'clock. As he hung up, the door went. I looked out expecting to see Gabriella, although it was ten minutes early for her to be here yet, but, to my surprise, it was Beth. I was pleased to see her, but it was the wrong time.

"Sorry Beth. I'm just about to go out. Can I pop over tomorrow? I would love to see you and the kids."

Beth looked dismayed and I hurriedly repeated how much I needed to catch up with her about what had been going on, as well as to fix a time for us to have a women's group meeting.

"Something dreadful has happened," she blurted out and I just needed to tell someone.

My mind raced over what might have happened. The kids had an accident? Please not another Gregory incident? I invited her in quickly as it was cold on the doorstep.

"My bloody ex husband has gone and sold the house. Right over my head, so it looks like I could be homeless. You remember the deal was instead of us selling and splitting the money, I owned half but could just live in it rent free with the girls and that would be alimony? Well he's met someone and want to get married and they would like to 'release the capital' in the house. He is saying he does not owe me any part of it because what he has done is taken the alimony as rent against my half so he has in effect bought me out. I don't't know hoe he did it – hi and his crafty solicitor, so now I have to see a lawyer and fight him in court. The thing is. He sold it without my knowledge and I just got this today."

Beth waved a piece of paper around angrily. "It is from the new owner who says he needs to come to speak with me over the matter of my residency in the house. I just don't know what to do. And, you never guess what? It's your landlord who has bought it. Apparently his father owned it before and sold it to my husband."

She burst into tears. I could see Gabriella getting off the bus on the other side of the road. I did not want to leave Beth in distress but I just could not handle anymore of anyone's dramas today, just as mine were beginning to settle and I so badly wanted just to go and do some Xmas shopping to take my mind off everything and feel a bit, well, 'normal' for a while. I wanted to say that I couldn't deal with this right now and that I needed some space from problems, but I couldn't. I hugged her and gave her a tissue as she was crying her eyes out. And of course at that moment the doorbell rang! I excused myself and invited Gabriella in.

On seeing her, Beth gathered herself, apologised and made to leave, but I held her back and said that I was seeing Feltz later and I would call her just as soon as he was gone. And that, definitely, I would be over in the morning and not to worry.

That seemed to settle her a bit and she said she had to get back to Benji as he was off school with a cold. Gabriella looked at me with a questioning look. "Don't ask," I replied. "Let's just get on our way."

I grabbed my bag, making sure I had my cheque book, put my coat on and grabbed some gloves and a scarf as Gabriella said it was freezing out there. As we left the house, the fresh air hit me, cold as it was though, I took a deep breath in, and then a few more, watching my exhaled breath curl its way into the cold air as if it were my troubles evaporating. We saw a 23-bus coming and ran for it, as we could take that up to Chepstow Road and then get a 28 or 31 to Kensington. It was a long time since I had been shopping.

Gabriella and I agreed not to talk about work. We planned out where we wanted to go shopping and what we had in mind to buy. I wanted a new dress from Biba and we also thought of going to Chelsea Girl. Then there were presents to think of

– perhaps the big stores, but they were expensive. Definitley Woolies for cards and xmas decorations, Marks to get something for my Mum. We shopped and chatted and hardly noticed the time until we started to feel hungry.

Finding a little coffee shop we sat down and then Gabriells asked if we could talk a little bit about work. I said Ok, as we did need to have a chat about the whole Bernadette thing, for which she apologised for not sticking up for me. Apparently, there was a case conference, which I already knew, but then she said that Jasper had been taken into care and was with foster carers in Chiswick. I imagined how heartbroken Bernadette must have been. She so wanted to make a go of being a Mum, but it was clear that, in her vulnerability, she had let the wrong man into her life and he – being Gregory - had abused her and Jasper. She had a history of this and had experienced violence when growing up and it seemed she just went from one abusive relationship to another. It was sad, very sad, but they said they were considering whether to work with the NSPCC for some intense family work and therapy, or whether to just get a court order to have Jasper adopted. It seemed unfair not to give her another chance to prove she could do it. You almost wanted to adopt her yourself to give her the right backing of a caring home where she could develop good mothering skills and make a better life for herself and Jasper, but that would never be an option. When they talk of 'mother and baby homes' that's what it should be like, not those punitive places run by cold hearted nuns where they put unmarried Catholic mothers. Oh. And another thing, as Gabriella added, after Sue said she knew him from her last job, they wanted details of his child and were going to look into that. Gregory had been arrested and charged, but if Bernadette denied it was him, then possibly he might get off. Honestly, that man seemed to have a skin like a snake,

However, this saddened me and I wanted to lift my spirits so we changed the subject and talked about the staff 'do'. This year it was going to be at the Town Hall for lots of the staff and their other halves. Gabriella said they laid on plenty of food and a fair bit of wine, but that the music was a bit grim. I half wanted to go, but after being suspended, I felt that their chicken vol-au-vents would just stick in my throat.

"Maybe I can give that a miss. I think Leroy has a party in mind. Would you like to come along?"

"It depends. I don't do Blues dances with all that weed smoking going on. And I prefer soul to reggae – which I assume is what Leroy means by a party? There's going to be a good night at the Q Club in Praed Street on New Year's Eve. It's about £5 but that includes food and there will be a band as well."

"I'm not sure what I will have planned with my Mum. You know my Dad died recently and we havn't had the funeral yet. It will be the first year my Mum has spent without him and I want to be with her as much as possible – also to protect her from my awful sister and her miserable husband! But I will let you know when we have sorted it all out."

"Oh, I'm sorry. I didn't think. But the invitation is open anyway."

We looked out and saw it was getting dark. "Goodness. It's half past four. The buses will be packed and I need to get back to Sharlette. She's at my Mum's"

We paid our bill and went out into the cold evening air. It felt damp and heavy as if it would snow soon. Ugh! I hated snow!

We sat separately on the packed bus back to Chepstow Road and then I walked down Westbourne Grove rather than waiting for the 23.

"When are you back to work anyway – we miss you?"

"I have the disciplinary hearing either tomorrow or next week, and then I want to have annual leave til January. I really need to rest as I have been under such a strain. It has been hell on all fronts, I can tell you."

"Ok, well here you are at your house. I am going to get along to my Mum's now. I hope all goes well for you and that we see you before Xmas for all the kids stuff. Our Xmas dinner is on the 21st. Hope you can come in just for that."

We said our goodbyes and I checked my watch. It was almost six, giving me just enough time to get in and get the heater on and start to prepare dinner. I thought we could eat when we came back from Leroy's, after meeting Feltz. I scoured the fridge for what I could make – it was a bit bare, but I had the makings of a Caribbean style macaroni pie and started to make that. It was quick as well. I boiled the pasta, fried the onons and tomatoes with some thyme, added a tin of sweet corn to the pasta when it was cooked. Broke an egg into it, beat it in well and added lots of cheese. Spooned it into a pyrex dish, more cheese on the top, and some slice tomatoes. Just as it went into the oven, Leroy arrived. Thank heavens for fast food, I thought!

I let him in and we greeted each other with hugs and a quick catch-up on our day. I could see he was hungry. He pulled a bit of a face when I said what was for dinner – no meat was a bit of an issue - but he was glad of hot food. I had boiled some carrots to go with the pie so it was a substantial plateful. Feltz was late and we were half-way through dinner when he arrived. He looked stressed. I offered him some dinner and to my surprise he said it looked tasty and agreed to have a portion, so we all sat down together. It was wierd to say the least. To sit and eat with your landlord, who, it appeared was about to deliver an eviction notice. It seemed best to wait until we had finished eating. Leroy took the plates and asked if anyone wanted 'haringe' as he cut and peeled a plateful of orange slices for us to dip into.

"My," said Feltz, "this is an unexpected treat. Thank you both. I know you must be keen to know the outcome of my note to you and for some explanation. As soon as I have finished this delicious orange and got rid of the juice which seems to be running through my beard, I can begin. May I use your bathroom?"

"Of course," I replied, rolling off some kitchen towel for him, "please do."

Leroy and I rinsed off our face and hands at the sink and I put the kettle on.

Then we settled with some coffee and Feltz began to reveal what had been going on since we had met with Frankie.

"Things have been really difficult for me. Frankie revealed things that I found hard to accept, although I do believe Frankie, from his experience, was telling the truth about my father's other life. After he died, there were boxes and boxes of his papers, which I kept, but I never had the time or inclination to go through them. I thought it was now high time that I did, so I started to put these boxes in order of date and place and then I started to sift through. You would not believe the stuff he kept – I suppose he had to for tax purposes when doing his accounts – but bus tickets? I ask you! So much of it was years upon years of receipts and, yes, many of these did indeed relate to the Soho premises. Then I found a box with some letters dated back to 1946, the year my father arrived here, from none other than Audrey. She had written them to his Soho address and her address was in Dover. Apparently my Dad was in hospital there when he first arrived in the UK and she was a nurse of some kind. It was clear they had a brief affair and Audrey had written to say she was pregnant. She seemed to think my father would marry her , so she obviously did not know about my mother and me. Then she wrote to say that she had been sacked from her job when they found out she was expecting and she got struck off the list of registered nurses for having an affair with a patient. She told him she was coming to London to join him. There were momentos like a handkerchief of hers and even a couple of photos – very pretty lady. The last letter thanked him for finding her somewhere to live – a flat in Greek Street, around the corner from his business. But I have no idea of what happened between them as the letter stopped there. So then I looked back in his accounts for that year and found books for his staff list in the strip club – Paradise Alley it was called – and her name, Audrey Jonson showed up as a receptionist/waitress from 1948. Then, right at the bottom of the other box with the letters was an envelope. On the front it said, 'Gregory Emmett Jonson'. Inside was a birth certificate, naming her as the mother, and my father as his father. There was also a small photograph of him as a baby and a lock of curly black hair."

We – Leroy and I – sat silent, stunned by this revelation. As we looked at each other, our eyes both said 'Marvalette was right'.

"So, you have discovered that Gregory is, in fact your brother, half brother. That must be a huge shock."

"Indeed. And I think of my life and his life. How different it has been and of my father's double life and how he unwittingly caused her death through that back-street abortion, denying my brother of not only a right to his father but to his mother also and I feel really angry. Not to mention how this double life meant he was lying and deceiving my mother and me too. Of how much I have had – love, material things, a home and family, education, inheritance - and my brother has had none of that. Children's homes with no love and no way for a good life."

Feltz was clearly distressed and his voice faltered as he fought back the tears.

"It nah your fault, boss. But dat is one sad story. Me sarry fe unno, fe true." Leroy placed a steadying hand on Feltz' shoulder.

"You know," I began slowly, as things started to click and fall into place in my mind, " Gregory seemed to know that was the case, which is why in some perverse way he has sought out your Dad to be 'close' to him and the ripping him off was the only way he could get what he felt was his. Maybe your Dad realized and that's why he did nothing. And since he died he has done nothing else but to try to get back into this house and get to be a thorn in your side – like he wants you to notice him."

"Ah. Miss Freud. Working out the psychological angle I see – you could well have something there."

I continued my theme. "Yes and we see how Gregory has modeled his life similarly leading a double life with a wife and child, with whom he appears to be the perfect Dad, yet making his money less than legally."

"But the analogy, I feel – I hope - stops there. My father , to my knowledge was never violent to anyone – although I admit a West End life does mean dealing with all kinds of nefarious folk and their behaviour, so I will never really know. I would like to talk more to Frankie and I have had a brief chat with him and we are going to meet tomorrow. But I need to get back now to my plan for the houses."

"And can you also tell us why you bought the house over the road, where my friend Beth lives? She is terrified she is going to be slung out and she's got three kids."

Leroy looked at me as if to say where did that come from. Reading his look, I quickly added she had popped in this morning and told me. Feltz went on.

"I know her ex-husband in a professional capacity – horrid, manipulative little man. He needed cash, so I offered a below market price for the house with Beth as a sitting tenant. Of course she is not, legally anyway, but she will be taken care of. I will speak with her first about that tomorrow and then she can tell you what I hope will be good news. But my letter also said I was putting this house and the one next door up for sale. Also, we have houses in Belsize Park and one in Shepherds Bush. All rented out. I am selling – or otherwise disposing of - all of them. I have spoken to my wife about this, and shared with her my plan, with which she agrees. I wish to try to make things right as much as I can with Gregory. He is due some inheritance and a final acknowledgement of the truth of his paternity. I shall bequeath him one of the houses. He can choose if he wishes. But I wish also to make some recompense to you. Because of my father, indirectly, you have suffered from Gregory's state of mind, as has Leroy. You will each have one of the flats in the newly converted houses in Belsize Park. Gregory, the house in Shepherds Bush – the whole house which he can live in or dispose of as he wishes.

247

It is a beautiful Edwardian Villa and is in good condition, recently I renovated it and brought it back as a four bedroomed family home.

"I will be selling these two houses and Beth will find out what I am doing with hers tomorrow. Then my wife and I and the children will be going to live in Israel. We want to start again, in a country where we don't have all this stuff for ever hanging over our heads. I hope you understand. Would Belsize Park suit you? It's not so near to your workplace, Jenifer, but there are buses. The flat I have in mind for you is in Belsize Park Gardens. It is the ground and lower ground floor so you have the garden too. There are two bedrooms, you could even make it three. Also a large kitchen leading to the garden and a huge lounge either upstairs or down – take your pick. It is very nice, modern and recently renovated. Or there is a three bedroomed mansion flat on the top floor but there's no lift. It's not so nice, and needs work, although the views are excellent. Leroy, for you, I have a small mews cottage in Belsize Mews with a garage/workshop space which I am sure you can make use of. The flt above has two bedrooms also, lounge, kitchen and bathroom and a small courtyard garden behind the workshop. I think you know both of these properties as it was you and your team working with my builders on the renovation. What do you think?"

Leroy and I were gobsmacked. Too taken aback to even speak, we both just nodded. Feltz took out some papers from his bag, and a bottle of what looked like, and indeed was, Champagne. The papers were a legal Notice of Intent to bequeath the properties to us. He gave them over and said we needed to see a solicitor as soon as. He then left the Champagne on the table, telling us to keep it until we had the keys. And, just like that, he got up to leave.

"Wait up, wait up! Jus' a minute boss. Dis offer, hmm, is very kind an' me no know wha' me can say towards it, excep' t'ank you, t'ank you very much. Me know de place yu mean - de mews cottage is one nice nice likkle place an' like yu say, perfec' fe me stuff an' me van fe keep it safe. Yu 'member 'ow it did get bruk into a few mont' back. Me feel like me need to pinch meself. Like is a dream. Me no know what to say, boss. T'ank you Mista Feltz, sah, t'ank yu."

Leroy had tears in his eyes as he looked at me as if to say go on thank the man, don't just sit there with your mouth wide open – which I was – too stunned to say anything.

"Mr Feltz. I'm sorry. I just don't know what to say. It's all so much to take in. Of course, I am so grateful. I still don't understand why you would want to do this – maybe you might regret it and say you didn't mean it when you come to your senses. This is a huge gift and I would be so grateful to you. I went to that area once and it is so lovely with all those regal looking houses. They must be expensive and you want to give us these amazing properties. Will we be able to see them?"

"Jenifer I want you both to have them. Both of you impress me as two individuals who want to get on in life, work hard and be good human beings. I've already covered the Gregory angle, but the final motivation is that when I sell all the properties I want to let go of, my tax bill will be enormous - it's capital gains tax and the rate goes up when you cross a threshold and I will cross that so if I take off a couple properties, would you believe it evens out. I would rather make you two happy than the tax man. I will make him happy enough as it is."

"Mista Feltz, we was jus' about to drive over to me yard in 'arlesden. Somet'ings me 'ave dere me wan' show Jen, but me also wan' show you too." Come. Let's go."

Leroy picked up his van keys and his coat and beckoned us both to the door. Feltz and I looked at each other but did as we were bid. Gathering my bag, keys and jacket too, we left the house and Feltz said he would follow Leroy's van in his car. Leroy said nothing on the way over. I tried to talk, but I could see he was still too choked up and I, too, still felt I was searching for words that were not coming freely as my mind too was still trying to process what had happened. It took about twenty minutes to get over to Rucklidge Avenue where Leroy had a ground floor flat. Feltz parked up behind us and Leroy let us all in.

"Dis ya me parlour," he said proudly of his living room with a black leatherette sofa, his music player, TV and a cabinet with glasses and a bottle of Advocat, which he later told me had been a gift from a happy client a year ago and, as he hated the stuff, it was still there. Then he led us down a passage with two steps which led to his back room and a kitchen with a bath in it and a separate toilet. It was all clean and tidy, apart from some of his stuff in the passage-way including shelves with tins of paint and other decorating equipment. But I was not really noticing that as he led us into the back room – which I had assumed was his bedroom. I was still unsure why he wanted to give us, particularly Feltz, this guided tour, but when we opened the door of the back room it all became clear. There was a large easel and canvases. A large table with drawing materials and piles of sketches, but what was most impressive was the two large finished canvases. One was a painting of a scene from, I thought, Jamaica, with little painted cottages and bright purple and pink flowers with kids playing along a dirt road. The other, a portrait I recognized immediately as Vinny with his wife, Grace and their two children.

"Dis me likkle secret," he chuckled. "Not you alone can do all de surprisin', boss!"

"Did you do this one for Vinny? Did they sit for you or what? It's incredible! Has he seen it? Are you going to give it to him for Christmas or something?" That was just the start of the questions. Leroy laughed.

"Nah. Look. Is a photo me use and den me jus' do so and fix it up like dis!"

"Just like that! Not like that. Just like that" said Feltz imitating Tommy Cooper's line. "Very lovely work Leroy. This is real talent. I am quite stunned. May I look at your sketches?"

"Yeah. De paintin' is a gif' fe Vinny, fe all 'im do fe 'elp me. 'Im sacrifice so much an' 'im was not much more dan a bwoy 'imself. As me get older, me get wiser and hunnerstan' better what 'im do. Yu like it?"

I nodded eagerly. The other painting he explained was of village life in Jamaica similar to where he came from.

Feltz was admiring the sketches and nodding his head. He looked again at the painting. "Stunning."

"Mista Feltz, sah. Me wan' yu fe carry dis one a Israel if yu can. A reminder of all o' we and the good that yu do. Yu would like to tek 'im?"

"Now it's me whose gobsmacked Leroy. I don't know what to say. I would love to have it and indeed it would be possible to ship it. It is beautiful, I might be tempted to change my mind from the deserts of Israel to the tropical lushness of the Caribbean! But my wife is set on Israel, so we have to follow where the missus directs!!"

"Well. Dat's dat. Yu wan' tek 'im now, or me can drop 'im off?"

"I would like to take it now if I may?"

"Right. Dat's sekkle den. Le' we get set." Leroy found an old clean dust cover he used for decorating and wrapped it carefully over the painting. Feltz was driving his estate car so he went out and lowered the seats to create space, clearing it so nothing could damage the painting. He was clearly touched by his gift and it was as if Leroy felt better about accepting the cottage as he was able to give something in return. Both gifts had come from the heart. Less important was their value, more important was the fact that they were given from a place of deep sincerity. As Feltz secured his car and made to say goodbye, Leroy held his arm gently and said:

"Yu' know. When a man grow up an' 'im nah know 'im fader and den 'im mudder die, it kill somet'ing inside and can mek de passage from bwoy to man a rocky road. Me know, car it 'appen to me. But me lucky, fe me did 'ave me brudder. 'Im see me t'ru t'ick n t'in. 'Im never give up and bit by bit, 'im love did get t'ru and mek me see sense. I jus' 'ope dat it nah too late fe Gregory."

"Me too," answered Feltz pensively. "And I think the terrible experiences my father went through killed something inside my father too. Perhaps that was why he had the double life. Who knows, but yes, I hope that I can at least try to put something right that went so wrong in my younger brother's life. Vinny is a special man indeed, Leroy. Good night."

I didn't hear what Leroy said in reply but he wiped his eyes a good few times.

"Yu wan' go 'ome now? Lemme get some gears and we cool to go." He handed me the keys to the van and beckoned me to get in. I waited, in the cold cold van I must add, shivering, for about ten icy minutes until he came out with his decorating gear and loaded it into the van. He also had a carrier bag, which he sat on my lap, containing his overalls and some underwear.

250

"Phew," I said. "Me know" he replied and just as on the way over, we sat quietly while the events that had unfolded that evening began to sink in.

"It's my Dad's funeral the day after tomorrow and I am supposed to be at my Mum's tomorrow. That means I won't be there. So sorry Leroy, I forgot all about that with all of this goin on. I will stay with her that night, so two nights and come back that day. Now yo've gone and packed your stuff to stay by me, and now I won't be there after tonight."

Leroy said nothing for a bit, then he said it wasn't a problem and he could just as easily go back home again. He asked if I wanted him to drop me over to Harrow tomorrow but he might be working so we agreed it was best for me to go by train. We thought it might be best for him to stay over anyway as the house was empty and he could look after my things. I agreed and said I would let Feltz and Francis know in the morning.

Even though we had eaten earlier, when we got in we were both still hungry, so Leroy nipped over the road for a couple of patties and a Nutrament. I asked him to get me some biscuits, but he came back with a packet of cream crackers. I was a bit disappointed and explained that was not what I meant by biscuit. He then admonished me for liking too much sweet things that were bad for my teeth. I pointed out that the Nutrament was full of sugar, and he scoffed that off saying it was a food replacement so was good for him. I said nothing further and buttered some cream crackers and had that with hot chocolate.

We started to talk about Feltz's offer. Was it real? Was there catch? Had we really landed on our feet? I could see Leroy was over the moon. The mews flat would give him a home and a place to do his painting, plus the workshop was ideal as a garage and store for his decorating stuff. He also saw the area as being as lucrative as Notting Hill and a good place to really set up a proper business and would I take care of the paperwork. Of course, I agreed, and said how lovely it would be to have a garden and learn to grow some flowers and vegetables, maybe have a chicken, like in the TV programme the Good Life. We laughed as we planned this new future. It was on that night by conincidence, so we watched it to pick up any tips, but of course it was all fiction anyway. When it ended we watched the news, which was tame compared to events nearer to home.

We were both really tired now and I just wanted to sleep. As we snuggled down Leroy told me that the painting of the Jamaican scene had really been for me, but he felt he wanted to give something back to Feltz and not to worry he would do me another one. I said I didn't mind and that his next picture would be even better! I think Leroy was telling me about how he started painting but, before I even knew it, I was fast asleep.

35 The Funeral

I saw Leroy off in the morning and got my stuff packed to go to Mum's. I left early so as to avoid getting drawn into more stories with Beth or Anthea. I was mentally exhausted and now wanted to focus on the ordeal of the funeral and get that over with. I got the 23 up to Paddington Station and from there went to Euston Square. I walked down to the main Euston Station and took the now familiar journey up to Watford Juction, catching the little train (as we always called it) on to Oxhey. I got to Mum's to find that Veronica and Ron were coming later that night as she was poorly with morning sickness. That meant we could have the rest of the afternoon together. We took a walk to the corner shop and got a couple of chicken pies that they could have if they were hungry, while Mum and I walked round to the fish and chip shop and got ourselves some supper. Mum was not in the mood for cooking.

We took our supper home and got cosy by the fire and were watching the television when the phone went and it was Veronica saying they were stuck on the motorway with a blown tyre. They were waiting for the AA and hoped they would be there before midnight,

"Veronica, I am sorry to hear this, but do you think you could find yourselves a little hotel. It would be better for you in your condition for one, and I don't want to have to wait up til midnight. I'm stressed as it is and I want to go to bed in a while."

"I can't stand the idea of a pokey hotel, Mum, my back is aching and I'm feeling sick so I just want to get home to you. Anyway, you've got Jen there, haven't you, so she could wait up for us. Ron will be hungry, but we could pick up something along the way, so she wouldn't have to do anything for us, just open the door."

Mum turned to me to relay with Veronica had said, rolling up her eyes. I said Ok I would wait up, snoozing on the sofa til they got here. I could see Mum felt bamboozled but she that this would be alright to Veronica and that she would see her in the morning and yes she did have Andrews if she had sickness in the morning.

Mum put the phone down with relief.

"What's wrong with the car?" I asked.

"I don't bloody know and I don't bloody well care. Blown tyre I think she said. You'd think Ron would have checked the car over before they left and carried a spare. Your dad always did. I tell you that man has got no sense. Now they've got to be disturbing your sleep, tonight of all nights."

"Don't worry Mum," I said, giving her a hug. It's no problem, really not. Why don't you go up and have a nice hot bath, set your hair and go to bed? Leave her to me."

"Thank you, Jenifer, you are such a darling girl. I will go on up then. I will let you know when I'm out of the bath. If you wait half an hour there will be hot water for you. Tell Veronica they are in me and Dad's room. I'm in the back and you are in the little room. Night night darling."

She kissed me and went upstairs. I gave Leroy a quick call and told him about Ron's car palava.

"Chupid man," he said, annoyed, "any damn fool know to check de car before a long drive and carry a spare tyre. Even me do dat!"

We said good night and I waited for mum to have her bath and for the water to heat up and then went up for mine. I had my nightie, and mum lent me an old dressing gown. I wound my hair into a bun so it would fall nicely tomorrow and then settled on the couch, watching the last hour of the TV and reading Mum's magazine's before I finally dozed off under one of mum's spare eiderdowns.

Eventually, I was woken by a loud kock on the door. I check the time. It was past one in the morning. Veronica must be wrecked. I opened the door. I was right. She was in tears and said she had been sick twice on the way down and all she wanted to do was get in bed. They had waited two hours for the AA and were freezing. Ron was tired and in a bad mood. I took them into the living room while I made them hot drinks. Ron was hungry, so I offered to heat up the chicken pie for him but he said not to bother, a cheese sandwich would do, which I dutifully provided. I made them a hot water bottle and when the two of them were fed and watered and had calmed down and warmed up, they went off to bed. I took my hot water bottle, and went off to the little room, from where I could hear them arguing. Then it went quiet. As I lay there I heard the bed springs bouncing for a few minutes, after which Ron got up, went to the loo and got back to bed. Now for some peace. And so it was until morning.

Mum would have loved a stressfree start to the day, but no. Veronica was sick (sick of Ron more like said Mum) for the first hour and had no breakfast. He expected Mum to make him a big cooke breakfast, but she just looked at him and went upstairs.

"Chicken pie?" I asked cheekily. "Mum hasn't got any egg and bacon; she hasn't had time to go shopping so it's that or toast with maralade or jam."

Ron grudgingly accepted toast and marmalade with a cup of tea, by which time Veronca felt better and asked me to make her some dry toast. I made some for myself, taking some up for Mum too, and went to get ready. Good job we had had our baths the night before, Ron emptied the tank, leaving no hot water for Veronica, so we had to wait for the water to heat up again. Meanwhile, Mum stayed in her room getting ready. I asked Veronica to boil a kette to wash up, seeing as I had made breakfast, to which she surprisingly agreed without a fuss.

I could see Mum was getting in a tizz.

"We have to be there is an hour Jen and Veronica has not got in the bath yet. I want to be there early; you know what I'm like Jen. The car is coming in a while and I wanted the three of us in the main car, with Ron coming in his car behind us. It's hard enough for me, coping with the funeral without these two."

"Mum. Try not to get worked up. When the car comes, we will just have to go in it and if they are not ready, Veronica will just have to go with Ron. I know it's not what you planned, but like you say, we can't be late."

Mum explained the revised plan to Veronica and Ron. That started an argument between them over him using the hot water and not taking responsibility for not thinking and him asking how was he to know. Anway that put a speed behind Veronica as there was no way she was not coming in the car with us. She was just getting her shoes on when the car came to take us to the Crem. Mum has streamlined (as she put it) the whole affair. "Crem, wake, done" she explained.

Of course Ron moaned, but Mum explained he would need the car to take us home after. I could see how minute by minute this was just adding to the stress of the day. Thankfully the journey went quietly with me and Veronica holding Mum's hands and Veronica trying not to throw up. We all got there in one piece and filed into the Crematorium, waiting while all the other guests came. There was lots of hugs and a few tears shed, but, soon enough, we were all assembled on time and ready to start,

The funeral passed without incident, as they say, with everyone – i.e me, Veronica and grumpy Ron the Racist, behaving and not causing any more tension, although it was still very much in the air. I was proud of the way I ignored Ron's provocative remarks and was pleasantly relieved to realise that ignoring him actually shut him up. This was Mum's day and I was not going to lose sight of that. The flowers were lovely, the service, everything was perfect. Neither Veronica nor I did a reading after all, but Dad's friend, Joe, did the Eulogy, so beautifully that it brought tears to my eyes. It was the first time I had been to a funeral as an adult, being aware of what was going on. Nevertheless, it was, I don't know, spooky, scary even, to see Dad's coffin go through the doors to the great furnace to be cremated. Mum was going to have the ashes interred, not scattered after all, with a headstone in Harrow Weald Cemetary so she could still come and sit with him, as she said. She said she wanted to do that alone in a week or so.

My mind wandered as I thought of my beginning relationship with Leroy, with a sense inside me that this was going to last the course and I hoped I would love him always as my Mum loved my Dad. I wondered then if she had trembled at his touch, let out cries of pleasure at her orgasm and if he had snuggled to her pregnant belly. So much love comes through these intimate connections of our bodies that they store these as deep memories. Held together by her smart black suit was a woman whose body ached and grieved in every cell as it recalled the long years and treasured moments of her married life to her husband, Ernest.

I squeezed her hand as the coffin went through and she returned the gesture, tears pouring now. I reached into my bag and found her a clean tissue (miracle) and blowing her nose, she composed herself. I slid my arm around her and hugged her as we stood there. I took my arm back before Veronica noticed and made an issue of it. We filed out of the Crem to the waiting cars. We travelled to the wake at the Working Men's Club in the same silence. I remembered Mum had asked me to help her with the wake but I had not got in touch as I had been so busy. I felt terrible – but at the same time she had not got in touch with me. Eventually, I spoke.

"So who organized the wake Mum?" I ventured with intrepidation.

"Mrs Blakewell and Mrs Clarke from the club. Mrs Coggins from next door helped too. Mr Blakewell said the club would pay for it all. You know he was very fond of your Dad. They served together during the war. Great pals they were. So yes, it was all done for me. That's why I didn't call you to ask for your help. In case you are wondering."

Sometimes it is not so much what people say but what they don't say and I knew my Mum well enough to know this was a tactful (so as not to trigger Veronica's input) and slightly barbed dig at me for not phoning her.

"I know. We will talk." I replied quietly.

"They've made us some of those Quiche Lorraine things. Should be a lovely spread and I'm hungry now. What about you Veronica? Ron?"

"I can't think about food right now." Veronica replied. "I'm still feeling sick a lot and today has been such a strain; I have no appetite."

"Well I'm not expecting so I will eat yours and drink your share too!"

Ron laughed at his joke, but it fell flat. Greedy bastard, I thought.

Thankfully we got to the club soon enough and yes, they had put on a spread to do Dad proud and a lovely display of photos of him as a child, him in his Army days, their wedding, us as kids and as a family together. A real celebration of his life. Mum was touched and we went round with her as she talked about the memories the pictures had for her. Our family's history encapsulated with images that would mean nothing to a passer by. But to Mum it was all significant – the dress she wore, the necklace, the ice-cream dripping down my frock. She recalled the ties she had bought him and the times we were at the seaside for our holidays, smiling at the picture of him in his shorts and 'Kiss me Kwik' hat that he had taken from her for the picture! Such small things but meaning so much.

Veronica had been threatening to throw up again. She was having a hard time with her pregnancy, I could see, and I felt quite sorry for her, especially as Ron seemed oblivious. I thought of how Leroy had been so attentive and compared that Ron's miserable lack of concern for my sister. I realized I felt quite angry towards him. Ron had not managed to down more than a pint so she said that she wanted to go home before he had drunk too much to be able to drive. She piled it on a bit saying she had a pain and wanted to be near her doctor just in case. So, Ron was persuaded to pull himself away from the Quiche Lorraine and the sausage rolls, his pints and his carping comments that no-one wanted to listen to. I wondered if the the real reason Veronica wanted to go was that Ron was embarrasing and was on course to be even more so. She said goodbye and told Mum they would pop back to the house to get their stuff but please could she have they key and that she promised to bring it back.

"I'll go with you,"said Mum, sealing off that conversation and I couldn't help thinking she was feeling that missing 15 minutes of the wake was a small price to pay for seeing the back of Ron.

We said our goodbyes and I was left talking to Susan, the Blakewells' 16-year-old daughter. She went to my old school, so we chatted aimlessly about teachers who were still there and what it was like now.

'It's a bit different now to when you was there. More coloureds. I don't much like them. Too stuck up. And they smell. Garlic – ugh. But some of them are good dancers. I've seen them at the Railway Club. You used to go there, didn't you? I know you used to dance with them. I did once with this coloured bloke. It was weird. I heard you left here and went to live with them. Coloured boyfriend and all. Is it true?'

My thoughts were to say piss off Susan, but I did not want to be rude to her.

"You know, Susan. When you get to know people who are different from you get to find out a lesson in life. That we are not all that different after all. You will find that out if you make friends and treat people the way you would like to be treated."

This wisdom seemed lost on her.

"They say once you've had black, there's no going back. Is that true? That you stretch down there so much you can't fit a white man."

"Well, if you are so interested, perhaps you need to find out for yourself. I'll see you later."

I really wanted to go home now. I wondered if that's what half of these adults thought of me too. Racism is so hard to comprehend. How it can make white people have almost split personalities. They can be good and kind and decent – salt-of-the-earth types like Mr Blakewell and his wife but bring anyone non-white into the equation then that goodness, kindness and decency goes out of the window and an ugly ignorance comes over them. Most of the things they thought about black people were completely untrue and I wondered where on earth it all came from. And these were the people that fought a war against facism. It was incomprehensible.

256

"Jen, you look all by yourself. Are you Ok?' Mum was back now and she linked my arm. 'Good send off isn't it?"

"Yes Mum, it's lovely. They've done you and Dad proud."

"Yes. So kind. But to tell you the truth I just want to go home and be in my own house. I've had Veronica and Ron up to hear and I need a week to get over them. Do you think they will be offended if I leave?"

"Well, Mum, the Quiche is all gone now, so I don't think they will mind. I will tell them you've got a headache and that I'm taking you home. Do you want to walk or have you got a lift or a taxis to call?"

"It's a bit cold to walk. I'm sure Joe will drop us round."

I went to ask Mr Blakewell if he could drop us home and that Mum wasn't feeling good. He couldn't have been kinder as he grabbed his keys and said not to worry, he understood.

We got back to Mum's in minutes and she said her goodbyes to Joe, then went to open the door. As I got out of the car he said:

"I was good friends with your Dad for many years. We talked about everything. He wanted so much for you. Don't let him down love, will you?"

Well , I knew exactly what that meant.

"No Mr Blakewell. I won't. My Dad was, is and would always be, proud of me. Thanks for the lift and everything you have done for Mum. Bye."

I followed Mum back into the house. She went to put the kettle on and then went upstairs to change into her nightclothes. A night by the fire then.

"Thank you for staying over love. It's been quite a day. Very lovely in many ways, but exhausting. I'm going to go to bed in a minute. Could you make me a cup of tea please? I'm going to go up and strip the sheets off my bed I know they were at it last night. I heard them. Fancy doing that in your mother's house, in your Mum and Dad's bed before his funeral of all things. Just no consideration."

I wanted to add something about how it didn't last long but did not want to appear bold to my Mum, so left it. I did feel sorry for Veronica on that score too. Last night it sounded like he just used her body for his own convenience as if he was entitled to it, regardless of how she felt. And it was clear how unwell and tired she felt. Somehow I think Mum probably thought the same but was not about to discuss my sister's private life with me.

I tidied up the kitchen and then thought to ring Leroy. He was at my place at that moment, thankfully, picking up a few bits to take home. I said I would be home tomorrow evening and we blew kisses goodbye to each other.

Mum appeared at the sitting room door. It was as if she had recovered a bit and was ready to talk.

"Right, my girl. You've got some talking to do. But before that, I have got good news. Mr Patel has found me a buyer (Veronica does not know yet, so keep schtum, won't you?) and he has also found me a very nice flat in central Harrow as you go up towards Harrow on the Hill. It's lovely and near to everything. If you can stay tomorrow I can take you to see it before you go home."

"I'd love to, Mum." I hugged her. We chatted about the flat for a bit, and then we settled down to my story. Well, selected parts anyway. Mainly to do with why I was suspended from work. I left off all the rest about Gregory and I thought I would leave off from telling her about Feltz offering to give me and Leroy the properties. I became aware of how far my life had moved from the narrow confines of Oxey and the small-minded attitudes of erstwhile good, decent and kind people like the Blakewells. She was at least relieved to know that I had been reinstated at work and exhonerated from the accusations. However, there was till the case conference that I was supposed to attend the next day. I told Mum how I felt I could not attend. Mum said she didn't think I was in any fit state and said she would ring them in the morning to say I could not come. I was grateful for her support and relieved not to have to go. It was late now, and we went to bed, me snuggling up with her in their double bed with its saggy mattress.

"Mum, I hope you are going to get a new mattress when you move."

"Darlin', I'm getting rid of the mattress the bed and the whole bloody lot. I want new and modern. I'm starting life over. I'm only 46 and I want to get as much out of life as I can. In Harrow I can get a little job, I can go to the cinema, meet people and I will go on holiday at least twice a year. I want to see the world before I fall off the mortal coil."

And with her dreams for her future as a derring-do widow, we both began to fall asleep.

"He's here, you know," Mum whispered.

"I know," I replied, "and he's happy for all your plans."

"Yes, he is that. Goodnight dear."

"Goodnight Mum."

I hate those nights when you fall asleep fast and think that because you are so tired you will sleep through like a log, but then something in your brain goes off like an alarm clock and you wake in the night with a restless mind, and it's only three am. This night was one of those. I snuck out of bed as I was too restless to sleep and didn't want to disturb Mum. Downstairs the living room was chilling as the fire was dying down. I pulled my/Mum's old dressing gown around me and went into the kitchen and made some hot milk. I found the last two rich tea biscuits and put the wrapper in the bin. As I opened it I saw a letter, torn in half. I don't know what sense of nosieness took over me, but I fished it out, put it together and read it and doing so, wished I hadn't, but couldn't stop myself.

> *Dearest Margie,*
> *I can't tell you the joy I felt seeing you again last week after so many years. Looking at your eyes across the table over dinner I saw that same shining blue that had so intrigued me all those years ago when you were just 18. I went off to the war and you then met and married the love of your life, Ernest. I also married Betty and we were happy until she died three years ago.*
> *I never forgot you and always wondered how you were doing. When we met again in '67 it seemed that our passions were still alive but there was nothing we could do that would have allowed them to flourish without destroying our family lives. How I've missed you.*
> *That was the only trip back to the old country from Canada that I made until now. I am staying a few months. I told you how I found out about Ernest when I went into the club and decided to try to find you.*
> *I am so glad that I did. Our meeting over lunch brought me much happiness and I hope that we can meet again. My mind has been racing with so many thoughts. I'd love to meet your girls and maybe you could come for a trip to Canada to meet my boys?*
> *Yes I know that's rushing ahead of myself, but I would very much like to meet you again for dinner.Maybe a show in the West End? – this time without air raid sirens and bombs dropping!*
> *Well you have my number of where I am staying at my sister Dorothy's and I will leave it to you to get in touch.*
> *With much affection*
> *George xx*

I wished I have kept my nose out and hurriedly put the letter back in the bin just as I had found it. It's strange to think of your Mum as having a life of her own. A secret life, full of romance and passion. I wondered what she made of this George. Perhaps his letter torn up in the bin said it all. I would say nothing and see what transpired. This distraction from my sleeplessness and the warm milk had made me sleepy so I crept back up to bed where I slept til morning, waking with Mum bringing us both tea in bed while we planned our day.

Mum called the social worker, and then Sue, in the morning and said I was not well enough to attend the case conference. They were not too happy, but Mum impressed on them that my Dad had just died and that the funeral was only yesterday. Well, they had to accept it and get on without me. We got ready to go to see the flat and Mum called Mr Patel to meet us there with the keys. We got to Harrow and met him in his office and he took us in the car to the flat. It was a low-rise modern block on Bessborough Road with large windows overlooking

Churchfields Park. I fell in love with it and I could see why she was impressed. Light and airy, with good sized rooms and a nice kitchen, I could see it would suit her to the ground.

"There's a bedroom for you or Veronica to come and stay anytime, maybe even my grandchild, but just for short stays. No moving back to Mum for either of you!!"

Mr Patel, it seemed could not do enough for my Mum. Well, she had brought him two sales. Or, as it now transpired – three!

"Now, here's the surprise. There's another flat over West Harrow. Mr Patel is going to take us over there too."

We all piled into Mt Patel's car again and drove to West Harrow to view a top floor one bedroomed flat in a rather elegant Edwardian house that had been a bit neglected.

"It's an investment. It needs doing up and a couple of Dad's builder friends have been over and taken a look. It's cheap and won't cost that much to bring it up to scratch. I'm going to rent it out and that will give me an income. Mr. Patel has shown me how it's better to do that than just live off the money left over from the house sale. Mr Davis, Dad's builder friend, has given me good advice. I know it all depends on getting good tenants, but here we go, this is a new venture for me and I'm sure I will learn. Margie McKay – Landlady."

I was taken aback, but Mum beamed at me and I knew it was going to be fine. The flat was nothing like the one she had chosen for herself, but she went through all what she was going to do and the quote for the work (yes, she had got that far) and all the sums added up, she said. Mr Patel looked even more pleased with himself. Three sales up for him! He asked us if we had plans and was I in a hurry to get back. We said we were free and asked why, wondering if there was another property he had in mind to sell. But no. He asked us if we liked Indian food and I nodded furiously, but Mum was a bit hesitant.

"Don't worry, don't worry. You will not have the hot stuff. I shall guide you in the delightful tastes of India – well Bangladesh actually, as many of our Indian Restaurants are run by people from what was formerly East Pakistan and is now Bangladesh and many of the recipes were made up here to suit English tastes!"

We nodded appreciatively.

"Ok, Indian lunch it is for my wonderful customer and her beautiful daughter!"

We drove down to Wealdstone to a small restaurant which looked a bit run down and we wondered where he had taken us.

"Oh, don't be put off by the frontage. They have only recently taken over this business and are doing it up. The Chef, I know him well, and he is very good. Mr. Saleem. You will eat well here."

I could see Mum was not sure, but Mr Patel was persuasive in a kind sort of way so we allowed ourselves to be led in. It was a different picture inside where recent decorations had made the place look attractive and inviting. There was a delicious smell coming from the kitchen and, being early, we were the first customers for lunch.

Mr Patel ordered for us, Tandoori Chicken (Mum loved that), Naan breads, rice, chicken curries, all sorts, it was too much for the three of us, but both he and Mr Saleem wanted to impress us. They both wanted to promote their businesses after all and this hospitality, as the phrase goes, was good for 'currying favour.' It was marvellous food and I was stuffed. Mr Patel was an interesting man. He did not have a strong Indian accent, but he spoke Panjabi with Mr Saleem and the waiter. He went to an English school in India and came here after the war to find work as an accountant for which he had qualifications gained in India. However, the best he could manage was finding work as a clerical assistant with the Post Office and gained promotion to a Clerical Officer but could not get promoted above that. So he decided to run his own business instead, choosing estate agent work rather than accountancy, which he said was soul destroyingly boring. He said he would help Mum find tenants and could even collect the rents.

I could see Mum was finding this a bit ingratiating, so she interrupted him and said it was very kind but she had someone in mind. A friend who had moved back from Canada was looking for somewhere and it would be just right. My ears pricked up at that but I did not let on. Anyway it did the trick and Mr Patel backed down, seeing he had rather over-stepped the mark.

"Jen, I need to stop off at Debenhams before I go home. Would you have time do do some shopping with me before you go home?"

I agreed and Mr Patel said he would drop us back at his office and we could walk round to Debenhams from there.

"He's a very nice man, Jen, but he can be a bit overbearing with his sales technique. But, before you say, yes I did try some other agents when I was looking for the flats, but he just came up with the right place at the right price and I am happy with that."

"So who is this mystery friend from Canada?"

"No-one," replied Mum with a definitive tone. "It was a made-up mystery friend to get him off the case. Your Dad said not to put all your eggs in one basket, otherwise people know too much about you. He already knows what I've got from the sale and how I had enough money for two flats, so it starts to get a bit too much if he starts knowing how much I am making as well on a rental. No. Time to pull back from Mr Pate,l methinks. I remember what my old Dad said about the

Indians. They could sell you a bucket with a hole in it and convince you it could hold water. He used to say they were great businesspeople but that you can't trust them. A bit like the Jews, really. They are good at business - could sell coal to a Geordie at twice the price. How do you think they got rich, nice houses and cars? Good at selling and can be a bit artful. My Dad knew the Indians from being out there til he got Malaria and had to come home. And believe me if you live round here, you get to know the Jews. So just like you are getting to know West Indians I suppose."

Hmm. I thought; how do I unpack that?

"Mum you can't say a whole race of people is a particular way because a few might be. Cockney barrow boys are salesmen and could sell you anything and they are artful too, but it doesn't mean all cockneys are artful dodgers. Why judge people negatively for being enterprising? Usually that comes from people who are jealous of what another person has got. People create a view of people and then believe it to be true and it's not."

"Oh well, I'm not arguing with you. I could do with a lemonade after all that greasy food. What about you?"

"No, my darling Mum. I have to get off and I thought the food was lovely. There's nothing greasier than fish and chips or roast potatoes!! But thanks for today. The flats are lovely. I will call you to see what you are doing at Xmas. Would you like to come to me and stay in my little place for a couple of nights, meet my friends and sample the life of Westbourne Grove?"

Mum looked hesitant. I dared her to be bold and she laughed and said yes as long as I didn't lecture her about her attitudes. I laughed, kissed her and said I would call her tomorrow. Fortunately I didn't have to go back to her place to get my stuff as I brought it all with me.

I walked towards Harrow-on-the-Hill tube station to take the fast train to Baker Street where I would change to go to Paddington and get the 23 bus. I went to the phone box at the Station and rang my number, then Leroy's. No answer, so I tried Francis and asked him to let Leroy know I was on my way back if he saw him. Francis said he would and then added a 'by the way' that Feltz had put a For Sale sign outside the house and did I know? I said we would have tea when I got back. Then I called Beth to see if she was OK and said I would pop in later. Part of me just wanted to go home and sleep, but I had been looking forward the catch-up with Beth that I had promised.

36   The Need for Boundaries

The thing with Leroy was that he was insecure after losing his Mum and possibly that was not the only thing. He got worried when I was not there and it made me uncomfortable. I could not go ahead with a relationship on the basis of being questioned where had I been from a standpoint of insecurity and not out of interest. And I told him so that evening when he came over, asking me where had I been and who was Mr Patel, did he chat me up, because you can't trust these Indian man dem. I told him he sounded as bad as my Mum to which he was not amused. Then he said Beth had called over last night with a message about some 'woman t'ing' and what was that about. I made some tea and suggested we talk about it. I explained my time with Mum and said how it made me feel when he seemed uninterested in how things went with his only concern being about the bloody estate agent. I told him about the women's group that we were planning and how this was important for me and I did not need either his permission or his approval to go. I said I was a free person and that a relationship could only thrive on trust and not suspicion which would strangle it. I said that if that was how our relationship would be it will end right now.

Leroy sat there, I did not know he was going to get mad, walk out or what.

"Well?"

"Jen, I can see yu point, i's true. I gets kinda jittery about t'ings like dis. Maybe yu have a point about my mom dyin' an' I felt so abandon' an' lost. But dere was more, as yu know, sometime, she would go off, off somewhere, me no know where an' me woulda go by Auntie dis or Auntie dat til she a come back. An' me ah fret. So me feel me could neva trus' her. An' I get dat same panicky feelin' like when me no know where me girl is. I can see how it mus' feel bad if yu feel me nah trus' yu. Me do trus' yu but dis feelin' sometimes get too strong. Me no know wha' me can do 'bout it."

Leroy slumped his head down on the table.

"Leroy. I am not your mother. That's the first thing. And you are no longer the abandoned child. You are an adult with a girlfriend you can trust. Just like I have to trust you. You meet women in your work, you are sometimes not contactable, but I can't start freaking out about that. You would leave me and so I am saying that this kind of jealousy will destroy us if you don't get in control of it. What happened with your Mum was traumatic and we can talk about that as much as you need but you have to keep telling yourself 'Jen is not my mother. I am not an abandoned child. I am an adult. I can trust my girl."

"Me will try. So if you gonna be out til 'alf ten-'leben o'clock, I may as well go up a me yard n sort out a couple two bit o' business dere an' come down in de marnin? Uno wan go shoppin' a Shepherd Bush an' pass by Cora an' dem? An' I t'ink Norman know 'bout some dance tomorrow fe a pre-Chris'mas t'ing. Dat's if yu wan' go out. Yu could all buy somet'ing in de market or we coulda go down Kensington?"

I hugged him and smiled .

"That would be great. And you know it's now OK for me to get down to some serious loving, don't you?"

Leroy kissed me. "All o' dat too! Me been waitin' long long."

"Something else we can discuss tomorrow is Christmas. How do you feel about my Mum coming Christmas Eve and staying over til Boxing Day?"

"Hmm. Not quite my kinda plan, but she is yu mudder and yu jus' los' yu fader, she 'usban', so it mus' be ok. But we will 'discoss', like Norman seh. An' fin' a way dat all o' we can be 'appy dis Chris'mas time."

The sun was shining again between us and we hugged again, put on some ska music and danced madly round the room. Then we kissed goodbye and I got ready to go to Beth's.

I made myself a fried egg and toast and thought I would get a cake and some fruit from the Everopen shop to take over with me. When I arrived at Beth's, she looked as frazzled as ever, trying to get her kids in bed. Anthea was there, shooing kids around and plumping up cushions. The kitchen was clean and tidy, as Beth proudly pointed out. I got busy preparing mugs and getting our snacks ready. The doorbell went again and to my surprise Jemma came in.

"Jus' dropped by to see what you lil ole white girls are all up to," she said in a Southern drawl, winking as she spoke.

"We are changing the world, Jemma. You are welcome to join us." Beth yelled down from upstairs, "I'll be down in a tic. Just getting the kids to bed. Jen and Anthea will get you some tea."

Before I could say anything to Jemma it was as if she read my mind. She laughed

"Don't look so surprised to see me. Kenneth told me you were meeting to talk about a women's group and he gave me Beth's number. I range her, so – here me is!"

"Well it's good to see you. I have no idea what we are going to be talking about. I suppose we are just planning. Anthea, this is Jemma. Jemma meet Anthea, my neighbour. She works for Underground News."

"Nice to meet you Jemma. I'm making tea – is that OK for you?"

"Yeah, yeah. Dat would do me. And planning..that sounds ominous. Where de cake an' biscuit dem?"

Jemma put the cake and biscuits on a plate while Anthea made the tea in a big flowery teapot and I got the mugs and the milk, washed the grapes and put them on a plate with the bananas. My mum would have put it in a jug, but I figured this was not the time or place. Beth came down from putting the kids to bed – frazzled she looked!

"Phew," she sighed, "they do feel a bit put out, especially Tammy, at having to vacate the sitting room and go to bed so early. I told Tammy she could sit up reading, but she's complaining about not watching TV and asking why she can't have TV in her room like Pru does. Pru is her friend from school. Parents have more money than sense. I said it was out of the question, of course. Oh thanks, girls for making the tea?"

"Girls?" questioned Anthea.

"Oh sorry. Sisters?"

"Sisters?" queried Jemma.

That was a cue for a discussion, but it felt a bit uncomfortable as we had not even sat down to break the ice. So I, in an attempt to be humourous, suggested "You lot?"

Beth laughed. "Thanks you lot!"

It seemed to work. Anthea carried the tray, Jemma the plate of goodies and I brought the bananas and grapes. Beth went to get some papers and magazines and followed us through to the sitting room. We sat down and Anthea poured tea and we started to munch and have a general chat. Then Beth said we ought to start to which we all agreed.

"Great. I do have to say I am not as organized as I'd like to be as there has been a lot of upheaval in my life this week, and no doubt I'm not the only one." She threw a glance at Althea and me when she said this, but then went straight on speaking so we did not open up the who Feltz subject.

"What I have been able to do is get in touch with the Women's Liberation Workshop office and they have sent me some bumf which will help us. OK so, first of all we should decide if we want to be a WLW group and if so, what we call it. Most people name it after their locality which helps women find a local group better. So for example we could be Westbourne Grove WLW or something like that. So when we decide that we tell the Office and then our contact details will be given out to women who want to join. We pay a small membership fee and get a newsletter, which groups can take I turns to produce – You's be good at that Anthea. Then.."

"Beth would you like me to take notes of the things we need to decide on at the end?" Athea interrupted. Beth nodded and carried on.

"Thanks, Anthea, yes. Ok, So, then we have a set of guidelines which we can use, although the idea is that each group develops in a way that is for the women as part of it, so you can start a campaign in the area for something – or against something even – which will improve women's lives, or we can be a Consciousness Raising or CR group. Or do a bit of both. I can talk a bit more about CR when I get through these few notes. So..oh yes..an important thing is about the structure of the group. Lots of formal groups have a Chairman, a Vice Chairman, Secretary, a Treasurer and they all CONTROL the activity and thinking of the group. WLW think that this is very patriarchal and typically in these groups, if they are mixed, the men have all the power and women stay quiet and make the tea. But even in the largest women's organization in the land – the old WI – they have this same patriarchal structure so usually the middle-class women rise to the influential posts and working class, or less educated or less confident women don't get a say."

"Nor Black women," interjected Jemma who was listening intently to what we li'l ol' white girls were getting up to and thinking if it had any relevance to her. No doubt she would speak her mind later. Meanwhile, Beth carried on speaking and Althea jotted away.

"Right, I expect so. Come to think of it, my mum is in the WI and they are all white women, although maybe being in Surrey might have something to do with that."

"And Socialist Worker groups – I can definitely say are predominantly white and yes the men have all the important roles and the women usually to the tea and typing duties."

"What about the Pumas?" I asked Jemma.

"Ditto," she replied, although I always thought she had a fair bit of influence if not power, but I didn't say so. Beth got back on track.

"So, sisters," she continued, when Jemma interrupted again.

"This sisters business. I'm not too cool wi' dat, yu know. Anthea – can you put it pon dat list dere please?"

"Sure," said Anthea, casting a glance at Beth who nodded.

"Nothing is to be off the table for discussion. Ok, where was I? Ah, yes. The structure of the group is totally democratic and everyone gets a say. Sometimes if we are having a campaign meeting we will need someone to co-ordinate and act like a chairperson, as well as someone to take notes. But those people will change so everyone gets a chance to develop skills in those roles. In CR groups, we have a different facilitator – that person also rotates – who makes sure we are all ok. More on that later. The democratic circle of power that we are all part of and included in is vital to Women's Liberation. None of us are free till all of us are free!"

She stopped to catch her breath and drink her tea, which as getting cold, with a mouthful of biscuit, she carried on.

"Finally, for today, mmm nice biscuits…. Sorry for talking through a mouthful, there are the Four demands of the Women's Liberation Workshop which we need to agree on or at least discuss and have a position on. These are:

266

1. *Equal pay*
2. *Equal educational and job opportunities*
3. *Free contraception and abortion on demand*
4. *Free 24-hour nurseries*

"We don't have to talk about them all tonight, but they are helpful to discuss as we do need to adopt them. So – got all that Anthea? Ok, so let's go round the circle – any comments, questions, thoughts, ideas?"

I had immediately flinched at the idea of 24-hour nurseries, but there would be time for me to say why later.

Anthea began.

"I really like the sound of the structure; we need to be freer to come into our own and as you say Beth, these are patriarchal power structures and we know they are oppressive, so we need to find our own ways. I am aware of how the patriarchal 'white male left' see women's issues, they weren't even keen on supporting the night cleaners and getting them unionised. It was women's left groups who did that work, supporting those women. The unions are still dominated by men, even though many workers, especially in factories, are women and are not protected by the unions at all. And that's before we think about office and shop workers – even nursery workers, Jen, and getting them into unions – which of course leads to the equal pay debate that we will discuss later. I am torn to some degree between the organising and campaigning side and the CR side. There has been criticism that this is just 'navel-gazing' on the part of more priviledged women, but I also know women in thos groups who say they get a lot out of it and have learned about the inner workings of oppression. By that I mean how sexism affects us psychologically and how our oppression does not necessarily begin in the factory but in and on our bodies which si why things like birth control and abortion are also important things to campaign for. I have to say I feel proud and excited to be in this time as a woman, to think of the possibilities of us coming together and making change to our whole lives that will fee not just ourselves but for future generations."

We all nodded, and even though I hadn't really thought about it that much, the idea that we were all at a pivotal moment in time did fill me with excitement and, yes, pride too, that I was part of it. Jemma shifted her position on the sofa and put her empty mug on the coffee table. We all sat back to listen to her.

"Hmmm. Where do I begin? For me, I am a Black woman first and foremost, with the emphasis on Black. My oppression as a woman is real, but it is in the context of racism that, as a member of the Black 'race', my oppression is magnified and I share more of that with my Black brothers perhaps than I do with you as my white 'sisters'. Plus history shows us how we have been oppressed to by white women, whether that was back in the days of slavery or even now as I walk down the road and white women 'pon de street in dem slippers dem wan' call me 'nigger' and 'black rubbish' and 'wy don't I go back to where I came from.' So a lot of bridges have to be built before I can get down with the white sisterhood and this is why I have a difficulty when white women want to call me 'sister', and the problem I have in calling white women 'sisters'. I wish that was different and we could all live in a nice pretty rainbow prejudice free world and be equal to all, but we are not at that day. I don't know how much you have all begun to think about racism and how it affects women like me, you know, or what it is like to live inside this skin. I have heard white women say how oppressed we Black women are by our Black men, whether it's womanising, violence or other bad behaviour – which actually all men are guilty of, or cultural things like polygamy in African cultures etc. So that is something dat me nah wan' 'ear at all, at all, yeah? So the choice is for Black women, how far we put being female experiencing sexism as our first priority or being Black and experiencing racism. Do we stand by our man, as the song goes, or go it alone? Do we ditch our brothers and join the white women's liberation cause, or stick with our menfolk, and sort out the gender stuff as we go? It is a dilemma and I hope unno can see that."

She sat back in her chair and Beth thanked her, saying she didn't have the answer, but that she felt her input was valuable and that she was welcome to hang with us to see how it went and that there was no suggestion in the group as far as we were concerned that she had to make a choice, we were not demanding it, that it would be up to her. Beth acknowledged that racism wasn't something that affected her and that she had hardly begun to think about it but knew that this was the time to do that, because we were not fighting for liberation of one kind of woman only here. To which Jemma asked how we defined liberation because our idea of it may not be that shared by black women – even the four demands. Anthea made a note – *what is liberation and who defines it?* And underlined *perspectives of oppression – white and black.*

"Well, Jemma, you have certainly given us a lot to think about and I can only apologise for the way you are treated here and slavery was appalling, but do you not think that is in the past now?"

"Not really. No, not at all Beth. We may be a long way from it historically, but we still live daily with its legacy – culturally and financially. Look at who is rich and who is poor in the world, yet whose countries have the resources whose doesn't. When we look at western – let's say specifically, British capitalism, we can see how it was built on the sale of Africans as slaves and their unwaged labour over centuries. Modern Britain was built on our backs and yes that oppression that is within our bodies, well yes, in slavery the master owned us to do what he wished with our bodies. For us, the enslavement of our foremothers and forefathers remains very much in our memories, as does the pain of it in our souls."

"Slavery was a huge bonus for capitalism," added Anthea, "it is true that it funded the industrial revolution as well as colonialism. So it is true that racism is not just about day to day prejudice – and that is bad enough- but it remains an economic mainstay of our capitalist economy. We cannot have a socialist revolution without dismantling it. And it is a terrible, terrible history, and as you said Jemma, especially for Black women. Mostly us whites are ignorant of it and the idea of our superiority is deeply embedded in our psyches."

268

"You can say that again," I chimed in, glad at last to be able to speak up as I was beginning to feel drowned out by Beth and Anthea. "That is my family altogether – my Mum is not quite so bad now, but this is the thing as I have learned. On the one hand white people who are really nice, honest, kind people turn into something else when faced with black people. It is such a contradiction. But it is true. Really brainwashed by society, through school, everything. We used to have comics when I was a kid that showed Black people with bones through their noses, preparing cooking pots to boil up white people and eat them! It's ridiculous, but it is taken as real when you are a kid – and as we all know, what you learn as a child sinks in and stays in. And from my experience of having Black friends, life in Britain is very hard because of racism, so yes we do have to think about it. I agree with Jemma. We can't have women's liberation without black liberation."

"And the liberation of the working class," added Anthea,

"But we ARE the working class," insisted Jemma. "It is our labour that underpins the prosperity of the West, it's not just about the good old working-class factory worker. It is the unpaid labour of all women that underpins even the working classes. It kind of criss crosses as we can see in the conversation. That is why I like to sit down and talk with you and for me this is consciousness raising. Not just all the orgasm and where's me clitoris stuff that leaves me a bit impatient. But anyway, we haven't heard what Jen thinks about the Women's Liberation group."

I was grateful for Jemma for making sure my voice was heard. She knew that not only was I the youngest, but that politics was still a new arena for me and there was so much I felt I still did not know about.

"I would like to have a group. Be part of a group," I said. "I like the idea of informal structure. Alice, our deputy at work, she tries to do that in staff meetings to get us all to contribute, otherwise people sit there in silence just waiting to go. I know this is different because we all want to be here, but still, I know that it works as Alice got everyone more involved and it was good. I am interested in the four demands and would like to discuss them. I also like the idea of different perspectives as we all have different views and what do we mean by liberation? I am just keen to learn. I am keen on talking groups, but I would also like to think about campaigning. I see a lot of women who have to endure violence – battered women and I think we could do something; I don't know what, but definitely something needs to be done."

"Great. Thanks Jen. We all seem agreed to go forward. Shall we call ourselves the Westbourne Grove Women's Liberation Workshop (WLW for short) Group?"

We all agreed, even Jemma who seemed keen to at least follow us down the road a bit more. Beth handed out a form to fill in to pay a yearly subscription of £3 for newsletters and a few leaflets about Women's Liberation.

"Do you know, I hadn't meant for this to be an actual meeting, but I'm glad it turned out that way. Can I ask that we meet here as a rule because of the kids?

Second Friday of the month. So we start in January, looking at the Four Demands. Is that agreed?"

We all nodded and wrote down the date for the second Friday in January. Beth said she would make us all tea, but would we like a glass of wine seeing as it was nearly Christmas? Jemma and I declined, but Beth and Anthea imbibed the wine and made us more tea. I went to help Beth.

"You seem to be taking to this like a duck to water, Jen. I hope you stick around, this could be really good. Now, what I wanted to ask you was about all this business with Feltz. You know he bought the house don't you, I mentioned the other day. But guess what Jen? I hardly believe it can be true. He is GIVING it to me! Anthea is still moving in though, rent free now, and to give me a hand, so I'm feeling good."

I picked up the tray and took it into the other room, Beth followed with the wine.

"It's great news Beth. I hope you will be Ok. Feltz has been generous to me and Leroy too – but there is something else. I know Anthea knows. Perhaps we can share another time?"

"Sure. Ok you lot. Here's the tea and wine. So what's everyone planning for Christmas?"

For the next half hour we chatted about Christmas plans and small stuff and around half past ten, we called it a night and said our goodbyes. I asked Jemma if she was Ok about walking home to Powis Square, she said yes. I noticed Leroy's van was there, so I said I could ask Leroy if she liked.
She declined, but I insisted at least she called me as soon as she got in and gave her my number. We said goodbye and she turned into Westbourne Grove in the direction of Ledbury Road. I made may way to my house and up the stairs, happy to know Leroy was there.

37   The Balance of Relationships

"Hiya! Before you ask Leroy, I was at Beth's talking. Anyway, it's good to see you. How's things?"

"Cho man, Jen. I'm glad you enjoy yourself. Dis serious. Denison 'ave a 'eart attack, man. 'Im in de 'ospital. Me was by Cora when it 'appen. Marvalette and Norman coming down in de marnin' fe pic she hup an' tek her to de 'ospital. You wan' come in the hafternoon? Me can tek you about two, t'ree o'clock when is visitin' time."

"Oh, my goodness! Cora must be in shock. You sure I won't be in the way?"

"Nah man. Dis is how we stay. When t'ings go wrong we does gather round that person, not leave dem by deyself. Come nah? Look Jen, bes' I don' stay de night. I was jus' waitin' to tell you, but me haffe go a me yard an' see about a few t'ings. Me pick you up about half twelve, OK? We could mek a quick spin roun' de market before we go. Bring yu' lis'."

"Ok. Will do. Poor Denison. What hospital is he in? Paddington?"

"Nah. Park Royal. 'im did collapse at 'im workplace over 'arlesden, so dey tek him dere. Neares' one. Ok. Me garn now. See yu' likkle more."

Something inside me wanted to tell Leroy no, that I wanted to him stay with me, but I thought it was best to let him go. I needed to have a clean up in the morning, and do some hand washing anyway before going out. I had been looking forward to staying at home for the day, but it was important to support him. I thought I should behave according to the expectations in a Jamaican family. It was clear I was regarded as an honorary member. I thought about what everyone would be doing. Food, for one. Cooking to keep up Cora's strength and to take some down to the hospital for Denison as the hospital food would not be to his liking. Oh well, so much for a lazy day tomorrow. I made a hot water bottle and got into bed. If there was anything I would like as a Christmas present, it would be an electric blanket like the one I had at Mum's. I went to sleep dreaming of endess warmth.

In the morning I buzzed around the flat cleaning, putting some washing in the bag to go to the launderette and doing some stuff by hand, letting it drip in the bath. Another thing on my list would be a little spin dryer I wrote out my shopping list and got ready fro Leroy to pick me up. I had some time to spare so I also wrote out some Xmas cards so at least I could get some posted. I phoned Mum, to see how she was and ask what she wanted for Xmas. Fine thanks, was her response and nothing this year – wait until she had moved. I metioned about the lectric blanket and she said she would treat me to that. We talked again about a Christmas plan and I said it looked like she could come here if she wanted to. However, I would want to see my friends and maybe go out one of the nights with my boyfriend. Mum said she knew all that was involved and was looking forward to it. I said Leroy and I would come to pick her up Xmas eve in the afternoon, and I could hear her falter a bit and then it was as if some cogs in her mind all moved forward at once.

'Jen. Let's do this. I'd love to meet everybody. I'm looking forward to lots of new chapters in my life, dear.'

Oh, my Mum could melt my heart at times. I just hoped nothing too awful was going to happen with Denison as that might affect all our plans very sadly, although I did not say as much to Mum.

I then called Gabriella quickly and we briefly chatted about work. I was going to invite her over on Sunday with Sharlette but then thought I should hold back til we found out what was happening with Denison. Finally, I was ready for Leroy to come, and with ten minutes to go, I thought of popping in to see Francis. I hadn't caught up with him since our talk with Feltz and I wondered if Feltz had made him an offer too. I wouldn't say anything, just wait to see what he volunteered.

I rang his doorbell and he slowly came down the corridor, he unlatched the bolts and I could see he wasn't at all well.

"Jenifer, darling, as you can see you have caught the old queen rather off colour and not himself at all. It's the flu'. Stay well away, is my advice. We don't want you coming down with this mighty humbler of men, now do we?"

I gave Francis all my sympathies and asked if he needed anything from the chemist. He told me a few things, which I added to my own list, and, wishing him well, I went up the steps to wait for Leroy – who soon came along, not in his van but his nice comfy car, which I was pleased about. I needed a bit of comfort right now!

We stopped off at Shepherd's Bush Market for some meat, veg, fruit and groceries on my list. There was a stall selling African stye things – carvings, clocks in the shape of Caribbean islands, clothing and bags in African print as well as books for adults and a few for children. I chose something for Aaron and as I was looking at the clock, Leroy said he had thought of getting one for Norman and Marvalette, so we agreed to get that between us. He also had been admiring a dashiki shirt with a look on his face that said it had his name on it, so I bought that too, which would be my present to him. Then we stopped off at the record shack and this is where I thought that we would never get away. The queue was long and everyone was saying to play them a piece of this or that record. Leroy looked at me to say this was going to be a long shop, raising his eyebrows as if to say was I up for it, to which I said any other day but we should get over to Cora as it was almost two o'clock. He agreed. Then he said he would prefer to go down Askew Road to get his records anyway because the market ones were often 'cratch-up'!

We took all our purchases to the car, piled them into the boot and made off to Cora's. She was in a state of distress and disarray. She said Norman had taken her to see him an hour or so ago so they were gong to skip the afternoon visiting time and gothis evening. She said they had only let her in this morning to bring him his pyjamas and shaving stuff, but he was still too unwell for it to be a long visit. The hose was as disarrayed as she was. Half it was packed into boxes and many of the rooms were empty as they were preparing to move. Marvalette, Norman and Aaron were already there with Marvalette deep into her cooking and Norman was with Aaron playing Ludo on the big Jamaican board. They were pleased to see me, and here my role was clear – to take over playing with Aaron while Norman and Leroy sat down to talk about football and music! The thought of new tunes was too much for Norman and, after a careful estimation of how long Marvalette was going to take, the two of them announced 'likkle more' and that they were just taking a short turn down Askew Road.

Marvalette and Cora raised their eyes together, warning both to stay out of the bookies – although they didn't have any intention of going there as neither were gamblers. That was Denison's weakness, although no-one could say it was a problem. He just liked a small bet now and again. After a short moan about West Indian men, the two of them now filled me in about Denison and that he had come round OK and how Cora had left him earlier on a heart monitor. She cried a while.

272

Just before the Christmas too, she lamented, adding that she worried that it was all the stress of moving that had caused it. Marvalette said no, it could not be that alone and if Cora didn't mind her saying it was all the rum Denison 'put down 'im t'roat'. Cora agreed and said she always warned him about that and those 'damn blasted cigarettes'.

Aaron wanted to watch TV to see the football, so I could now sit in the kitchen and we all talked, catching up with our lives. I decided not to say yet about what Feltz had offered me and Leroy as he might not yet want them to know and I didn't want to say before it was all signed and sealed. But we did talk about that damn man Gregory and all the trouble he had caused me and everyone who had the misfortune to step in his pathway. Again, I kept quiet about the fact of Feltz discovering they were brothers. I did mention the women's group, however, and I told them about what we had planned.

"Oh, can I come to your group? Me have PLENTY to say for my contribution! But I hope this is not just about man hating because I also want to say a word about de good man dem. Don't forget that Jen. Look at Norman – if Aaron grow up half as good, then that is another good man to put into the world. We need more of them. I think my dear cousin Leroy is starting to come good and what he needs is a kind woman who is strong enough to put her foot down – I hope that's you Jen! Denison too – he had his hardship too and came good. We mustn't forget how our men – our Black men – have had their trials and tribulations and they need our support to stay strong. Too many of them fall by the wayside and drag the woman down with them – and the kids. Like that Trinny man and his wife that you had living upstairs."

"Oh yes," came in Cora, "did I tell you I saw Vida? Oh Lord. That girl will never learn. She tell me that the council took her boys and put them in a home and she can't even see them. Imagine that! I didn't know the council could say that a mother can't even see her own children. It doesn't seem right. And I was just starting to feel sorry for her and tell her drop round any time, when she tell me she living with another man now who takes care of her and is having his baby. This girl is not even twenty-one yet. On her fourth child and she still doesn't know A from bull foot. No job, no education. What kind of life is that? And if the man gets fed up with her and slings her out, what then? Dear me, I've got no time, no time. Needless to say, I didn't invite her round. Goes to show you can't always feel sorry for people. Maybe the kids are better off in a home. At least they get fed."

"But they also get abuse' Cora love. I know dis. I <u>know</u> dis. Yes, the council can seh she can' see dem if dey t'ink she not a fit mother. Maybe dey will have dem adopted but you can't find many nice kind white people wanting to adopt three little Black boys, is it? Anyway, I thought them was already with two lots o' foster family? "

Cora shook her head.

"Seems like they moved them on. I think that might have been just an emergency stop. But Vida definitely said they are all three in a home. Who knows what will happen to them? There's not enough Black families coming forward to adopt or even foster black children and Lord knows it's needed. I was talking about this to Denison the other night, saying how when we move maybe it should be to a three-bed house instead of two, then we could adopt. I don't know. It seems like a right thing to do if you have a home to offer and some little child needs it badly. He seemed keen enough, but now the heart attack might make them think against accepting him. You know you have to go through a damn great rigmarole and they look into everything."

"Yes, me an' Norman was talking about the self-same thing the other day too. We talk about it a lot actually. 'im wasn't keen at firs' but me work me likkle magic 'pon 'im and 'im now seems to quite like the idea. Especially after what happened after the march. He's really feeling how important it is that we as Black people stick together and look after our own. That's why Jen, for us as Black women, our women's lib can only come when we get 'black lib' as a whole people. But I would still like to come to your group just to see what you are all saying."

"I'd like that Marvalette and I can tell Beth. You know some of the women who could join might be lesbians, don't you?"

"Oh Lord!" exclaimed Cora, who was a tad old fashioned about these things.

"Me no care one bumba claart 'bout who dem wan' share dey tings wid as long as dem not after mines!" laughed Marvalette.

"Ooh. You're very accepting of this lesbian or homo thing, Marvalette. I'm not sure myself. God made Adam and Eve not Adam and Steve, is what the preacher used to say. And it seems a bit sinful still in my mind."

"It's funny how two people loving each other is a sin in God's eyes, when a man can bash the hell out of a woman or rape her as a child no one bats an eye as if that's ok. It's not even a crime to rape your wife. And when you get married women still have to promise to obey! There seems to be a double standard here somewhere." I was getting a bit het up.

"Ooh slow down, George. Let's keep it at a slower pace eh?" Marvalette kept me in check.

"Sorry. I've just seen so much at work about real torment that women experience so for me everything is up for questioning. I am really looking forward to our meeting to discuss the Four Demands."

I listed each demand and said we were going to discuss them at the meeting,

"I don't believe in abortion either," she laughed, "So I am not sure I would fit in, but I do think birth control is good."

" Yeah, agreed Marvalette, "It would have saved Vida and her little ones. Remind us when the meeting is again and I will see if I want to come. Meanwhile can you just check that rice for me. I think this fish is done steam now."

Cora was making tomato and watercress salad – Denison's favourite – to add to the meal of steamed bream with okra, rice with split peas and boiled green banana. There was enough for all of us.

"We might as well have ours now – or should we wait a bit longer for the happy wanderers?" Cora mused, but she need not have worried for at that minute the door went and the happy wanderers came back with a parcel of records for us to enjoy later.

Marvalette's dinner was delicious and even though I struggled with the bones, it was really nice to eat fish cooked in this way. She could read my mind.

"So Jen. Is it recipe time?"

I laughed and nodded, adding that I was actually going to ask advice for cooking a shoulder of lamb joint. Marvalette said Cora was the one for that.

"You have garlic? Rosemary? Clove? Pepper? Just pound them down and mix with oil and salt and rub into the meat tonight and then you cook it slowly in the oven til the meat fall off for about 2-3 hours. Add your tomatoes and onion half-way for the gravy. When it's done, put it on the stove top and strain off the fat as lamb can be too fatty like that, then add your oxo and stir up the gravy with some water til it comes how you want it and boof – done!"

"I hope you not gonna be one of these white women that takes down all black women's recipes and then sticks them in a pretty book- making lots of money for white woman and Black woman go hungry?" inquired Marvalette, jokingly, but with a hint of seriousness.

"Nope. I'm gonna make you write them down and you put them in a pretty book and you make loads of money and when you are famous I can say how I knew you back when and how you taught me."

They laughed. "You think I'm joking, don't you? I'm not. You will be on TV as one of those chefs like Fanny Craddock."

"Yeah. I can see Norman acting like Johnny Craddock!"

"Is who dat? Dis Craddock man? Me not goin' on no TV wearing no apron. Y'hear."

We were all laughing and messing about joking, and it seemed to help Cora keep her mind off her worries. Lovingly she put out food for Denison in a Pyrex dish and said we needed to get a move on before it got cold. She got some orange joice from the fridge that she had made that morning and wrapped the hot food in some towels to help keep it warm. She went in the car with Marvalette and

Norman and Aaron said he wanted to come with me and Leroy. So, off we all went them to the hospital.

Denison was lying in bed in a side ward strapped up to machines that beeped and flashed. Cora knew what they all were, and she checked the clipboard at the bottom of his bed knowingly.

"You're doing OK, me ole darlin'," she said to him, giving him a kiss. "Blood pressure coming down anyway and your temperature has been stable. Heartbeat is a bit erratic but out of danger zone. You hungry? We got food for you."

"I'll 'ave a bit then. Bleedin' food in 'ere is diabolical. Nurses are a bit of allright though!" He winked at Cora.

"Hmm. I see you are well on the mend then."

Just then a nurse came in and said we should not have Aaron there as children who were not relatives were not allowed on the ward. I said I would take him down to the shop to get a comic or something and Leroy came with me. There was a place to have a cup of tea, like a small café, next to the shop and of all people, Marion from work was sitting there in tears. I went to say hello, while Leroy bought something for Aaron. He saw me say hello to Marion, and sensing my concern, said he would walk Aaron outside a while so I could talk to my friend.

'It's my bloke. Dennis. He's had a heart attack. I'm trying to find out what ward he's on, but no-one will tell me. It was one of his mates said he was in here.'

I don't think I could stand any more shocks, revelations or secrets today. I had my suspicions she meant Denison. After all it was too much of a co-incidence. But Denison? Why would he have an affair? He loved Cora to bits and she loved him. I decided not to let on anything to her. After all there was a chance it was not him. A slim chance.

"Is that your bloke and his kid? He's nice? I think black blokes are right tasty, don't you?"

"No, on all counts." I replied. "Look I've got to go. I hope you find your boyfriend."

I felt sickened. Leroy sensed something was wrong. I told him I would tell him all later. Which I did in the car going home after we left the others at the hospital.

"Blouse an' skirts!" exclaimed Leroy. "Yu know her? Don't tell Cora. Cho' Denison will be in big trouble – 'im would 'ave a nex' 'eart attack fe true."

"But Leroy, you remember we talked about honesty and trust in a relationship. Why would Denison do that? Cora is lovely. She would be devastated to find that out."

"Jen. Man is man. Maybe 'im feelin' like 'im getting a bit ol' now and 'im wan prove somet'ing. Like de grass greener pon de other side o' de fence. I's jus' a likkle dalliance. No big 't'ing."

"Except that it's deceitful and a betrayal of Cora's trust."

Leroy went silent. So did I, as I thought of Beth saying how 'hubbies liked their seccies' and how their wifies were relieved. But I didn't see Cora and Denison in that way. Plus, it seemed to me their sex life was none of my business, so I didn't venture down that road with Leroy. But he, surprisingly, did.

"Yu know, Jen. Sometimes a man an' a 'oman can love each other bad, but t'ings not right inna de bedroom. Then if a man takes his t'ings from an outside 'oman, den it's no big t'ing. Denison would never leave Cora or let a 'oman put any problem down inna 'im 'ouse. Like he mek sure t'ings cool, den."

"But what about the outside woman? Marion didn't seem cool. She looked like a woman desperately worried about someone she loves. Not that I've got any particular sympathies with Marion, but it seems she does not know about Cora. So that's two women being deceived. I can see what you are saying Leroy and I don't know the answer. In my mind, if that is the situation then the man should be honest with both women."

"Is 'ow me see it too, Jen."

"But what if it was the other way round? That things were not right in the bedroom and it was the man leaving the woman without? Should she get some outside loving? Should she keep it to herself? Or be up front?"

"Dat's different. T'ings different for a woman."

"Oh?"

"Well. Is 'ow me can hexplain? De 'oman coulda get sheself pregnant and den wha'? Or, she might aready 'ave pickney. Is 'ow she gwine carry on her likkle dalliance? Plus, man can tek advantage. Look at my mudder – a case in point?"

I decided to leave it there. I didn't want Leroy dredging up too much about his mother. I could see how much harder it would be for a woman to have an affair, and that there could be repercussions, but it was the old double standard again. I'd had enough.

"Oh well. It's their business after all and I can assure you I won't say a word to Cora nor Marvalette, although if Marion clocks it all, and blows it up, I could then be in trouble. However, that's a problem for another day. Poor Francis is ill, and I need to take his stuff down for him. Then it's me, you, the lamb joint to season and a night in together at last with no dramas to come between us."

Leroy agreed, and we did exactly that, although we didn't actually end up watching what was on TV as we were far more interested in each other. We moved my little record player to the bedroom and I ran a bath for Leroy. He invited me to join him, which would have been more romantic if the bathroom was warmer, but I had never sat in the bath with a man, my man, before and could not resist this new experience. To be looked at so intimately and vice versa, to kiss as we washed each other felt so nurturing and personal. And yes, to dry each other and cream each other's skin as we lay on the bed, admiring, smoothing, stroking, kissing. It was all so lovely and as he took me, or as I took him into me, we seemed to ride this pleasure wave and I experienced for the first time one climax after another until we were both spent, and it was nearly dawn. After half an hour lying there together, we decided we were hungry, so we got up and made a massive breakfast of eggs, beans, toast and fried plantain. We celebrated with orange juice and confirmed to each other that this was the beginning of our journey together, in love, as we we laid gently into each other's arms, falling into a deep, nurturing, secure sleep.

38   The Year Ended.

To the true soul you just have to cling. *To be true to one another*
To be kind and gentle to each other
To give your best when it's asked of you
To do what you have to do when you're supposed to

You've got to feel it You've got to feel the soul down inside of you You've got to feel it

If you're to feel it, you've got to be clean
Then you will feel it Feel the soul inside of you
You've got to feel it

If you're to feel it, you've got to be clean
You've got to make it straight, you can't be lean
To share the joys togetherness can bring
To the true soul you just have to cling

Then you will feel it
You'll feel the soul inside of you
You've got to feel it
Feel it deep down inside of you
You've got to make it straight, you can't be lean
To share the joys togetherness can bring.[xiii]

We agreed with my Mum that she could come for Xmas and that Leroy would not sleep over while she was there. However, Mum said she would go home Boxing Day after lunch so we could go out to a party and enjoy ourselves. Leroy would bring her over and take her home again and he would spend Xmas lunch with us, then take us round to visit our friends – well, everyone was planning to be at Marvalette's new house for Christmas day evening. She had kept that quiet!

Marvalette was happy that I was bringing my Mum, it would only be for a while, so Norman could have his smoke in the car! Then Leroy would take us back.

So, Xmas shopping was done, presents wrapped, cards posted. Oh, and we went to the market got a small tree and set it up with lights and it looked lovely. Feltz came over with 2 bottles of Champagne and Cora gave us a cake, drenched in rum. Denison came home and was recovering. Cora said no more bloody fags and forget the rum, mate. He complied. Absolutely. Which Leroy and I had thought not possible. We never mentioned Marion again. Whatever Denison got up to with her, it was clear that him and Cora were solid. They found a house and started the process of being approved to adopt a child. However, Marion was dumped without a word and was bitter and angry for a long time. She moaned away about how Black men can't be trusted, to which I suggested, tongue in cheek, that she try to find a white man that she *could* trust. I felt guilty about holding the truth from Cora but, the way things worked out, that seemed for the best.

Marvalette and Norman had moved to Kensal Rise, not the two bedroomed house, but, because of her inheritance, they got their three bedroomed house after all. Leroy had helped with the decorating and they went hell for leather to get it ship-shape for Christmas. A new sofa, a dining table and sideboard for the dining room and a bar – for Norman.

Meanwhile Feltz was true to his word and we got a letter inviting us to see the properties he had in mind for me and Leroy. We couldn't believe our luck. We sorted out a solicitor and the transfer to us would complete, we hoped, in January.We discussed whether to live together in one and rent the other out, but Leroy and I both agreed it was too early to do that and that we would bed hop between our places for a year until we were ready to see if we wanted to go to the next stage.

Feltz also sorted out Beth's house and the deeds were made over to her. It now belonged to her. Freehold and all. And Francis? He didn't want to stay in the house. Feltz offered him a flat, rent free for life. Francis asked if the offer was transferable as he would prefer to move to Belsize Par k too. He was given a rent-free place on the top floor of the house that I was to move to. The last person to receive Feltz's generosity was Gregory. They had met up. It was, Feltz told us, a difficult meeting, with Gregory, who was out on bail, being very angry and threatening Feltz, who became emotional, saying how sorry he was and that he wanted to make amends, thus helping Gregory in this way, so that he could be the father he really wanted to be. He told him he would always regard him as his brother and Gregory's son as his nephew. He suggested Gregory had psychiatric help as he and Gregory both recognized how his mind had been so messed up. This perhaps would help with his court case regarding Bernadette and Jasper, although I felt that there was no excuse for his behaviour and to try to build a case of mitigating circumstances was pushing the meaning of 'justice' to a rather odd dimesion. Gregory said he couldn't handle any of it right now, but after Christmas he rang him and invited Feltz to go to his house to visit him and meet his sister-in-law and nephew. It seemed that things were going to work out there after all, although sorting out Gregory's head was going to be a long haul. But their deal was sorted out and before long we had a call from Feltz to say all the rest of his properties had been sold and he was going off to live in Israel. We never heard from him again; whether Gegory did was another matter. We heard no more about Gregory either, except a snippet to say he had been found guilty of assaulting Bernadette and Jasper and had been sent to prison. How long for we did not know until one day I saw Bernadette, who had not come back to the nursery, because they had taken Jasper off her. She said Gregory had been given six months in prison but that she had been given a life sentence and she had committed no crime. She said she was still at the flat and still going to college and that at least no one could steal her dream of being a chef one day. I admired her strength and told her so, expressing how sad I was to hear about Jasper. But she seemed to think he was better off where he was. I hugged her and wished her good-bye, but I had tears in my eye when I walked away. That was four children, all Black children, even though one was mixed race, all gone into care because there was no support, by which I mean the support of a loving and caring family, behind the mothers to help them cope. Support from the council, or the state, was one thing, but it could not replace the need mothers have for love and support from the families. As Cora said, "that would never have happened in the Caribbean."

Mum bought her flats and got a tenant in to flat two, so that gave her an income. Nevertheless, she went back to work and decided to train to be a nurse and I suspect this had been influenced by Cora. Her and Cora had got on well over Christmas and they kept in touch. This was made easier by Cora and Denison moving to Harrow Weald. Denison and Leroy helped my Mum with the decorating and gradually my Mum's attitude changed towards people of colour and her view of 'good decent people' like the Blakewells. Mum would pop in to see Cora when she had been to 'visit' Dad at Harrow Weald Cemetery where she had interred his ashes. They would chat and go shopping together. During these chats, Mum had spoken of her interest in training as a nurse because she wanted to be of use to society now she was no longer needed by her family. Cora had helped her on the road to achieving her ambition and Mum applied to start a course later in the new year.

My work? Well, after what happened with the disciplinary, I never really wanted to go back, so during the time I was off, I wrote to the Town Hall to say I was handing in my notice. I applied for a job at a new style nursery called a Family Care Centre not far from where I lived and got the job. That would be dog the kind of work I was interested in, alongside social workers and other professionals to helpf families cope better. I knew I had lot more learning to do and if I could help children and their families, especially help mothers feel empowered to stand up for themselves and thought of doing more training at some stage.

Before Feltz left, he, Denison and Leroy met together to talk about 'consolidating' their businesses into one, so that Denison could work a bit less and so that Leroy could buy him out of the partnership if and when Denison fully retired. They appreciated his business advice and set themselves up in a proper partnership where they could both boss each other about and argue until they agreed!

I continued meeting with our Women's Liberation Group at Beth's. It was a trek, but I would stay overnight and Leroy never made a fuss. He knew where I was going and I had told him a bit about the group. I never told him about what we discussed unless it was public information. We had decided to start a campaign to give advice and information to women experiencing domestic violence and as the forst women's refuge opened in west London; Beth and Marvalette started volunteering there and our campaign group seemed no longer necessary. We decided to carry on meeting as a Consciouness Raising Group and put a time limit of six months and to be committed to that. Marvalette did join for a while, but Cora declined. A lesbian couple and an Indian woman also became part of the group. It went well while we were focussing on an external campaign but when in the CR group we had to be more open about ourselves we ralised where there were cracks in our 'sisterhood', not that we ever used that expression like before after what Jemma had said. It could not be taken for granted. But we did begin to get a political oversight that drew together the threads of our experiences without generalising for the other or assuming that what was true for us was the same for someone else. We learned to listen, to feel, to empathise from the heart. We read and read, learned abour Marxism and each other's struggles. I learned about slavery, about Jim Crow, about civil rights, about colonialism and the harm it had done from the experiences of those affected by it. I learned about sexuality, and about patriarchal oppression of women's beings and bodies. We learned about becoming empowered to make choices about our lifestyles, relationships and what struggles we could support. We were learning, growing and finding our strength. We knew we would end up going our own ways, but this was like a developmental springboard and healing fulcrum. We would never see the world in the same way as before. We were recreating our identities as liberated women. We were the revolution and it was taking place within us individually and within the way we saw and related to one another.

Jemma persuaded Leroy to go to some Puma meetings which he and Norman did, with Marvalette going along too and so a women's Puma group came into being – not without some arugument though it seemed. Gabriella even joined for awhile. Sometimes we would all meet for Sunday lunch at each other's houses and discuss all our perspectives as they were also growing and changing and then we would spend time playing music, eating and just having a nice time. I knew I could not be in the Pumas, but Leroy and I wanted to do something political together, so we got involved in the anti-apartheid struggle and went on demos together. We had many heated discussions as we, too, were in a process of our own evolution, confronting our deep seated oppressed/oppressor. Our relationship was like a crossroads where these things were confronted within it and within ourselves. Our love and understanding grew. We were happy.

The end

i I'll Be Waiting. Alton Ellis Lyrics by Alton Nehemiah Ellis
ii Perfidia. Phyllis Dyllon Lyrics by Phyllis Dillon
iii Baby Why . The Cables Lyrics by The Cables
iv People Get Ready. The Uniques, Lyrics by Slim Smith
v Blood and Fyah Lyrics by Niney
vi Pressure Drop. Toots and the Maytals. Lyrics by Toots Hibbert
vii Sunday's Coming. Alton Ellis. Lyrics by Alton Nehemiah Ellis
viii Band of Gold. Marcia Griffiths. Lyrics by Edythe Wayne and Ron Dunbar
Universal Music
ix Better Mus' Come. Delroy Wilson. Lyrics by Delroy Wilson
x Queen Majesty. Techniques Lyrics by Curtis Mayfield
xi Stranger in Love. John Holt Lyrics by John Holt
xii If it Don't Work Out Pat Kelly Lyrics by Pat Kelly
xiii Feeling Soul. Bob Andy. Lyrics by Bob Andy

Printed in Great Britain
by Amazon

55212266R00163